Copyright © 2020 Christopher J Kappler All rights reserved

The characters and events portrayed in this book are fictitious. Any similarity to real persons, living or dead, is coincidental and not intended by the author.

No part of this book may be reproduced, or stored in a retrieval system, or transmitted in any form or by any means, electronic, mechanical, photocopying, recording, or otherwise, without express written permission of the publisher.

ISBN-13: 979-8511665948
ASIN: B08RP9TXM1

Cover design by: Azmat Munshi and Chris Kappler
Library of Congress Control Number: 2018675309
Printed in the United States of America

D0167503

I dedicate this work, as I have all of my pursuits for the past 30 years, to Michelle Frachetti Kappler, who has taught me most of what I know about life. There aren't words to thank you for what you have given me.

The Ghost of Sphinx

Act-I

Emergence

1 - The Champion - Nov 2109 -

Kuala Lumpur, Malaysia

Jacqueline

Jacqueline let go of her grandmother's hand and took a step forward. Placing her fingertips on the edge of the table in front of her, she leaned in to get a closer look. Across from them, one of the race technicians was positioning a fresh battery pack onto the spine of Jacqueline's quadcopter. He connected the leads and tucked them neatly along one side, then tightened the black velcro band down over the top. As a final check, he slid his fingers along the edge of the molded red brick and gave it a quick twist.

"There you go, young lady," he said, lifting the quad and holding it in the air just in front of her, "one fresh battery pack."

Jacqueline extended her hands, and he placed the drone gently onto the surface of her open palms.

"Good luck, now. I'll be rootin' for ya."

Jacqueline felt her mother squeeze her shoulder tightly, and she looked up from the drone to the man's smiling face.

"Thank you," she said, then turned to look at her mother, who nodded approvingly.

"Not at all. That's what I'm here for."

"Come now, *sayangku*," said her mother, turning to leave. Jacqueline stole a glance back at her grandmother, then quickened her steps to catch up to her mother. A little smile came to Jacqueline's face as she did. The bright lights in the tech support tent made the colors in her mother's outfit seem even more brilliant. Her dress faded from one shade of lime green at the bottom to a lighter shade at her waist where it disappeared into a thin purple sweater. A tie-dyed blue and white shawl hung loosely around her neck.

As they stepped out onto the field, leaving the incandescent white of the tech tent behind, Jacqueline looked up at the night sky and let her eyes adjust to the dark. The stadium lights were low, and the November stars over Kuala Lumpur were stunning. She let her gaze drift down to the bleachers of the stadium. Other than the hint of a few screen-lit faces in the distance, she couldn't make out the spectators, but she could hear the murmur of thousands of people gathered in one place. As she scanned the crowd, she began to feel her heart thumping in her chest.

Taking a deep breath, she turned her eyes away from the grandstand and looked past her mother at the intricate lighting design of the drone course. It was like a miniature roller coaster with swooping hills and helix turns. At the very center of the snaking white structure rose a dark medieval-looking tower that seemed to absorb all of the ambient light around it.

Jacqueline's mother took two steps up onto the competitor's platform, but Jacqueline still needed to set up her quad on its launch pedestal. She stayed on the turf and kept pace with her mother, walking along the length of the low structure. Based on her qualifying times, Jacqueline had been assigned launch position three for the final race. She approached pedestal three and gently placed the drone onto it with the first-person cam pointing toward the starting gate. Switching on the drone, she adjusted its footing one more time before walking back to the steps to join her mother on the platform.

Jacqueline's grandmother and Mr. Raban had taken longer to arrive from the tech tent and were only a few steps ahead of her. When they reached her assigned station, Mr. Raban put his bag on the ground and opened it. He pulled out Jacqueline's first-person view headset and handed it to her mother, then bent back down to retrieve her flight controls.

Jacqueline took her seat in the pilot's chair and looked up at her mother. "Don't mess up my braid," she said as her mother began to slide the stiff band of the goggles around the crown of her head.

"Your braid took me a half an hour to do this morning. I'm not going to mess it up."

Still smiling, Jacqueline squeezed her eyes closed as the goggles slid onto her head. She felt her mother's fingers in her hair, just as she had that morning. When Jacqueline opened her eyes again, the scene was dim, but soon she could see the edge of the pedestal and the starting gate. It looked much higher from the drone's point of view. At multiple points along the gate were miniature traffic lights that shone red, discoloring the turf in small pools of light.

Jacqueline felt a tap on her arm, and someone handed her the haptic flight controls. She guessed that it had to be Mr. Raban. The touch was quick and efficient - just enough to signal what he wanted.

She felt a cable slide over her left shoulder, and a muffled click told her that he had connected the goggles to her flight controls. There was one last squeeze of her shoulder, and Jacqueline knew that the three of them would move off onto the sidelines until the race was over.

Now she just had to wait. Before long, the countdown reached 100 seconds to the start of the race. Jacqueline slowed her breathing and studied what she could see of the racecourse through her drone's FPV camera.

The final seconds ticked down accompanied by staccato beeps, and the red lights began to flash. A longer, high-pitched tone followed, and red gave way to blinking yellow. Finally, with a piercing electronic shriek, the signals flipped to green.

Jacqueline and her competitors punched their controls, and six X-shaped quadcopters lifted off from their launch pedestals and pitched sharply forward towards the onramp to the track.

Jacqueline left her body behind. Her senses were teleported into her little quad and the force feedback of her flight controls let her feel every bump and tilt. The only sensation lacking was the wind in her face as she watched the white slats of the racetrack streak by underneath her.

In less than 30 seconds, the racers had navigated more than half of the course, and a multi-quad collision in one of the low underpasses had already eliminated two contenders. Jacqueline was in third place and had a clear view of the two quads ahead of her, but as she was beginning her climb toward the tower obstacle, the telltale whine of a quadcopter became audible in her left ear. Another drone was trying to overtake her from behind.

She pitched backward instinctively, sacrificing speed for a few centimeters of lift, and the high-pitched sound in her headset went silent, punctuated by a plasticky clatter. Jacqueline winced, knowing too well that it had been the invisible prop wash from her own quad that had driven her opponent down into the rails.

She finished her climb, then plunged down into the black interior of the tower. Jacqueline held the dive as long as she could, trying to regain lost time, but as she sailed out the base of the tower she could see that the two racers ahead of her had widened their lead.

Jacqueline knew that she could play it safe and go home with the bronze, but another idea was forming in her mind. Taking one

The Ghost of Sphinx

last deep breath, she locked her eyes on a point high and to the inside of the final corkscrew turn then executed a sharp roll to the right, putting her copter into a sideways freefall. Using only throttle and pitch, she clung to the center of the helix.

Within a second, she executed two full rotations around the inner post of the corkscrew, then righted her quad and looked around to get her bearings. There was no one in front of her.

It was a straight shot to the finish line, but Jacqueline could hear the other drones nearby. The audio wouldn't be enough this time if one of them tried to overtake her, but she only needed to stay in the lead for a few more seconds.

Everything faded away except for one brightly lit circle on the turf, just past the finish line. She aimed for it, maintaining a slight descent in order to gather what little speed she could. The target was growing larger in her field of view, but a sudden squeeze on her shoulders and an eruption of voices jolted her back into her body. It was over.

Letting go of her flight controls, Jacqueline watched the ground rush up to meet her, then shoved her goggles onto her forehead and swung around to find her mother and her grandmother laughing and clapping. Even Mr. Raban was showing an uncharacteristic smile.

A few electronic notes chimed over the loudspeakers, then Jacqueline heard the announcer declare, "Ladies and gentlemen, twelve-year-old Jacqueline Binti Abdullah from Sarawak, Malaysia takes the title of drone racing champion, 2109!"

His last words were still ringing over the sound of applause when four fiery streaks of light shot across the night sky. The crowd went quiet, and a blinding flash of white detonated overhead, lighting everything around them for a half a second. Jacqueline squinted her eyes. The lights seemed too far away to be fireworks, and there hadn't been any sound.

Mr. Raban tugged Jacqueline up out of her pilot's seat and began yanking the cables off of her. His eyes were wide. "We need to get some cover!" He jumped down off the competitors' platform, pulling her with him, then turned back and called sharply to Jacqueline's mother, "Ms. Wan! Follow me! Quickly!"

A loud clack echoed, and darkness took hold of the stadium. Raban's grip tightened painfully around Jacqueline's arm, but when she looked up at him, his head was still turned away from her. Jacqueline followed his gaze and saw her grandmother, staring transfixed as glowing red streaks cauterized fresh slashes across the night sky. The eerie glow was the only light around them.

"This way!" Mr. Raban pulled Jacqueline as fast as she could run, diagonally off the sporting field and towards the concrete base of the stadium. A few people were running in other directions, but Raban didn't falter. He kept stealing quick glances at the lights moving across the sky, as if something there could tell him which way to go.

As they reached the wall, Mr. Raban yanked Jacqueline around sharply and dropped to one knee. He took her shoulders and pushed her back up against the wall. "Stay here," he ordered, then sprang to his feet and set off again. Jacqueline's eyes followed him. He was running back toward where they had come from, toward Jacqueline's mother and grandmother. The women seemed so far away. One of her mother's arms extended back as she dragged her own mother across the field.

Jacqueline clapped her hands over her ears reflexively as an explosive wave of energy consumed the stadium. Blinking, she fought to keep her eyes open only to watch in horror as Raban and the two women were lifted off the ground. The white race track shredded into spinning fragments that crushed into the stands at the far corner of the stadium, lacerating the turf along their path.

Mr. Raban lay motionless a short distance away, partially shielded from the blast, just as Jacqueline had been. Beyond him though, there was no trace of her mother, her grandmother, or practically anything else between Mr. Raban and the jumble of wreckage across the field from them.

Jacqueline called out but she couldn't hear her own voice. Time seemed to slow down, and the ground rumbled again beneath her. She tried to stay against the wall where Mr. Raban had placed her, but the urge to run to him was too strong.

Before Jacqueline reached the spot where Raban lay, he had begun to push himself up onto his hands and knees. He twisted around and lifted his head towards her. There was a wide scrape down one side of his face that seemed to get darker each time she looked at it. The pocket of his shirt was torn and hanging. He looked like he was saying something, but she couldn't hear him.

Finally, his words became intelligible through the ringing in her ears. "Are you hurt, miss?"

Shaking her head, she pleaded, "We have to go back, *lah!* For *Ibu* and *Nenek!*"

Mr. Raban turned his head back over his shoulder to the devastation and chaos at the far corner of the field. He paused for a long moment, and Jacqueline dropped down next to him and yelled again, "I don't see them anywhere!"

Raban looked back at her, then got to his feet and took Jacqueline's hand. "Yes, come." He was limping, but they moved quickly toward the center of the field.

Hundreds of people were pouring onto the turf from the grandstands, and Raban squeezed her hand looking around and said, "Stay close to me, miss."

They passed the area where the racing platform had stood just minutes earlier. There was practically nothing left of it other than deep scars that raked diagonally across the field. Over the heads of fleeing spectators, Jacqueline could see the ruins of the event, a mass of white pilings that the shockwave had plowed up into the stands at the far corner of the stadium.

There were people moving all around them now, shoving and clawing their way towards the exits. One man tried to pass in between Raban and Jacqueline, but Raban dodged quickly in her direction and lowered his shoulder. The movement caught Jacqueline off guard and she lost her footing, but Raban quickly lifted her arm to keep her from falling. Something sharp scraped her ankle, and she looked down to see what it was. There was a twisted piece of metal sticking up out of the ground.

Jacqueline tried to start walking again, but Raban held her where they were. "Stop here, miss," he said, frozen in place and staring out at the field ahead. After another moment he blinked his eyes, then began to inspect the faces around them.

A Western-looking woman in her late twenties was stumbling past them, unsteady, but in better shape than many. She was holding her head with one hand, and a streak of her hair looked like it was wet with blood.

Mr. Raban spoke to her in English. "Excuse me, sister. Would you stand here for a moment with my daughter?" Jacqueline looked up at him and scrunched up her face. Raban wasn't her father...

Before she could react further, he was talking again. "I only need a minute. Just over there," he said, pointing with his chin toward what seemed to be a hole in the crowd with people walking all around it.

The young woman stopped and inspected the two of them. She turned her head slowly to one side and narrowed her eyes. After a few seconds, she nodded and bent down slightly to take hold of Jacqueline with her free hand. Surprised, Jacqueline looked down at her own hand, then let her eyes follow the woman's arm up to her face. The woman's other hand was still raised to her forehead, and her arm was trembling slightly.

As Raban moved away, Jacqueline saw the woman squeeze her eyes shut several times, staring in his direction, before letting out a sigh and looking down at her.

Jacqueline turned away, directing her attention back to Mr. Raban who was jogging unevenly and pushing through the crowd. She saw him come to a stop, 20 meters away. He bent down and looked at something. At Raban's feet there was a hint of color. Bright green and purple.

Jacqueline lurched towards him, but the woman closed her fingers firmly around Jacqueline's hand and held onto her tightly.

She called out as loudly as she could. "*Ibu!*" Her own voice sounded muffled.

Raban must have heard her, because he straightened up, glanced back at them, and held up his palm.

"Your dad will be back in a minute, sweetie." The woman's voice came to her dimly. "Just wait here, OK?"

She tried again to free herself. Her eyes were fixed on Mr. Raban, but the crowd squeezed in on them, blocking her view. When she finally caught sight of him again he was facing her, limping back towards where they stood. His hollow stare pierced straight through her.

As soon as he reached them, Mr. Raban dropped to his knees and took hold of Jacqueline's shoulders. "Allah forgive me. I have failed you, miss."

She looked back at him and waited for him to say something else, but he closed his eyes slowly and let his own head hang down. Jacqueline tried to see behind him, where he had come from, but there were too many people. She turned toward the young woman who had been standing with them, but she had already been swallowed by the throng.

Briefly, through the crowd, Jacqueline spotted her again. She was walking unsteadily towards one of the stadium exits, still holding her head. Jacqueline thought that she saw the woman look back at them one last time before passing through an archway and out of sight.

2 - The Architect - Nov 2109 - Houston, TX

Colleen

It was just after 4 a.m. when Colleen woke to a soft chime. She sat up and turned on the light, then reached for her Augmented Reality glasses and put them on.

"Dr. Pastor, I'm sorry to do this but I'm afraid I have to recall you. How soon can you be back on campus?"

"Hmm, I don't know," she mumbled. Speaking slowly, she added, "I think that the commercial carriers are still grounded."

"I see. Well, we need you here. I'll have Colonel Crespin reach out to you to arrange military transport."

Oh, that sounds comfortable...

"Yeah, ok. That's probably our best bet," said Colleen. "What's this about, Director?"

"I'm sorry Doctor Pastor," answered Tinghir, "but I think it would be safest to get you back here before discussing it. I can say this though, I have a feeling that you won't be disappointed."

****

Colleen opened her office door and stepped slowly inside. It seemed surreal. She could almost hear herself pounding her fist on the desk, warning that it was just a matter of time before one of these main belt asteroids would catch them by surprise.

She dropped her bag on her desk and tapped the rim of her glasses to display the time. It was 9:30, and she had told the Director that she'd meet him before 10. She touched her temple and shot off a quick message to Director Tinghir. "I'm here. I'm going to get a cappuccino then I'll come to your office."

Colleen made her way to the canteen and placed her cup on the counter in front of the gleaming espresso machine, then bent down slowly to pull a small bottle of milk out of the short fridge that sat beneath it. As the black espresso started to dribble into her cup, and the steam wand hissed into the stainless-steel pitcher of milk, the sounds resonated painfully with the throbbing in Colleen's head.

What the fuck am I doing back here?

Director Tinghir was standing in his office to greet her. "Colleen, thank you for coming back. I'm sorry to have interrupted your sabbatical, but as you can imagine, most of our plans for the coming year have been overtaken by events."

"Yeah, seriously..." said Colleen as she lowered herself gingerly into one of the chairs in front of Director Tinghir's desk. "OK, so what's up?"

Tinghir nodded and looked at Colleen straight on for a moment before answering. "We need you to take immediate steps to operationalize GhostMap. The joint chiefs have given you carte blanche to move as quickly as technically feasible to get us up and running."

Colleen straightened her back and sat wide eyed for a second. "Holy shit. That *is* serious. Do they understand what that means?" she asked. "I mean, don't get me wrong, I believe that this is the right move, but do they really get what we're talking about here?"

"They will soon enough," said Tinghir. "We've got a meeting with Colonel Crespin tomorrow to give him the full scope of the mission. He'll be your military counterpart on this going forward."

Colleen nodded silently and kept her face as expressionless as she could.

****

"Good morning, Doctor, Director," said Crespin. "In preparation for today's meeting, I've taken the liberty of reviewing your technical specifications for the vehicles, training devices, and personal protective equipment associated with the new mission."

Colleen raised an eyebrow and tilted her head. "That's great. So, what do you think?"

Crespin looked back at her. His face seemed to change expression more than once before he said, "My chain of command has asked me to make this program successful, so that is what I intend to do."

"That's excellent, Colonel," said Tinghir. "Tell me then, which parts of the program are you most comfortable with?"

"Hehm, let's see," said Colonel Crespin. "I find the PPE to be a logical extension of the G-suit that we use for fighter pilots, and the hyperloop training facility seems straightforward to understand as well. Both follow naturally from devices that I have used in the past."

"Nice!" said Colleen. "We're almost halfway there then. If I'm not mistaken, you've personally participated in launching lightsail craft as well, during the SpaceChips program?"

"Yes, ma'am," responded Crespin. "They were small craft, though. Less than one kilogram each."

"Sure, but the principle was the same. You had to put a high-powered propulsion station in orbit to bombard the lightsail with photons. That allowed the SpaceChips payloads to accelerate without any onboard propellant."

"Yes, ma'am, but again, scaling that up from one kilogram to one tonne, and placing a human pilot inside the lightsail craft changes the equation significantly," said Colonel Crespin. "Surely you agree."

Colleen looked at him a moment. Had she imagined the combative tone in his last question?

"Colonel, a hundred thousand people are dead precisely because we didn't have a system like GhostMap deployed. I have been trying to get this program off the ground since we observed the first orbital decay of a main belt asteroid five years ago. Your technical concerns are reasonable, but you have to weigh them against the threat of a global extinction."

Crespin's mouth twisted into a smirk, and he held Colleen's stare for another few seconds.

"What are you smiling at?" she challenged, realizing too late that she had raised her voice slightly.

"If I can be so bold, Doctor, didn't your last video game have a similar title?" asked Colonel Crespin.

"Oh, fuck this guy," mumbled Colleen, standing up.

Director Tinghir grabbed her wrist and held it firmly. Colleen wanted to cry out from the pain but suppressed it.

"Colonel," said Tinghir, "I see that you are aware the Doctor Pastor's first career was in the gaming industry. I hope that you can appreciate that in the civilian branch of the Space Agency, we value brilliance and creativity just as much as any private company would. We didn't hire Doctor Pastor to follow orders, we hired her to create a future for us that's better than the one we have today."

With that, he let go of Colleen's arm. Somewhat at a loss, she caught Tinghir's eye and gave him a short nod of thanks.

The Ghost of Sphinx

"The irony is not that an ex-game-designer would become a mission architect with us," added the Director. "The irony is that a brilliant astrophysicist and engineer went to work for a gaming company for more than a decade before returning home."

Colleen sat back down and looked over at Colonel Crespin. "My last game was called Galactic Extermination."

She slid a pair of AR glasses across the table towards him and said, "Here, put these on." Director Tinghir pulled out his own pair of glasses and slipped them on as well.

Colleen clapped her hands together, and disks appeared around them like cymbals. She pulled her hands apart and the cylinder between the two cymbals filled with two different colors of glowing objects. There were what looked like electric blue strands of twisted barbed wire and a train of little green circles that floated like smoke rings back and forth between the two cymbals.

"So let's get to the other vessels in GhostMap. We have these two propulsion stations, the Nest close to Earth and the Outpost deployed out in the direction of the solar Apex. The barbed wire is meant to represent the Galactic Halo Substructures that have been stirred up by the stellar stream. They're invisible to us, but the effect of their gravity has been steadily increasing to the point where it's dragging asteroids out of stable orbits. The little green rings depict the gravitational probes that fly between the two propulsion stations under the control of the pilots in our lightsail craft."

She looked at Crespin and waited for him to make the next move.

"Is this to scale?" he asked.

"No, good point," with a jerk of her hands, like flicking water off of her fingertips, Colleen threw the cymbals, and they flew out to each side of the room. The tangle of luminescent blue barbed wire grew to fill the entire space, and the train of green disks circulating between the two propulsion stations stretched out, opening wide gaps between the circulating rings.

"So the concepts are simple. We propel one of the lightsail craft up to relativistic speed, and it deploys a ring of gravitational probes. Traveling at that speed has two crucial side effects. First, obviously, it can cover hundreds of times more distance. More importantly though, the relativistic effects allow the dark matter detector to have 500 times more area without loss of sensitivity.

Conventional spacecraft would be four to five orders of magnitude less effective."

Director Tinghir interjected. "Colonel, the design of these gravitational probes is really quite ingenious. They are based on the same principles of interferometry that enable detection of gravitational waves here on Earth, but flown in precision formation with 360-degree coverage and an aperture eight times wider than Jupiter."

Crespin nodded. "I see. Let me raise my main concerns then, Doctor. I can accept that there are scientific reasons for why you want these craft to travel close to light speed, but I can't understand why these need to be manned missions. My obvious concerns are for the safety of both the crew of the remote space station and the pilots of the lightsail craft."

"Both are reasonable concerns," answered Colleen. "It comes down to unknowns and reaction time. We need to pilot each formation of gravitational probes in real time. The scope of the search area is vast, and we can no longer afford to ignore the structure or currents in the dark matter that lies in the path of our solar system."

"We have reason to believe that even on this small scale we're going to encounter a tangle of dense filaments, similar to those measurable in the cosmic web. That means that pilots will have to use their instincts and make quick decisions to follow high-value trails. It just isn't possible to control probes like these remotely. The distances and speeds involved create months of transmission delay for any form of communication."

"And the crew of 50 on the remote space station?" asked the Colonel.

"Yes, the Outpost is the only way for these lightsail ships to execute a braking phase at the end of their outbound run. The station will house the pilot for a brief recovery period and then re-launch them homeward. Lightsail ships can't accelerate or decelerate without external propulsion, and the pilots of the lightsail craft will need the support of a full ground crew before and after each sensor run."

Colonel Crespin took off his AR glasses and placed them on the table. He lifted his hand to his eyes and squeezed the bridge of his nose.

After a moment he lowered his hand and looked up at Colleen. "OK, I have a sense for how you're viewing this mission." Turning to Director Tinghir, he asked, "It would seem as if you're willing to bet on the operational suitability of this ... research, Director?"

"Yes, Colonel. I am."

Crespin nodded with pursed lips and looked down at the table. Colleen watched him and waited. She suspected that saying anything else would only aggravate him.

"I want to make myself clear then," he said finally. "My orders are to facilitate the safe deployment of this technology. I will need to maintain veto authority over every aspect of the program. Make no mistake. This is a military mission."

Turning to Tinghir he added, "Director Tinghir, I expect that you will follow proper channels in opening this plan up for comprehensive scientific review by Congressional experts and by all funding agencies. Some of the dual-use technologies are classified and need-to-know, but that should not get in the way of proper   oversight."

"Doctor Pastor, you should be prepared to hold quarterly program reviews with my staff to generate up-to-date safety and risk estimates. Put simply, I will not expose my personnel to unjustified risk. I promise you that I will shut you down if I discover that your plan can't meet my safety standards."

3 - The Captain - May 2111 - Troy, NY

Liam

For just a moment, as he watched Christopher crouch down onto the frozen turf, Liam allowed himself to remember the warm, wet smell of springtime and the sound of the birds returning to the northeast. Such memories seemed distant now. Impact winter was entering its 500th day.

In June 2110, seven months after the meteor strikes, summer in parts of the northern hemisphere simply never came. Historians compared it to another event, a volcanic winter in 1816 that had done the same thing across a swath of North America, Europe, China, and Russia.

In December 2110, more than a year after Sphinx, the pattern repeated itself in New Zealand, the tip of Argentina and the Falklands. Feed stores from the previous year dwindled as farmers were unable to plant crops in the frozen soil. Ranchers were forced to slaughter livestock in an effort to realize what value they could before their herds starved.

Now, in mid-May 2111, Liam found himself standing on a frigid sporting field in Troy, NY. The trees that lined the field were dormant and leafless. For the second year in a row, there were no signs of spring.

Liam barely took note of the persistent dry fog that reddened and dimmed the daylight. What he did notice was that his team had been decimated. Almost a quarter of the squad had left school as their family farms and businesses failed. College tuition had become a luxury that some could no longer afford.

As team captain, Liam tried to focus on the one thing that he might actually be able to control, scoring. It was their final game of the year. A victory would mean finishing the season with a 6-5 winning record, and with only 20 seconds left on the clock, Christopher's face-off might be their last chance.

The official blew his whistle, and Christopher clamped his lacrosse stick down over the ball. He forced all of his weight forward and knocked the opposing player backwards before scrambling to his feet.

As soon as Liam saw that Christopher had the ball, he drove hard towards the offensive goal, leaving Paul to receive the pass.

Liam reached the last defend

see Paul arc around for a str

The goalie was moving in

Liam switched to a left-hand

out of the air before it ente

momentum was carrying hir

again, he slung his own stic

a close range shot behind hi

official blew his whistle aga

Paul, Christopher and the

share in the moment. Liam

looked around at his teammates and lifted his chin. "Let's go
thank our opponents for a great game."

As they walked toward the opposing sideline, Paul looked
around at the players of both teams lining up to shake hands.

"I should enjoy this while it lasts," he shot to Liam. "There's no
way things are going to go as well next year."

Liam looked sideways at him. "You guys are going to be fine.
You'll see."

"Nah, it's not gonna be the same. These guys would follow you
to the gates of hell."

Each team had formed into a line and the players shook hands
walking past each other. On the way back to their own sideline,
Liam tried to change the subject. "Hey Paul, do you think that I
can get your help tonight on this programming assignment for my
fluid mechanics class?"

Paul laughed. He was younger than Liam, but he was a computer
science major so the programming that Liam needed for aero-
space came easily for him. "Yeah sure. Why don't you come over
to our place after you get cleaned up, and we can work there. Mericiel's coming over for dinner, but we can eat and work at the
same time."

****

Liam stopped by the grocery store on his way over to Christopher and Paul's apartment to pick up something special. He hadn't
told any of them yet that this was likely going to be their last
weekend together.

When he finally arrived and rang the bell, Mericiel opened the
door for him. "Hey, there. You hungry? We were just going to
order some food."

...hat you haven't ordered yet. I brought us

...ay from the door and let him in with his grocery ...had barely closed the front door behind him when ...walked through the living room wearing only a towel. ...curly hair was wet from the shower. "Oooh, what'd you

...iam slapped Christopher's hand away from the edge of the bag. It's for everyone to share."

Christopher pouted, so Liam pulled out an apple and handed it to him. Then he took out cartons of fresh blueberries and cherries and placed them on the table, followed by several plums. As a final flourish, he let three more fresh apples spill out of the bag and roll across the table. Christopher, Paul and Mericiel gasped. "Oh my god, where did you get all of this stuff?!"

The reaction was exactly what Liam had been hoping for. He had chosen items that had become scarce after two years without a northern growing season. "I wanted us to have something special tonight, so I went to that high-end all-natural place and spent a little bit extra. The sign said that the apples came from South Carolina."

Mericiel looked at the fruit and whispered to him, "That's more than a little extra. I haven't seen a fresh plum in over a year. You shouldn't have."

"Oh, come on," Liam said, waving them off. "You guys are like family to me."

Paul motioned Liam over to the computer, and the two of them got to work on Liam's programming assignment while the others snacked. Both the fruit and the program were polished off in 45 minutes.

"Thank you, Paul. I owe you," said Liam when they closed out the code editor. "Hey, I have an idea. Christopher and I are going flying in the morning. Do you guys want to come?"

Stuffing a handful of blueberries in his mouth, Christopher mumbled, "I'm going to be Liam's first official student."

Mericiel turned to look at Liam. "Official? Are you an instructor now?"

"Yeah, I just finished my Flight-Instructor Airplane rating a few weeks ago. This guy is going to be my first victim."

"Thank you for the offer," Paul said, lifting his hands in front of him with his palms facing Liam, "but small planes aren't really my thing."

"Yeah, and now that I'm thinking about it, I don't really want an audience tomorrow for my first lesson," said Christopher.

Liam smiled apologetically at Mericiel. "Sorry, I'll have to take you up by yourself some time."

She just shrugged and returned his smile.

****

"OK, put your yoke about there. Just use one hand. Keep your right hand on the throttle. Yeah, now work those rudder pedals with your feet."

Their seats bounced a bit as the small plane picked up speed on the runway.

"Good, now pull back, a little more... Hey, you're flying."

Christopher's eyes were wide, and his mouth was opened into something between a holler and a smile.

Liam heard a change in pitch and looked down at the twin throttle controls between their seats. "Oops, keep your right hand on the throttle. It can walk back on you."

Christopher quickly lowered his right hand and applied a bit of pressure. The sound of the engine corrected itself, and he shot Liam a quick grin, flinching the muscles in his neck.

They continued to climb at a steep angle for another 90 seconds, and the look on Christopher's face was priceless. When Liam saw the altimeter hit 800m he said, "Great, level off here." Christopher pushed forward on the yoke and the horizon came back into view in front of them.

"Here, use your right hand to adjust your trim so that you're not fighting with the yoke to keep your attitude."

"Haaaa," said Christopher letting out a long breath. "This is so cool. Thank you for taking me up. It's really beautiful. I can see why you love it so much."

Liam shook his head and let his eyes run over the wispy surface of the grey clouds that extended above them in a dual horizon. "I wish that you could have come up with me a few years ago. All this cloud cover at 1000 meters wasn't there, and the sky was blue. I used to go up to 2500 meters on almost every flight."

"Oh, that's high," said Christopher, breathing in through his teeth. "We're at 800 now? I think that I'm OK here."

"Ah, you say that now, but you haven't seen it. I'll show you a video when we get home. One time, with my instructor, I went up to 4000 meters. It was like going to heaven."

"You can't do that anymore?" asked Christopher.

"No, the clouds are too thick and there's no visibility. If you're instrument rated, you can fly up into the soup, but there's nothing to see."

Liam was dividing his attention three ways. He was checking the instruments, and he was keeping an eye out for their heading and for other planes, but he couldn't stop looking over at Christopher. Christopher was so distracted, he didn't even notice that Liam was studying him.

Maybe up here, he'll understand...

Liam opened his mouth to speak, then closed it again. He took another scan of the instruments and the sky around them, then said, "Christopher, I have to tell you something, and you're not going to like it at first, but please give me a minute to try to convince you. I think that it's a great opportunity for us."

"OK…"

Liam scanned around them again, then looked back at Christopher. "It's about our plan to go to Boston next year. I…. I was contacted by a recruiter from the Space Agency a few months ago and I haven't been able to stop thinking about it."

Christopher's eyebrows creased together. "The Space Agency?"

"Yeah," answered Liam. "I think that you know that going into space has always been a dream of mine, but I never really thought that it could happen. But this recruiter said that maybe it could. Maybe even both of us could."

Christopher wiggled his fingers slightly, adjusting his grip on the yoke. "You've been thinking about this for a few months? That's a long time without saying anything to me."

"I know, I'm sorry that I didn't say anything until now," said Liam. "I guess I've been trying to talk myself out of wanting this, but I can't fight it anymore. This is the first time that I've had the courage to say anything because the screening process has progressed and it's getting to a point of no return. I want you to come with me."

Christopher's eyes were still forward, but he was shaking his head. "How? How am I supposed to come with you? I can't practice even basic counseling without at least a Masters, and I was planning on going for my MD. I got accepted at one of the best schools in the country for psychiatry. Do I really need to tell you all the reasons this doesn't make sense? We have a lease on an apartment in Boston. I've taken out student loans, and my father is expecting me to come join his practice when I finish."

"Christopher, I know. You're right, I do know all of those things, and I'd understand if you didn't want to put any of those plans on hold. I guess I was just hoping that you'd consider delaying by a year, two tops. This mission, the one that they're planning to protect the planet from future asteroids, they're recruiting for it now. If you come with me, we could try out for it together. We'll miss our chance if we wait four or five years. The ships will already be deployed."

For the first time since they had taken off, Christopher turned his head and looked at Liam, but his face was inscrutable.

Liam quickly checked their heading then tightened his own grip on the yoke. "I looked into it. The Space Agency has these officers called Behavior Scientists or Human Factors Scientists. I don't know the difference. They specialize in the stresses of long-term deployments, living in confined spaces, stuff like that. You could take your psych degree and apply it there, with me. Maybe even get your Masters at the same time. Then, if we don't get selected for the mission, we can go back to plan A and move to Boston."

Christopher turned back towards the instruments, then looked out the windshield again. His eyes seemed to be scanning the sky and the terrain in the distance.

Liam watched him and waited. He applied a little pressure to the yoke, gently guiding their heading a bit to the west.

As soon as he did, Christopher let go of the yoke and folded his hands in his lap. He closed his eyes and leaned his head back onto the headrest of his seat.

"I can defer for a year," he said finally. Opening his eyes again, he turned his head and looked at Liam. "You should have told me."

"I know. I'm sorry," responded Liam.

Christopher gave a quick nod. "If in a year's time, things aren't working out, I'm going to Boston, with or without you."

"It's going to work out," Liam said. "I can feel it."

4 - The Prodigy - Aug 2128 - Corinth, NY

Edward / Mericiel

Edward woke in a sweat with his blankets tangled around him. His heart was still pounding, but as he looked around his room, everything was quiet. He sat up and pushed his damp hair out of his eyes.

His parents had asked him to try to stay in his bed at night, even when he had his nightmares, but Edward knew that they didn't understand what it was like. The images from his dreams didn't just fade away when he was awake. If he didn't check on them, he would never be able to go back to sleep.

As quietly as he could, Edward slipped into the cool hallway then across into the warmth of his parents' room. He had learned to move slowly and to stay at the foot of their bed to avoid waking them up. He stood there and listened. His father's breathing was slow and deep. Edward closed his eyes and tried to match the rhythm with his own breathing, then he turned his head a bit to try to hear his mother. Her breathing was different. The pitch was higher, and each breath was quicker. He stayed for another minute to listen to them, then quietly turned and left their room.

Now that he was awake, he knew he didn't have any choice. He wouldn't be able to get comfortable again until he went downstairs and double checked that everything was OK. He stood at the top of the stairs and listened, but the only sound he could make out was the faint echo of the kitchen clock. He took one step and waited again, straining to hear any other noises from below. Slowly, stopping to listen with each step, he made his way to the bottom of the stairs, then stood as still as he could and searched the shadows for any sign of movement.

Just beyond the base of the stairs was the front door. Edward checked that the bolt was locked. He pushed on the door to feel if it was firmly shut. One night, he had found that it wasn't even closed all the way. The bolt was just resting against the doorframe. He went into the study and touched each window. All were closed and locked. From there he went into the living room at the back of the house and lightly slid his fingers over each window lock, confirming they were all flipped to the left. The back door was locked, and so was the door to the garage.

There... Edward took a deep breath and let it out slowly. Finally, he went back into the kitchen and checked that the stove was off and the toaster unplugged.

He thought about going back up to his bed, and immediately felt an urge to recheck the front door. Glancing toward the front of the house, Edward noticed the faint glow of blue light spilling into the hallway. His computer must have turned on in the study.

I'll check the doors one more time, then I'll go back to bed.

****

When Mericiel got to the bottom of the stairs, she found Edward there in the study playing one of his computer games. "How long have you been up?" she asked him.

"Um, not long, like maybe 45 minutes," Edward answered.

In so many ways, Mericiel expected Edward to act like an adult. He argued like an adult when he wanted something, but she had to remind herself that he was only 10, and that he didn't have a feel for time. He would say weeks, when she knew that he meant months, and he never really knew how long he had spent on the computer.

Paul was coming down the stairs behind her. "Hey bud, you saving the world for us?"

"This game is so stupid sometimes. You can't even really win it. You do everything right and then the earth is destroyed anyway because they make you steer your ship back to the Outpost."

Mericiel could hear Edward's voice trembling when he answered. He was upset. She was pretty sure that he hadn't slept enough, and he probably needed to eat something. "OK, honey. Let's leave the game alone for a while and eat some breakfast, OK?"

"Mom, I'm in the middle of a mission! If I leave it now, I'll have to start over!"

Paul took a step into the study and looked at the screen. "Hey buddy, I have an idea."

Edward turned to look at his father, and Mericiel could see the little muscles in her son's shoulders and face relax. It was so frustrating. She and her friends had talked about how their kids controlled themselves so much more when talking to their fathers, but let their emotions run wild with their mothers.

"This is one of those Phocis games, isn't it?" asked Paul. "What if we make a mod for it, so that you don't have to steer your ships that way?"

"Really? You know how to make our own mod?"

"Well, I don't know yet, but I can try. Which one of these ships isn't doing what you want?"

Edward started pointing to objects on the screen. "Here, this one. You see this little ball and the big ring? So, I'm in the ball, that's the NLS ship, and the ring is for finding stuff and it follows me. But watch, I'm finding something over here, but then I have to leave it because I have to land on the Outpost station or I'll die. I just want the ring to keep on going without me. I don't want it to follow me to the Outpost."

Paul nodded. "OK, I think I understand. So listen, this is going to take me at least a half an hour to figure this out. Why don't you go with your mom and eat something, and I'll call you when I'm ready."

Edward paused for a moment, then turned from the screen to his father and nodded. He hopped up from the desk, walked over to Mericiel, and looked up at her expectantly. When she didn't move, he lifted one eyebrow.

Mericiel had to fight the urge to roll her eyes. *So not fair,* she thought to herself.

Once he was eating a piece of toast, Mericiel asked Edward. "What's this game called again?"

"It's called 'After the Sphinx'. It's so cool. Giant clouds made out of dark matter fly through the solar system and mess up the orbits of asteroids and comets and stuff. The first one is Sphinx. Do you want to see it?" Edward's speech had grown rapid, and he was looking at her intently.

"Sure," she answered.

He walked over to a computer in the living room and said, "Here. I'll just show you the video that plays when you start. OK, there. Do you see the planets and the sun? OK, now watch. Do you see that asteroid? It's called Sphinx-896. It's going around on its orbit but then look, it just turns."

As he spoke, Mericiel noticed the time and date on the screen. It read January 2109. The hours and days were rolling by fast, as if time was sped up in the video.

"Did you see it turn?" asked Edward. "A dark matter cloud flew through the solar system and messed up Sphinx's orbit. Wait, this is cool too, look. Sphinx starts going faster and faster towards the sun. Do you see it?"

Mericiel tried to answer, but her voice caught in her throat. She had never taken the time to watch Edward play this game before.

"OK, watch this now," said Edward. "When the Sphinx gets close to the sun it starts to glow, like it's turning into lava, then it flies back out from the sun and slams into Earth. It's still all melted and glowing."

The date on the screen froze on November 10th, 2109. There were red dots punctuating strike zones up and down the Pacific region. The screen went dark, then came back to a model of the solar system with planets and asteroids orbiting around the sun. "Isn't it cool?" asked Edward.

Tears had started to stream down Mericiel's face. It was too late to hide her reaction from her son, but he was old enough now to hear the truth. "Baby, I remember that asteroid. It was such a sad day for me. It killed so many people, and everything, even the weather, was crazy afterwards."

She was openly crying now, remembering that global trauma. She was speaking slowly, watching to see if he was understanding. "I was in college, and I was supposed to have my French exams that day, but they cancelled classes. The news was playing in every building, all day. I can still picture my friends' faces as we sat around watching it. Some of them had family members in the countries that got hit."

Edward was shaking his head. "But mom, this isn't that. This is a survival game," he said. "The goal is to fly your ships out to where the dark matter is coming from and see where it is. For each cloud you find, the program draws an arrow of where it's going so you can tell if it'll come near us."

He reached up and squeezed one of her crossed arms with his small hand. "You see? This makes it better."

She could feel the heat from his hand, and the warmth spread through her whole body. Just seeing how excited he was actually made Mericiel feel better. It was nice to see him being so positive for once. Usually he worried about everything.

She took a deep breath, then let it out slowly. With it, the memories and emotions that had overtaken her so suddenly began to recede. She ruffled Edwards' hair and said, "I didn't see the dark matter. Why did that Sphinx asteroid turn like that?"

Edward rolled his eyes. "Mom, you can't see dark matter. It's dark. But when really big clouds of it get too close to stuff like asteroids, then it makes them turn."

"Asteroids, huh?" replied Mericiel. "You're like 'Le Petit Prince'. Do you want to live on an asteroid and fall in love with a rose?"

"I'd rather have a boa constrictor," he said with a grin. Mericiel hugged him tightly and held him for a few seconds. She took another deep breath, letting the last bit of sadness leave her. She was so blessed to have this little guy in her life. She and Paul had tried for a long time before Edward came along.

Just then, they heard Paul's voice from the other room. "I think it's ready!"

Edward was back at his father's side in seconds, and Mericiel followed him into the study. Part of his breakfast was still in his hand. "What is it that you're doing for him?"

"It's a mod, a modification to the game. This company, Phocis, makes games that support patches. The patches can modify how the games run, so it's kind of like he'll have a private version of the game."

"But you can share them," added Edward. "I want to share mine with Colin."

"The actual behavioral change didn't take too long, but the rest of it, bundling it up into a mod and exporting it, was a little bit more --" Paul lifted his hands in the air and leaned backwards as Edward squeezed himself between his father and the computer and started controlling the little spaceships.

He had barely played 30 seconds, then groaned. "No, it doesn't work. The sensors still follow me when I turn back to the Outpost."

"Oh, no, you have to hit the D key to detach before you head back," answered Paul.

Edward lifted an eyebrow and went back to playing. As he did, Mericiel saw cloud shapes appearing behind the rings. It reminded her of making soapy bubbles with a big hoop in the yard. "What are those swirly cloud things?" she asked him.

"Those are the clumps of dark matter," he answered. "When my ships fly back and forth, I can make them light up, so we know where they are."

"Dad, it worked. Look, that ring is still finding stuff over there, but I can land on the Outpost now! Cool! It's finding stuff that I couldn't see before."

"Ahem," Mericiel cleared her throat, catching Edward's attention and raising her eyebrows.

"Thank you, dad. This is awesome!" said Edward. He gave his father a quick hug around the neck then went back to playing the game. Mericiel and Paul exchanged a smile. She loved seeing Edward so happy with something that his father had done for him.

"You know," Paul said, "your mother and I know some people who joined the Space Agency after college. They might be on one of these ships."

"Cool!" said Edward as his fingers tapped keys, but he was only half listening. "Dad, it's really working. Can you share the mod with my friends so that we can play together?"

"OK," answered Paul. "What should we name it?"

Edward turned and looked at him, then tilted his head to one side.

Paul was going to be on his own. "OK, so you're in that ball, looking for stuff, so it's kind of like an eyeball. And that ring helps you, like eyeglasses. How about Monocle?"

"OK," said Edward. Mericiel wondered if he was following Paul's logic.

Paul clicked a few more buttons on the game site, and the upload started. He showed it to Edward on the screen and told him. "There it is. Now anyone can download it. You just have to tell your friends the name."

"Monocle," murmured Edward to himself as he read the screen. Suddenly though, he lifted his hand and let his fingers run over the text under the icon, then he turned to his father and looked at him quizzically. "Dad, you put my name on it."

Paul smiled, and exchanged another look with Mericiel. She was actually surprised that Edward had even bothered to read the details on the screen.

"Yeah, buddy," answered Paul. "This was your idea from the beginning. I'm just the lead programmer on your engineering team."

"This is the coolest thing ever," said Edward, touching the spot on the screen again where his name was displayed. Then, looking back and forth between his parents, he asked, "Can I call Colin and tell him about the mod so that we can both play?"

"Um, it's still kind of early," replied Mericiel. "I vote that you curl up on the couch and try to close your eyes for a little while. I still don't know what time you got up this morning."

To her surprise, Edward nodded. He rubbed one of his eyes as he stood up from the desk.

****

It was after midnight when Mericiel heard the noise. She was about to wake Paul when she recognized Edward's voice. She got out of bed and went downstairs. He was there, playing the game.

"Edward, what are you doing up? It's 12:30."

When he turned to look at her, his eyes were gaunt, and his face was drawn. "I can't stop them. They just keep coming."

"What, honey. What keeps coming?"

"The asteroids. I don't want you to be sad again, Mom, but no matter what I try, there's always more of them."

"It's OK sweetie. We just have to live our lives. We can't worry about things that might happen."

He didn't seem to hear her. Mericiel never forgave herself for crying in front of her son that day. His fears got so much worse after that.

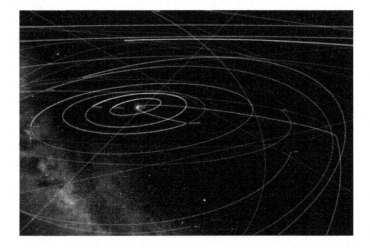

5 - A Patriarch - 2114 - Sarawak, Malaysia

Jacqueline

At first Jacqueline couldn't see anything, but as her vision cleared it was obvious that she was on the ground. She could make out every detail of the cracked asphalt beneath her. In the distance, beyond a growth of low weeds, loomed an abandoned two-story building of red brick. The windows on the first floor were boarded up. On the second floor, granite sills underscored the empty window frames. The building was dark, but looking up at it from the ground as she was, Jacqueline could see through the upper windows to slivers of blue sky where the roof had given way. Blue sky was one of the things that she had missed most during the past few years.

In the center of Jacqueline's field of view, resting peacefully on the boundary between the asphalt and the weeds, was a young woman. She sat cross-legged among a jumble of poorly stacked cinder blocks, her thick black hair gathered forward over one of her bare shoulders. Jacqueline barely recognized herself from this angle. Most of her face was covered by her goggles, and the tawny bronze tone of her arms and legs seemed to exaggerate the sculpted lines of her athletic frame.

She closed her eyes for a moment and took an unsteady breath.

It's ok. It's no different from the game.

This was the fifth day in a row that Jacqueline found herself here. She hadn't managed to get off the ground yet. Each time, she had lost her nerve and given up.

Six days ago, she would have never believed that she would be holding the controls of a real drone again. The online games that she secretly played weren't really flying, they were just games, and she was very careful that no one in her house ever knew about them. The package from America had almost betrayed her. Anyone could have seen it there, just sitting on her bed waiting for her to get home.

If Jacqueline had realized that it was possible to win a drone by playing video games, she would have never played. A brief wave of nausea passed through her stomach, so she closed her eyes again and waited for it to subside.

Just move your fingers.

A high-pitched whine rose in Jacqueline's ears, and when she opened her eyes again, she saw that the scene in front of her was trembling slightly. The sound grew louder, and her perspective rose up as the quadcopter lifted off the ground. She hadn't even realized that she was smiling until she saw her own face through the drone's first-person view camera.

A second later though, movement caught her eye. The smile vanished and the sick feeling inside of her came surging back. The gait of the man walking toward her was unmistakable. He had just rounded the corner of the brick building and was coming straight for her.

Quickly, Jacqueline landed the quadcopter in the same spot from where it had lifted off moments earlier. She switched off the controller and took off her goggles. Placing the controller and the goggles at her feet, she got up from where she was sitting and stood to meet Mr. Raban as he approached.

Raban was in charge of security for Jacqueline's grandfather, and his presence here was a sign that something was wrong. She immediately suspected that her trainers had notified Mr. Wan that she hadn't shown up to the gym this past week.

Raban stopped a few meters away. Jacqueline knew that he preferred to keep a respectful distance, even more so at seeing her bare arms and legs.

"Ms. Wan, are you alone?" Raban asked, looking at the equipment that Jacqueline had with her.

"Please don't call me Ms. Wan," she replied. "If my grandfather can't tolerate hearing the name 'Binti Abdullah', then just call me Jacqueline. You have known me for my whole life."

Raban did not seem to react. "Miss, are these your belongings?" asked Raban, indicating the drone and the controllers. "If your grandfather learns of this he will be quite displeased with me."

Jacqueline didn't know how to answer. She didn't want to tell Raban about the package that had turned her life upside down a week ago. Ultimately, she decided to say nothing at all.

It worked. Raban changed the subject. "Your grandfather wants to see you immediately, but I think that it would be better for both of us if he doesn't see you looking as you do."

"Thank you, Mr. Raban. I will gather my things here and head back to the compound. I assume that he is at home?"

"Yes, miss. You can come back with me," he replied.

"No, I'm fine. I have one of the private cars with me," she said. Raban nodded, but he didn't turn to leave. Jacqueline realized that he would watch her pack up and that he would insist on riding back to the compound with her, like a good soldier.

"I'll send my car back then," said Raban. Arguing would be pointless. Jacqueline didn't even bother wondering how Raban had located her. Keeping track of her comings and goings was just part of his job.

****

On the drive back to her grandfather's estate, Jacqueline tried to prepare herself for what she would hear. *'This was the best team in the country, and if she wanted to qualify for the SEA games, she would listen to her coaches. Who was she to doubt the word of such people? They were professionals and champions. She needed to learn how to win, how to be relentless. It was the only way that she could succeed one day, when she would hold the reins of his empire.'*

Maybe he would surprise her. Jacqueline didn't think of her grandfather as a kind man, but she kept telling herself that above all, he was the only family that she had left, and so he was going to have to listen to her eventually. She tried not to pay attention to the voice in the back of her mind that said that her grandfather would never yield.

Jacqueline had confided once in Amah. She had told her about how bad things were at the training facility. Amah took her in her arms and held her, but Jacqueline understood that silent sympathy was all that Amah could ever offer. A servant was in no position to risk repeating such charged words in Mr. Wan's house. Jacqueline's grandfather had little tolerance for impertinence.

"Very well," said Mr. Raban to Jacqueline as they arrived. "I assume that you will need to change your clothes. I will inform Haji that you will be down in 30 minutes."

Jacqueline nodded, imagining the scene that would follow. It wasn't as much time as she had been hoping for, but she knew that she had probably exhausted Raban's generosity.

Jacqueline slipped off her sandals on the front porch then stepped through the great doors. As she walked silently toward her room, her mind raced to think of how she would explain what she had been doing with her days for the past week. She knew that she couldn't tell her grandfather about the quadcopter. As she rounded the corner at the top of the stairs, the sight of Amah waiting in her bedroom door gave Jacqueline a start.

Amah had picked out a conservative sundress, with long sleeves. Raban must have called ahead and asked her to help Jacqueline change.

The walk to her grandfather's study in the east wing felt like the longest in her life. *It's Saturday, so he shouldn't have people in his office this morning.* Still, if her assumptions were correct, and he had heard from her coaches, he was going to be even more angry than the last time that Jacqueline had tried to broach the subject of her gymnastics regime with him.

Jacqueline's pace slowed as she got further and further from the part of the house that she and Amah occupied. She was little more than a visitor in the east wing, and the sights and smells were foreign to her. The marble floors felt like ice on her feet, and the large doors that awaited her at the end of the hall were more intimidating than any in the whole house. Worse yet, they were closed.

She had only ever knocked on the closed doors of her grandfather's office once before. It was the day that she had come home from the drone championship in Kuala Lumpur. Returning to her grandfather's house without her mother or her grandmother had felt like walking out into the sea with the sound of thunder on the horizon.

Five years had passed, but the estate still felt empty without them. If they had come home with her that day, things would be different now. They would have done something to help her.

She lifted her hand and knocked hesitantly on the door with her knuckles. The sound was faint, and Jacqueline started to doubt that he would hear it. Now that she had knocked though, she didn't dare knock again in case he *had* actually heard her.

She was frozen, not knowing what to do as long seconds ticked by, straining to hear any sound coming from within. Her mother would have just pushed the doors open and strode in, insolent and oblivious to Mr. Wan's judgment.

You weren't afraid of anything.

Jacqueline had only been 12 years old when she'd come back to live alone with her grandfather. She had never gotten over the feeling that he blamed her for his wife's death.

The Ghost of Sphinx

"Your mother brought shame into this house," he said to her, "and your grandmother allowed it. It will be up to us to make this right."

Jacqueline had started to cry, but Mr. Wan waved the back of his hand at her, and Mr. Haji ushered Jacqueline out of the office and back to the west wing. She didn't even bother to wonder what other shame her mother had brought to the house. The message was clear enough, even to a 12-year-old.

For the past five years, Amah and the rest of the household staff cared for Jacqueline, but none of them would talk to her about how things had been before.

"Mr. Wan has certain expectations that must be respected," they would say. Jacqueline had heard those exact words countless times.

There was still no sound from inside the office and Jacqueline was working up her courage to knock a second time. She stood mere inches from the imposing doors with her hands at her sides. Just as she had started to bend the fingers of her right hand to knock again, the door opened. Standing behind it was Mr. Haji, who served as Mr. Wan's valet and secretary.

"Ms. Wan, your grandfather is expecting you," said Mr. Haji, "but you must be brief. He has a call with the head of the Samling group in less than an hour, and he must prepare."

Jacqueline heard her grandfather's voice, and Mr. Haji stepped back, sweeping his left hand toward the deep hardwood book-shelves that lined the inside of the office. She lowered her eyes and kept them low as she entered, but as soon as she had a clear line of sight, she stole a glance up at her grandfather sitting behind his desk. On either side of him were floor to ceiling doors leading out onto the terrace. The light that came in through those doors was sharp, even painful in contrast to the dark wood tones inside the office.

Mr. Wan's desk was sculpted from a single 74 cm thick kidney-shaped cross section of a giant sequoia, red brown and strikingly beautiful. Years earlier, her mother had told Jacqueline that there were over 1000 rings visible on the desk's surface, and Jacqueline had often wondered what had become of the rest of that ancient tree.

Mr. Wan's wealth and power were rooted in the timber business. His influence on the local economy and politics had grown over the years as the rainforest of Sarawak diminished. The sequoia that had given its cross-section to this desk was not even indigenous to Malaysia, and Jacqueline knew without asking that very few people in the world could have obtained something so rare.

Jacqueline's steps had begun to slow, but the sound of Mr. Hadji clearing his throat snapped her to attention. She looked back at him, and he flicked his eyes toward the center of the room. She pulled herself up as straight as she knew how, lifted her chin, then turned and strode toward the redwood desk with the confidence and presence that gymnastics had trained her to deliver.

The effect was immediate. Mr. Wan leaned back in his chair and looked at her with half closed eyes. There might have even been the hint of a smile for a moment. Gymnastics was one area where Jacqueline could earn his approval. On the few occasions when she had exchanged polite conversation with her grandfather, Mr. Wan had repeated the refrain that he saw a pathway for her in gymnastics. He told Jacqueline that competing in the South East Asia Games would teach her more about how to succeed in business than any book ever written. It was ironic that her training should work to Jacqueline's advantage, today of all days.

The warmth of his features didn't last. "Jacqueline, sit," he said curtly, leaning forward and lifting a small hand-written note from his desk.

Jacqueline started to sit, but then stopped herself. She took a deep breath and tried to straighten her back and hold his gaze. She didn't want to be small. She wanted to stand her ground, but after only a few seconds of hesitation, she sat down.

His eyes followed her as she sat, and he leaned further forward and tilted his head down toward her. She knew that even her short delay in obeying his order would be unacceptable to him.

"It has been brought to my attention that you have shown yourself irresponsible in regard to your training schedule. Given the magnitude of the investment that I am making in your career, I have come to a decision. Coach Yeien is willing to accept you in the team's boarding program. It is the only way to guarantee that you meet the demands of your training."

Jacqueline felt the blood drain from her face. Her lungs tightened, as she tried to find her words.

"Grandfather, no, please. I don't want to live there. The trainers treat us like they own us. They know that I don't want to compete in the SEA Games, but they're trying to get me qualified anyway because they don't want to lose you as a client."

He placed the note back on his desk and sat up straighter.

"Don't let them deceive you," she said, but she heard her own voice trail off as she realized that she had gone too far.

He raised his eyebrows and shook his head slightly. "Your mother was prone to exaggeration," he said. "It is unfortunate that you have inherited this trait."

How can you talk about her that way?

The image of Jacqueline's mother flashed through her mind, and it made her eyes and nose sting.

"You should not underestimate me," he said. "My investments in this team are strategic. To compete in the SEA Games, you must simply try out. The rest is taken care of."

Suddenly, Jacqueline had clarity. He had already bribed the officials to get her qualified. Mr. Wan and some of the other timber tycoons of Sarawak were among the richest people in Malaysia. Of course he had bribed the committee. He had been talking to her about the South East Asia Games for years.

Jacqueline nodded for a moment out of respect. When she replied, she tried to keep her voice soft but firm. "Please, grandfather. I will be 18 years old in two months. I know that you value a competitive spirit, but I could compete at university. It's not fair that you let Ibu go away to study, but you won't even consider letting me do the same." She kept her eyes low. This was no time to risk angering him further.

"No. I will not make the same mistakes with you that I made with my daughter and I have decided that it is time for me to correct the errors that she made with you. She over-indulged you right up until her last day in Kuala Lumpur."

Acid rose up in Jacqueline's throat, and her gaze hardened on her grandfather. "If she were here, she wouldn't let you do this to me. She would fight you."

Jacqueline knew. She knew that she couldn't go back. Slowly, she rose from her chair, held herself tall and said, "I won't be their prisoner."

Mr. Wan stood. He took off his glasses and placed them on the magnificent sequoia desk. He walked all the way around it until he was in front of her. He stood uncomfortably close to Jacqueline, but she met his gaze and even drew herself up a little taller.

As he looked at her, his mouth twisting into a thin line, and she realized that as terrified as she was, it wasn't enough for him. He had expected her to cower. He had expected to frighten her back into her chair. As the idea came to her, she couldn't help but smile, ever so slightly.

She watched his eyes as he studied her. Slowly, Mr. Wan's head tipped down and Jaqueline saw the shadow of a jagged vein on his brow. He brought up his hand and slapped her violently across the face. "Get out of this office and do as I have instructed you. We will correct what your mother has corrupted in you. One way or the other."

Jacqueline didn't turn her head back towards him after the force of the slap. She knew instinctively that to do so would have been more defiance that his pride could endure. She turned away from him and walked quickly out of the office, brushing past Mr. Haji as she rushed through the door.

Once in the hallway, Jacqueline broke into a full run. Her face was still stinging, and she didn't know how long she had before they would come for her. She thought back on Haji's words and hoped that he would wait to deal with her until after the business call that he had mentioned.

Amah was waiting for her at the top of the stairs, and when she saw Jacqueline she breathed, "Oh child, what have you done? Why are you crying?"

Jacqueline knew that she was dooming Amah along with herself, and she heard her own voice tremble as she said, "They're sending me away." Amah put her arms around Jacqueline and as their heads touched, she heard Amah's muffled breath as the two of them cried softly.

She released Amah from her tight squeeze, and let her hands run down her soft arms. This woman, who had cared for her for so long, was going to suffer Mr. Wan's anger too, collateral damage in the battle over Jacqueline's future. They both knew it, but there was no blame in Amah's eyes, only sympathy and fear.

Suddenly though, the fear came into sharp focus. Jacqueline heard a noise behind her and realized that the dread on Amah's face was for her. She slowly turned and saw that Mr. Raban was coming up the stairs. She adjusted her feet and stood to face him for a second time. There was an envelope in his right hand, and he clearly had Jacqueline in his sights as he walked, eyes alert, jaw set.

Jacqueline was trapped. If Raban was here, then she had missed any chance. Raban had always been able to find her. Even this morning, he had just appeared with no warning. She had never minded before, that she was such easy prey for Mr. Raban, that he could track her movements effortlessly, but now, the thought overwhelmed her. She was ready to run away from her grandfather, but she had never really considered what it would mean to escape Mr. Raban's reach.

Jacqueline let her shoulders slump forward and imagined what it would be like to step back into the training facility, with her coaches looking smugly down at her. Raban reached the top of the stairs and took a final step toward her. He had not been this close to her since the day that her mother had died, and the room got a little darker as he leaned in.

He lifted his hand, slowly, and brought the large manilla envelope up into the narrow space that remained between them. He arched his head forward slightly, his face just inches from her hair. When he spoke, it was barely a whisper. "Take this, miss. Haji has called me, and I need to make my way to Mr. Wan's office. I believe that this will be the last time that I may be able to do anything kind for you. I only wish I had acted sooner."

As Jacqueline slowly took the envelope from Raban's right hand, she felt something strange. This stoic man who had not stood closer than two meters from her in the past five years had lifted his left arm and was, ever so softly, touching the crown of her head with the fingertips of his left hand. It was so light that Jacqueline wasn't even sure that she had really felt it.

"You deserve so much more than this one thing that I can offer you. I am giving you a head start. Please don't ever let me find you again."

Within seconds, Raban had turned and was heading back down the stairs. As he walked away, Jacqueline saw him touch the side of his head before saying, "Yes, I'm on my way to you now."

6 - An Observatory - 2112 - Houston, Texas

Colleen

A thin smile crossed Colleen's lips. She had been whispering in Tinghir's ear for six months before he finally set Katherine loose on the project, and today would make it official. Her checkmate move had come and gone more than three weeks ago, but Crespin still didn't realize it. He was so busy going after her pawns that he probably even thought he was winning.

Colleen knew that Tinghir was ambitious. She knew that he wanted to sail out on a high note, and the GhostMap program had all of the hallmarks of Big Science. It was a big-budget project, and it had the world's attention. In the past year alone, over 50 research papers had been published in major journals creating a theoretical foundation for the first GhostMap measurements, but in spite of everything, there was still something lacking. It didn't fit into the same research ecology that drove other Big Science projects.

Colleen was half-way to the conference room when she noticed that she wasn't wearing her AR glasses.

Shit, they must be in the lab.

She felt naked without them and quickly changed direction to get another pair from her office. It was going to make her late, but she couldn't go into a meeting with Tinghir and Crespin without her notes.

As soon as she stepped through her office door, Colleen spotted the spare pair of glasses sitting on her desk. She picked them up and plucked an up-to-date memory pin from its data socket, then set out again towards the conference room named *Schwarzschild*. As she walked, Colleen tried to insert the new pin into the stem of the glasses, but it took her several attempts. Her fingers were trembling, as if she had gone too long without a cigarette.

She saw the Director look at his watch as she entered the room, but she knew that he wouldn't say anything. Colleen took a moment to look around as the airman in the corridor closed the door behind her. Colonel Crespin accorded her a small nod. Katherine Othoni, the Space Agency's general counsel, was present as well. Colleen did a quick calculation and decided to place herself next to Colonel Crespin rather than across from him.

I'll wear my sheep's clothing today...

Director Tinghir began to speak before she was even seated. "Well, we're all here then. Today we will be conducting an administrative review of several aspects of the Galactic Halo Substructure Mapping mission. As you all know, the GhostMap program is the most ambitious and costly mission that this Agency has ever undertaken, and the risks involved are significant."

Everyone nodded and Tinghir's voice was somber, but Colleen couldn't help but see the Agency's investment in her plan as evidence of their confidence in her.

"Let's start with our simulation models of mission scenarios," said Tinghir. "Dr. Pastor, can you tell us how things are going there?"

"Well, we have successfully built our first-generation models," said Colleen, "but we're hitting roadblocks in collaborating with both academic and industry partners. The administrative hurdles required to share information seem to have multiplied in the past few months."

Colonel Crespin spoke up. "If you are referring to the recent veto of your plan to open up mission details to gamers, then I concur, Doctor. I and others in my chain of command have serious reservations about the safety of leaking mission details for no other reason than to allow the public to play more realistic games. I'm afraid that I will have to insist on maintaining an acceptable level of information security."

"Colonel, crowdsourcing has been used for hundreds of years to take advantage of the public's knowledge and creativity," said Colleen. "If you really have concerns with that concept, then you should probably move your retirement savings into gold, because the stock market runs on the same principle."

Colleen turned in her chair and faced Crespin directly. "We have the opportunity here to get millions of people to role play the types of choices that our pilots and crew are going to face up there. Our existing gaming partnerships have already helped us identify promising candidates for the Near Light Speed training program."

"Case in point, Doctor," said Crespin. "These games of yours are a constant source of distraction. We have a two-year deadline for creating a squad of flyers who are capable of surviving the inhuman conditions that your engineering team is offering us. We don't have time for these fanciful methods."

Turning to the Director, Crespin continued. "Just this week I learned that Dr. Pastor has drawn up a list of potential civilians who she believes will demonstrate some secret advantage over well trained military personnel. Most of them aren't even citizens."

Colleen snorted. "Oh please, have you really taken the time to look at the dossiers that you're referring to? I believe that these candidates fit the bill of materials for the NLS mission perfectly: lightning reflexes, pilot training, small lightweight stature, and enough physical strength to withstand the requisite g-forces."

"I have made myself clear about the flaws with this mission plan," the Colonel shot back, "111 hours at 75 g... It's solitary confinement, a strait jacket, and a death sentence rolled into one. You should leave the recruiting to us, Doctor, and focus your energies on finding better technical solutions to these problems. Very few human beings can do what you're asking of these pilots."

"Now we're agreeing. You need the right type of humans," responded Colleen. "I have confidence that the candidates I have identified will perform better at almost every aspect of NLS training than more traditional candidates."

"And your position is that these superhumans are sitting around playing video games?" he asked.

Colleen knew that Crespin already had this information. Was he trying to bait her?

Turning towards Katherine, she explained, "Players who perform well enough in the games are shown an ad to apply for a spot on the mission. Once they offer us their identities, my contacts at the FBI look into their background and see if they have the right physical characteristics."

Director Tinghir looked Colleen in the eye and gestured to her to stop. The exchange was escalating, and both the Director and Colleen knew that the most important part of the meeting was still ahead of them.

"Dr. Pastor, let me remind you that this is a military operation, funded by a military budget," said Crespin. "There is no more room for your experimentation in the recruiting and training of our pilots."

"Yes, about that, Colonel," said Tinghir. "I need to inform you that the GhostMap program is being reclassified. As of today, the

Nest and Outpost propulsion stations as well as the NLS ships are to be categorized as components of a large-scale scientific observatory. As such, this will no longer be, strictly speaking, a military mission."

This is what she was waiting for. Colleen was dying to see the look on Crespin's face and had to fight the urge to turn towards him.

"Director," said Crespin, shaking his head. It took him another few seconds to formulate his objection. "That would be a mistake. Labelling a fleet of vessels as *An Observatory* and leaving all decisions up to conference rooms full of ivory tower scientists is going to lead directly to a loss of life. You can mark my words."

"Well," countered Tinghir, "by reclassifying, and by bringing in more partners, we gain access to vital resources to get the job done more quickly. I think that this too can be crucial for saving lives, don't you?"

Crespin crossed his arms and leaned back in his chair. "I think that the joint chiefs will have something to say about this."

"I'm afraid, Colonel, that reclassifying the GhostMap program is the current plan of record," said Tinghir. "I have been in touch with the Pentagon, and the decision is made. Katherine has already drawn up the legal framework. In effect, this will alter the authority structure of the operation from predominantly military to predominantly civilian and scientific in nature."

Crespin was shaking his head, but Tinghir pressed on. "The Pentagon is taking steps to activate a new recruiting squadron that will be searching for specialists in the fields of astronomy, nuclear power, optical physics and the like. They are even creating a new ROTC program, working with universities to offer graduate research positions on the Nest and the Outpost."

"We're not forming a study group here, Director. These people will need military discipline if they want to survive on a twenty-year mission." Crespin looked at each of them in turn.

Doesn't he get it? It's already done.

Colleen turned to Katherine and asked, "Have you already begun the process of re-classifying the GhostMap program as an observatory?"

"Yes, I filed the necessary paperwork a few weeks ago," replied Katherine. "As of this morning, we have signed memoranda of understanding initiating official collaborations across no fewer than 18 scientific institutions, 11 of which represent international partners and three of which represent private business."

"That is very impressive, Katherine," said Tinghir.

"Director, if I may," said Colonel Crespin, "I don't find this impressive at all. Decentralizing all decision making is nothing less than a dereliction of our duty to lead."

Turning to Colleen, he added, "I am not naive, Doctor. I know that you are behind this, and I will not sit idly by while you squander the lives of my people. If this arrogance results in so much as a single unnecessary death, I will personally see to it that you be held accountable."

7 - A Commission - November 2112 - Houston, Texas

Liam

Breathing was becoming harder, and Liam's eyes had gone out of focus again. He heard one of the engineers in the control booth acknowledge his last command. "70g confirmed, Captain. Your current speed is 4716 kilometers per hour, 5 rpms. Awaiting your status."

Liam needed another second to reply. The instruments were going in and out of focus as the optics in his helmet adapted to the latest deformation of his corneas. Each change in g-force came with a corresponding change in prescription, and the helmet's retinal scanner took three or four seconds to measure it accurately. Once he was able to see clearly again, Liam directed his gaze to the icon for the temporal link and double clicked his teeth to select it.

"Roger that, G-loop. Status is nominal. Vision clear. Airway clear. Maintain speed at 4716. Over." Liam's mouth guard made speaking impossible, but the temporal link in his helmet was enough to send text messages to his flight test engineers. At 70g, he was completely immobilized, so his helmet's ability to track his eye movements and transcribe his thoughts was critical. Reinforcing his neck so that it didn't snap was another key feature.

Liam was, once again, setting a record for the highest g-force withstood by a human. Today's test not only brought him to 70g, almost 50% more than the long-established 46g human limit, but he was going to endure the g-force for two hours and carry out basic tasks by moving only his eyes, his jaw, and his fingertips.

"Captain, be advised. Colonel Crespin has requested a meeting with you. Shall I schedule it after your post-flight MR scan?"

"Roger that, Airman Skotadi. Thank you."

After another second, Liam sent a follow up message. "Rhea, how do things look on your end? Do you need me to do anything before I begin my test sequence at 70g?"

"Stand by," answered Airman Skotadi. When she opened the channel again, Liam could hear the voices of several of his crew.

"Captain, we'd like permission to try a new program in your COFLEX," one of them said.

"It's supposed to offer improved circulation in your forearms and calves," added Rhea. "What do you say? Are you up for a massage?"

****

A little more than two hours later, Liam climbed out of the pod with his helmet in his hand. He spotted the pink shock of Colleen's hair from across the room and made his way over to her. "Hey, I didn't know you were here. I wanted to talk to you about my next G-loop test. I think that I'm ready to go up to 80g."

"I'm not here to chat, and you are scheduled for an MR scan," she answered. "I don't want to get all involved in a conversation then have you stroke out on me just when I get to the good parts. I hate repeating myself."

Liam turned his palms up and shot her a look. His flight test engineers were all watching the conversation, and some of them were smiling.

"Page me when you're ready and we'll get dinner," she said stepping in close. She wasn't even looking him in the eye. She had placed one of her hands on the exaggerated pectoral section of his body armor and was lifting his arm with the other hand, squinting to inspect some detail or other of the shoulder joint.

"I have to meet the Colonel first. He wants to see me about something."

"Fine," she said, "just come find me after that then. That'll give me time to look at your MRI results before we talk about going any faster."

Liam nodded, moving towards the exit, bowing his head to avoid hitting it as he left the control hut. Once outside, he placed his COFLEX helmet on the passenger seat of Colleen's golf cart, then set off at a jog back to the main campus.

****

Colonel Alesandro Crespin had his hands clasped behind his back as he looked out the window of his office, surveying the training field.

Liam knocked on the frame of the open door. "You wanted to see me, sir?"

Crespin turned his shoulders slightly and raised his chin. "Captain, yes, please come in."

As Liam entered, Crespin turned to face him and gestured towards a chair. "Have a seat, son. I have several things that I'd like to talk to you about."

Liam sat, straight backed, and waited attentively.

The Colonel had taken a seat as well and reviewed some information on his desk before continuing. "I see here that you've been able to speed up progress on the test runs of the G-loop. Let's start there. How'd you manage it?"

"Yes, sir. As you know, both the COFLEX body armor and the high g-force hyperloop are experimental, and we couldn't prove out the capabilities of the COFLEX without the g-loop. The Flight Test Engineers had put together a very conservative schedule to control for all risks. Obviously, as the first test pilot, I appreciated that. However, as I sat with each of them, it became clear that they hadn't considered the possibility that the test pilot would be able to take an active role in correlating the human experience inside the pod to their engineering projections. Once I took the time to document their goals and their concerns and connect the dots for them on what I planned to look for in my maneuver-by-maneuver test plan, we all agreed that we could speed up the process without compromising safety."

Crespin narrowed his eyes slightly. "And how do you find working with the civilian staff, the scientists? They seem to think very highly of you."

"I enjoy it very much, sir. Having studied engineering myself, we have a common language, but the caliber of the engineers on this project goes well beyond my own level of study. I am satisfied with the degree of mutual respect that we have established."

"Excellent," said Crespin. "I've asked you here to discuss what comes next for you. In spite of your effective command of the g-loop, I don't see your name on Dr. Pastor's list of NLS pilot candidates. That fits well with my plan for you. I'd like for you to consider--Is there a problem, Captain?"

Liam realized with a jolt that he had let his attention wander. He forced himself to make eye contact again with the Colonel. "I'm sorry sir. I didn't mean to be disrespectful. If I may, sir. Did you say that I'm not on the list of NLS candidates?"

"Yes, I did," answered Crespin. "I take it that our friend Dr. Pastor hasn't informed you that she left your name off the list?"

"That's correct, sir. I apologize if I seemed distracted. Please continue."

"Regardless of what I think of that decision, I called you here to recruit you as an officer for the Outpost station. The leadership that you've shown over the military and scientific staff of the g-loop has been exemplary. To my mind, it's exactly the type of leadership that will be required on the Outpost."

Liam straightened up in his chair. "The Outpost, sir?"

"Yes. Because of the prolonged duration of the deployment, we can't draw from our experienced officer pool. We need someone young, but who can effectively manage the military and scientific crew of that station. Since the Outpost is a propulsion station, we would ideally want someone who can understand the stresses and the mindset of the NLS pilots. You have proven yourself in both regards."

"I'm honored, Colonel. With your permission, sir. This is a big decision. Would it be appropriate for me to request a few days to think it over?"

Crespin's eyebrows pinched together for a moment. "Yes, take a few days, but when you come back to me, I'll need a firm commitment. We don't have the luxury of investing in anyone who can't offer 110% to this mission."

"Yes, sir. Thank you, sir. I understand."

Liam waited for the nod that would imply that he was dismissed, then he stood and left the Colonel's office.

****

Liam could see Colleen brushing a lock of tinted hair off her brow as he walked up to her office.

She looked up and saw him approaching. "Hey, what'd Crespin want?"

Liam relaxed the expression on his face and breathed deeply. "Colleen, did you leave me off the list of potential NLS pilots?"

"Ah, fuck. Yeah, I did. I'm sorry that you heard about it from someone else."

"Why? Why would you do that when I'm so close to meeting the mission criteria? I am literally the only person in the world who has survived the g-forces required for the mission."

Colleen shrugged. "Well, that's true, but I think that the gear that we built for you had something to do with that. We can make that gear for other people too."

Liam just stared at her.

"To be honest, you really shouldn't have done as well as you have done," she said. "For starters, you're too big. What do you weigh, like 100 kilos? The kids that I'm looking at to be NLS pilots are closer to 45 kilos, and they're wired differently from you. You don't fit the neuropsych profile that I'm targeting. You grew up in the real world, playing lacrosse, flying planes, and driving cars. Heavy machines move slowly. I need people who have been doing e-sports in simulated worlds with freaky physics. More importantly, I need people who have been doing them since they were 5 years old so that it's baked into their brains."

"Why?"

"It's hard to explain, but when you're traveling that fast, it screws with time," explained Colleen. "The amount of time that you feel passing and the amount of time that is passing outside your ship are off by a factor of 20. I need people with twitchy reflexes so that they can react fast enough to situations that might come up."

She leaned forward in her chair and looked at him directly. "Liam, the Outpost mission is prestigious. It's the tip of the spear for combating this threat. We need officers like you and Christopher to set up and maintain a durable social dynamic."

At the mention of Christopher's name, Liam lifted his gaze and started looking Colleen in the eye again.

"You showed us, in bringing the hyperloop online with the flight test engineers, that you can lead. We can't afford to squander someone like you by sealing you up in a steel ball for 12 months at a time. That's what I need from the kids that I'm tracking for the NLS mission. They have to be solo performers."

Liam tipped his head forward a little and looked at Colleen through his eyebrows. "What does that mean, 'the kids that you're tracking?'"

"Here, I'll show you," said Colleen. She sat down next to him and handed him a set of Augmented Reality glasses. As he put them on, he saw her reach behind them and tap the control pad.

Hundreds of photos and videos appeared in front of them in simulated piles. Each pile contained photos and videos for a different candidate. In front of each pile was the candidate's name, country of origin, and something called an excalibur score.

Liam worked the AR display, using three-fingered gestures to move the piles as he slowly perused them, and two-fingered gestures to swipe individual photos off of the stacks. He paused, looking more closely at some photos, and flicked away others, which re-joined their piles at the bottom.

"What does the excalibur number mean?" Liam asked as he shuffled through some of the photos.

"Oh, that. Heh, that's just a little joke of mine that I got from an old movie," said Colleen. "The score ranges from 0 to 100 and indicates how close they are to mastering the NLS tasks in my video game mods."

Liam studied the images. He was shuffling through the stack of photos and videos labelled 'Jacqueline'. Her age was displayed below each item, and the file followed her from age 12 to 15. The recent photos were all from gymnastics competitions.

"She's remarkable, isn't she?" said Colleen. "I actually saw her compete once."

Liam didn't say anything, but Colleen continued anyway. "She has the highest excalibur score of any of the recruits and, as you can see, she's in amazing physical condition."

Liam flipped through some more images. "She plays video games?" he asked, finally.

"No, she flies drones, or at least she did. She seems to have given it up a few years ago, but I've been tracking her for a long time. I've actually been thinking of having a modern quadcopter delivered to her anonymously to see if she'll start up again."

"She's tiny," observed Liam.

"Yeah, that's actually an asset. The g-forces are tough on the body, and small people tend to do better. This girl has hard landings all the time. She's probably experienced over 50g on her joints in a random week of gymnastics, but it's not only that. Don't underestimate the importance of the fact that she weighs less and that she even uses less oxygen than others. That all means that we can shorten the acceleration time and make the whole craft lighter." explained Colleen.

"How do you find them based on nothing more than a video game download?" asked Liam.

"Never mind that. Are you going to accept command of the Outpost or not?"

****

"What's all this?" Christopher asked as he entered the apartment to find Liam setting the table with a bottle of red wine and candles.

"It's kind of a celebration," said Liam. "I've been offered a promotion, but whether I take it or not depends on you."

Christopher furrowed his brow. He scanned the table again then looked back up at Liam. "I don't understand. Are you saying that you're quitting the Near Light Speed program? I've been assuming that I'd just go back to Boston once you deployed."

"Some stuff has happened. Let's serve ourselves and we can talk about it."

Liam handed Christopher a plate then carried his own plate to the kitchen and took the lids off of the pots, revealing several courses of food. He thought that he saw an impressed look on Christopher's face, but maybe he was imagining it. When they were both seated at the table, Liam served the wine. "You guessed correctly. I learned today that I'm not going to be offered a spot in the NLS program."

Christopher lifted his head sharply and looked Liam in the eye, but as soon as they made eye contact, he lowered his gaze again and shook his head. "I'm sorry to hear that. I think that you deserved a place on that mission."

"It's OK. You don't have to hide your relief. We both know that two-year-long deployments in an NLS would have been extremely hard on us. The thing is, the new mission might not appeal to you any better. I've thought about it though, and I don't think that I can accept it if you don't come with me."

"I don't understand," said Christopher.

"They are offering me the command of the Outpost, partly based on how well the team did with the g-loop. But you and I both know that you were coaching me every step of the way on how to wrangle that group."

"Isn't the Outpost supposed to stay in space for 20 years?" asked Christopher.

"Yes. That's why assembling the right crew for the Outpost is so important. It's more like founding a small city. Every stage of the mission is going to demand perseverance. You would shine at keeping a crew like that together and healthy. Once the vessel reaches a safe distance, we would set up a braking and re-launch station for Near Light Speed ships. There is no NLS mission without the Outpost."

Christopher still wasn't eating. He looked Liam in the eyes. "Liam, I understand that a mission like this doesn't sound like a big deal to you, but do you understand how much I've already hurt my family? I actually had to agree to let one of my father's colleagues evaluate me for perspecticide last year after I came here with you."

Liam took a sip of wine, then put the glass down and tilted his head. "I don't know what that word means."

"It's a type of emotional abuse that happens in dominating relationships. He has patients who have lost all sense of their own beliefs and goals in life. They believe what their partner wants them to believe."

"I'm not asking you to give up your beliefs or your family. Everything that you already are is what this mission needs. I can't even imagine an Outpost crew succeeding without someone like you."

"Liam, you're underestimating the effects of your own history here. You have basically had to build a family for yourself over and over again, wherever you went. That's why this seems normal to you. I understand why you distanced yourself from your father. He was abusive and his alcoholism only made it worse. The fact that your mother never did anything to protect you just reinforced your idea that family is something that you shed when you need to."

Liam was shaking his head, but Christopher went on anyway. "I can see how that makes you a good candidate for the Outpost, but I don't share that history with you. It's not how I'm built. I have a family down here, and they are counting on me. I respect the things that make you strong, but I think that I'm going to have to let you go without me."

"Christopher, you're right, we don't have the same history, but your history is more compelling than mine in this situation. What was the point of us joining the Space Agency if we don't sign up for missions like this? This was the opportunity that we were hoping for. I don't think that anyone believes that they should assemble a crew for the Outpost made exclusively of people who had broken families growing up."

Liam took a bite of the dinner he had prepared. He kept his eyes on Christopher and waited until he did the same. They were both silent for the next minute.

"Listen," said Liam, "I love your dad. You know that I feel closer to him than I ever will to my own father, but part of what I admire about your dad is that he has literally saved people's lives with his work. Over the lifetime of his practice, he's probably saved thousands."

Liam took another sip of wine and waited, but Christopher didn't respond. They looked at each other for another minute, and Christopher took a deep breath without looking away.

"If we do this," Liam said, "we could be the ones who save the lives of millions of people. What if the best way for you to honor your family is to take the gifts that they gave you and use them to protect everyone and everything that you love here on Earth?"

8 - A Recruit - August 2114 - Arlington, Texas
Jacqueline/Colleen

Jacqueline was cold, and the bright sunlight coming in through the window made sleep impossible. She wrapped her arms around herself to try to warm up. Looking to her right, she could see that other people on the plane were starting to stir as well. In the past, she had enjoyed flying, but she was feeling impatient for this leg of her journey to be finished. Jacqueline had been in airplanes and airports for more than 24 hours from Sarawak, and had passed through Singapore and London.

Stepping off the second flight into the London Heathrow terminal had made Jacqueline's heart quicken. She was so close to where her mother had gone to university. For the entire layover, she looked up into the face of every blue-eyed man that crossed her path. She knew it was ridiculous, but she couldn't help but wonder if she would feel it in some way, if the man that her mother had fallen in love with so long ago were somewhere nearby. Her mother had told her once that it was his eyes that had first captivated her, but long before Jacqueline boarded her final flight, she had come to her senses. She hadn't felt anything at all, and she had seen more people with blue eyes in those short hours than she had seen in her entire life leading up to that day.

The curved wall of the airplane was cold to the touch. Jacqueline couldn't stand it any longer. She bent down to get a sweater from her bag under the seat. As she felt around inside the canvas backpack, her fingers brushed the manila envelope that Mr. Raban had placed in her hand almost two weeks earlier.

Jacqueline closed her eyes and thought about how those last moments had felt. The gentle hand that he had placed on her head. The sound of his voice as he leaned over her to give her the envelope. Mr. Raban had always been a fixture in her life, and he was the one person who knew what she had lived through. She would never forget the way that he had protected her the day that her mother died, but over the past few years she had told herself that he was just doing his job. The powerful right arm of Mr. Wan operated with absolute efficiency in looking after her grandfather's interests. Except for this time.

'Please don't ever let me find you again.'

Did that mean that she should hide from him? It didn't even make sense. He had given her the envelope with the money and her passport. He had even given her a name of the person who would arrange her passage out of Malaysia. How was she supposed to hide from the person who orchestrated her escape?

Her hand finally found the thin cashmere sweater in the bag. She pulled it out and placed it on her lap, then bent back down to slide the manilla envelope out as well. It was heavy. Even through the thick paper, Jacqueline could feel the outlines of her travel documents and a thick wad of cash. It was in mixed currencies, but mostly American dollars. She reached into the envelope, fishing around until her fingers found a single piece of paper. She pulled it out, and her eyes drifted over Mr. Raban's handwriting, fluid and neat to a fault. He must have written the note while she was in her grandfather's office. She had read and re-read it countless times in the days that followed. In keeping with Raban's nature, the letter contained few details that could identify him as its author. There was no greeting and it was unsigned, but it was perhaps the most personal exchange she'd ever had with him.

> *It would seem that Allah wills it, and only a journey may bring you the freedom to live your life. Here is what you must do now:*

- *Turn off your devices and leave them in the house. Please do not take any of them with you.*

- *Leave your bank cards too. Do not take any of them with you.*

- *Go out through the kitchens. Ask them to call a car to pick you up at the service entrance.*

- *Go to the waterfront bazaar in Kuching and find a youth hostel. You can stay there until you have arranged to leave the island. Please do not contact anyone that you know. You must stay hidden.*

- *In the Kuching bazaar, go to the stall that sells spices and lentils and ask for a Mr. Teoh. Tell him that I sent you and tell him where you want to go next. Pay him in cash.*

- *I have put some money in for your trip, but it won't last long. Your priority must be to find a way to use what you know. You will need to earn money to live.*

  I know that you are not my daughter, but I will keep your memory close to me, just as I have always done with the memory of your mother. My wish is that one day, you may once again know what it is to have the family that you deserve.

  May you seek refuge in Allah from the cursed Satan.

Jacqueline pushed the note back into the manila envelope, then slid the envelope into her bag. Tears had come to her eyes reading it, and she wiped her face with the back of her hand. A minute later, the flight attendant came down the aisle handing out steaming towels for passengers to freshen up before landing. The timing couldn't have been better.

Jacqueline wiped her face with the warm towel, then pulled on the sweater that she had retrieved from her bag. The warmth of the towel and the sweater soothed her frayed nerves, and the view through the window drew her attention to what awaited her on the ground. She had never seen such expanses of land with no water in sight.

They would be arriving soon, and the man who had called himself Mr. Teoh had told her to use her real passport to get through border security. It was too risky to use a forgery for entering the United States. Once out of the airport, she could use the new passport that he had made for her with a changed name. The new document also made her a few years older so that she wouldn't have restrictions placed on her for things like hotels, cars, or even looking for a job.

Jacqueline had never had a job, and she had only come up with one idea for how to get one. Her best shot was going to be this week in Texas.

****

It was almost 11pm when Colleen received the notification that Special Agent Elenora Voskos wanted to talk to her. For the past two years, Elenora had been Colleen's point of contact in the FBI for carrying out the requisite background checks on her NLS recruits.

Colleen stood up and closed the door to her office for some privacy, then went back to her desk and opened a video chat with Elenora. "Hey, it's late for you. What's up?"

Before the video link was even stable, Colleen saw something strange in Elenora's expression. Her stare was more intense than usual as she said, "You're not going to believe this, but we have eyes on the Binti Abdullah girl. If my intel is right, she passed through US border control just before 1pm in Dallas."

"Are you fucking kidding me?" asked Colleen. "How did you find out?"

"That's where it gets complicated," responded Elenora. "She's been declared missing by her maternal grandfather in Malaysia, a mister Aquil Wan. Interpol has filed a Yellow Notice on her. That's the reason that she was flagged."

"*Interpol*? She's just a kid!" said Colleen.

"That's just it. They've filed a global alert for a missing minor. Any unexplained disappearance of a minor can be escalated to Interpol if law enforcement believes that an abductor could have taken them out of the country."

"Wait, they think that she was abducted?" asked Colleen.

"Well, from our end, it certainly doesn't seem to be the case," said Elenora. "She was flagged by passport control in Dallas. I requested surveillance, and they've managed to keep tabs on her all day. I'm still waiting for the report from the behavioral analysis unit though."

"You're not planning to detain her, are you?" pressed Colleen.

"No, nothing like that. We'll try to observe her out in the open to look for any signs of trouble. Here, I'll send you over a picture." There was some clicking on Elenora's end of the call, then a photo popped up on Colleen's screen.

"Wow, she's really grown since the last photos that I'd seen. She's so athletic," said Colleen as she did some clicking of her own. "Any intel on why she came to Texas?"

"No," responded Elenora. "She hasn't done much since arriving. She checked into a low-end hotel in Arlington, walking distance from the football stadium, but she hasn't contacted anyone, and we don't know why she chose that area."

"Actually, I might know," said Colleen. "There is a drone racing championship in Arlington this weekend. I bet that's why she's here."

"Ah, that makes sense," replied Elenora. "That's a good lead. We'll keep tailing her until we can get a clearer picture."

"Elenora, you know what I'm going to say next don't you? The others start training in six weeks."

"Let's not get ahead of ourselves," cautioned Elenora. "She is still only 17 years old. First thing tomorrow I need to notify the Office of Children's Issues at the Department of State. Her missing-person status trumps everything else. Once we know that she's safe, we can talk about next steps."

"Of course, Elenora," said Colleen dryly. "No one has more respect for your protocols than I do."

****

Colleen gave Elenora her most charming smile when she spotted her in the airport in Dallas. "You look gorgeous. I'm so glad that you decided to come."

Elenora's eyes had fire in them. "I'm only here to keep you in check. I notified you as a courtesy, but to be honest, I regret telling you anything at all."

"Don't be that way. This recruit is really important to me," answered Colleen.

Elenora stopped and looked at Colleen. "Can we talk about that for a minute? I've worked with you on how many recruits? To be honest, I was always a little bit surprised by how calculating and unemotional you were in your evaluations. Why the personal interest in this recruit?"

Colleen wasn't ready to answer that question. "Come on. Let's keep walking." After a few steps, she said, "You're right, this recruit is different from the other ones. I think that it's because she was one of the first candidates that I identified, and some of my designs for the mission sort of formed around my idea of her."

A car pulled itself up to the curb as the women exited the doors of the terminal. Colleen climbed in first and slid over. "Have you gotten any updates?"

"Yes, she's been at the stadium all day," answered Elenora as she climbed into the car.

The sun was starting to set outside as they drove, and the sky was taking on a reddish tinge.

"OK, here's what I've been thinking," said Colleen. "She's only a month shy of her 18th birthday. The way I see it, we just need to put her up somewhere until she's an adult, then the whole missing minor thing goes away."

"No, Colleen, that's not how this is going down. I'm a federal agent, and once I can confirm the whereabouts of a person who has been declared missing, I have to report that she's been located so that people can stop looking for her."

"So what's *your* solution, just send her back to Malaysia?" asked Colleen. "Come on, Elenora, work with me."

The car pulled up to the stadium and waited in a line to drop them off. Both women got out and walked along the sidewalk that led to the stadium. The edges of the parking lot were lined with brightly painted trailers belonging to the different racing teams.

"No, we don't have to send her back to Malaysia," said Elenora, "You're right about one thing. She can probably be emancipated, since she's practically an adult. But regardless, we will have to inform whoever filed the report that she has been located. We need law enforcement in her home country to close out the Yellow Notice with Interpol. There are ways to protect her privacy, but lying isn't one of them."

Colleen had already purchased tickets for them to enter the drone races, but getting through security with Elenora's standard-issue sidearm took several minutes and a verification call to her home office. Even then, some of the guards still eyed her suspiciously.

The sun was almost completely set when Elenora and Colleen were finally cleared to enter the stadium. They walked through the ground-level indoor corridors of the arena, following signs towards the section where their seats were located. But as they emerged from the hallway's wash of white light and headed through the characteristic triangular wedge tunnel that led out to the field, Colleen faltered.

The roof was open on the stadium, and bright stars were starting to show through the red of the evening sky. The stadium was full of people on the edge of their seats, straining to get a better look at the drone racing track. It was a winding knot of twisted white latticework, and the drones whizzed around, leaving streaks of colored light behind them.

With each step the white light from the corridor faded, and the sights and sounds of the stadium enveloped Colleen. She started to feel dizzy and even leaned up against one of the cement walls to try to steady herself. Her head was spinning, and for a moment, Colleen wasn't sure if she could make herself continue. Each time she tried, her heart beat faster, and she felt short of breath.

Elenora had kept walking for several meters before noticing that she was alone. She stopped and walked back to where Colleen was standing. "What's going on? Are you feeling alright?"

"Yeah, I'm OK, I just need a minute." Colleen pushed herself back off the wall and took a slow deep breath. She could see that Elenora was going to need more, so she added. "I get anxious in public sometimes."

Elenora twisted up her mouth and narrowed her eyes, but she didn't ask any more questions. They started walking again, albeit slowly, and they came out into the stands to see the full spectacle. There were support teams, and tech tents with electrical repair tools and computers. There were vendors selling videos, food, and even small quadcopters that would follow people around if they put a special key fob in their pocket. The scope of the event was remarkable. Down on the field, the track, the racers, and the open night sky formed the centerpiece of the spectacle.

Colleen got control over her breathing and began to look around at the attendees. The majority of drone pilots were either overweight, undermuscled, or both, to the point that some were having trouble carrying their own gear. Most of them had long hair and what might be charitably described as indoor complexions.

Elenora was the first to spot Jacqueline and she touched Colleen on the shoulder. "Colleen, look over there. It's her."

Her athlete's build made her stand out from the group surrounding her. She was down on the turf with the racing teams. Judging from her outfit of white pants and a T-shirt with a team logo on it, Colleen surmised that she must have joined one of the racing teams' support crews. She was intently staring at a display with the first-person video feed from six different drones.

Colleen lifted her chin. "Check out that display in front of her."

Jacqueline was standing, her eyes riveted on the screen. As she watched she was cringing a little, and she leaned into each turn. Just then, she threw her hands back, and a second later, Colleen heard a collective gasp from the crowd. She looked from

Jacqueline to the track to try to understand what had happened. As she did, she saw two quadcopters crashing into the turf.

"She knew that they were going to collide."

As Colleen looked back from the fallen drones to Jacqueline, she saw her excitedly cheering for one of the remaining racers. Colleen was shaking her head in awe. "This girl is tracking six drones in time and space from a single display."

Elenora looked sideways at Colleen, wrinkling up her nose. "You don't really believe that, do you? There has to be another explanation."

"That's exactly what I believe," said Colleen. "Come on. Let's go talk to her."

Without waiting for an answer, Colleen started walking down towards the field, and Elenora had to trot a few steps to catch up to her. The two women made their way along the edge of the turf to an open section, and they each showed their identification to the security guards who controlled access to the competitors' area. After a little persuading, they were allowed down onto the field, and they doubled back towards where they had seen Jacqueline. Stopping a few meters away from her, the two women waited for the next race to end and for Jacqueline to look away from her monitor. When she finally did, Colleen spoke first.

"That was very impressive, the way that you were following along with the FPV feeds from all of the drones."

Jacqueline spun around when Colleen spoke to her and she looked quickly to her left and right before looking back at Colleen and answering, "Oh, I think I just got a little caught up in the excitement."

Elenora put her hand on Colleen's shoulder, then took a step forward and slowly opened her ID to show it to Jacqueline. "Excuse me, but are you Jacqueline Binti Abdullah?"

Jacqueline's eyes narrowed as she looked at the badge, and she took a small step backwards. Elenora seemed to take Jacqueline's reaction as answer enough. "I'm Special Agent Elenora Voskos with the Houston office of the FBI. Your grandfather, Mr. Wan, has reported you missing with Interpol. I'm going to have to request that you come with me so that we can clear this matter up."

Jacqueline took another step backwards. She looked up from the badge, but she wasn't making eye contact with Elenora. She seemed to be scanning the area behind them. "Is he here with you?" she asked in a low voice.

Colleen took a step to one side in order to distance herself from Elenora. "No, Special Agent Voskos didn't bring anyone here and she's not going to send you home. You have my word."

Colleen's statement made Elenora spin around, but Colleen didn't break eye contact with Jacqueline. "I'm not with the FBI. I actually came here to recruit you as a pilot. I'm a mission planner with the Space Agency, and I've been recruiting pilots just like you for over a year."

Elenora's head tipped forward, and she drew her shoulders back. She spoke calmly, but firmly. "I warned you, Colleen. This isn't one of your games. She's a minor and the subject of an active investigation. If you try to interfere, then you're the one who's going to end up in custody."

Colleen closed her eyes for a second and sighed. "Elenora, think about it for a second. You know that trillion-dollar mission I'm working on? The one that you've been helping me recruit for? Have you thought about why governments around the world are willing to invest so much? It's because we're not going to survive the next asteroid strike! Not a single goddamn one of us."

She could hear the strain in her own voice. "Do you even realize the magnitude of what happened the night that Sphinx hit us? If the fucking thing hadn't been burnt down to a stub on its way around the sun, we'd all be dead now."

Her voice started to trail off. "One minute things were fine, but then… The sky just..."

The images that Colleen had pushed out of her mind 30 minutes earlier were forcing their way back in. The stadium, the flash of light, the bodies, the feel of the young girl's small hand, trying to pull free from hers.

Colleen lifted her own hand to her eyes for a moment and tried to squeeze the tension from her brow. "I will do whatever it takes to keep something like that from happening again."

She could still hear that poor child so clearly in her mind. *'Ibu!'*

She took a deep breath and slowly swept a dark pink lock of hair back with the hand that had been covering her eyes. For a moment she had actually forgotten that Jacqueline was standing there, but as Colleen turned back towards her, their eyes met, and she could see that the girl had recognized her.

She had gone ashen, looking up at Colleen. A stream of tears had started to roll down her cheeks. "You were there." Her voice sounded small and vulnerable.

Elenora looked back and forth between the two of them. "Colleen, what's she talking about? Have you had previous contact with--"

Elenora's words stopped short when she saw Jacqueline reach out and place her hand in Colleen's. Several more seconds passed before anyone spoke.

"I'll come with you," Jacqueline said softly, looking down at her hand.

Jacqueline lifted her head and turned to face Elenora. She looked her in the eyes and nodded. "It's ok. I... I know her. I'll come with you, like you said."

Colleen hadn't wanted it to happen this way, but it was done now. She closed her fingers firmly around Jacqueline's hand. "Where are your things?"

Jacqueline pointed, mutely with the other hand. There were tears reflecting in her eyes.

Colleen led Jacqueline towards one of the stadium exits, still holding her hand. She looked back one last time and caught Elenora's eye before stepping off the field and out of sight.

9 - Hemispheres - February 2114 -
High-Earth Orbit
Liam

On the outside, the Outpost and the Nest were exact replicas of each other, and together they were to form the bookends of the GhostMap mission, propelling NLS vessels into deep space, then back into Earth's solar system. Inside the stations, however, there were significant differences.

Colleen had warned Liam from the beginning, "No one has ever tried to sequester a crew on a twenty-year mission before. We are going to have to be creative."

Given what was at stake, Liam's push for a dedicated Human Factors Scientist was easily accepted. The crucial importance of morale and resilience among the Outpost crew easily justified the decision to allocate full-time psychiatric support. Once the post existed, Liam had relied on Colleen to secure the position for Christopher. Colonel Crespin would have preferred a different candidate based on experience and pedigree, and Liam couldn't risk appearing biased.

Christopher's presentation to the Chiefs quashed all questions of his inexperience. His psych roadmap for the Outpost crew had been as comprehensive as it had been daunting to implement.

"We're going to have to offer some benefit in every area of life:" he had told them, "physical fitness, short work days, optimal career opportunities, creativity in their work and hobbies, and five-star leisure activities. Two things that are absolutely not negotiable, we are going to have to offer world-class food, and we are going to have to lift the ban on shipboard romances."

Even during this past month, when preparations had been so stressful, Christopher had organized their first full-crew 10k around the outer loop of the station. He also sat with each member of the crew, even Liam, and asked them what type of creative or aspirational work they wanted to do in their off hours. "You want to use both hemispheres of your brain," he had said, "the analytical and the creative." That's when Liam realized that he wanted to stay connected to the NLS training program somehow.

Colleen immediately keyed in on the idea of leisure activities. "We should have gaming stations in every cabin and as many full haptic VR rigs as we can fit." There was a light in her eyes. Liam hadn't spent much time in immersive games, but it sounded like a way to get outside the space station, if only virtually.

During construction, the Nest and the Outpost had begun life as one 50km clamshell of dense carbon-black latticework. Having a single object in orbit at forty-thousand kilometers above the Earth's surface simplified planning and operations. The crew of the Outpost was recruited early and participated in every phase of construction of the twin space stations, perfecting their understanding of the design along the way.

"Even that will reduce anxiety," Christopher had said. "If they know how it's built, they'll feel more in control."

The crews of the Nest and the Outpost were certainly not exact replicas of each other. For the past three months, it had become painfully clear to Liam that members of his crew were going to run into serious challenges training their counterparts on the Nest.

As soon as the Nest had a competent crew, the two parabolic stations would separate, and the Outpost would begin its journey to a vantage point deep in interstellar space. However, for weeks on end, the crew of the Nest had been unable to demonstrate that they could operate their propulsion station with the mastery that Liam and his crew expected of them.

"You're just spoiled," Colleen had said to him. "We gave you a crew made up exclusively of young, passionate, triathlon racing, PhDs that read Kant, cook frittata and spout Keats. Sorry buddy, but the well is dry. All of our good eggs are in your basket for now. We can keep improving the Nest, but the same isn't true for the Outpost. It'll be years before we'll be capable of replacing anyone on your crew. Leave the Nest to me. It's time for you to set sail."

Liam knew that she was right. He had been spoiled. The Outpost crew was truly extraordinary. They were by far the best and brightest that the Space Agency had ever seen. Anyone good enough to be on the crew of the Outpost was already on the Outpost. By extension, the crew of the Nest was bound to come up a little bit short in comparison.

The Nest would have the whole planet to support them. If they ever got stuck and didn't know the answer, they could just have one of the experts down on Earth tell them what to do. The crew of the Outpost knew that they needed to be completely self-reliant. At one light-year from home, getting even the simplest question answered would take a minimum of two years.

Liam watched on giant monitors from the Nest's Command deck as video feeds streamed from each of the 16 "Bugs". The exoskeleton-like maintenance vessels had six articulated arms for manipulating and repairing the machinery along the surface of the carbon-fiber mesh. The vehicles were being piloted by Nest crew members as they completed a visual inspection of cabling, lasers, and ion thrusters along the scaffolding of the Nest's propulsion disc. The inspection was going according to plan today. *Finally! Maybe it really is time to set sail.*

Captain Kett looked over at Liam. "What do you think?" she asked.

"I like what I see," he said, and they exchanged a satisfied nod. Liam was the last of his crew left on the Nest. There was a Bug waiting for him in the Axle, and he looked forward to getting into it.

Liam surveyed the new crew of the space station that would stay behind. They were buzzing with energy, ricocheting between tasks and stations, and it took him several beats to capture their complete attention. He cleared his throat.

"All of you now control the most powerful light source in our solar system, other than the sun itself. I am proud to hand over this station to Captain Kett and to all of you. I know that every member of the Outpost crew has personally signed off on your readiness, and today they sleep easy knowing that you will be our partners in this adventure."

The Nest crew cheered, and their counterparts on the Outpost could be seen applauding over the video links. Liam knew that encouragement was perhaps more important than absolute accuracy when trying to inspire a crew.

He shook hands with Nest crew members as he made his way out of the Command deck and into the corridor of the outer ring of what people affectionately called the Wagon Wheel. The habitable portion of the space station occupied much of the empty 1km center of the propulsion disk. As its name implied, the Wagon Wheel spun at roughly 1.5 revolutions per minute to create 1 g of simulated gravity in the outer ring. Liam entered the elevator and took it "up" toward the cargo ring and the Axle launch bay.

Liam had to climb a ladder from the cargo ring to the Axle. From there, he followed a guideline across the zero-g bay over to his Bug. Strapping himself in, he sealed the Bug, and requested permission to enter one of the launch tubes.

"Granted," came Captain Kett's voice over the comm. It was unusual for a captain to personally grant permission, but this was a special occasion. Up until the launch tube was fully evacuated, Liam could hear the clicks and hisses of the airlock mechanism, but soon it was silent.

He waited for a final rush of air that would eject him from the airlock, then fired a small burst of ion thrust to start his silent glide along the 45km center of the clamshell to reach the Axle of the Outpost.

It would take about 20 minutes for Liam's Bug to float across the span between the two space stations, and he planned to use every last second of it to soak up the blue of Earth with his own eyes.

When he was safely clear of the Nest, Liam let go of the controls, let his hands float free, and stared in disbelief - disbelief at the panorama extending out in front of him and disbelief at the decades long journey that lay ahead. The white and blue light from the Earth, stars, and sun filtered in through the ball of black latticework that curved in around him on all sides.

The shadowy woven framework of the Nest and the Outpost, covered in their uneven placement of lasers, thrusters, and tangled wires, looked more organic than mechanical, more primitive than modern. These titan structures, floating in space, were awe inspiring, and Liam was gliding right through the center of the two.

Here and there, Liam stole quick glances at his display where members of the Outpost crew were taking turns on the big screen to talk to their counterparts on the Nest and to wish them luck. It was a proud day for the two crews, and it was the last time that they would be together for a long time.

The crew of the Outpost had readied the station for departure by the time that Liam boarded. He proceeded to the Command deck and gave the order to engage thrusters. The two parabolic disks began to separate.

For the next few months, the Outpost would still be close enough to home to pitch in with final training of Nest crew members and debugging of Nest systems, but with each passing day, the round-trip-time for sending messages would become more and more difficult to manage.

Liam had anticipated that the tipping point would come at roughly one week delay to get an answer to a question. He and Christopher agreed that it would be at that point that the crew would truly start to feel as if they were on their own.

Liam recalled Christopher's words to the director, "Extreme environments and situations can stretch people's minds to the edge of sanity. I think that we're ready, but a sequestered crew like this can go either way. They'll either join together or tear each other apart. The officers of the Outpost will need to remain vigilant."

Specifically to Liam, he had warned, "You're the Captain. These people are going to look to you as sheriff and judge, as their mother and their father, their brother, their priest. You have to be ready for that."

Father, brother, priest. Liam had never really had any of those things. Christopher was right about one thing. Soon, the crew of the Outpost would fall under no one's jurisdiction but their own, as astronomical stretches of space and time unfurled in their wake.

The Ghost of Sphinx

Act-II

The Mission

The Ghost of Sphinx

10 - Orientation - 2114 - Houston, Texas

Jacqueline

"Good morning, recruits."

The sharp greeting came from behind them, and it made Jacqueline's whole body flinch. She closed her eyes, splayed her fingers, and waited for the goosebumps to dissipate.

She had been daydreaming about the drone racing team, wondering where she would be right now if she had stayed with them. There was no doubt that moving from city to city with the racers would have felt safer than hiding in that hotel for a month, but Special Agent Voskos had told Jacqueline she would be detained if she crossed state lines.

Was she just trying to scare me?

As the military man made his way to the front of the room, Jacqueline heard the sound of a heavy door click shut behind her. He didn't speak again until he reached the narrow wood podium and turned to face them.

"I am Colonel Crespin, and I am the senior military officer in charge of the mission for which you have been recruited. Soon, one of my civilian colleagues will be introducing you to the technical details of the operation, but first I would like to prepare you for the challenge that lies ahead of you."

The Colonel had black hair and a neatly trimmed mustache. His movements reminded Jacqueline of Mr. Raban, right down to the way his eyes seemed to take in the entire room. His manner of speaking was different though. It reminded her more of her grandfather.

"There is no question that the majority of you will be cut from this program. The only disagreement has been over which traits will be most crucial to your success. At this time, I will ask each of you to take a look at your peers. What you may notice is that this group is the product of a compromise."

He paused, and Jacqueline did as he had asked. The five men sitting straight and still in the front row were lean and muscular with short hair, but the rest of the group didn't fit a mold. One of the young women looked like a trained gymnast with lean muscle in her shoulders and neck, and Jacqueline thought that she recognized one of the other women from the drone races in Arlington weeks earlier. As Jacqueline turned her head again, a thin man with a dark complexion was looking at her. Their eyes met for a moment and he smiled, but before she could respond, the Colonel drew her attention back to the front of the room.

"Let me speak plainly," he said, "my goal is, and will remain, to find any available pretext to eliminate you. It is my duty to expose you to physical and mental stressors here, where the consequences of failure are non-fatal. You will also undergo regular medical examinations designed to detect any bodily risk factors that may emerge as training continues. I take no pleasure in these things. For those of you whom we cut from the program, you can rest assured that in so doing, we have probably saved your lives."

Someone coughed.

"This week will begin with immersive training materials," continued the Colonel. "By the end of the week, you will have been tested for tolerance of 25g accelerations, tolerance of enclosed spaces, and you will have had an individual fitness assessment. Those of you who remain in a few weeks' time will undergo a procedure to implant a gastrostomy tube in your abdomens."

The Colonel's eyes flicked over several of the recruits. His gaze fell on Jacqueline and remained there as long seconds ticked by.

"Are there any questions before I hand you over to my civilian counterpart?" asked the Colonel.

The front row responded immediately and forcefully. "NO SIR!" Their synchronized reaction was just loud enough that it startled Jacqueline and several of the other civilians.

One recruit, the drone racer, raised her hand.

"What is it, miss?" asked the Colonel.

"Did you say … surgery? For us?" she asked.

"Yes, for those of you who show yourselves capable of mastering the mission requirements, we will want to have your gastrostomy tubes implanted as early as possible to give your bodies the maximum time to heal before your first training exercises at 50g and above."

"Can I refuse the surgery?" she pressed.

"Yes, ma'am," said the Colonel. As he said it, he gave a slow nod and a smile, and Jacqueline wondered if he expected her to be cut before that.

Colonel Crespin let the smile fade and stood a little straighter. "At this time, I will leave you in the hands of Dr. Colleen Pastor. She is leading the scientific portion of this mission."

Jacqueline saw Colleen approaching from the right, but the Colonel didn't look in her direction. He turned away from her and strode past the recruits along the same path he had entered. As he passed the airman at the back of the hall, the two men exchanged a short nod. Jacqueline had expected the younger airman to salute, but he didn't.

Colleen took the podium and looked at each face before speaking. When she looked at Jacqueline, she smiled, and lifted her chin slightly.

"Great, let's get started then," she began. "The asteroid that hit Earth in 2109 was called Sphinx-896. To get a sense of scale, Sphinx measured 12 km in diameter before losing most of its mass in a close flyby around the sun. In contrast, we estimate that the asteroid that caused the extinction of the dinosaurs was only 10km across. If Sphinx had hit us directly, it could have ended all life on the planet."

Jacqueline had spoken to Colleen a handful of times over the past few weeks, but neither one of them ever brought up the topic of Kuala Lumpur.

"This is where all of you come in," she said. "You have been recruited to fly Near Light Speed ships as part of the GhostMap program. The term GHoSt is used to refer to Galactic Halo Substructures. These are dense, gravitationally bound accumulations of dark matter in the halo that surrounds the Milky Way. We tend to think of gravity as the thing that keeps us down on Earth, but stable gravity is also what keeps things like asteroids up in their orbits. In the past ten years our solar system has begun to traverse a powerful stellar stream, and the gravitational influence of GHoSts has increased sharply. This poses a clear danger to Earth."

Colleen paused to take another survey of the faces in the room, then continued. "Your flight path will be largely determined by the placement of our two propulsion stations, but as pilots you will have significant control over where you scan for GHoSts. We need you to travel at very high speeds to take advantage of relativistic effects, both on your bodies, and on the dark matter clusters that you will be hunting. Inside your ship, relativity will slow down time significantly. From your point of view this will shorten the trip so that you don't go crazy or run out of air."

Jacqueline's hands were still in her lap, but she found herself leaning further and further back as Colleen spoke. She glanced over at the thin man who had smiled at her earlier, and the look on his face mirrored Jacqueline's own reaction. His eyes were wide, and his mouth was open slightly.

"At the same time," said Colleen, "relativity is all about point of view. Looking out from your ship, the dark matter clusters will be moving past you at nearly the speed of light. That will increase their inertial mass 20-fold and make them easier for our probes to detect. The gravitational probes, which you will pilot alongside your ships, use precision laser signals to detect the curvature in space that accompanies gravity."

Colleen waited for a moment then said, "All of this is covered in your training materials, but I'd be happy to answer any questions if you have them now."

One of the recruits spoke up immediately. "When you talk about slowing down time for us, I don't know what that means. How long are these trips?" It was the same drone racer who had spoken up a few minutes earlier.

"That's a good question," said Colleen. "Once the Outpost reaches its target distance of one light year, you will have what feels like 15 days to pilot your probes, and there will be a combined 9 days of acceleration and deceleration, where you will probably choose to sleep."

The recruit's face twisted up, and she looked around at the other recruits, then back to Colleen. "How can we travel one light year in fifteen days? That doesn't seem possible."

Colleen shook her head. "No, first, it's not 15 days. There are 15 days when you're awake plus 9 days of sleep, so 24. Second, it only feels like 24 days to you. During the same period, those of us down on Earth would experience the full year."

The recruit was shaking her head. "I'm still confused. If I fly 24 days out and 24 days back again, are you saying that I miss out on two years of my family's life?" Her voice rose significantly at the end

"Yeah, in point of fact, we'll actually have you stay on the Outpost for at least a week to recover before coming back, but everyone ages at the same rate during those weeks."

The Ghost of Sphinx

Jacqueline furrowed her brow and looked back and forth between the scientist and the recruit. Colleen's conversational tone seemed out of step given the obvious concern in the recruit's voice.

During the preceding weeks, after Special Agent Voskos had placed Jacqueline in the hotel and had ordered her to stay there, it was Colleen who had checked in on her to see how she was doing. She had even brought her a small cake on her 18th birthday. This seemed like a completely different Colleen.

"The easiest way to remember the effect of light-speed travel on your timeline is to remember 6-1-12," continued Colleen. "For every six round trips, an NLS pilot ages by one year and travels for 12 light years. This is a huge breakthrough, and you've been chosen to be the pioneers of a new age in human space flight."

Twelve years?

Every doubt, every nagging question that had been forming in Jacqueline's mind went quiet. Her jaw sagged open, and she slowly turned her head away from the exchange between Colleen and the other recruit.

'Don't ever let me find you again.'

There was no way that Raban would keep looking for her for twelve years, and in twelve years her grandfather would be a very old man.

Two months of images swirled through Jacqueline's head: Raban's note, weeks hiding in the bazaar in Kutching, the drone track in Arlington, more weeks hiding in the hotel in Texas. She looked back at the other recruit, the drone pilot, at her sour expression, but her only thought was, *'Twelve years.'*

The relative safety of traveling with the drone team meant nothing in comparison. If she did what Colleen was asking of them, she could just vanish for two years at a time, and she could keep vanishing again and again until it was safe to stop.

Silence hung in the air for most of a minute, until one of the military recruits raised his hand. "Yes," said Colleen, looking at him.

"So once we find these dark ghost things, how do we destroy them?" he asked.

"You can't," said Colleen. "Dark matter doesn't interact with ordinary matter and it's immune to most forms of radiation that we know of. Even the fiery, dangerous part of a nuclear blast wouldn't have any effect on it. All you can do is detect its gravity and plot its course so that we can see when and where it might hit something."

Jacqueline looked from Colleen to the military recruit who had asked the question. He was nodding slowly, and finally said, "Yes, ma'am."

"OK, let's stop there," Colleen said. "As I mentioned, most of this information is in your training videos. Airman Nino here will escort you to your bunks, where you can suit up for training before heading to lunch. Please proceed to the media center after that to begin your first instruction modules. I'll look forward to seeing all of you during your training exercises."

She stood smiling at them as the recruits got out of their seats slowly and started to wander towards the airman at the back of the room. They all filed out through the heavy door without exchanging another word.

The quarters for all ten of the NLS recruits were located along a single wide corridor. Airman Nino showed them their bunk assignments and instructed them to suit up in a training uniform then return to the corridor.

Jacqueline slipped off her shoes and stepped into the room that Airman Nino indicated. She stood there for a moment and let her eyes adjust to the light as the door slid closed behind her. The polished floor felt gritty under her feet as she surveyed the small room. The first thing that caught her attention were socks, bedding, and other items folded in neat piles at the foot of the narrow bed. She took a few steps toward the closet and opened it to find three sandy brown camouflage training uniforms hanging there. She pulled out one of the uniforms and turned to see it better in the light that entered through a small window to her left.

How did they know my size?

Jacqueline tossed the uniform onto the bed and then unfolded and spread out one of the sheets next to it so that she would have a place to sit down.

She got changed quickly, and put on a pair of socks, but when she stepped back into the corridor with her boots in her hand, three of the soldiers and the other gymnast were already waiting with Airman Nino. Jacqueline bent down to put on the boots and as the last five recruits made it into the hallway, she laced them up.

The canteen was a short walk from their quarters, and Airman Nino made a point to show them the media center along their path. Jacqueline wasn't very hungry, and the brown meat that was being served for lunch didn't look appealing. She continued to think about Colonel Crespin's words as she placed a small portion of rice and a spoonful of vegetables onto her tray.

Jacqueline sat by herself, but she couldn't stop stealing glances at the other recruits as she ate. She wondered how each of them had been selected, and she wondered if any of them knew about her own encounter with Colleen and Special Agent Voskos at the drone races in Arlington, Texas.

Careful to call as little attention to herself as possible, Jacqueline finished eating, slipped out of the canteen, and began to retrace the path that the airman had taken them from their quarters. When she reached the door that he had pointed out to them, Jacqueline breathed a sigh of relief that she had found the media center again without having to ask for help. She pulled the door open tentatively and stepped inside.

"Hi, are you one of the new recruits?" asked a young man. He was sitting at a desk in front of a set of high shelves that were packed with thin journals. He wasn't dressed like other men his age on the base. He had on denim jeans and a polo shirt.

"Yes, I think that I'm supposed to watch a training video."

"Sure, follow me please. I'll get you set up." He stood and walked around his desk, then directed Jacqueline to follow him as he walked past a row of grey cubicles. When they reached a second row of cubicles, he turned and gestured for her to enter one of them. The cubicle had a shallow desk built into one end. On the desk was a tablet and a pair of Augmented Reality glasses. "Put those on, then select the trainings that you want from this tablet here," he said, pointing at the devices.

"Thank you," she said, and he raked his fingers through his hair and gave her a quick smile before turning and walking away.

Jacqueline sat down and looked at the devices, then slid the glasses slowly onto her face, not quite sure what to expect. As soon as she did, a menu popped up on the tablet offering her NLS flight training units 1 through 6. She extended her finger toward the first option, but it vanished as her hand approached it. The wall behind the desk disappeared and was replaced by a scene of another cubicle like hers. Seated on the other side of the virtual desk was a tall man with broad shoulders.

"Hello," said the projection, "My name is Liam Fourtouna, and I am the Captain of the Outpost propulsion station. I will be taking you through the training units on piloting Near Light Speed ships, deploying your lightsails, and piloting gravitational probes."

Jacqueline had to look up to see his face. When she did, she felt a flutter in her stomach. The Captain's dark complexion and blue eyes reminded her of the image that had formed in her mind years earlier, when her mother had tried to explain how she had fallen for a man that she barely knew. Jacqueline felt her face flush, embarrassed by the hours that she had spent in the London airport trying to sense her father's presence.

"In this module, I will explain the g-forces required by your mission and the technology that we use to protect you during the acceleration and deceleration phases."

The air over the table between them seemed to come alive. With each technical detail, complex and even beautiful 3D animations moved, turned, became transparent, then opaque again. Jacqueline tilted her head in to get a closer look, and she learned how to grab parts of the scene with two hands to stretch and squeeze the models to different sizes.

The Captain was plainspoken, but the technical information was dense, and given the number of times that Jacqueline had to scroll backward and re-listen to sections of the material, the 60-minute training took her over two hours to complete.

The chapter on g-force was full of numbers, and a quiz at the end of the section asked her to rank the 75g acceleration of the NLS mission relative to other human experiences like a roller coaster ride. Jacqueline positioned it between the long-standing 50g human safety limit and the 100g traumas suffered in nearly-fatal car crashes.

For a moment, the ideas of a rollercoaster and a car crash fused into one, and a nauseating scene flashed through Jacqueline's mind of white pillars flying into the crowd in Kuala Lumpur. Since the drone races a few weeks earlier, long forgotten details about that night in 2109 had begun to resurface.

Jacqueline shook her head and blinked, trying to clear the thoughts from her mind, then hurried to click submit on the quiz question before the timer ran out.

"To enable you to withstand these extreme accelerations, there will be a few basic countermeasures that we will employ. The first is the Cradle, a gyroscopically mounted harness that will pivot to keep you lying flat and facing the direction of the g-force at all times." Jacqueline studied the projection, taking in the details of the Cradle, how it attached to the shoulders, arms, and legs of the small pilot figure, and how it rotated around different axes to keep the pilot facing into g-force.

"The second is the COFLEX or Compressive Fluid Exoskeleton. This is a special kind of body armor that will be custom built for each pilot. The suit will assist with your breathing under severe g-force, and it helps in maintaining normal blood flow in your extremities." The body armor looked thick and uncomfortable, and the differences in the female version seemed to be inappropriately exaggerated.

"The final countermeasure designed to keep you safe during flight will be your diet. To avoid the risks that solid food or waste would pose to you, a Gastrostomy Tube passes directly into the stomach and permits a liquid diet to be continuously fed to the pilot during flight."

The Captain delved into each. The subject matter was strangely intimate. Phrases like "your body", "your eyes", "your abdomen", "the muscles in your arms and legs" were repeated so many times that it left Jacqueline feeling exposed. She turned her eyes away the first time that small 3D projections of anatomically correct male and female forms faded into view, but in the end, she had no choice but to skip backwards and take a closer look just to answer the questions.

You're just making it harder for yourself.

She looked up from the technical material and watched Captain Fourtouna. With the small movements and gestures that he made, the muscle development of his shoulders revealed itself under his uniform.

After the fourth and final quiz, the 3D visuals between Jacqueline and the Captain faded away. "This is the end of NLS training module number one."

The image of the Captain leaned forward over the desk. "Listen, I know that this might seem pretty terrifying, but I want to assure you that I have done all of these things myself before I took command of the Outpost. We have selected you based on our assessment that these challenges are within your capabilities. I would only ask that you try. Try for yourself and see if you can do this. I believe that you can."

Jacqueline fought the urge to lower her gaze. He was staring straight into her eyes as he leaned in. *It's only a recording...*

She held his gaze for another few seconds, then turned her head and looked out from her cubicle, scanning what she could see of the media center from where she sat. As she did, she thought about Colonel Crespin's words from earlier in the day.

Jacqueline squeezed her eyes shut and shook her head. It seemed odd that the two military men were taking such opposite positions. The Colonel was openly trying to eliminate them, while the Captain seemed to want nothing more than for her to succeed.

It was almost funny, and the hint of a smile formed on her lips, but when she turned back toward her training video, he was gone.

11 - Pipes - 2114 - Houston, Texas

Jacqueline

Jacqueline stood up from where she had been sitting for the past two hours and stretched her back. Stepping out of the cubicle, she turned to walk back toward the front desk and the door through which she had entered the media center.

The young man who had shown her to her cubicle was no longer sitting behind his desk, and his chair sat empty in front of the high stacks of academic journals. She pushed open the door that led back out to the corridor, then crossed over to look out through the windows on the far side.

Her shoulders were stiff from sitting for so long in a single position, and she lifted one hand to the base of her neck and squeezed the tight muscles. Her mind was filled with images of body armor, g-forces, the faces of the other recruits, and all of the strange science that Colleen had told them about. The transition from weeks alone in the hotel to this firehose of information was jarring, and each time she let herself imagine the crush of people who surrounded her on the Space Agency campus, her chest tightened.

Inhaling deeply, Jacqueline looked out the window past the green of the open field. A pair of airmen jogged a slow arc, 100 meters away from where she stood. They were wearing matching blue shorts and grey T-shirts, and Jacqueline remembered that the same athletic wear had been in the pile on the foot of her bed. It was decided. She headed back to her quarters to change. A run was exactly what she needed to clear her head.

Once suited up, Jacqueline slipped out through a pair of doors, walked onto the grassy field and began to stretch. When she was warmed up, she stepped onto the brick red surface of the track and picked up a slow jog in the same direction as others were moving. By the time Jacqueline had started her second lap, she was at a comfortable pace, and the events of the day were all but forgotten. Just off the path, an obstacle course and other structures on the training grounds captivated her attention. She tried to picture what it would be like to tackle some of those physical challenges.

If what the Colonel said was true, you'll find out in a couple days.

The track was marked off in 100 meter segments, and it measured 5K around. After three laps, Jacqueline was feeling herself again. The sun was still up, but it was angling lower in the sky. Breaking to a walk, she stepped back onto the grassy field that separated the jogging path from the main campus buildings. Walking to cool down, Jacqueline passed close by the outside of floor to ceiling windows of the canteen, and she smelled something cooking. They must have been preparing dinner.

Jacqueline hadn't had much of an appetite at lunchtime, but she was genuinely hungry now. However, she couldn't exactly go into the canteen dripping with sweat. She was going to need a shower. Hopefully the pre-dinner hour would mean she might have some relative privacy.

Heading first to her quarters to get what she would need, Jacqueline located the shower area at the end of the same hall. She was relieved to find that each stall had a full door, a place to hang one's clothes, and enough space inside to dry off without exiting.

Refreshed and back in her training uniform, Jacqueline began making her way to the canteen. Her appetite was gnawing at her stomach as she stepped up to the counter. To her relief, there was some chicken among the entrees, and Jacqueline wasn't shy in filling her tray. Her impatience was growing as she made her way into the seating area. She was about to sit at a table near the windows when she saw someone waving to her.

Jacqueline was in no mental state to make conversation. She was completely focused on the food in front of her, but four of the NLS recruits were eagerly waving her over, and she knew that they had seen her make eye contact. There was no way to feign ignorance.

As she neared the table, Jacqueline noticed that none of the soldiers were present. The thin recruit with the dark complexion stood as she approached. "Hello, please join us. I am Cemil."

Jacqueline smiled back at him. "Hello, I'm Jacqueline. Thank you for inviting me over."

I'm so hungry. Please don't talk to me.

Jacqueline sat down and quickly took a mouthful of food before anyone else could speak to her. She was just in time.

"Hi, I'm Kirin," said the young woman who looked like a gymnast to Jacqueline.

"Antoni," said another one of the recruits.

"I'm Lanxi," said the drone pilot.

Jacqueline was just finishing her bite and thought of something quick that she could say to divert attention away from herself. "I actually recognized you, Lanxi, from the World Air Sports championship. You were there a few weeks ago racing, I think."

The plan backfired. Lanxi looked visibly excited and asked, "You fly drones too?"

Jacqueline lifted her hand to cover her mouth as she finished her bite. Finally, she managed, "No, I don't race. I was working for one of the teams."

"But you used to race, and you were a competitive gymnast, like me," said Kirin.

Everyone turned at once to look at Kirin. She pulled her shoulders back and tilted her head down slightly. "Don't tell me that none of you even thought to do a little research on the competition?" She raised her eyebrows and looked around at the others. "We all fit the same profile. First, we're all athletes. Cemil is a free diver. Antoni does extreme sports. Lanxi is a rock climber, and Jacqueline and I are competitive gymnasts. Also, we're all involved in e-sports. Lanxi and Jacqueline fly drones, and the rest of us are gamers."

Cemil was nodding. "You were right to show interest in your peers, but we are not your competition. From what I understand, they will need many pilots for this mission."

"Everything is a competition," Kirin said with a sideways smile. Cemil responded in kind, and his own smile reached his eyes.

"I agree with her," said Antoni. "The people who spoke to us today? They are not running a kindergarten. They seem to bet on us, like we are dogs who race."

"I got the feeling that the Colonel places more faith in the military recruits," Jacqueline offered. "I think that he assumes that we will be the ones who fail."

"No one underestimates me for long," said Kirin.

"The Colonel is easy," said Antoni. "You know that he is telling the truth because it is not covered in sugar. It makes me trust his words more than hers, the Doctor."

Cemil nodded. "When Dr. Pastor speaks, I find that I am both inspired and alarmed. Technology seems to be her religion. She needs to place humans inside her machines, but I feel that the machine is what interests her the most."

Kirin leaned in and added, "If what Dr. Pastor said is true, then the women have an advantage. We're lighter and we consume less of everything; air, water, nutrients."

"I am not happy with any of these people," said Lanxi. "They hid information from us until we were already here. If they wanted us to have surgery, then they should have said so before we signed up."

"Surgery? Oh, the G-tube," said Kirin. "It's not real surgery. When I was a little girl, my friend had one. She had cystic fibrosis, and she was always fighting with her parents about eating enough. Once she got a G-tube, everybody was happier."

"I don't have to agree to what they want," said Lanxi, crossing her arms. "I can just say no. They don't have the right to force me." She was looking straight at Jacqueline.

Jacqueline thought back to the visits that Colleen had paid her in the hotel while she waited for training to start. *How could I have been so naive? I never asked her any questions like these about the mission.* She kept the thought to herself. She had no desire to explain to the group how she had spent the last two months of her life. "I guess I'll just do it if that's the only way to stay in the program."

"And what about the travel time?" pressed Lanxi. "Are you really going to let everyone you know just get older without you?"

"This mission is extreme. That is the only reason that I am here," said Antoni. "The things that make you worry are the things that make this interesting. Where I go, others can not follow. It has been this way for me for a long time."

"My parents are already very old," said Lanxi. "I don't like the idea of letting them grow older without me."

The edge was starting to come off of Jacquline's hunger, and she found herself mulling over Lanxi's words. They were all quiet for a moment until Cemil spoke.

"We should try to remember why we are here. If my body is adapted to this struggle, then I shall accept my place in it and do what is needed of me. We don't do this for ourselves."

Jacqueline nodded in agreement. "I grew up in Malaysia. The meteors of 2109 caused many deaths in my country. I suppose that if there is something that I can do to prevent that from happening again, it would be worth the cost."

Cemil looked around at the others. "I would like to propose a pact among us, and even among those of us who are not present at this table. We have come together to prepare and to offer ourselves for the good of others. Let us each do whatever we can to ensure that at least one of us is successful."

Jacqueline raised her water glass to join Cemil, but no one else followed suit. To Jacqueline's surprise, it was Kirin who rescued the moment.

"It's simpler than that. They needed the best for this mission, and they found it," she said, raising her water glass. It broke the deadlock, and Antoni and Lanxi raised their glasses, laughing.

****

Jacqueline awoke to the sound of Airman Nino's voice over the PA system. "Attention NLS recruits, please assemble in front of your quarters for training assignments."

She got out of bed and put on the same training uniform that she had worn the day before. She pulled her hair back into a ponytail and walked out into the hallway to put her boots on. The four soldiers and Kirin had gotten ready faster than she had. She smiled. *I'll beat one of them tomorrow.*

"Five of you are going to medical for an MRI, and the other five are coming with me to the pipes. After lunch, you'll switch and do the opposite," announced Airman Nino when they were all assembled.

"OK, Binti Abdullah, Daws, Demir, Espinosa, Kolpo, you're with me. The rest of you, report to medical for your MRI."

Jacqueline's group followed Airman Nino out across the training grounds at a comfortable jog. As they neared the far end of the training grounds, they saw two airmen, a man and a woman, each wearing the same uniform as Airman Nino. On the ground in front of them, five sets of what appeared to be scuba gear were laid out.

"Good, you're all here," said the larger of the two, "I am Airman Fovos. Please take a moment and familiarize yourself with the equipment in front of you. When it is time to suit up, the overalls will go on first, followed by the knee and elbow pads. We will ask each of you to test the respirator briefly, but I don't want you to consume the air until you are actually in the pipe."

Jacqueline looked down at the gear. She could already tell that she was going to have to roll up the arms and legs on the overalls. They were much too big for her.

Her concentration was broken when the other airman introduced herself. "Good morning. I am Airman Skotadi, and I will be assisting with today's exercise. The pipe is modeled after a training used by firefighters to establish your ability to function in enclosed spaces. We have three pipes, so you will enter in two waves, with the second wave following 20 minutes after the first wave enters. Each of you will need to crawl a distance of 100 meters, and the only light that you will see will come from the small lamp attached to your mask."

Jacqueline looked casually to her left and right. She wasn't alone, several of them were staring slack jawed at the pipes behind their trainers. Airman Skotadi continued her introduction. "The diameter of the pipe tapers quickly, and there will come a point where you will have to lie in a prone position to proceed. You will push your air supply in front of you as you make your way. Please do not remove the respirator mask from your face. This is hard work, and you will need more oxygen than the air in the pipe can provide to you. Now, who wants to start?"

Antoni and two of the soldiers stepped forward quickly, leaving Jacqueline and Cemil to wait and enter in the second wave. The two of them watched their peers suit up, then get down onto their hands and knees and enter the circular holes in the hillside in front of them.

When they were out of view, Jacqueline tried to break the silence. "I can't decide if I would have rather gone first or second. I don't mind waiting, but now I'll have more time to sit and worry."

"When I dive, I go 75m down then 75m up again. That is more than this and I have no air with me. I think that you will be OK here."

Jacqueline nodded, the knot around her insides loosening. They suited up in their gear and sat together for another ten minutes without speaking, and Jacqueline thought perhaps that she should say something else.

She was about to ask Cemil more questions about free diving when a loud banging began. Airmen Skotadi and Fovos made quick eye contact and then ran out of sight to the left of them

The Ghost of Sphinx

before Jacqueline could fully process the sound's origin. When a man's voice joined the metallic pounding, she understood. It was coming from inside one of the pipes. The banging got louder.

Sitting at least 10 meters from the entrance to the pipes, it wasn't clear to Jacqueline which one was the source of the noises. At least, it wasn't clear until the screaming started. It was loud and full of panic, and it was coming from the pipe on the right. There seemed to be words, but she couldn't make them out. Jacqueline couldn't remember who had entered which pipe, but this was definitely a man's voice, and the banging was strong.

The screaming got quieter, and the banging slowed. After another minute, things were quiet again, but then from the same pipe they heard another sound, like the high-pitched whine of an electric motor followed by metallic clanking and scraping. Those noises subsided as well after a short time and there was quiet.

As Jacqueline and Cemil stood exchanging nervous glances, their trainers came back into view, walking calmly. Airman Fovos called to them. "First Lieutenant Demir, you're up. Please put on your respirator mask and enter the pipe on the right."

Cemil gave Jacqueline a thin smile as he shook out his hands, then moved forward to begin his crawl. Jacqueline knew that he would make it. After Cemil moved away, Airman Skotadi approached her and looked her firmly in the eye. "The other guy is fine, he just panicked. We pulled him out and he's OK. You should try not to worry about it. It's unfortunate that you had to hear all of that before starting your own crawl. Just forget it, and you'll be alright."

Cemil vanished into the pipe and Jacqueline had to wait another five minutes before it was her turn to enter. They waited in silence, which suited her. A voice came over the radio saying, "three is clear". Airman Fovos, who had been silently looking at the ground, lifted his head and made eye contact with Jacqueline. With an open hand, he indicated the pipe on the far left and said, "First Lieutenant Binti Abdullah, you can proceed. Please put on your respirator before entering the pipe."

Jacqueline attached her respirator mask and took a few slow steps toward the pipe. She got down onto her hands and knees and placed the respirator tank on the ground. For the first ten meters or so she could crawl on her hands and knees, dragging the tank of the respirator on the ground under her. Soon, however, the pipe was too narrow for that. She pushed the respirator out in front of herself and lay on her stomach. The tubes pulled differently on her mask when the kit was out ahead of her. There were some shiny surfaces on the respirator apparatus, and the light on her mask sometimes reflected back into her eyes painfully.

She shoved the kit forward as far as the tubes would allow, then she shimmied her body behind it. With each five-meter segment of pipe, the diameter got a little narrower. Jacqueline paused, and briefly considered turning back, but when she tried to turn her head to look behind her, she couldn't see past her own shoulder. Her breathing was fast and shallow, and she wondered how long the air in her respirator was meant to last. Jacqueline began to feel light headed.

She had only been at the Space Agency for 24 hours, and for the first time, she was starting to doubt that she would have the strength to stay.

You're so stupid. You even never thought about failing out, did you?

She would have no idea how to contact the drone racing team again, and they probably wouldn't accept her call given that she had quit after only three days' work.

There is only one way out of here, and it's forward.

Jacqueline closed her eyes and imagined herself back on her run from the night before. She focused on her breathing and tried to make each breath deeper and to hold it for a fraction of a second before breathing out.

The air around her grew silent. After another long moment she continued her forward motion. Breath, push, shimmy, over and over until she got into a rhythm. The cycle of sounds began to remind Jacqueline of a song from home, and she began to hum in time with her clunks and scrapes.

Breath, push, shimmy; Breath, push, shimmy; Breath, push... push...

Something was wrong. She tried to push her respirator kit forward, but it was caught on something. She pushed it again and again, but it wouldn't budge. Her breathing was getting faster, and the air had a metallic taste to it. She couldn't see past the kit to free it from whatever it was caught on, and she knew that there was no way to turn around. Jacqueline grunted, pulling back on the respirator kit and slamming it forward again. It was no use.

She was going to have to choose between staying stuck and calling for help, and either option would mean failure.

As she lay, paralyzed by the no-win scenario, a painful wash of blinding light suddenly replaced the blackness ahead of her in the pipe, and she screwed her eyes shut. When she opened them again, she saw Airman Nino's face, silhouetted. "I'm sorry Lieutenant," he said as he reached in to pull out her respirator. "I was busy pulling out some of your crewmates and you got here faster than I expected you to. I was supposed to have had this end opened up so that you wouldn't bump into it."

Jacqueline slid forward and allowed herself to spill out of the pipe and roll onto the ground. She lay there for a minute with her eyes closed, breathing deeply and waiting for her heart rate to slow down. When she finally opened her eyes, she could see Cemil and Antoni, but one of the military recruits was missing. "Were you singing in there?" quipped Cemil.

She *really* wasn't ready for conversation. "Uh, I don't know."

When she opened her eyes again, he was still looking at her, so she tried again, as casually as she could manage. "The rhythm of the crawl reminded me of a song that I used to know. I didn't realize that anyone could hear me."

Sitting up again to face the three pipes, Jacqueline twisted slightly so that her back was to Cemil. Each pipe had a dome-shaped hatch door at the end. Airman Nino was sealing them back up again, presumably in preparation for Lanxi, Kirin and their group to enjoy the same ride after lunch.

12 - Signals - 2136 - Princeton, New Jersey
Edward

Edward took a deep breath, and let it out slowly, staring into the perfect blackness inside of his VR goggles. With a gesture of his hand, the clockwork motion of the solar system appeared to his right, zooming around the Milky Way at 800 thousand km/h with its orbital plane tilted back like a car's windshield. Each of the swirling objects left a spiral streak of light behind as the disk moved through space.

The model had been finalized almost nine months prior at the University of Cambridge, where Newton himself developed the theory of gravitation.

Edward gestured again, and brightly colored volumes began to grow along the solar system's path, like crystals in some kind of home science kit. They represented the gravitational scans of the GhostMap mission, and they were derived from the Space Agency's own telemetry data. Every few seconds, tiny flashes of white sparked like fireflies inside of the colored crystals. The flashes represented NLS detections of massive dark matter clusters in the galactic halo.

A final gesture activated the display of Edward's own research. His algorithms could recognize the shape and size of each invisible GHoSt and track them across multiple NLS scans to calculate their heading and velocity. Taken together, the combined system would predict where and when new dark matter clusters would disturb asteroids in the main belt.

Since Sphinx, no fewer than nine asteroids had fallen into the sun, averaging one event every few years. Even now, there was no scientific consensus on how long it would take for the solar system to pass through the stellar stream that was triggering these events. The only thing that seemed certain was that sooner or later, Earth was going to suffer another hit.

Running at its current speed, the simulation retraced two decades of GhostMap scans in just over a minute, but Sphinx and its recently fallen peers were poorly covered by these models. The Space Agency had no measurements at all of Enigma, the dark mass that had disrupted the orbit of Sphinx-896, and though some limited data had been collected along the path of asteroids like

Sethos and Nicomachus, GhostMap's gravitational data was too sparse to fully explain their orbital decays.

Edward wasn't trying to explain past events though. His research was aimed at predicting future threats. Rolling his chair around to the right, he stared through the disk of the solar system and down the barrel of the brightly colored GhostMap scans. The swarm of blue GHoSt detections flew towards him like the pellets of a slow-motion shotgun blast.

It took another 13 minutes for the simulator to trace 250 years into the future, and the gravitational forecast from Edward's algorithms had led to at least 30 asteroids falling out of orbit in the Cambridge model, but with each passing minute, Edward saw fewer and fewer events.

Edward squeezed his eyes shut for a moment and lifted both hands to his head to massage his temples. He had been in the lab for over 15 hours. The answers he was looking for were close. He could feel it, but something was off.

He got to his feet slowly and put his hands forward with his fingers cupped towards the center. Turning his wrists, he rocked the whole scene vertically in front of him. The disk of the solar system hovered at a slant at waist height, and the column of brightly colored gravitational scans stood roughly as tall as Edward himself.

Can that be right?

Looking down toward his feet, most of the blue GHoSts had stayed close to the brightly colored traces that detected them, but as he ran his eyes up the column of gravitational scans, he could see that some of the GHoSts had drifted well outside the radius of the main belt. More than half of the detected masses were gliding towards the galactic center, well outside of the danger zone for Earth.

Why are we tracking objects that aren't even going to hit us?

Edward let himself drop back into his chair and stared up at the display for a second, then he pulled off his VR goggles and placed them on the table next to him. Letting his arm slide along the table's surface, he caught the edge of his tablet with his fingertips and pulled it toward himself.

I'm going to need to...

With a shaky hand, Edward slid the stylus out of the side of the tablet and lowered it toward the grid-lined page. He sat there for a minute, creasing his brow, but nothing was coming to him. By force of will, Edward lowered the stylus and started to draw the curve of where the GHoSts were positioned, but then he stopped, sighed, and slipped the stylus back into the edge of the tablet's case. He locked the screen with a swipe of his hand, closed his eyes again, and bent his head forward to stretch the muscles in the back of his neck.

It was already 2am, and Edward could feel his whole body grinding from the lack of sleep. The acrid taste in the back of his throat told him that he had already had too much caffeine. Whatever the answer was, it would have to wait till morning.

Slowly, he spun his chair around, bent down, and picked up his backpack. Edward slid the tablet into the bag then stared at his belongings for a minute while he mustered the energy to keep packing. One by one, he gathered the rest of his things, then zipped the bag closed and got to his feet. At first, he couldn't remember where he had left his coat, but he finally spotted it thrown over a chair in the next row of seats.

Edward stepped out into a cold New Jersey night, leaving the computer lab behind, but images continued to swirl around in his mind as he walked towards the dorms. He *knew*, in his core, that there was danger hiding in the galactic halo, but somehow his simulations were telling another story.

He tried to come up with a list of possibilities, but a sudden gust of wind sent a blast of icy air up under his coat. Edward hunched forward, bracing himself against the cold, but straightened up again when he heard laughter off to his right. He turned his head and squinted his eyes to get a better look at a group of stumbling undergrads. At least one of them seemed to need help walking and had his arms draped over two of the others.

Slowing his pace, Edward shook his head and scuffed his feet quietly on the snowy ground, watching them. They looked like they didn't have a care in the world. He used to try to tell people about his work, but he had learned better. The best-case scenario would be some kind of condescending advice like, *'You worry too much. You should relax and have some fun.'*

It wasn't just the students though. Edward had seen his share of researchers publish optimistic findings, especially when they represented what people already wanted to believe.

I can't show these results to anyone until I figure out what's going on.

He pulled his coat tightly around himself and started walking again, trailing the group at a comfortable distance. Edward wasn't surprised to see them enter his residence hall. Most of the students in the dorms were undergrads. Edward was in a Ph.D. program, but school policy required any student under the age of 18 to live in university housing.

By the time he reached the building and looked through the glass doors, the group in front of him was safely out of sight, so he went in, crossed the lobby, and headed for the stairs.

Edward stepped inside his dorm room and stood in the shadows for a second as the wedge of light on the floor slowly narrowed then disappeared. He let his bag drop down next to his feet, then took a few distracted steps toward the corner of his bed and sat down. The plastic basket that held his toiletries and his toothbrush was sitting on the desk across from him, but he was already losing the argument with himself about picking it up and walking back down the hall to the bathroom.

****

Edward didn't remember lying down, but when he woke up, he was still wearing his coat and his shoes. His heart was pounding, so he sat up and blinked his eyes a few times then squinted to look out the window as the macabre images slowly faded from his mind. It was just one of the typical meteor-strike dreams with his parents' house leveled by a fiery blast, but he couldn't shake the sick feeling in his stomach that he should have done something to stop it.

You're no closer to protecting them then you were a year ago...

Looking out the window, he could see the path that he had walked the night before, and it made him purse his lips.

Edward thought about the year that he had spent painstakingly verifying every last detail of his models, and a shiver ran up his back in spite of his heavy winter coat. The worst-case scenario wasn't actually a failure in the simulation. The worst-case scenario was that the simulation was right, and that the GhostMap mission was wasting time detecting objects that would never hit them.

Looking back at the clock, Edward could see that he had already missed breakfast service in the dining hall, but he had worked through dinner the night before, so he couldn't wait for lunchtime. He was going to have to walk across campus to the student center and buy something.

Plucking his toothbrush out of the basket in front of him, Edward put a small dab of paste on the brush and stuck it in his mouth, then got to his feet and walked to the door. He picked up his bag from where he had dropped it the night before and left his room.

Edward had practically finished brushing his teeth by the time he reached the bathroom at the end of the hall. Pushing the door open with his shoulder, he slid inside to spit and rinse off his toothbrush in one of the white porcelain sinks. His mind was still on his simulation as he clicked the brush on the edge of the sink to get the water out of it.

It's not just that they're missing us. It's as if something is pulling them all in the same direction.

As Edward opened his coat to stash the toothbrush in his inside pocket, he caught a glimpse of his orange T-shirt in the mirror. It read "English is important, but Math is importanter," and it was one of his favorites. It occurred to him that he'd been wearing the same T-shirt and jeans for a couple of days, but that was no reason to delay breakfast.

Edward made one more stop in the bathroom before heading out into the hallway, down the stairs to the lobby of the dorm, and outside for the walk to the student center. The campus looked bright and sunny, and Edward pulled his shoulders back as he joined the columns of students walking along the paths that criss-crossed among the academic buildings. Anyone out there, headed to class on a winter morning couldn't be all bad.

When he reached the student center and pulled open the heavy doors, he immediately smelled food, but in spite of his hunger, he paused there and surveyed the crowd for a moment before stepping inside. More than once in the past few years Edward had had run-ins with older students there. If he had known what it was going to feel like to go to college at age 16, he might have taken his parents' advice and stayed in high school.

There were several stations inside the cafe, but Edward went straight for his usual combo of coffee and two burritos, then headed for a table in the back corner of the seating area and tore into the wrappers. Over the course of the week, he had eaten the same meal several times, but it tasted even better today. The first burrito lasted less than 60 seconds, and half way through the second, his whole body started to relax.

The problem is that there's no way to check the predictions of the model against the original clusters.

Edward looked out the window of the student center and sipped his coffee. His eyes came to rest on a spot where three walking paths converged across the street from him. One of the paths was cracked where the roots of a nearby tree were lifting the cement.

The roots...

There was something nagging at him as he stared at the buckled sidewalk. He looked up and down the trunk of the tree, then looked down at the ground and imagined the thick roots of the tree snaking deep under the surface. His eyes narrowed and he could hear his own heart beating.

What would it take to track their paths beneath the orbital plane?

Edward stood up quickly and almost knocked over his coffee. He slid his bag over his shoulder, then picked up his cup and wrappers and hurried out of the student center. On the way up the hill towards the astro building, he threw away what was left of his coffee and broke into a jog.

Passing through the same doors that he had exited the night before, he could see through the wall of glass that the computer lab was full of students. Edward hurried past the lab and up three flights of stairs to where Dr. Oldfield had his office. As he burst out of the stairwell and along the corridor, he caught sight of his professor heading away from him.

"Professor! Professor," shouted Edward, weaving to avoid other people in the hallway, "I need to discuss something with you."

Oldfield stopped, turned, and looked towards Edward, but he didn't acknowledge him right away. He folded his arms and waited. "Edward, I'm on my way to teach a class in five minutes. I thought that we agreed that you would make an appointment on my calendar the next time that you wanted to talk to me?"

Edward opened his mouth to speak, but nothing came out. He was out of breath and his mind temporarily went blank. Oldfield's demeanor softened. "OK, walk with me. What did you want to discuss?"

"It's the merged simulation," Edward blurted. "The initial results are making me think that there could be an important area that's not being scanned by GhostMap, but I would need a new dataset to prove it."

"Oh!" said Oldfield. "The simulations have finally started working? I have to tell you, I was more than a little concerned. This is actually good news. Put an hour on my calendar for later today and you can show me the working simulation."

"No!" said Edward. "I mean, the results are inconclusive. It's too soon to show them to anyone."

Oldfield stopped walking again and turned to look around them, then back at him. "Edward, as principal investigator, I'm responsible for progress on this grant, and we have promised to publish initial findings as soon as we have them."

"But it's too soon," said Edward, "The models can't be validated without augmenting the gravitational probe data."

"Augmenting? What does it mean to augment data that was measured in space, decades ago?"

"Well, the current data was only measured between the Nest and the Outpost," Edward answered. "What I realize now is that I could verify the findings if I had data from the other side of the Nest, below the orbital plane of the solar system. It's the only way that I can think of to test the model's predictions."

Oldfield was shaking his head. He started walking again. "This isn't making sense to me. Between the Nest and the Outpost is the only data. There is no other data, and even if there were, why would you want data that doesn't correspond to the GhostMap search area?"

"No, no!" snapped Edward. "There's got to be more data, from after the point that the probes pass us. Maybe we can get it from SETI."

"From SETI? As in the Search for Extraterrestrial Intelligence?" asked Oldfield. "Edward, I think that you should focus on making progress with the data you have. If you're going to be successful in research, you are going to need to make progress based on limited information."

Edward let out a sigh and shook his head. "Garbage in garbage out. What's the point in making decisions based on bad information?"

Oldfield stopped walking again, and his expression changed as he turned to look at Edward. He lifted his jaw and narrowed his eyes. "Edward, I think that I have an idea. How would you feel about working directly with the Space Agency on this?"

Edward furrowed his brow and studied the sharp look on Oldfield's face. "Do you think that they'll be able to get me the data that I need?"

"We'll see. I actually have a meeting with the Director of the Space Agency at 1pm in my office. Since I don't have any simulation results to share, you might as well attend and try to articulate your plan for her." After a pause he added, "Calmly…"

Edward's face lit up. "Yes! Yeah, I can do that."

"OK, but listen," replied Oldfield. "You have to go get cleaned up. You look like you've been sleeping in the lab. I'll see you back in my office at 1 sharp."

"OK, I'll be there. Thank you." Edward turned back toward the stairwell, and once he was out of sight, he bent his arms up in front of him and bumped his fists together, "Yes!"

Still smiling, he scurried down three flights of steps and retreated onto the paved campus path that led away from the astro building.

****

After his shower, Edward stood in his dorm room and tried to decide what to wear to the meeting. He knew that Dr. Oldfield would never forgive him if he offended his colleague, so among his T-shirt options, he decided not to put on "Sarcasm, it's better than killing people," and equally opted against "I haven't got the time or the crayons to explain this to you." He finally chose a shirt with an attractive arrangement of the fundamental particles positioned in a circle, with the Higgs Boson at the center.

Clean, fed, and rested, he walked back to the astro building, and was moving down the hallway towards Dr. Oldfield's office a few minutes early. The door was closed, so Edward leaned on the wall to wait for him. Tilting his head back, he let his eyes drift closed for a moment. The sound of a woman's voice surprised him. It was loud, and he opened his eyes to see where she was. There were a few people scattered in the hallway, but no one was talking.

With his head turned, Edward heard her voice again through the wall. "John, I don't understand. Why are you trying to push this off on me? If you want me to keep signing your grants, then I suggest that you just stick to the script."

Edward heard Oldfield's voice, but he couldn't make out the words. After another pause, he heard the woman say, "Fuck it, fine, but to be clear, the money follows the student. Don't bother sending me any research proposals for a while."

Edward pushed off the wall and moved to the other side of the corridor. He had just turned around to face the door when Oldfield opened it. "Oh, good. You're here. Come in."

Edward walked into the office and sat down in the seat that Oldfield indicated. His professor's hand seemed to tremble slightly with the gesture. Oldfield took a seat next to Edward then said, "Thank you, Director for your time. Director Pastor, I'd like to introduce you to Edward Kaiser. He's one of my brightest research students, but he also has an unquenchable thirst for data. At this point, I feel as if he should start working directly with you on his new idea."

Dr. Pastor squinted. She had an unusual look to her with a bright pink lock of hair almost covering one of her eyes. She wasn't what Edward would have expected as the Director of the Space Agency.

"Hello Edward," she said with a tight smile. "So tell me, what kind of data are you looking for?"

"Um, Hello. I would like to access 20 years worth of signals data from SETI in the 8GHz band. I'm looking for any data that I can find on Enigma or any of the other nine clusters that have already passed through our solar system, so that I can check them against the current alignment of GhostMap."

Dr. Pastor looked at Oldfield then back at Edward. "SETI? You realize that dark matter clusters like Enigma don't interact with electromagnetic waves. SETI can't help you."

No, you don't understand...

Edward closed his eyes and took a slow breath in. He knew that this might be his last chance to salvage his research, so he chose his next words carefully. "Director, let me back up one step and start with a question about the GhostMap mission. Each time an NLS ship decelerates and lands on one of the propulsion stations, what happens to the gravitational probes that were flying with it?"

"They're abandoned," said the Director. "It wouldn't be worth the cost to try to recover them, so when the NLS deploys its lightsail for braking, the probes just keep going at their last speed and heading."

"OK, good. That's actually what I was hoping for," said Edward. "If you can get me the SETI data, then I think that we might be able to recover red-shifted and time dilated signals from those NLS gravitational probes flying below the orbital plane of the solar system."

Director Pastor looked back and forth between Edward and Dr. Oldfield, but then let her gaze drift offscreen.

"If I can recover any trace of masses like Enigma, Discord, or Tiye after the point where they interacted with Sphinx or the other asteroids, it may allow me to verify that the alignment of the GhostMap Observatory is correct."

Her initial reaction was barely audible, and she was clearly lost in her own reflection. "They're still flying..." After a moment, she straightened herself and looked back at Edward and Dr. Oldfield.

Speaking clearly this time she said. "Signals, interesting. This is quite a theory Edward. I had assumed that we were going to talk about the astrophysical models today. John, have you informed Edward that you're asking me to take over as his thesis advisor?"

Edward turned to look at his professor, but Oldfield kept his eyes on the screen and answered, "Yes, we discussed it earlier today."

Edward looked back at Director Pastor and tried to keep his expression neutral. Judging from what he had overheard in the hallway, he wasn't sure if this was a new opportunity, or if he had simply managed to get himself kicked out of his research group.

The Ghost of Sphinx

13 - Magnets - 2114 - Houston, Texas

Jacqueline

"Is he kicked out?" whispered Lanxi.

Jacqueline turned her head to see if any of the other recruits were nearby. There were people all around them in the canteen, so she signaled with her chin and led the way to a table against one of the walls.

"I don't know what happened to him," she replied, shaking her head. "I don't know if we'll get second chances or not with these training exercises."

"We lost one too," said Lanxi. "The doctors wanted to talk to him after his MRI, and then he went to talk to someone else. They told us that they're looking for anything in our brains or blood vessels that might make the g-force unsafe for us."

Jacqueline took a bite and chewed it, but there was almost no flavor.

"I can't believe that we might lose two people so soon," she said. "At this rate, none of us are going to qualify." She closed her eyes for a second, and the memory of dragging herself through the dark pipe came back to her. "How are you in tight spaces? This pipe thing that I did this morning was pretty intense."

"I'm OK I think," said Lanxi. "I have climbed in caves before."

Jacqueline gave her a thin smile and nodded. She wondered if Lanxi was taking her warning seriously. She took another bite, but it wasn't even worth eating.

"I'm not very hungry," she said. "I guess I'm going to finish up here and go over to the medical bay. I want to get this over with."

Lanxi gave her directions to medical, and Jacqueline dropped her tray off on the way out of the canteen. Ten minutes after that, she was sitting in a cotton gown filling out a questionnaire about her medical history.

Jacqueline had never had an MRI before, and the experience was closer to climbing through the pipe than she would have imagined. Even though everything in the room was bright white, the tube in the center of the magnet still felt cramped and dark, and the machine's loud clicks and chirps seemed to grow louder with each passing second, drawing out her thoughts.

Every minute that passed inside the machine seemed like an hour, and her skin felt like it was covered in a layer of grit and dust from the morning crawl. She tried to stay as still as she could, but her muscles were cramping up and she was aching to get to her feet and stretch.

Finally, the metallic cot that she was lying on began to slide out of the magnet, and there was a nurse waiting to talk to her when she sat up.

"You're all set. You can get dressed and drop that gown in the hamper. It'll be faster next time because we have a baseline scan for you now."

It took Jacqueline a moment for the nurse's words to register. "Thank you," she said, flashing a quick smile, then slid off the cot and retraced her steps to the dressing room where her dusty uniform was hanging. She entered and closed the door, then just stood there for a second taking deep breaths.

The whole time that Jacqueline was getting dressed, she half expected to hear a knock on the door to tell her that they had missed something, and that she had to come back to talk to the doctor.

Leaving medical on the way back to her quarters, she looked over her shoulder to see if anyone was trying to come after her. None of the medical staff were looking in her direction, but she quickened her steps anyway, down the hall and away from them.

****

Jacqueline stayed under the warm water of the shower for a long time, washing away the dust and sweat from the day. She let her head hang down, closed her eyes and just let her mind go blank. She would have liked to go straight to her quarters and wrap herself up in her blankets, but there was a training video that she had to watch before tomorrow, and the last one had taken her two hours.

After suiting up in a fresh uniform, she walked to the media center and sat down in the same booth that she had used last time. Putting on the AR glasses, she selected NLS training module number two and waited for the cubicle wall to vanish as it had done before. When the image appeared, she took a quick breath in and opened her eyes a little wider. The tall dark form of Captain Fourtouna was sitting across the table from her, and she felt the brief flutter in her abdomen as their eyes met.

"So, I suppose that congratulations are in order. If you're sitting here, it means that you made it through the first day of NLS training. We needed to be sure that both your body and your mind could handle what you'll be doing next. You are going to get your first taste of high g-force in our hyperloop centrifuge."

As he spoke, a 3D model appeared over the desk showing a human figure standing in an archway. In the distant background, a curved wall was visible with several more archways cut through it. Soon, the view zoomed out and Jacqueline saw that all of these passages were cut out of a single large circular wall, like an arena. At that scale, the tiny human figure was almost too small to see. The base of the wall faded away, leaving only the white halo that had crowned the top of the structure.

"The hyperloop is a sealed tube with all air removed from it," continued Captain Fourtouna. "This allows a pod to be propelled through it with no wind resistance. Both the propulsion and the frictionless support for the pod are magnetic. The first day of G-loop exercises will expose you to 10g then 25g accelerations for a few minutes each. Your trainers will be monitoring you closely, and if there is any sign of trouble, we will stop the hyperloop and pull you out."

Jacqueline wrinkled her brow, remembering her last training video. *Wasn't 10 g the limit for fighter pilots?*

"You won't need a COFLEX for 25 g. The G-loop is equipped with a pressurized pilot's chair that has tall side supports for protection. Since you'll be lying flat, all of the g-force will be +Gx, so there should be no risk of blackout."

Jacqueline closed her eyes for a second and tried to remember which direction was +Gx. She had trouble opening them again, and regretted her decision to come straight to the media center rather than taking a nap first.

The 3D model zoomed in to one section of the loop, and the tube wall became transparent. A small bullet-shaped pod was traveling along the inside of the loop. Soon, the pod became transparent too, and Jacqueline could see a small human figure lying flat in a large reclining chair. As the pod picked up speed, it rotated within the tube so that the reclined pilot's chair was flat against the outside wall of the hyperloop.

"As I mentioned before," said the Captain, "I've done all of these exercises myself. The most important factor for your first exposure to the G-loop will be to lie still and let your body adapt to the pressure of the g-force. You might be able to move your arms or legs a little bit at 10 g, but it's unlikely that you'll be able to move at 25 g, so don't fight it."

The little human figure looked comfortable, lying in that big chair. Jacqueline slid down in her own chair and let her neck bend back until her head was resting on the seatback. Taking a deep breath, she let her muscles relax and her eyes close.

Just for a second.

"You shouldn't feel any lightheadedness during the exercise, but if you do, just try to tighten the muscles in your calves, thighs, and abdomen. You squeeze these muscles on and off to keep your blood moving. There are breathing exercises that we…"

Jacqueline wasn't really listening. Her eyes were closed, and she was imagining how the pressure would feel, pushing her down into the deep chair. She thought about pointing her toes and squeezing the muscles in her thighs and stomach. She lost her train of thought for a moment but then found it again and pictured herself quietly concealed in the little pod, the deep cushions surrounding her limbs.

Fighting to open her eyes half way, Jacqueline tried to see if the image of the Captain was still there. The 3D animation was running, and as her eyelids fell closed again, she let her knees relax and sank deeper into her chair, imagining the feeling of pressure pushing down on her. She heard his voice again, but she forgot what he said almost as soon as he said it.

You're missing it.

She tried one more time to open her eyes, but they flitted closed again after an instant. She could hear him speaking to her in a low, steady voice, but it seemed slower this time. "You just have to surrender to it," he said. "The pod will be traveling at mach two. During your first few laps you'll want to …"

It's fine. I'll rewind it later. I just need to close my eyes for a minute…

It took Jacqueline a moment to remember where she was when she opened her eyes. Captain Fourtouna's voice had stopped, but his image seemed to be looking straight at her. His blue eyes daring her to look up into them.

Abruptly, however, he vanished. Jacqueline realized that she was slumped down in her seat inside the cubicle, so she quickly sat up and straightened her uniform. No one was close enough to see her, but she was feeling a little flushed nonetheless. Her hair was dry now, but it hadn't been brushed and she worried that it must look tousled.

Quietly, Jacqueline stood up and headed back to her quarters. She knew that she would have to re-watch the entire module, but first she needed to lie down for an hour.

****

It was 4:45 am when Jacqueline woke up, and her heart started to pound as soon as she realized what had happened. Her plan to take a short nap had accidentally turned into more than eight hours of sleep. She had not only slept through dinner, but she still hadn't completed the training module for the G-loop exercise that was scheduled for the morning.

As quickly as she could, Jacqueline got up and got dressed, hoping that she wouldn't find the media center locked when she got there.

She grabbed her boots in her hand and slipped out of her room. Without even lacing them up, she pulled them on and set off. Rounding a corner, Jacqueline stood a little taller seeing that the lights were on inside the media center and the doors were open. She also detected the smell of freshly brewed coffee coming from the direction of the canteen.

Her stomach was hurting a little, and she wondered if she should try to eat something to avoid being distracted again. This would be her last chance to watch this training module.

Hoping that there might be some bread or something else to snack on, she walked past the media center and continued on toward the canteen. Once inside, however, she couldn't see anything prepared besides the coffee. The rest of the surfaces were wiped clean.

She could hear people hard at work in the kitchen, but no one was in sight. Jacqueline was just turning to leave when she heard, "Can I get you something, Ma'am?"

She turned back and saw one of the enlisted kitchen staff walking towards her. He had a thin frame with keen eyes, and he was smiling broadly.

"Oh, thank you. What time does breakfast start?" asked Jacqueline.

"It's going to be another hour ma'am, but we have some cut up fruit in the back," answered the young airman. "I could get you a bowl now if you want. What do you like?"

"Oh, thank you. Anything would be fine with me: durian, mangosteen, cempedak. I like everything."

The airman looked confused. "Uhm, did you say mango? I don't know if we have that. I could bring you some melon."

"Melon would be great, thank you."

He was back in under a minute with a small bowl of cut melon. Jacqueline thanked him and accepted the bowl. She popped a melon chunk in her mouth and started walking again towards the media center. As she passed the windows in the corridor, she noticed that the sky outside was a brilliant orange. She paused and opened the door to the training yard to get a better look. The color was even more striking without the glass filtering it.

It was cool outside. Jacqueline stepped through the door and sat on the cement steps that led down from the low stone patio to the field. She took another wedge of the orange melon between her fingers. It made her smile, noticing how the color of the fruit matched the light on the horizon. There was a fresh breeze, and she started to hear the sound of birds as the sun came up behind the trees.

Jacqueline was lost in her thoughts, finishing off her bowl when she heard a metallic sound behind her, followed by voices. She rushed to get to her feet, but before she could even turn around, she heard, "Well, well. If it isn't the competition."

Three of the military NLS recruits were coming out of the same door that she had used. Jacqueline was struck again by how muscular they were.

The surprise coupled with the fact that there were three of them had made the hairs stand up on her arms, and her heart was pumping. It took several seconds for her to realize that they were all smiling at her, waiting for her reaction. That was also the first time that she noticed that these men were not as tall as most of the other airmen on the base. They were all about the same height, and that was only about 6 inches taller than herself.

They must have realized that they startled her, because one of them walked up and extended his hand. "Hi, I'm Ben."

"Oh hi, I'm Jacqueline." she managed. "I've actually been meaning to introduce myself to all of you. I didn't even know the name of the recruit who left my group after the pipe yesterday."

The other two put out their hands in turn.

"Joshua," said the second with a smile.

"Andrew," said the third. "The guy in the pipe yesterday was Marcus. He and I did BMT together in San Antonio, but he's gone now."

"Oh, you knew him before coming here?" asked Jacqueline.

"Yes, ma'am. We were in the same training class in Texas, and we got recruited together for this program."

"So, you are all American?", asked Jacqueline.

They all nodded, and Andrew responded first. "Yes, ma'am. I'm from Florida, and Marcus was from Georgia."

"Kentucky", added Ben.

"Seattle, Washington." said Joshua.

"We were just going for a run. Do you want to join us?" asked Ben.

"Uhm, I would like to, but I can't. I need to re-watch the module for today's training." Seeing the surprised look on their faces, she added. "I fell asleep watching it yesterday."

They all nodded sympathetically, and Joshua added, "Yes, ma'am. I think that we all feel the same way about the Captain and his videos."

Jacqueline smiled and nodded, but she sincerely doubted it.

14 - The Loop - 2114 - Houston, Texas

Jacqueline

Jacqueline rewatched the training for the hyperloop and answered all of the quiz questions. It was roughly 6am when she arrived back in front of the trainees' quarters to find Ben, Joshua, and Andrew there, talking to Airman Nino. She joined them, noticing that Kirin wasn't with them.

She's going to be mad that I beat her today.

Within a few minutes, Kirin, Cemil, Antoni and Lanxi were in the hallway as well. Airman Nino addressed them, "NLS recruits, I will be taking you on a short 5.5K jog this morning to the far side of the G-loop where we will begin acclimating you to high g-forces. There are eight of you, and you will each spend roughly 15 minutes in the G-loop. Following the high-g exercise this morning, we will have lunch here, then split into groups like yesterday for a new MRI exam and for your individual fitness assessments."

He paused, then added, "Are there any questions?" Jacqueline and the other recruits looked around silently at one another.

"Alright, then, please follow me."

From the main building, they jogged across the field and onto the paved running track. After a few hundred meters, they branched off to the right and followed a narrow dirt path through the woods. The jog along the wooded path took them another two or three minutes before opening onto a green field. Across the field stood the 10m high wall supporting the G-loop. An archway, just as in the AR animations, opened in the wall 50m from them. The structure seemed to be made of rustic stone, but as she approached, Jacqueline noticed that the masonry pattern repeated every few meters. Airman Nino led them at a jog through an archway and into the interior of the loop.

If it hadn't been for the bright metallic white pipe that Jacqueline recognized as the hyperloop on top of the stone wall, she could have believed that they had entered a medieval walled city. Farming fields and uncut grassy areas extended out in all directions, with simple dirt roads creating the rectangular sections. There was an idle tractor on the far side of one of the fields, but for the moment, the air was silent and fresh.

They jogged for 25 more minutes along the dirt roads to arrive at the far side of the circular wall. Their destination was a rectangular building abutting a 25m section of the wall and fashioned in the same rustic stone exterior. The roof of the building was made of white metal, like the hyperloop tube, and from a distance, the building blended in with the rest of the grey and white structure.

Airman Nino slowed to a walk as they approached the building. The recruits had spread out a bit during the run. Jacqueline was near the front, as was Kirin. Joshua had kept up with the front of the pack as well, but Jacqueline could see that his cheeks were flushed and as soon as they stopped, he hunched over to rest with his hands on his knees.

By the time the rest of the trainees arrived, Joshua was standing upright again. He smiled at Andrew and quietly jibed "Hey, nice of you to join us."

Andrew turned his head to look at Airman Nino. His back was to them, and he was watching the approach of the other recruits, so Andrew turned back to Joshua and said, "I'm exhausted. I didn't sleep enough last night and I kind of blame you. I could hear you right through the wall. You were snoring half the night."

"Yeah, nice try," responded Joshua. "I don't snore."

"No, dude, you really do. I'm guessing that you've never had anyone in your bed to complain about it, so it's a well-kept secret." Jacqueline didn't mean to listen in, but when she laughed out loud, both men turned to face her as an informal referee to their sparring.

As the last of the recruits arrived, Airman Nino straightened up and started to look more alert. Andrew and Joshua followed suit, and in a moment, Airman Skotadi emerged from the hyperloop building, followed by Colleen. She had a smile on her face, and Jacqueline thought back to the reaction that the other recruits had had to Dr. Pastor during their orientation.

"Welcome to the G-loop," said Colleen. "This hyperloop was designed with the express purpose of preparing all of you for the 75g accelerations that this mission demands. It became operational two years ago and has already taken a select few individuals up to maximum g-force."

Two years, thought Jacqueline. Did that mean that the NLS training modules had been recorded within that time frame?

"As your training continues," said Colleen, "we will be constructing COFLEX body armor for each of you, but for today that won't be necessary. The pod is equipped with a pilot's chair that can keep you safe up to 40g, and for this morning we are only taking you to 25g. We will be monitoring your vitals throughout the exercise. Let's proceed alphabetically." She paused briefly to look at a name on the tablet that Airman Skotadi was showing her. "First Lieutenant Kirin Ballis, you will be leading the pack today. The rest of you are welcome to come inside to observe in the control room behind me or to enjoy the sun out here." Colleen looked one more time at Airman Skotadi's tablet and added, "First Lieutenant Jacqueline Binti Abdullah, you will be up next, so please be inside in 15 minutes so that we can get you ready for your run."

Jacqueline watched Kirin enter the little building and tried to decide what to do. Cemil came up beside and said, "I guess you are next. My last name is Demir, so maybe I will follow you. Will you be singing for this training too?"

Jacqueline folded her arms across her chest, turned her head slightly and looked at Cemil through the side of her eyes. "You were never meant to hear that."

She turned back to look at the building and added, "I think that I'd like to go in and observe. Are you staying outside?"

"OK, I won't keep you." he answered. "Yes, I think that I'm going to wait here for now."

Jacqueline walked over to the small building. The door was made of glass, but there was a reflective coating that prevented her from seeing anything inside. Opening the door slowly, she bit her lip and stepped inside. At the center of the space was a stairwell leading up to what looked like a platform beside the hyperloop tube. To the right of the stairs was a medical bay. To the left was a bank of technical displays with staff looking at them and discussing the information. There were desks and chairs, but Colleen and her peers were all standing. Kirin was in the medical bay with Airman Skotadi, and a nurse was attaching electrodes to Kirin's forehead. She must have had others attached to her chest because there were white wires dangling stiffly from her shirt collar.

Jacqueline slipped through the door, then stood there, out of the way. Colleen handed a tablet to one of the technicians, then looked over and saw her. She motioned Jacqueline over to the control area, and as she approached, Colleen smiled warmly and extended her hand. "Jacqueline, welcome."

As they shook hands, she said, "It's a real kick for me to finally have you here. You know, the brass still isn't 100% sold on opening training to non-military pilots, and I'm counting on you to prove that we're right. We'll have to see how soon we can get one of you up to 75g."

Jacqueline opened her eyes a little wider and raised her eyebrows. "Is it hard?"

"Well, no one's been up past 50g since Liam Fourtouna shipped out."

"The Captain?" asked Jacqueline.

"Ha, yeah, the Captain," Colleen said with a smirk. "I'll tell you something. It took me showing him videos of you and the other recruits that I had been following, before he finally understood that he wasn't going to be able to keep up with you."

You showed Captain Fourtouna videos of me?

Colleen was looking over at the team of technicians as she spoke. "I owe him a lot, though. He brought this G-loop online as a test pilot before taking command of the Outpost."

Colleen's voice trailed off as she pronounced the last word, and she put a finger in the air and strained to see something across the room. "Carrie, could you tell them to re-attach that oxygen monitor? We're not getting a reading."

Colleen looked back at Jacqueline. "Look, I need to pay attention. Let's watch your teammate here do her first loop."

Jacqueline nodded, and the scientist walked over to a microphone and pushed a button. "OK, Kirin, we're ready to start. It'll take about 30 seconds to get you up to speed, then you'll take 13 trips around at 10g. After that, I'll ask you how you're doing, and if everything is OK, we'll take another lap to speed you up to 25g and you'll do 20 laps at that speed. It'll be about 6 or 7 minutes at each setting. Are you ready to start?"

Through the monitors, they could see Kirin give a thumbs up, and Colleen pushed the button again. "OK, I want you to use your voice to talk to us because in a minute, you're not going to be able to move your hands. Can you give me a verbal response?"

"Yes, I'm ready," replied Kirin. Her voice cracked as she spoke, and Jacqueline took a closer look at the monitor. Kirin's eyes were moving quickly from one spot to another, but Jacqueline couldn't see what she was looking at.

Colleen nodded to members of her staff in the control room, and they began pushing buttons on the touch screens. There was a sound like an air-piston releasing with a hiss, followed by a clunk and a high-pitched whine that reminded Jacqueline of the MRI. The sound seemed to move away, quickly, then about half a minute later the high-pitched whine was audible again behind them and a palpable whoosh went overhead, making the hairs stand up on Jacqueline's arms. She couldn't help but duck down and look around, but no one else seemed concerned.

Jacqueline kept her eyes on the display with the circular model of the G-loop. There was a flashing red indicator that traveled around the loop. Each time the red dot swung around the bottom of the display, the powerful whoosh went overhead again.

After three or four minutes, Colleen turned to Jacqueline and said, "You'd better head over to the other side and get prepped. We're going to be ready for you in 10 minutes."

Jacqueline followed Colleen's direction and turned to head over to the small medical bay. As she made her way around the stairs, she heard Colleen's voice say, "Kirin, things are looking good. We're ready to take you up to 25 g. Are you OK?" There was a pause, then Jacqueline heard "Is she nodding? Kirin, I need a verbal response. Is that OK?"

Then Jacqueline heard a faint reply. "Yes, I'm OK."

"Good, bring her up to 2800 km/hr."

In the medical bay, two nurses were waiting for Jacqueline. "Hi, I'm Tina. Would you lie down here please? We're going to stick a few sensors on you. Two on your head, two on your chest, and one on your left ring finger. Would that be alright?"

"Yes," replied Jacqueline, climbing up onto the examination table.

"Would you unbutton the top two buttons on your shirt for me?" asked Tina. "I need to place one of these leads on your skin right here and here." The nurse pointed to her own chest indicating the locations.

Jacqueline nodded, and Tina slid a lead under her shirt and attached it just below her left collar bone. She repeated it on the right, then pulled the wires together in front. "OK, you can button back up now."

She turned to pick another lead, then faced Jacqueline and gently smoothed a few fly-away hairs back toward her ponytail. "OK, now on your forehead." She said, sticking one lead on her left temple, then again on the right. "And finally your finger." With that, Tina took Jacqueline's left hand and stuck a more bulky sensor on her fingernail, with the wire tracing back over Jacqueline's hand and up her arm. All of the leads converged in front of Jacqueline's left shoulder.

This whole process was punctuated by an unnerving whoosh overhead every 20 seconds. As Tina finished with the electrodes, the other nurse connected a small box to all 5 leads, looked for a moment to see if everything was working correctly, and clipped the box onto a loop on the shirt of Jacqueline's uniform.

Jacqueline got back on her feet and followed the nurse to the base of the stairs that separated the two halves of the G-loop building. As she arrived at the foot of the stairs, she saw Airman Skotadi descend a few steps toward her.

"Please come this way, First Lieutenant."

Jacqueline climbed the stairs up toward her, and Airmen Skotadi led the way up to the platform next to the hyperloop tube.

Where the platform reached the white steel tube, there was a bulkhead door with rounded corners, similar to the door on an airplane. Jacqueline approached the door, curious to see what was visible through the small window, when "woosh", the pod went by projecting a bright beam of light that swept across the walls behind Jacqueline. She reflexively ducked and raised her hands, as if to protect her head. The sound was much louder on this level.

"That was the last lap." commented Airman Skotadi. "It won't be so loud when you're inside the pod."

Within a minute, the high-pitched whine could be heard coming back around as the pod slowed to a stop in front of the bulkhead door. The gaskets and seals hissed again, and the door swung open. As it opened, Jacqueline saw the pilot's chair holding First Lieutenant Ballis. It was facing the rear of the pod, and the side-walls of the chair were deep enough that only a few hints of Kirin's hair and uniform were visible from the door.

Airman Skotadi entered the pod to help detach the restraints that held Kirin in the chair. Jacqueline heard a low hum as the bulky surrounding sidewalls of the seat deflated, making space for whatever body type might occupy the seat next. Kirin stood slowly and checked her balance, then lifted her hand and wiped it across her chin. Carefully, she straightened herself then walked unsteadily around the chair to exit the pod. As she reached the platform, she stopped next to Jacqueline and said, "Good luck. It's not that bad. We can compare notes when you get out."

Airman Skotadi gestured for Jacqueline to enter, so she stepped into the pod through the bulkhead door. Up close, the chair didn't look very impressive. It could have been a coin operated massage chair in a shopping mall. It was rounded and wide, and there were hollow padded areas for legs, arms, and head. Even with no-one in it, the chair looked like a chubby robot. Jacqueline turned and sat down, then leaned back into the seat. Airman Skotadi detached the small box with the electrode leads from Jacqueline's uniform and slid it into a slot on the side of the chair. She attached a belt over the front of the chair near Jacqueline's waist then adjusted large discs down around her shoulders. Finally, she pushed a button, and the side walls inflated with the same humming sound to apply an even pressure to Jacqueline's back, shoulders, arms, and legs.

"The chair will stay in this position for a minute, but it will recline when you hit 2g," said Airman Skotadi. "As you go faster, the whole pod is going to rotate, but you won't be able to tell because all of the pressure is going to be towards your back. How do you feel?"

Jacqueline nodded and said, "I'm OK."

"Alright, I'm going to head out now and close the door. Ready?" asked Skotadi.

"Yes."

Jacqueline heard footsteps, then the hissing of the bulkhead door. Once the door was closed, there was a hollow thud, and the pod started to bob slightly, as if it were floating in water. Colleen's voice came over the speaker near Jacqueline's head and said, "Great, Jacqueline, just like you saw before, we're going to take you to 10g for 7 minutes, then to 25g for 7 minutes. Are you ready to start?"

"Yes, I'm ready," replied Jacqueline. She heard the high-pitched whine, and since she was facing backwards, she felt herself pulled slightly out of her chair as the pod accelerated. Within 10 seconds the chair started to recline, and the air cushions around Jacqueline's arms, legs and head inflated a little more, squeezing her slightly. The skin pulled back on her face and she felt herself pressed down deeper into the seat. Jacqueline had trouble closing her mouth to swallow.

The pressure was strong, but manageable. Jacqueline heard 10 clear beeps, separated by about 30 seconds each. She guessed that they indicated laps around the loop. Colleen's voice came on again and said, "Things look good, Jacqueline. We're going to take you up to 25g now, OK?"

"Yes, I'm fine," she replied.

The chair's side cushions inflated even more, squeezing her very tightly now, and the pressure on Jacqueline's back and face got stronger. The beeps were closer together and Jacqueline's breathing felt labored. She counted about 20 beeps, and then the high-pitched whine changed. The pressure started to decrease. Within a minute, the chair was pivoting back upright, and a new, quieter noise engaged until the pod came to a stop, bobbing and floating like before. With a slight vibration and an electric whining sound, the pod latched onto something and stopped moving all together. A final pressurized hiss and Jacqueline smelled a blast of fresh air from outside the pod.

"How do you feel?" asked Airman Skotadi.

"Fine, actually," replied Jacqueline. Once the straps were unhooked, she stepped out of the chair, which had fully deflated its side cushions, and shook her hands to try to make the tingling stop in her fingers. She looked towards the bulkhead and saw Joshua standing there waiting. She gave him a thumbs up and walked out towards him onto the platform.

"Good luck," she said to him. "I'll see you when you get out." Joshua smiled briefly back at her, but his eyes were trained on the interior of the pod.

Jacqueline walked down the stairs and turned left toward the medical bay to have the wires removed. The nurses were there, ready for her, and had everything off of her in less than a minute. She heard the woosh of Joshua zooming around the loop overhead. "Thank you," she said, with a smile and headed outside.

"How'd you do?" asked Kirin. Her stare was intense, but she was smiling.

"It hurt my face," said Jacqueline, laughing.

"I know, I couldn't swallow. I think that I drooled on myself," answered Kirin.

They both laughed, and Jacqueline saw Cemil looking at them. "I'm up next. Any advice?" he asked.

"Don't drool," she said, and they both laughed again.

Cemil smiled and replied. "I'll do my best."

"Come on," added Jacqueline. "I'll walk in with you and tell you what to expect while you get wired up with sensors." Cemil offered her a little bow.

As they entered and turned towards the medical bay on the right, Jacqueline heard Colleen say, "Joshua, things look good. We're going to take you up to 25g, OK?"

"Roger that," came back the response from Joshua.

The woosh went overhead, and Cemil ducked. Jacqueline was used to it now and didn't react. She explained. "That's the pod going past us. It happens every 20 or 30 seconds. You get used to it."

The nurses were putting electrodes on Cemil and running the leads over to his left shoulder when an electronic alarm sounded from the control area on the other side of the stairs.

"Dr. Pastor, we have a problem inside the pod. Subject's EEG Alpha and Beta frequencies are spiking," said one of the controllers. "Heart rate increasing sharply," said another. "Blood oxygen levels are dropping. Something's wrong."

Colleen's voice cut through the noise. "He can't breathe! Slow him down, now."

Jacqueline put her hand on Cemil's shoulder and looked him in the eyes. "Go" said Cemil, and she turned and ran up the stairs to the platform. Airman Skotadi was there waiting as before. The whining sound told them that the pod was arriving. It connected to the bulkhead with a grind and a hiss. The door opened and Airman Skotadi rushed in, followed by Jacqueline.

Joshua's eyes were wide, and he was breathing heavily. He looked at Airman Skotadi. "I couldn't breathe. My throat closed up and I couldn't breathe."

She nodded and put her hand on his shoulder. "You're not the only one. We've seen this before. Dr. Pastor will give you your options, but for right now let's get you out of here."

Jacqueline stood next to the pilot's chair and waited for Joshua to get to his feet, then followed him out of the pod and downstairs. He was a few steps ahead of her on the stairs, and she reached forward and put her hand on his shoulder. Joshua turned his head toward her and gave her a small nod then let out a deep breath and continued down the stairs. Below, in the control room, Colleen was waiting for him.

"Joshua, how are you feeling?" she asked. "Do you want some privacy?"

"I'm fine. No, they can stay. Everything was going well at first, but after I started going faster, I couldn't breathe. My throat closed up."

"Yeah. My guess is that you have an obstructive apnea. I can ask the doctors to take a closer look at your MRI. This should have been detected there. It basically comes down to the shape of certain craniofacial structures and if they can close up when squeezed by a high g-force."

"Am I out?" asked Joshua.

"Well, for now, we can't bring you back up to 25g or higher unless you have surgery, and even then, it's no guarantee. We'll have you circle back with the radiologists who administered your MRI and ask them what the next steps are for you."

Joshua nodded then looked down at the ground for a few seconds, then lifted his head to see Cemil standing by the stairs.

"OK, I'll head back outside then, ma'am, so that the others can go," said Joshua, then turned to leave. Jacqueline followed him. As she reached the door, she turned back and saw Cemil at the top of the stairs, ready to enter the pod. He looked down at them, and she gave him a small wave, and twisted up her face in an apologetic smile as she passed through the door leading outside.

Airman Nino was waiting for them outside, and Jacqueline could tell from the way that he looked at them that he had already been informed of the situation. Talking to Jacqueline, Joshua and Kirin, he said, "Why don't the three of you jog back to the main campus, the same way that we came. You're all due to have a follow-up MRI after the 25g exercise to look for any new signs of stress. After that you can get some lunch and head over to do the next training module in the media center. First Lieutenant Cleveland, while the others are doing the training, you should make an appointment to talk to the docs about your follow up medical plan."

"Roger that," said Joshua. The three of them looked at each other briefly, then Joshua broke into a jog, followed by Kirin and Jacqueline. No one spoke as the three NLS recruits jogged through the fields in the center of the G-loop. Jacqueline couldn't think of anything to say, and she couldn't imagine how Joshua was feeling, running back toward the campus. It took them 25 minutes to jog across the diameter of the hyperloop. From time to time, they could hear a faint woosh of the pod racing around the tube.

As they passed, Jacqueline looked at the fields with their dirt roads and thought how strange it was that she had just been doing mach two around the outside of this peaceful country setting. She looked back at Joshua and wondered if it was worthwhile making friends in their squad if they were going to keep getting eliminated from the program.

The Ghost of Sphinx

15 - The Message - Sept 2115 -

70 Light-Days from Earth

Liam

Liam entered the game that Colleen had sent him, and he found himself standing on a replica of the Space Agency campus. Real or virtual, setting foot back on campus made his breathing quicken. He lifted his eyes to take in the blue sky and took another deep breath trying to smell the mud and the grass around him, even though he knew that he couldn't.

Colleen's leather-clad elfin avatar was there, and the two of them were standing in front of the training grounds. "Hey Liam. I have updates on training status of the NLS recruits and on our upcoming flight plans. I would like to get a status update from you regarding the crew of the Outpost, and I can chat about some personal items as well. What should we talk about first?"

Liam wasn't in a hurry to answer. He knew that the avatar would just wait for him to speak, and there was something confusing about the swarm of recruits tackling the obstacle course.

Which squad is this?

As he looked closer, he realized that what looked like 50 people running the course were actually just multiple copies of each recruit spaced out along the course. It had the effect of making the squad seem many times larger than it really was.

Most of the structures on the course were made of thick logs, though some were supported by metal girders. Ropes and netting hung in places where recruits needed to climb, and barbed wire kept them low in the parts of the course where they needed to crawl. In all, there were 20 obstacles connected by a muddy serpentine path.

Liam looked around to see if Christopher had arrived yet. There was still no sign of him, so he said, "Let's start with the update on your flight plans."

Colleen's avatar took a moment, then said, "It's good news. By the time this message reaches you, we will be ready to launch our first manned NLS vessel. It should reach you in November. I'll send the precise schedule to Chief Karabi to coordinate Navigation and propulsion."

"Finally! Who's the pilot?"

"First Lieutenant Jacqueline Binti Abdullah will make the first NLS flight. At this time, only Jacqueline has qualified for 75g. She might even get up to 100g later this month. Andrew, Kirin, Antoni and Cemil are all making slow weekly progress up from 65g."

Liam took a step back and surveyed the recruits on the obstacle course, then turning to Colleen's avatar, he asked, "Where are Ben and Lanxi? You didn't mention them, and I don't see them here."

Colleen turned to face him. Her eyes fluttered as she processed what he had asked her. "First Lieutenant Lanxi Wu exercised her right to refuse the gastrostomy tube procedure. She has resigned from the program. First Lieutenant Ben Palm suffered from space sickness during multiple rounds of parabolic flights simulating zero-g. He has been sent on to other assignments."

The way that Colleen's avatar answered questions was almost robotic.

"That's too bad," said Liam. "So we really are down to five."

He looked again at the recruits and noticed that Jacqueline was clearing several of the obstacles faster than her peers. One copy of her caught his attention as she reached the top of what was essentially a four-story building with no walls. Instead of climbing down the corner supports, she lay on her stomach and put both arms over the ledge of the top platform. She flipped forward, letting her legs swing over and down to the level below. Just as her feet swung to their farthest point, she let go with her hands and landed on all fours on the floor below. She immediately lay down on this next level and repeated the action. Three more flips in 15 seconds and she was on the ground.

Impressive...

As she got to her feet and walked out from under the tower, he said, "Pause it." All of the recruits froze where they were. Some were even suspended in the air, mid-jump or mid-fall.

He walked up to Jacqueline and stood for a second, looking down at her. Her hair had been cropped into a rounded bob since the last images that Liam had seen. There was mud on her face, and instinctively he started to lift his left hand towards her when he heard Christopher's voice.

"What the hell is this?"

Liam felt his face flush, and he laughed, "Good, you're here. I was expecting you half an hour ago."

Christopher just crossed his arms.

"Colleen sent me an interactive update on the NLS recruits," Liam said. "They will be doing their first manned launch any day now. We'll be welcoming First Lieutenant Binti Abdulah here on the Outpost in November."

Christopher still didn't respond. He just looked back and forth between Liam and the image of Jacqueline standing half a meter away from him.

Liam took one step away from Jacqueline and cleared his throat. "Colleen needs a status update from you on the Outpost crew."

Christopher rolled his eyes then looked around at the obstacle course then back at Liam. "Any answers we give here will take more than two months to reach her. What's the point?"

Liam didn't want the exchange to escalate, especially after how well Christopher had done recently. In his role as Human Factors Scientist onboard the Outpost, Christopher had laid the plans that were proving so successful in keeping the crew healthy and engaged in their mission. While Liam used his discretionary work time to invest in the NLS training program, Christopher had all but finished his doctorate in the social and psychological effects of group isolation. He leveraged his own cutting-edge research and expertise to find ways to keep the crew thriving.

"OK, give me the update then," Liam said. "I haven't asked you for a report in a few weeks."

Christopher looked again from Liam to the image of Jacqueline, then shook his head and turned to Colleen's avatar. "Colleen, the further we get from Earth, more and more members of the crew seem to be going through their own period of mourning for losing their connections to home and family. From my professional assessments of these individuals, we need to do more to help them grieve."

Liam tilted his head to one side. "Grieve?"

"Yes, they've suffered a loss, and the realities of this deployment are starting to have negative effects. In spite of everything that we did to try to make this station habitable, and in spite of all of the psychological preparation that we gave them, some members of the crew hadn't really come to terms with what an extended deployment like this was going to mean for them. From my perspective, I'd say that many of them were in denial."

"I see," said Liam. "In retrospect, that was even true for me"

"Now, 20 months in, I'm seeing some crew members who appear to be experiencing a range of grieving responses including anger, bargaining and even depression," said Christopher. "A few are angry at the Space Agency for little inconveniences, but I would say that the most common response that I observe is bargaining. They're rationalizing their loss. Some of them tell me that it was the only way to carry out their scientific work. Others say that they're willing to isolate themselves out here if it will protect Earth from future threats. But the bargaining is clear when they use terms like, *'If I can just do this, then it'll all be worth it.'*"

"Isn't that healthy, though?" asked Liam. "They are here to do a job. If they do it well, then their sacrifice *will* be worth it."

Christopher was shaking his head again. "My concern is that bargaining could just be a phase. If this idea is right, then the concern would come if more of the crew started to move towards depression. If they follow the most common patterns of grieving, and if grief is really what we're dealing with, then it could reach a critical point if we're not careful. Our main job should be to get them through these phases and towards acceptance of their new reality."

"What you're saying makes sense, but how will they react to a big event, like Jacqueline's arrival?" asked Liam.

Christopher blinked and seemed to miss a beat. "You're betting that everyone feels the way that you do. Remember, most of the crew don't identify with the NLS pilots as much as you do. Why would you think that one more mission milestone will change things for people who have left everything behind?"

"I think that you underestimate their dedication," said Liam, "especially if you consider how many of the crew are scientists and scholars. They have been waiting for almost two years for her to get here."

Christopher just stared at him.

"What?" asked Liam.

"Your first responsibility is to this crew. You are the captain, and your mind needs to be on us. There are 50 people on this vessel, including me. I have stood by your side and followed you for the past four years. I can't tell if you're obsessed with all of the NLS pilots or just this one, but either way, it has to stop."

Liam took several deep breaths and waited for his pulse to slow back to normal. He didn't want to respond in anger to Christopher's words, but regardless he didn't get a chance. Before Liam could say anything, Christopher pursed his lips and shook his head slightly. "That's all of the status that I have to report." After a moment, he put his left hand to his eyes in a C-shape, then vanished.

Liam turned to Colleen and said, "Save progress. I'll come back in later and we'll finish the exchange."

Like Christopher, Liam put his hand to the side of his face and vanished from the immersive world by pulling off his VR goggles. Colleen's avatar waited stoically, unfazed by their dematerialization.

****

"Attention, Crew of the Outpost." Liam's voice came over the global comm channel. "First, let me congratulate you again. Since reaching our top speed last month we remain the fastest E-class vessel in the galaxy. At our current speed of 0.2c you are all adding one week to your lives for each year that we travel. You are breaking records every day, and you have reason to be proud."

There was some applause and one or two hoots, but the energy in the room was lacking.

"Next, I have some exciting news. First Lieutenant Binti Abdullah is now certified as the first NLS pilot and she will be launching from the Nest very soon. Following a two month flight path, she will be the first of many NLS pilots that we will welcome here on the Outpost. This means that the researchers and astrophysicists among you will have gravitational probe data to analyze before the start of the new year!"

This time the applause was sincere and heartfelt. Liam exchanged a look with Christopher who, though he was keeping his distance at the back of the room, gave a smile and lifted a hand toward the excited crew in acknowledgment of the scene.

"What you have worked for, what we have waited for begins now. With the launch of the NLS pilots, the GhostMap Observatory becomes fully operational. Our entire focus in the coming weeks needs to be on preparing for her safe arrival on the Outpost.

I hope that she will come to think of this station as her second home."

Cheers rose up again.

Liam clicked off his comm and stepped toward the group that was facing him. Several crew members approached him, excitedly asking questions and sharing ideas. Liam looked around briefly, trying to find Christopher, but all he saw through the crowd were broad shoulders leaving the Command deck. They didn't speak again for four days.

16 - The Nest - Sept 2115 - High-Earth Orbit
Jacqueline

The sound of the helicopter shifted, and the rapid thud of the blades rose to cover the whine of the engine. They lifted off the tarmac then tipped forward, and the ground fell away. Jacqueline looked down and saw a few slivers of lush green sweep by beneath them, but soon, there was nothing but the blue of the open Pacific for as far as she could see.

Jacqueline and the other nine passengers in the back of the helicopter wore heavy headsets with thick, black boom mics. Some of them were engaged in polite conversation, but Jacqueline switched off her audio and lost herself in the view. Given the early hour, the sun cast an elongated shadow of the helicopter across the waves outside of Jacqueline's window.

It had been a day and a half since leaving the Space Agency campus. Her journey had started with an eight-hour flight from Houston to Honolulu, then another three-hour flight brought her south, and she spent the night on one of the Line Islands of Kiribati. Jacqueline was scheduled for an ascent on the South Pacific International Space Elevator, affectionately referred to as "spice". Reaching the Nest in high earth orbit required Space Agency personnel to travel via one of two international space elevators located at nearly opposite points on the earth's equator.

When Colleen had told Jacqueline that she would be the first NLS pilot to launch, her mind filled with questions, and the two of them stayed in Colleen's office for over an hour while Colleen took her through what to expect in the coming weeks.

Later, however, when Jacqueline was alone, she let the reality sink in.

'Please don't ever let me find you again.'

She tried to remember when exactly she had stopped looking over her shoulder, but thinking back over the previous year, all that came to mind were the various stages of her mission training.

On the afternoon of her departure, Andrew, Kirin, and Cemil had come to see her off. They were all that remained of Jacqueline's NLS squad, and Andrew in particular had been the only traditional recruit to make it to the final stages. He and Jacqueline had carried on doing early morning jogs, even after the others were gone.

"By the time I get back, you'll all be flying," Jacqueline said. Pulling her arms tightly around herself, she added, "After that, none of us will ever be on the stations at the same time."

Kirin didn't say anything, but she lifted her hand to the back of her neck and pulled at the ends of her recently cropped hair.

"Perhaps," said Cemil, "but we will see each other's trails when we fly. I will study the sensor trails that you have traced for me and I will know that you were there."

He raised a finger and looked over his shoulder. "In fact, I shall go today to suggest to Dr. Pastor that she assign a different color to each of us for our sensor trails. This way, I will know how to recognize all of you along my journey."

It was a beautiful idea, weaving a braid of color in space, together in the exploit if not in actual dimensions.

Jacqueline stepped towards Cemil and extended her hand. She had seen Colleen do it countless times, and these people meant everything to her. The weight of the gesture wasn't lost on Cemil. He took her hand and shook it gently, then placed his other hand on top of it for a second as they exchanged a final smile. The others took a step in, on either side of Cemil, and put their hands in as well.

Though none of them said so, Jacqueline knew that it was the last time that the four of them would ever be together.

Jacqueline's focus came back to the open blue of the Pacific, and as she turned her head, something caught her eye over the pilot's shoulder. A vertical black segment, that she had assumed was part of the helicopter's windshield, changed position slightly. Her heart skipped a beat as she imagined the consequences of having part of the windshield break free from the fuselage of the helicopter. Jacqueline groped for the switch on her headset to re-activate her microphone and looked around at the other passengers to see if they had noticed it too.

Her finger found the rough edge of the switch to turn her sound back on, and she was about to speak when she heard a voice in her headset. "Two minutes to platform. Cleared for landing on south-west helipad."

Jacqueline leaned to her left and hunched down to get a better look. The view out the windshield of the helicopter was still obscured by the two pilots, but from the new angle, she could see that the vertical black line was not part of the helicopter. It was their destination. The carbon black of the elevator cable faded from view as it rose into the sky. Lifting her chin, Jacqueline could see where it reached the water. The cable was socketed to the Earth by an enormous square platform. It must have been 200m on a side and it stood two and a half stories out of the water. The artificial island of steel was painted in the familiar haze grey typical of naval vessels.

In three corners of the top deck of the platform were bright yellow circles marking helicopter landing pads, and in the fourth was a small structure that Jacqueline imagined must house a command deck. As the helicopter began to circle the platform, she saw two small ships docked on the south and west edges of the platform with wooden crates stacked like toy blocks alongside them.

It was hard to see much more, leaning forward from the passenger cabin, so Jacqueline sat back in her seat and closed her eyes. They were almost there.

****

Jacqueline was unprepared for the assault on her senses as she stepped down onto the space elevator platform. Rising from its center was a 10 meter thick cylinder of black braided graphene cable that vaulted straight upward, disappearing into the sky. The cable seemed so unnatural, so bewilderingly massive, that Jacqueline felt a sharp sense of wrongness, as if a giant spear had been thrust down from space and driven straight into the core of the earth.

The sun was hot on her skin, and the top deck of the platform was swarming with crew and machines. There were cranes, forklifts and belt loaders moving cargo into the lower rings of the climber vehicle, and a small elevator was taking passengers up to the top ring for boarding. The forklifts in particular seemed to be burning some kind of fuel, and acrid fumes were wafting across the deck. Beneath the chemical smell was a smokey odor of charred meat that must have come from some below-deck kitchen. Her stomach turned, and Jacqueline stood up straighter and opened her mouth to breathe.

Turning her head, she caught a glimpse of the SPISE crew unloading her large aluminum trunk and placing it near the rail of the platform. Finally a cool breeze passed over her face from the direction of the rail, and Jacqueline smelled the salty humid air. She breathed it deeply, and the familiar smell transported her mind back to Sarawak, searching for a youth hostel in the water-front bazaar in Kuching.

The humid air and the smell of home easily overpowered twelve months of relative safety and anonymity as her senses dragged her back into the mind of that scared teenager, hiding from everyone she had ever known.

Jacqueline took a few unsteady steps in the direction of her trunk and let herself sit down on top of it for a moment. She closed her eyes and thought about everything that had happened in the past year, everything she had accomplished. Her hands hung at her sides, and her fingers brushed over the texture of the aluminum. The Space Agency decal was rubbery and she held her hand on it for a moment. Tilting her head down, Jacqueline's eyes scanned the other markings of the case that indicated that the trunk contained a COFLEX that was not to be subjected to X-rays.

Her eyes were still on her case when she heard, "Excuse me, ma'am. I'm sorry to bother you, but is that a COFLEX in that case?"

Jacqueline looked up at the voice. A wiry young airman with thick glasses was standing a few meters away from her. He hadn't been on her helicopter, so she assumed that he must be working on the platform.

Jacqueline nodded.

"So, you're an NLS pilot?" he continued. His voice cracked a little with this question.

Well, am I?

Feeling as if heavy chains had just fallen off of her shoulders. Jacqueline stood up and took a decisive step toward the airman, and for the second time in a week, offered her hand. "Yes, I am. My name's Jacqueline Binti Abdullah. What's yours?"

"Airman Tharos, ma'am. It's an honor to meet you," he said, shaking her hand. "A bunch of us are going up to the Nest today. I guess that we'll be on the same climber."

Jacqueline lifted her gaze to the three story cylindrical vehicle that surrounded the base of the graphene cable. The sun glinted sharply off of its smooth service, making her squint her eyes, and she wondered why there weren't any exterior windows on the

The Ghost of Sphinx

climber. She had been counting on the view as a distraction during the three day climb.

Taking a final lungful of salty air, she nodded and said, "I guess we will. Should we get moving?"

"Yes, ma'am," said Tharos nervously, and turned to rejoin his group.

The SPISE crew had already taken most of the luggage from Jacqueline's helipad over to the cargo loading area. Looking toward the passenger elevator, Jacqueline could see that people were boarding with their smaller bags and leaving their larger items to be loaded by the crew, so she took hold of her personal suitcase and moved to join the short line of passengers who were waiting to be brought up to board the climber. After a few steps, she paused, wondering if she should have told anyone about her COFLEX case, but when she turned to look back toward the helipad, she saw that two of the platform crew had already picked it up and were carrying it around toward one of the belt loaders at the far side of the climber.

Inside the small passenger elevator, no one spoke, but once she had crossed over the small bridge to the climber she caught sight of her own name on a display screen followed by the words 'Cabin 12' and an arrow to the right. She followed the aisle around the circular passenger level until she found her door. It was narrow, and she had to turn sideways to enter, but the cabin widened, like a wedge, to roughly a meter and a half at the outer wall. A reclining seat faced outward toward a 25cm wide stripe of virtual window that extended from floor to ceiling. Scattered through the cabin, grey metal hand grips protruded a few centimeters from the wall and ceiling, presumably to facilitate moving around the cabin during the zero-gravity portions of her climb.

Jacqueline attached her personal suitcase in the corner against the outer wall and sat down facing her virtual window. There were dark clouds looming on the horizon to the east.

After a few announcements, the climber lifted off gently. The platform and the ocean fell away, slowly at first, but with increasing speed. Within 90 seconds Jacqueline was eye-level with some of the clouds and in another minute she was looking down on the storm that had darkened the horizon minutes earlier. Lightning flashes backlit some of the blue and gray clouds, temporarily erasing their shadowy texture. Jacqueline spent several minutes just studying the swirling mass of the storm's surface. It seemed almost alive as it rolled and churned.

Her view rotated around as they rose, and she could see that, most of the Pacific was still blue and sunny, and Jaqueline wondered if she'd be able to see Malaysia as they climbed higher. Sadly, even the most eastern tip of Borneo stayed just around the curvature of the earth, invisible, even from space.

At dinnertime, Jacqueline slipped back out through her narrow doorway and took a walk around the aisle that separated the cabins from the inner cylinder of the climber. At different points along the curved inner wall, she found the bathrooms and concession stations. The outer wall of the corridor had at least 30 cabin doors along its length, and Jacqueline passed by two open seating areas before finding herself back in front of her own cabin door. The wedge-shaped common areas had tables for eating, and the view through the panoramic floor-to-ceiling virtual windows was so realistic that it almost looked as if a section of the outer wall was missing.

Jacqueline took a seat in one of the open areas and found herself tilting her head to one side as she stared at the thin blanket of atmosphere that followed the curvature of the Earth. She breathed slowly and scanned the scene for any visible sign that the blue ball was shrinking. Behind her, she heard people talking about the choices of the boxed meals, but Jacqueline wasn't hungry. She just sat quietly, looking out the window and wondering about the mechanisms that must be at work at the center of the cylindrical climber.

Perhaps it was how she was sitting, with her back to the room, but no one spoke to her during the hour that she stayed in the common area. She didn't mind, though. Her appetite for company was just as blunted as her hunger and her thirst.

Jacqueline looked out over the darkened Pacific and imagined the island of Borneo just beyond the western horizon. She lifted her chin and felt the strain in her neck as she tried to swallow. With each passing hour, she was moving farther and farther away from anyone she had ever known.

Somewhere high above her in orbit, there was a metal ball with her name on it, and in less than a week's time, she was going to seal herself inside of it and let them launch her out into empty space.

Is this really the freedom that you were looking for?

****

By the time the climber reached its summit station, 36 thousand kilometers above the Pacific, Earth appeared to be no larger than a soccer ball outside of Jacqueline's window. For the past 12 hours, there had been essentially no gravity inside the climber, and Jacqueline kept herself fastened into her seat for most of the trip.

Upon arrival, the passengers were requested to stay in their cabins for an additional hour while the summit station crew transported all of the cargo and baggage off of the climber. When it was finally time for the passengers to disembark, they did so, pulling themselves along the walls, ceilings, and floors. Several of them looked ill, but others had easy, even playful, movements, pushing off walls and floating perfectly towards their intended destinations.

Jacqueline and roughly 15 Nest crew members boarded a small orbiter shuttle for the four hour trip from the elevator summit station over to the Nest. Once everyone was seated in the shuttle, and before detaching from the summit station, the shuttle commander, a young pilot with sharp eyes, passed hand-over-hand among the seats, confirming his passenger list and verifying that everyone was securely buckled.

"OK, next stop, the Nest." he said with a smile once his inspection was complete. He pushed off and floated back to the front of the shuttle before strapping himself in.

Jacqueline noticed Airman Tharos seated a few rows ahead of her. He offered her a warm smile and wave. She responded in kind. Other airmen, three women and two men, were stealing glances at her as well.

It looks like I'm the main event this week.

Jacqueline almost laughed thinking about it. The propulsion station, with its searing lasers, would be much more efficient than any volcano for offering her up to the heavens.

There were virtual windows in the ceiling of the shuttle, but the Nest was still hard to see. Woven from a black carbon scaffolding, it was like a bowl-shaped shadow floating in space, blocking some but not all of the stars. The spinning Wagon Wheel at the center of the Nest seemed no larger than the mechanism in the middle of a clock face.

As the station came into clearer view, Jacqueline looked over its curved exterior. She had just spent three days in the cabin of a round climber, and now she was taking a shuttle over to the circular space station. Even her NLS was spherical. It was strange. She had spent 19 years living down on Earth where buildings, rooms, and furniture were all straight and rectangular. Up here, everything was round.

They got closer, and Jacqueline could see the eight pie-slice segments of the giant parabolic laser array. White lights flashed around the edge of the donut-shaped fusion reactors sitting at the center of each slice. Colleen had told her that the carbon mesh was covered in thousands of tiny ion thrusters to hold each gridpoint in place and to counter the backward pressure from the laser array, but even now, Jacqueline wasn't clear on what it all had meant.

As the shuttle approached the center of the Nest's Wagon Wheel, the overhead windows dimmed. Jaqueline felt a sideways motion in her stomach and she got a little bit dizzy. Soon, there was the sound of thruster exhaust, and Jacqueline was jerked forward a few times in her seat.

"Thank you everyone for your patience," said the shuttle commander. "We are safely docked on the Nest and we will start disembarking with the rows closest to me. If this is your first time on the Nest, please wait for me inside the Axle and I will give you a quick orientation."

Jacqueline and the 15 other passengers on the orbiter shuttle unbuckled themselves and waited their turns as the shuttle commander had requested. Once the path in front of Jacqueline was clear, she floated out through the front of the vessel to join the others.

Some of the passengers were gliding off in their own directions, but Jacqueline, Airmen Tharos and a few others waited for the shuttle commander to join them.

"Welcome aboard the Nest," he said when he arrived. "You'll find your baggage down below in the cargo ring. It's much safer to have you claim it there since that level offers 20% gravity, so your bags will stay where we put them. Please do be careful. The cargo ring is full of robotic palettes that move around on their own to keep the wagon wheel balanced."

"We've got some safety cables here behind you, please clip onto this guideline and follow me," he said, then pushed off toward one of the outer walls of the Axle, letting the guideline and the safety cable do the work of directing him toward a spot on the outer floor of the cylindrical hangar.

"OK, you can probably feel that the outer wall of the Axle has some light gravity," he said when the group was re-assembled below. "Those wide holes that you see in the floor have ladders that you can climb down to the cargo ring. The elevators in the cargo ring will take you to the other rings. The sleeping quarters are located on the middle ring at 50% gravity, and the outer ring is where the science and command decks are located. More importantly, the outer ring is where you'll find the mess hall. The chow is good on this station, so don't be shy."

Jacqueline looked around the hanger as the commander spoke. There were airmen gliding in several directions across the hangar of the Axle and she even saw someone pop up out of one of the wide bulkhead openings to the cargo ring.

"OK, that's the end of my little tour. Some of you are scheduled to meet Captain Kett on the Command Deck. Please go to her first. You can come back to the cargo ring to claim your bags after that."

Jacqueline and the others split into two groups in order to fit into the tight elevator. The change in gravity, as the elevator descended to the outer ring, felt strange, but the sensation dissipated as they stepped back out into the corridor.

They found the Command Deck and Captain Kett who was waiting to welcome them onto the Nest. The Captain was tall, much taller than Jacqueline, and she stood as straight as anyone Jacqueline had ever seen. The curl of her short auburn hair struggled bravely to free itself from the tight bun at the back of her head.

"Welcome aboard the Nest. I am Captain Kett. For those of you who will be joining my crew, let me say that I am eager to meet each of you one-on-one, and I will do so in the coming days. We also have the honor today to welcome our first NLS pilot, Lieutenant Jacqueline Binti Abdullah. In preparation for her launch, the next 48 hours will take this station to full operational readiness."

Jacqueline's heart was racing. These giant machines, this crew of airmen, another identical set of both a billion kilometers away were all waiting for her to drop into one of these NLS spheres and get shot out of the cannon. Her stomach twisted and she quickly looked around the room for a distraction just to keep from throwing up. That thought alone brought a little smile to her lips. She would hate to let this room full of people see how terrified she really was.

The Captain rattled off the names of her new crewmembers and assigned each to other Airmen who took responsibility for them. When there was no one left, Captain Kett walked over to Jacqueline and extended her hand. "It really is an honor to have you on the Nest. I'll escort you to locate your bags and then to your quarters, and we can talk about what needs to happen over the next 48 hours leading up to your launch."

They made their way back toward the elevator.

"From my side, the crew is ready to take you through your preflight procedures," said the Captain. "From what I understand, the doctors will start you with a full GI cleanse, and they'll set your dosages on the medications that you will need for the flight. I believe that you will be switching to taking nutrition from your gastrostomy tube, so we won't bother trying to throw a big dinner for you."

Jacqueline nodded. "Yes ma'am."

They got out of the elevator on the cargo ring, and Captain Kett pointed to one of the large motorized yellow palettes where the baggage was stacked. Jacqueline found her small hard-sided suitcase and her large aluminum COFLEX case. In the reduced gravity, the case lifted easily off the floor, so she didn't waste any time trying to extend the rolling wheels.

"What else are you going to require?" asked the Captain as they moved back toward the elevator.

Jacqueline thought for a moment then said. "At T minus eight hours I'll suit up in my COFLEX and I'll start self-checks of all of the micro-mechanical components to verify that the suit is flight-ready. Before that, I might like to be shown the NLS vessel so that I can familiarize myself with it."

"Excellent," said the Captain, as the elevator opened. "Yes, the NLS is moored just above us in the Axle. You may have seen it when you arrived. It is your vessel, and you have full access to it beginning immediately."

Tipping the COFLEX case on one end, Jacqueline slid into the elevator as Captain Kett held the door. Once on the middle ring,

Jacqueline followed Captain Kett to find the quarters that had been assigned to her. When they reached the door, Captain Kett turned and looked at her.

"Here we are. I'll leave you with one final request. There are 50 people aboard this station, and they've been working towards this goal for some time. These people are deeply invested in you. If you would consider saying a few words to the crew of the Nest before your departure, it would be phenomenal for morale."

Jacqueline blinked her eyes a few times as she thought how to respond. She had competed in front of crowds, but she had never spoken to a group larger than three or four people.

"I have to confess," she said, "I don't know if I'm ready for that. Would it be OK if I give you an answer tomorrow, Captain?"

"I understand. Yes, let's speak tomorrow and you can tell me what you've decided," confirmed the Captain. "I'll leave you to it then. Good luck, Lieutenant."

"Thank you, Captain."

****

Jacqueline could see herself projected on the large screens of the Command Deck. The COFLEX body armor amplified her frame. It wasn't feminine, but she liked it. She felt strong wearing it. With her helmet under one arm, she stood and waited for Captain Kett to tell her that it was time for her to speak. The two had agreed that a few short words would be sufficient, and the Captain had proposed speaking from the Command deck where she would only have to face a few individuals and a camera. Four hundred meters from the spot where she stood, engineers in the Axle ran final checks on her NLS.

A tone signaled that an all hands announcement would follow, and the voice communications from Jacqueline's suit were connected into the Nest's global comm channel. Jacqueline closed her eyes and kept them closed while she spoke her first few words.

"It's finally time for us to launch," she said. "My squad and I have been training for this, but ultimately, I'm in your hands. I want to thank you for taking responsibility for me and for the others. I'm ready to fly to the Outpost, and I'll tell them that you sent me."

There was silence for several seconds after she spoke, and she looked over at Captain Kett. Maybe they had been expecting more.

The first sounds of the crew's reaction didn't come from the officers on the Command deck where Jacqueline stood, but as echoes from the far corners of the Nest. The screens on the Command Deck switched to show groups of ten and twenty throughout the station celebrating and congratulating each other.

The officers on the Command Deck rose to their feet and began to applaud as well. Captain Kett looked satisfied, and executed a short bow in Jacqueline's direction.

Jacqueline took a step toward her and raised her hand in salute. Captain Kett responded with a crisp and precise salute of her own. With a final wave to the room, Jacqueline made her way to the elevator and took it "up" toward the center of the space station. From the inner ring she passed through one of the overhead bulkheads into the Axle. Standing on the outer wall of the Axle, she clipped onto one of the guidelines, bent her knees, and leapt upward towards the center of the empty 150 meter diameter cylinder. Between the added strength of the exoskeleton and the 17% gravity on the sidewalls of the Axle, Jacqueline rocketed towards the NLS and had to slow herself by squeezing the clamp of the carabiner around the guideline. The braking action caused her to flip around with her feet moving first towards the NLS.

It wasn't intentional, but she was glad for the feet-first orientation as she came to a stop near the hatch of her small spherical ship. Pausing for a moment, Jacqueline realized that there were people standing on the Axle walls above her, below her, and in all directions. There must have been 30 of them. They were all looking up at her. She stood there, holding the guideline with her feet on the surface of her NLS and waved. Another round of cheers broke out. She waited for it to quiet down, then waved one more time before directing her attention to the hatch near her feet.

Alone, she slid down through the hatch and looked around the small space that she would occupy for the next few days. One button push brought the lighted controls and displays to life, and another closed the hatch above her head.

You can do this, Jacqueline.

There was a high-pitched whine as the hatch sealed tightly on the four meter sphere.

It's just like in training.

She scanned the space around herself inside the small vehicle and thought back on the AR videos that she had seen with Captain

Fourtouna. She wondered what it would be like to finally meet him when she reached the Outpost.

Jacqueline fastened and sealed her helmet as she had done so many times in training, then positioned herself on the cradle, and buckled in. She was ready. She took one more deep breath and closed her eyes, "Axle Control, this is NLS-1 requesting air-lock access."

It was another 5 minutes before the outer door opened on the airlock, and a small puff of air sent Jacqueline's Near Light Ship floating silently forward into space. Eighteen months of training had led her to this moment, and the sound of that puff of air hitting the outer fuselage of her vessel almost made her smile, like being blown a kiss goodbye. What was coming next would be anything but gentle, and she had been working to acclimate her body to withstand it. The crushing force on her NLS ship from the propulsion array was about to begin, and once it did, it would last for four and a half days.

When she had achieved a safe distance from the Nest, Jacqueline used a voice command to deploy the lightsail that would be targeted by the Nest's hundred thousand propulsion lasers. She fired off several tiny ion thruster bursts to establish an ideal targeting position and vector at the center of the propulsion array.

The Nest lasers focused on her, and ramped up slowly over 75 minutes, adding 1 g per minute until her acceleration reached the full 75 g. Jacqueline knew that her vitals would be monitored to ensure that she was handling each step up in acceleration. In her trainings, she had learned that the multi-wavelength lasers would emit mostly red light on that first day. On subsequent days they would have to shift to yellow then to violet, consuming more energy from their reactors and projecting their coherent light further into space to target Jacqueline's lightsail.

Jacqueline didn't like being immobilized, and within an hour of reaching 75 g, she gave the voice command to start her long sleep. Though she could technically communicate with earth during those first few days, there wouldn't have been much to report. By the beginning of the fourth day, Jacqueline's ship was moving at 86% the speed of light and the outside world would have sounded like it was running at double time. It was only during the final 14 hours of acceleration that Jacqueline's clock would slow further to where each of her hours was practically a full day at home.

The same speed that warped her time, warped the mass of the dark matter GHoSts that she was hunting. If the invisible structures that scientists blamed for her mother's death were really out there, she was determined to find them.

As the sedatives took hold of her, the ghosts of her past and the ghosts of her future swirled around each other. If she survived this first trip, there would be more, and once the Outpost reached its final position, she would be asked to travel a distance of nearly a full light year, 356 light days, in this little ship that was only designed to keep her alive for 600 hours.

The Ghost of Sphinx

17 - Her Shadow - Sept 2115 - Austin Texas

Colonel Alessandro Crespin

"Colonel, he's here," said Airman Fovos.

The Colonel looked up from the documents that he was reviewing and made eye contact with the enlisted Airman. "Thank you, Fovos."

The first thing that Crespin noticed about his visitor was his suit. The cut was slightly different than one would see in the U.S., but regardless, it looked expensive.

Ah hell, this is probably the family lawyer.

He stood up from his desk and tugged slightly on the shirt of his uniform to straighten it. As the man entered, Crespin noticed that he carried himself more like a soldier than a lawyer and his eyes seemed to take a quick tactical inventory of the office as he passed through the door.

"Thank you for seeing me, Colonel," he said, extending his arm.

Crespin did the same and they shook hands. The bright white of the man's shirt cuff cut a sharp contrast against his light brown wrist. His grip was strong and the skin on his hands was coarse. As the two men exchanged a quick smile, Crespin noticed the traces of several thin parallel scars running down one side of the man's face. The skin between the raised lines seemed tight and even slightly reflective.

"Of course, Mr. Raban," said Crespin, "please have a seat and tell me what I can do for you."

After another quick visual scan of his surroundings, Raban sat in the chair that Crespin had indicated with his gesture. Crespin picked his documents up again and waited.

"Yes, Colonel. I've come on behalf of the family of Jacqueline Binti Abdullah. My employer received a letter, roughly two months ago, referring to her 'pre-deployment support'?" Raban's voice went up at the end, as if he were unfamiliar with the term that he had just used.

"I see," said Crespin. "May I ask if you are a member of the First Lieutenant's immediate family?"

"No, sir. I am not. I am only a representative. I have been granted special Power of Attorney for the sole purpose of receiving this pre-deployment briefing, described in the letter that you sent to Mr. Wan."

Crespin tilted his head and lowered a thick brow. "Mr. Raban, I'm afraid that the pre-deployment phase has passed. First Lieutenant Binti Abdullah is already deployed."

Raban nodded. "Certainly, Colonel. I understand, but my employer would still like for me to obtain as much of the offered information as I can. Specifically, the letter indicated that we would be able to learn more about deployment stresses and support for an eventual reunion."

As he spoke, Raban pulled out the letter that Crespin himself had drafted two months prior. Recognizing it, Crespin asked, "If I may, Mr. Raban, why are you responding to this now? We reached out to you some time ago."

Raban was nodding. "Yes, Colonel. To be honest, we didn't believe that the letter was authentic. You see, we have had no contact with Miss Jacqueline for over a year, and her grandfather is a very wealthy man. A letter, claiming to be from the American military and offering information about a Malaysian citizen seemed fraudulent. My employer is frequently targeted by dishonorable individuals, and he is especially vulnerable regarding his granddaughter. I was personally charged with determining whether or not Miss Jacqueline was in Houston, but verifying her presence here has proven difficult."

Crespin consulted his documents one more time. "I see. Well, I'm afraid that at this time I am not at liberty to give much information about First Lieutenant Binti Abdullah, other than to confirm that she is deployed and that she is an outstanding pilot. Her role is critical to the mission, and for all of our sake, we should hope that she is successful."

"She's a pilot?" asked Raban. Crespin thought that he heard a catch in Raban's voice as he spoke, and there was a brief change in his expression, but he corrected it before Crespin could read it.

"Yes, sir," said Crespin, "She is one of our best pilots, and she was first in her class for this mission."

Raban was still a moment, seemingly absorbing the information. "Is she in any danger?" he asked, finally.

Crespin tightened his lips. "Again, sir, I apologize, but at this time, I'm not at liberty to say. I can say that we have done, and we will continue to do, everything in our power to keep her safe."

To Crespin's surprise, Raban stood. "Thank you, Colonel. I don't think that I need to take up any more of your time today."

Crespin followed suit and stood as well. "I see. Would you like for me to deliver the Power of Attorney documents that you mentioned to our head counsel?"

"That won't be necessary. I will reassure Mr. Wan that Miss Jacqueline seems to be where she belongs. That is already a great comfort."

"Very well, then. Let me show you out."

Mr. Raban made a slight bow of his head, and Crespin walked around his desk and towards the door to his office. The sun was setting outside, and warm orange light was filtering in through the window behind Crespin. He stopped at the door to his office and gestured with his hand, encouraging Raban to pass in front of him.

Crespin closed and locked his door, and the two men began walking through the corridors, towards the main entrance.

"Could you tell me when she is expected back?" asked Raban as they walked.

"All that I can say is that you should expect significant periods of time where no contact will be possible. You can always direct communication to me, and I can forward it appropriately."

They turned a corner, and Crespin spotted Dr. Pastor entering a hallway that led to the civilian wing of the Agency. "Oh, Doctor," he called. "Do you have a moment?"

Colleen stopped and turned towards them. Crespin noticed that she already had a sour look on her face, but it didn't last. As she came to a stop facing the two men, her expression went blank.

There was something unnatural about seeing her so still. She was usually an unruly jumble of nervous ticks and technobabble, but for some reason she just stood there looking at them without speaking.

"Doctor, I'd like for you to meet Mr. Raban. He came to see us regarding Lieutenant Binti Abdullah's Family Readiness briefings. Mr. Raban, this is Doctor Colleen Pastor. She is the scientific lead on the First Lieutenant's mission."

Mr. Raban put out his hand to shake, and after a moment, Colleen accepted it. The handshake seemed oddly slow to Crespin. Neither of them spoke, but their eyes remained locked for several seconds.

"It is a pleasure to make your acquaintance, Doctor Pastor," said Raban at last.

Crespin was looking back and forth between them, waiting for Colleen to respond, but his mind wandered to the pile of work that was back on his desk.

After ten or fifteen seconds more of silence, Raban asked, "Excuse me if this sounds odd, Doctor, but have we met before?"

"Yes, I believe that we have," said Colleen. "It would have been at the drone racing championships in Kuala Lumpur."

Raban finally let go of Colleen's hand with a nod. As his right hand fell back to his side, Raban lifted his left hand to his face and slid his fingers lightly over the hairline scars on his cheekbone.

"Yes, that's it," he said. "What a remarkable pleasure it is to find you again," then turning back to Crespin, he said, "Thank you again for seeing me today, Colonel. I think that it's time for me to go."

18 - Her Web - Sept 2115 -
Five Light-Days from Earth
Jacqueline

Jacqueline slowly blinked her eyes open. The dull gray walls of her capsule were bathed in uneven yellow light as the optics of her helmet tried to come into focus. As the sedatives continued to wear off, Jacqueline realized that her whole body was sore. She wondered if she had sustained any injuries during the acceleration phase. She was dizzy, but zero-g could cause that. Her limbs tingled with pins and needles, but it had been the same on the G-loop during her trainings. The lining of her COFLEX was still massaging her arms and legs, trying to restore normal blood flow.

She struggled to remember her instructions over the lulling, systematic beep of the controls before her. The effort was more than she could face, and she let herself slip back towards sleep. She had been sleeping almost continuously for over 110 hours. How could she be so tired?

****

When Jacqueline opened her eyes again, something yellow was flashing on the ship-control display in front of her. She could see the rotating image of her spherical NLS ship. It was drawn in blue, but the gravitational probes were flashing yellow. The 24 bullet-shaped probes slung around the centerline of the sphere reminded Jacqueline of a bandolier full of bullets, as if her Near-Light ship were some kind of old-west villain.

Of the three large displays across from her, the one to the left seemed eerily dark and lifeless. The controls that sat below the dead screen brought back memories of the ones that she had used years earlier to pilot drones.

Yellow words flashed on the center screen below the NLS: "Deploy Gravitational Probes", "Deploy Gravitational Probes". She wondered how long she had been at zero-g, trying to climb out of her barbiturate-induced stupor.

The probes would have to wait while she freed herself from the cradle. Jacqueline's COFLEX was attached to the netting of the cradle at eight points. The bindings at her wrists could be released with a voice command, then she used her hands to detach her shoulders and head, freeing her entire torso. Finally she bent at the waist and released her knees and ankles.

The sedatives must not have been fully worn off yet because Jacqueline was already thinking about how she would re-attach her hips and shoulders for her next nap in the cradle.

This isn't even a full length flight. You can't waste any more time.

Jacqueline tried to recall her flight plan. '*As the first NLS pilot to fly to the Outpost, your early flights will be the shortest of the mission,*' Colleen had told her. In September of 2115, the Outpost was 69 light days from the Nest, but the flight plan showed that Jacqueline would only experience 3 days of dilated time at zero-g to do her work before strapping back in for deceleration. The idea of two different timelines didn't feel real. These were just numbers after all.

She removed her helmet and took a breath before remembering Captain Fortuna's words from the final training module. '*Before taking off your helmet in the NLS ship, it is extremely important that you check the center display to confirm that the NLS is safely pressurized, oxygenated, and temperature controlled.*'

"Well, I'm not dead yet..." she whispered into the dry air around her.

Jacqueline focused back on the yellow flash of the screen across from her. She swung her arms forward and the momentum carried her over to the center console. This time she did check the relevant display before acting. She confirmed her ship's x,y,z orientation on the navigational display to the right before tapping "Begin Deployment Sequence" with her gloved hand. Even traveling at this incredible speed, Jacqueline couldn't tell which way was forward without that display. Soon she heard what sounded like a dentist's drill, then another. The sound moved through 24 points around her as the band holding each gravitational probe was retracted in turn.

OK, so far so good.

Gently, nervously Jacqueline touched the radial thruster control for a fraction of a second. It was enough. Her center display showed the probes separate out from the NLS in every direction. They would keep moving outward for the remainder of her three day run.

Once the sensors were deployed, the display on the left came to life, and confirmed that all 24 probes, Alpha through Omega, had begun to establish laser communications with the NLS and with each other. The link status of all 24 probes was displayed in columns at the lower border of the panel. Most of the lights in those columns had turned green, but the lower four lights of each column were flashing red.

Jacqueline was floating parallel to the floor of her cabin, gripping the handhold with her left hand and pushing buttons with her right. She switched hands to glide herself over to gravitational sensor displays on her left in order to investigate. The display showed a graphic representing the 24 probes as a circle, with a mesh of green lines crisscrossing among them to represent laser signals. The outer portions of the laser mesh looked normal, but a small circular section at the center was still black. The dark circle was shrinking slightly as the ring expanded, but it wasn't going away.

Ah, I'm the problem... Jacqueline realized that her NLS, at the center of the expanding ring, was blocking any line-of-sight communication across the middle.

She placed her hands on the probe-piloting controls and tapped forward with the left joystick. That did it. The laser mesh began to move forward and away from the NLS. Within seconds, all of the status lights were green. The weave of green lines between the probes was so dense that it played tricks on Jacqueline's eyes, making her see woven bands of dark and light rather than straight lines cutting across the circle.

Finally! Oversleeping, Forgetting to check life support, and now forgetting how to deploy the probes correctly... When they see the flight log, they're going to wish that they had sent someone else.

It was far from textbook, but she still had most of three days to perform her primary goal of looking for GHoSts in the dark matter halo. She let go of her handholds and let herself float back towards the center of her little ball. Now she just had to wait.

****

Jacqueline had been biting her lip for so long, she was starting to taste blood. The hours were slipping by with nothing to show for it, and she had a growing suspicion that she had made some kind of mistake in deploying the probes. She twisted midair and directed herself back towards the gravitational sensor displays to double check their readings. Other than the expansion of the ring, making some of the lines slide slowly over each other, it was quiet. Hours passed staring at that display, but nothing was changing. The total detected mass stayed stubbornly frozen at 0 Kg.

****

The feel of the cradle's netting against her cheek was the first thing that she noticed. Jacqueline hadn't even realized that she had fallen asleep. She wasn't attached to anything. *Ugh... Did I hit any of the controls free floating like this?*

When she looked over at the displays to see if everything was still on track and reading normally, she noticed the total detected mass had climbed to over 2500 Kg. *I can't believe that I slept through a detection!*

Jacqueline pushed off the cradle and grabbed the handhold next to the detection displays, then touched the controls to rotate the view back towards the path she had traveled. There were several wispy traces floating behind her like sliced segments of cirrus clouds. Each of them seemed to flow down and to the left. *I have to find it again.*

Jacqueline's orders had left some room for interpretation. This first trip was assumed to be a straight flight with no lateral diversions. *But maybe they assumed that I was going to have lots of detections.* At that moment, she decided that if another one of those things flew through her web, she was going to change course to see if she could capture more of it.

Jacqueline mentally reviewed how to pilot the formation as a whole. She pushed herself over to the rightmost panel, which displayed her heading as a crosshair symbol to create an intercept course with the Outpost. Two numbers labelled Y deviation and Z deviation were both 0.

Her fingers felt ice cold as she reached for the controls. The idea of activating thrusters on all 25 vessels of the formation at once suddenly seemed reckless to her.

I might not be authorized for this, but there's no way to get new orders out here.

I can't just let this disappear without going after it.

She would just have to wait for the mass to reappear, but this time, she wouldn't fall asleep.

****

It took five more hours before it happened. Without warning, the animation of the laser mesh came alive with movement. A small region of the circle of intersecting green lines bubbled backwards, away from the plane of the probes, as the gravity of the dark mass elongated the path that the lasers followed. The bulge in the net let off a blue mist trail behind it to mark the path of the dark matter current.

Jacqueline could already see that the protrusion in the mesh was sliding from the upper right edge, towards the center of the ring. This was it. If she was going to follow one of these GHoSts, this might be her last chance.

Nervously, she pushed the thruster control diagonally down in the direction that the bubble was moving. She wanted to match its speed, but the only effect that she noticed was that her feet began floating upward and to the right as she gripped the handhold of the console.

Beads of sweat were forming on Jacqueline's upper lip. She wasn't even sure anymore if she was moving the right control. She dialed the units up past newtons to kilonewtons and pinned the thrust control diagonally down in the 7:00 position as far as it would go. Her feet slammed into the ceiling of the NLS and she lost her grip on the handhold. Her heartbeat was hammering in her ears as she pushed herself back down to look at the display.

At least this time there was a visible result. The bubble, which had been sliding quickly down the laser mesh, had slowed to a crawl. There was more texture appearing now that the detection was stable between the sensors. The shape fluttered, leaving turbulent swirls and bumps in the dark current trace behind her.

The intercept crosshairs on the navigational display vaulted away from the center of the Outpost, and the accumulated Y and Z deviations counted up hundreds of kilometers per second like two car odometers on fast forward.

As the warped section of the laser mesh slowly approached the bottom left edge, Jacqueline knew that she couldn't bear to break off the chase just yet. Her mind was made up. Holding on more firmly this time, she repeated her previous maneuver, pinning the thrust control diagonally down. *10, 9,* she counted down straining to maintain her grip with her left hand. *8, 7, 6-* she released the joystick. It was clear that she had reversed the motion of the bubble back towards the center of the laser mesh.

I've got you.

Jacqueline practiced with the thrusters, keeping the bubble towards the center of the laser mesh, so that even when it turned abruptly, she could apply thrust and follow it. The reading for total detected mass was climbing almost as fast as the Y and Z deviation odometers. It was accumulating several hundred kg of dark mass every minute.

****

When the mission clock read 15 hours remaining, a warning started to repeat itself on the navigation screens to the right. "Warning, course correction needed. Remaining mission time insufficient for rendezvous.", "Warning, course correction needed. Remaining mission time insufficient for rendezvous."

Jacqueline had been following the dark current for over 2 hours, and she knew she should calculate how to put herself back on an intercept course with the Outpost. Given the accumulated effect of all of the thruster blasts that she had been applying to follow the dark mass, her current heading was unsustainable.

She had barely started to do the calculations, when everything on the detection displays went solid blue. The mesh of laser lines between the probes was completely drawn back into a giant twisted windsock. If this was a dark current, then it must have been larger than the radius of the sensor ring itself.

What if this is the one that they're looking for? Can I really afford to give up on it after making so many other mistakes?

Slowly, Jacqueline reached towards the button that would silence the warning alarm. Her finger hovered over it for a moment as she weighed her options. Finally, deliberately, she pressed the button that muted the alert. She had made her choice. She would continue on her hunt, even if it meant missing the Outpost.

If nothing else, they'll get my data, and the others can pick up where I left off.

****

For long minutes, nothing changed. Jacqueline kept her breaths slow and deep as she clung onto the handholds on either side of the gravitational display. Finally, some of the probes flipped from blue back to green and the detection mesh began to flatten out signaling an end to the event. Jacqueline pushed out a final breath through pursed lips.

She pulled her feet to the right, then shoved off with her left hand to pivot over to the navigation controls. Her course correction calculations were complete, and she hurriedly brought her feet down to the wall of the NLS under the controls and hooked them there. She gripped the handhold hard with her left hand, jammed the joystick toward the 1:30 position and held it there for over a minute and a half, watching the Y and Z odometers as they slowed to a stop then reversed themselves. Her COFLEX squeezed her limbs to counter the g-force of her maneuver.

It didn't look good. The crosshairs weren't moving back to the Outpost as fast as they had moved away, and for some reason, the thrust had felt weaker near the end of her burst. Jacqueline pushed herself over to the center display and tried to find the problem. She inspected all of the gauges, and finally saw that the ion thrusters along the bottom left of the NLS were depleted.

She checked the readings back on the right to see how far off she was. It was tens of millions of kilometers, almost half of the distance between the sun and the Earth.

Why would they make a ship that could run out of propellant on one side if it still had reserves on the other?

That's it!

She pushed quickly back to the navigational controls. It was actually the spherical shape of the vessel that had confused her. Flying drones, there had always been a clear up and down, left and right, but on the NLS she had been ignoring roll completely.

She fired off a millinewton of left roll and waited for a few seconds until the NLS was rotated by 90 degrees before firing some right roll to cancel the rotation. Her thrusters at 10:00 and 11:00 should have more than enough propellant to finish the job.

Bracing herself, Jacqueline jammed the thrusters to 4:30 until she was almost out of propellant in those thrusters. She let off the joystick and waited to see if the crosshairs directed themselves back toward the Outpost. They did, and she was getting closer. She rolled her ship another 180 degrees, and gave another long thrust toward 10:30 until the destination display finally showed that she was back on an intercept course with the remote space station.

To her own surprise, Jacqueline let out a hoarse laugh and realized that there were tears in her eyes. She let go of the controls and floated backward for a moment. She tried to stop the shaking in her hands, but her heart was still pounding, and her breath was uneven.

Opening her eyes again, something didn't look right. A few of her probes at the bottom of the ring had gone offline. Four rows and four columns of link status were blinking red, and the mesh looked sparse, missing almost a third of its crisscrossing weave.

Jacqueline spent the next hour trying to pilot the disconnected probes back into position to get them in alignment with the ring. With lots of trial and error maneuvering she was able to get two out of the four back online, but by the time that the mission clock read 13 hours, all traces of dark currents were gone.

Jacqueline could barely focus her eyes, scanning the displays. It was going to have to be enough for now. She clipped herself into the cradle and slept for almost 6 hours.

****

When she awoke and unclipped herself, Jacqueline took a moment to just float there in the middle of her steel ball. She emptied her mind and let her eyes run over every wire, every pipe inside the curved hull. Finally, she kicked her feet and directed herself back to the screens. The navigational display looked OK, and the ship status display was quiet. Finally, she floated over to the detection display.

Jacqueline spent several minutes reviewing the traces that she had collected. Zooming out, she looked back and forth over the path that she had swept with her probes.

Viewed on that scale, it wasn't much. It was like a silk strand of a spider's web stretched over the grand canyon. Jacqueline placed her finger on the control to make dark mass detections brighter. Sliding the knob up and down brought the image to life, and short sections of her silken path glinted in the changing light.

The Ghost of Sphinx

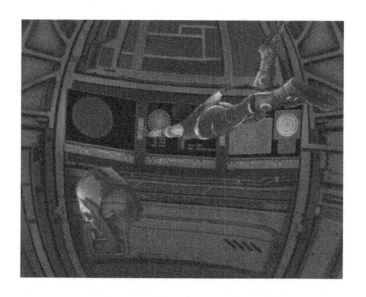

19 - Her Captain - Nov 2115 -

81 Light-Days from Earth

Jacqueline/Liam

"So, Lieutenant, tell me," he asked. "What was going through your mind when you silenced those alerts that were meant to notify you that you were passing a point of no return? Did you realize that you might have no way to get back to the Outpost?"

Jacqueline was seated on the edge of an examining table. Her COFLEX was standing empty by the wall, and the micromechanical gel was in a glass jar next to it, swirling to clean itself. Jacqueline's feet didn't reach the ground, and the narrow paper sheet on the table made crinkling noises whenever she moved. Second Lieutenant Christopher Ellis, the Outpost's Human Factors Scientist, sat a few meters across from her on a grey stool.

"Well, for most of my trip there was nothing, and I had made so many mistakes during the early hours of the flight," she said, looking down at the floor. "If I came all this way without finding anything, then maybe it was because I did something wrong." She looked up at his face, but he didn't seem to react to what she had said. He just looked back at her.

"But then I got another chance, and there was finally something worth following, … I mean how would it look if I just ignored something like that? Back in training, when people couldn't do what was needed, they ended up getting cut from the program."

Lieutenant Ellis was taking notes on a tablet. He paused for a long moment before speaking again. "So, are you telling me that you are worried that you might be eliminated from the NLS program?"

Jacqueline wasn't looking directly at Lieutenant Ellis. "Not really, I mean, it just felt like everyone was watching this first run, expecting…" Jacqueline looked around the room to see if the other medical staff could hear what she was saying. "It wasn't as if I was putting the whole mission at risk. You would have still gotten the data even if I missed my landing on the Outpost."

Lieutenant Ellis put down his tablet and looked Jacqueline in the eye. "OK, Lieutenant. I'm going to give you some homework while you're on the Outpost with us. I'd like for you to ask around while you're here. I'd like for you to ask as many of the 50 people onboard this station as you can, how they would feel about both scenarios. How they would feel about an NLS flight with no data versus a flight that yielded amazing data, but resulted in the loss of an NLS pilot. I'd like for you not just to ask them, but to really listen to their answers. I think that you will be interested in what you hear. I think that they will be shocked to learn that you would take such risks. I'll wager that every one of those scientists will place infinitely more value on the life of the NLS pilot, on your life, than on the data."

Lieutenant Ellis raised an eyebrow, but she wasn't sure what to say. When she didn't respond he asked directly, "Are you willing to try that exercise for me?"

"OK," responded Jacqueline.

Lieutenant Ellis stood. He was tall, and Jacqueline's eyes followed him. With her neck strained backward, looking up at the officer, and with her feet dangling 30cm off the floor, she felt like a child in a pediatrician's office.

"Excellent. I'm all set here. Maybe I'll see you in the mess hall at dinner time."

Jacqueline slid off of the examining table with a loud crinkle and placed her bare feet on the floor. It was colder than she had expected it to be. She looked around for the doctors who had been handling her post-flight checkup, but they were nowhere in sight.

Not knowing what to do next, she looked back at Lieutenant Ellis.

"Oh, let me get you some socks." he said "The Captain will be here in a minute to welcome you onboard. He will also show you to your quarters."

"Captain Fourtouna is coming here?" asked Jacqueline.

Lieutenant Ellis stood upright again, empty-handed and turned towards her. The cabinet that he had opened to retrieve socks stood unsecured behind him. "Do you know the Captain?"

Jacqueline felt the blood rushing to her cheeks and turned to look back at the table, as if she were going to collect her things, but there was nothing there.

"No, I've never met him," she said, turning back, "but we watched all of his training videos."

Lieutenant Ellis didn't respond for a moment. He just looked at her, letting his eyes move up and down over her.

Jacqueline folded her arms in front of her and rounded her back a little.

The cloud over his expression lifted, and he smiled brightly, turning back to the cabinet. "Right, so let me find those socks for you."

He finally closed the cabinet, and was handing a pair of warm socks to Jacqueline when something caught his eye behind her. "Oh, Captain, your timing is perfect. Captain Fourtouna, this is First Lieutenant Binti Abdulah. She is ready for you."

The Captain was just as tall as Second Lieutenant Ellis. The two of them towered over Jacqueline. "Thank you, Christopher." said the Captain, then to Jacqueline he said, "First Lieutenant, it is such a thrill for me to finally meet you. I wanted to personally welcome you onboard. Come. I'll show you to your quarters where you can get into uniform. You're going to cause enough of a stir already without walking around in a bathrobe."

Lieutenant Ellis had been smiling as he introduced her, but his expression grew more serious as the Captain spoke. Jacqueline glanced at each of the men. One was looking at her with the brightest of expressions, while the other looked at him, expressionless. She didn't want to call attention to what she was seeing, so she quickly followed the Captain's gesture and began walking towards the door without taking time to put on the socks.

As soon as the door opened leading from the medical bay to the corridor, she froze. There was a commotion in the hallway, and Jacqueline found herself standing barefoot in a bathrobe, staring into the faces of no fewer than 20 Space Agency personnel.

There was a brief pause, as if the crowd was as embarrassed as Jacqueline to have come upon her in this unfortunate state of partial undress. Regardless, the silence only lasted a moment. Applause rang out, and the crowd compacted into a tight semi-circle around the door to the medical bay. There were shouts of "Welcome aboard!" and "Congratulations!"

Jacqueline wilted backward a few steps, and Captain Fourtouna confidently slipped out in front of her. Rather than facing the crowd, he turned and joined in for a moment, clapping along with them. With a broad smile, he looked to his left and right and exchanged pleased glances with his crew.

He had to speak loudly to be heard over the noise. "They were right, not to wait," he said, still clapping. "This is no time for protocol. It's a big day, for all of us."

When the applause started to die down, the Captain turned to face the crew gathered in the hallway and addressed them. "I'd like your attention for a moment, please. As you can see, First Lieutenant Binti Abdulah has not actually had a chance to finish her medical check-in. In a moment, I will ask you all to give us a respectful about-face, at which time, she will be led discreetly to her quarters where she can don a proper uniform."

"On three, One, Two, About Face!" With his words, every person in the hallway spun around with military precision, and where there had been a sea of smiles and eyes, Jacqueline now saw tightly pressed uniform shirt collars, neat haircuts, and ponytails. Precision aside, there was still a ripple of conversation and friendly laughter throughout the crowd.

Jacqueline worried that it would be rude not to speak. As she and the Captain slipped along the unoccupied edge of the hallway, she said over her shoulder, "Thank you. I'm really glad to be here." That was all it took for military discipline to evaporate. The crowd was at ease again, clapping, laughing and turning to face her. As she walked away from them, she realized that she was still holding a pair of socks in her hand.

While on the Nest, Jacqueline had grown accustomed to the slow upward curvature of the floors in these long corridors. They had only been walking for 15 or 20 seconds, but already, when she turned to look back at where they had come from, only the feet of the people who had welcomed her were still visible. She knew that her quarters wouldn't be on this level. All crew sleeping quarters were located in the middle ring, at 0.5g.

The Captain turned towards Jacqueline and raised an outstretched arm to indicate the path. "The elevator is just up ahead." Jacqueline looked in the direction he was pointing and saw the elevator, but her glance quickly moved back to notice how the Captain's shirtsleeve strained against the solid muscle underneath.

As she followed the Captain the few remaining steps, Jacqueline remembered how small these elevators were. The door opened immediately, and they entered. It was cramped inside, and after days alone in the NLS, Jacqueline was surprised by how sensitive she had become to things like the smell of another person close to her. She was suddenly glad that she had had a chance to shower in the medical bay. Her robe was slightly damp which had made it feel heavier on her shoulders and back, but it grew lighter as the elevator brought them from the 1 g outer ring to the 0.5g middle ring of the Outpost.

The ride took less than a minute, and soon they were making their way to Jacqueline's quarters along a corridor whose floor had even more upward bend to it. She could only see 10m of hallway in front or behind her as she walked, and walking in half gravity was awkward. The Captain seemed accustomed to it, but Jacqueline had only spent two nights on the Nest before boarding the NLS. Nervously, she kept her arms at her sides to keep the white bathrobe from moving too much. She could barely feel its heft anymore, and the sensation was unsettling.

Captain Fourtouna came to a stop in front of one of the doors. "Here you are, Lieutenant. Your things are already inside. Now, I'll leave this up to you. I'm available for the next hour if you'd like a tour of the Outpost, but if you're tired from your trip, we can schedule it for another time. Either way, why don't you suit up and you can tell me your decision when you're ready."

"Thank you, Captain." Jacqueline slipped past him and into her quarters. She closed the door gently, pushing it with both hands. As the spring lock clicked, she relaxed her elbows and let her whole body lean up against the door.

Jacqueline bit her lip and took a slow breath in, then pushed herself back upright and turned around to look at her quarters. The familiarity of it all struck her. There was nothing in that room that would indicate that they were 80 light days from Earth. She looked down at the floor and tapped her foot lightly, trying to imagine how thick the hull was between her foot and the emptiness of space outside. There was no one who could help them if one of the station's systems malfunctioned, but that also meant that nothing unwelcome could reach them out there either.

Them...

He's still waiting for my answer.

Quickly, Jacqueline made her way over to a small set of drawers where one of the crew had placed her suitcase. She put the thick socks that Lieutenant Ellis had given her in the top drawer, and opened her suitcase to find a clean uniform and her normal athletic socks that would fit into her sneakers.

She sat on the bed to get dressed. The mattress was thin, but at 0.5g, it felt deep and soft. Jacqueline raked her fingers through her hair, pushing it over to one side, and headed for the door, sneakers in hand.

He was exactly where she had left him, but the expression on his face made her narrow her eyes.

He already knew. The smug bastard knew that I would say yes.

"I'm ready for my tour, Captain."

****

Liam was waiting in the hallway outside of Christopher's quarters when he saw him approaching in his shorts and running shoes, dripping with sweat. His clothes clung to his broad frame and his long hair clumped into chords that swung slightly as he moved. The 2.5k length, not to mention the full gravity of the outer loop made it an ideal running track for the crew of the Outpost, and Christopher had one of the best times for their monthly 10k.

Liam had been wondering where he was. "It's late for a run. Are you on a diet or something? Why did you decide to skip dinner?"

"I need a shower. Can we do the third degree later?" responded Christopher as he went inside. Liam followed him.

"Christopher, seriously. What were you thinking? Tonight was Jacqueline's last real meal on the station, and the whole crew was there to see her off. You're one of my senior officers. What kind of message does it send if you're a no-show?"

Christopher wasn't making eye contact with Liam. He was collecting up his towel and clean clothes to bring with him to the showers. "I doubt that anyone other than you even noticed. Don't make a big deal out of it."

"Something is off," Liam said. "You should be ecstatic. For months, you've been telling me that you're worried about morale and that you think that the crew is going to sink into a depression."

He waited for Christopher to react, but nothing came. "So, have you noticed that for the past seven days, every member of the crew has been in the best spirits that we've seen in a year? Everyone but you. You're aggravated about something."

"Frankly, I'm surprised that you can even remember what I said to you about the crew. I guess you were right. Ignoring the problem worked out fine. You should stick with that strategy going forward."

This was going nowhere. Liam walked over to Christopher. He put his hands on Christopher's solid shoulders and looked him in the eye. "What is going on?"

Christopher tried half-heartedly to pull free, but Liam held him there. He finally answered. "This is an illusion. They're not better. You ignored the problem before, and now you're hoping that your little golden girl has magically cured them, but you're fooling yourself. No one's problems have changed. No one's except mine."

Liam turned his head slightly, straining to hear Christopher's last sentence.

"Christopher, this crew is lucky to have you, and I am too. You have kept us going and you will continue to be our voice of reason. The mission achieved a major milestone this week, and you played a key role in that. This is your success too."

Christopher took a few seconds to answer. When he did, his voice was unsteady as he shook his head. "No, I never would have signed up for this." After another pause, he added, almost to himself, "I guess I'm the one who was in denial."

Liam had been concerned as an officer, but now he was feeling something else. He knew that Christopher was intuitive, but he thought he had been so careful. Had Christopher really guessed? Maybe it would be best to just let him cool off.

Liam let go of Christopher's shoulders and let his hands drop to his sides. Christopher just looked at him. Liam saw his expression change. The intensity in his stare faded and his eyelids drooped. He tilted his head down and looked at something off to the right.

"Like I said, you might as well stick with that strategy."

Christopher turned to leave the stateroom, but before he reached the door he turned back. "So I guess you're going to deal with this the way you deal with other problems, but let me just say one last thing to you. If you sleep with her, it'll mean the end for us."

He turned back without waiting to see Liam's reaction and left the room.

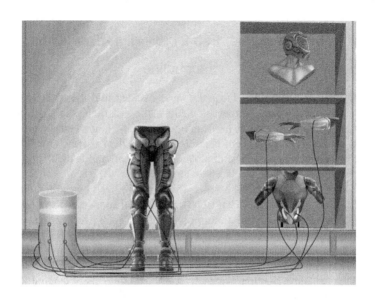

20 - His Game- Feb 2116 - High-Earth Orbit

Jacqueline

Just like last time, Jacqueline was buckled into the cradle, but she knew what to expect now. Just like last time, she signaled Axle Control to move her ship into one of the launch tubes where a small puff of air sent her ship floating silently away from the propulsion station. She deployed her lightsail and waited for the Outpost's propulsion lasers to target her.

Within two hours she was at 75g, immobilized by the force of the acceleration, her COFLEX's exoskeletal support assisting her breathing. Jacqueline thought about the Captain for a moment, and she wondered if the quick flutter that she suddenly felt would set off warning lights for the engineers who were monitoring her vital signs. She was infinitely more confident on this run than she had been on her first, but each time she thought about leaving the Outpost behind, her stomach twisted into knots.

She hadn't felt this way about leaving Earth. She hadn't been worried that she might never return. *It's only four days of awake time to the Nest, eight days on that space station, then five days to come back here.*

You can wait two more weeks, Jacqueline.

It didn't make her feel any better though. She knew that her timeline wasn't the problem. She moved her eyes over the menu options and selected the mission schedule. It projected inside her visor.

It's not two weeks for him. It will be more like six months... Whatever I thought I saw in him, it won't last six months...

Mercifully, the sedatives were taking effect, and Jacqueline didn't have to dwell on that thought for much longer.

****

This run is going to be flawless.

Jacqueline woke with an hour of 75 g remaining and went through a mental checklist of her deployment sequence. As soon as the NLS was at zero-g, she checked the center display to confirm that the life support systems were nominal, then she removed her helmet and detached herself from the cradle in under a minute.

Checking the NLS orientation, Jacqueline saw that it was off slightly, so she fired a millinewton of right yaw and downward pitch, then after a few seconds, she fired both thrusters again in the opposite direction to stop her rotation. *There, that looks perfect now.*

She tapped "Begin Deployment Sequence" and listened as the 24 bands retracted. In another five minutes, all 24 probes were deployed out in front of the NLS with solid link status and a fully connected mesh.

Jacqueline checked her records from her last flight and banked hard towards the region where she had last seen the large diameter dark current. Colleen had explained to her that the goal of the mission was to map out how the GHoSts were moving through interstellar space so that they would be able to predict which ones were on a collision course with Earth's solar system. "You can't just find them once." she had said. "You need to find the same ghost twice, so that we can measure its direction and velocity."

During quiet hours, Jacqueline practiced at bumping her probes out of alignment with the formation, then recovering them. She wondered how many she could dislodge before the remaining mesh would be too sparse for her to recover.

I'll leave that experiment for another run. This one is going to be by the book.

****

With 18 hours of zero-g time left on the mission clock, Jacqueline had once again broken off her pursuit of a dark current. It was a different one than last time, and it fit neatly inside her ring of gravitational probes. She had followed the silken trace of her previous run, but all of the detections had been new ones.

Jacqueline liked weaving a new strand, distinct from the first. Somehow, two small strands of web seemed like the start of something in a way that one hadn't. Her trails were green and had the glint of blue where dark currents had been detected inside them.

The third trail startled her. There was nothing but empty space, then suddenly, a third trail, gold in color, extended out ahead of her as far as she could see.

How could it just appear like that?

Jacqueline pulled up the mission plan again and saw that Andrew had departed the Nest about two weeks earlier. His trail was a different color than hers. *Cemil...* He must have convinced Colleen to give them different colors.

'You need to find the same current twice...'

Jacqueline pushed herself over to the detection displays and pored over Andrew's data. She wanted to find a dark current with a distinctive shape that she could pick up again. Then maybe Colleen could map out the speed and direction that she wanted.

Ha, there... The cloud of dark matter looked like a lumpy foot, with five puffs on top and a rounded trapezoidal base. Trailing behind it were several wispy puffs that could have been a leg attached to it. Jacqueline laughed out loud as she looked at it.

If there were ever going to be a detection well suited to be recognized again, it's this one.

She hooked herself in with her legs, held tightly with her left hand, and leaned on her thrusters. The formation of NLS and probes deformed for a moment, but as the probes caught up to the NLS, Jacqueline smiled.

You've got this...

****

Just like last time, Jacqueline used her last minutes before strapping into the cradle again to look back over her run. She couldn't wait to hear what Colleen would have to say about the second detection of Andrew's foot cloud. It had deformed slightly between the two detections, but it was still recognizable.

Time was up. Jacqueline put on her helmet and sealed it. She pivoted the NLS so that her back was towards the Nest and deployed her lightsail. Finally, she hooked into the cradle and waited. According to the mission plan, the Nest's propulsion lasers had started firing almost 68 hours prior, but the first photons wouldn't reach her for another 30 minutes of her time.

Buckled in and calm, Jacqueline let her mind wander over the past few weeks. It had been so exciting. She thought back to all of the things that Captain Fourtouna had said to her while she was on the Outpost. She could still see the intensity in his blue eyes when he asked her, "Do you realize how special you are?" No one had ever used words like that with her before. Well, maybe *Ibu*, but that was so long ago.

More and more, when she tried to remember her mother's face, she couldn't. So much had happened. She had broken her promise to herself to give up flying as penance for their deaths, but in her heart, she wanted to believe that she was doing the right thing.

The Captain had said that she was the soul of the mission, and that she had done more for morale in one flight than he had done in 3 years. That man knew how to get the most out of people.

All he has to do is ask...

****

The eight days that Jacqueline spent on the Nest were torture. All she wanted to do was to get back into the NLS.

Are you really trying to further the mission, or are you just anxious to get back out there?

Either way, sitting and waiting for clearance was making her crazy, so getting a call from Colleen was the highlight of the first four days. "Hey, sweetie, how are you holding up?"

"I'm OK." answered Jacqueline. "I'm eager to make another run. How have the detections been so far?"

"Are you kidding me? I am completely serious when I tell you that this is beyond my wildest expectations. I really needed this too. Crespin's lackeys have been looking up my ass with a microscope and all recruiting is frozen until your class shows results."

"Really. Do you mean that there are no other NLS pilots in training right now?" asked Jacqueline. "How many of us are there?"

"Well, you know, Andrew flew out last month, and Cemil will be on his way to SPISE in a day or two, but he won't get to the Nest in time to see you."

"What about Kirin?" asked Jacqueline.

"She is close to graduation, but she still needs a little bit of time to acclimate to 75g. Hey, don't worry about anything. Your detections alone should be enough to get those assholes off my back. Seriously, doll, you cannot imagine how important you are to me right now."

****

The day before Jacqueline was scheduled to fly again, she received an invitation to play an immersive game on the Nest. Jacqueline had been into the games once or twice with Colleen, and she knew that the crew on the Outpost lived a dual existence, partly inside and partly outside of their artificial worlds, but the crew of the Nest was different. They were close to Earth and they could come and go and even take leave to see their families.

Jacqueline tried to imagine who would have sent the invitation, but no one came to mind. She had largely kept to herself on the Nest for the past few days. Rolling onto one side, she got up off of her bed and sat down at her desk to use the VR headset that had been hanging on the wall, untouched since her arrival.

She strapped on the headset and entered the game.

The sun was bright, and she had to squint her eyes. After a moment, though, she recognized where she was. The illusion had brought her to one of the dirt pathways, next to a recently plowed field. All around her was the stone wall of the G-loop, and she could see some of the trails leading through its arches. The detail was extraordinary, right down to the sound of a gentle breeze. The sights and sounds were almost enough to fool her senses into smelling the overturned dirt ten meters away from where she was standing.

A tall figure was walking toward her. Jacqueline wasn't familiar with the game controls, so she waited where she was. Before she could even see his face, she knew that it was Captain Fourtouna. He stopped a little bit further away from her than she was expecting. "Hello. Thank you for accepting my invitation." He turned and looked around himself at the fields and the circular stone wall. "I miss this place. I was so full of hope, the first time that I came here."

"How is this possible?" Jacqueline asked. "The Outpost is over 100 light days from the Nest right now. How are we talking?"

There was a pause, and the Captain froze for a second. "It's a trick." he said, moving naturally again. "Colleen came up with it a few years ago. She calls it a scripted game. You're not actually talking to me in real time. This game that I invited you to play has 75 pre-recorded responses that I narrated over the course of a day. It's like role playing. She says that it's more fun than sending long written reports. As long as you say and ask things that I was able to anticipate, it can feel very natural."

"Can anyone else see us?"

"If you're asking about privacy, then let me say that this game can only be accessed by you. Each time that you enter, it will be a fresh start. I've set up this game so that it doesn't record anything and it doesn't keep any record of what happened inside."

The idea was tempting. Could she really say whatever she wanted to the Captain with no fear of the consequences? *No, not yet.* "May I ask why you sent me this?"

"If you're asking why I invited you to this scripted game, it's because I wanted to ask you a favor. It might be better if we talked about other things first. I don't want to rush into asking this favor of you."

"What's the favor?" asked Jacqueline.

The Captain's mouth twisted up and his nostrils flared for a moment. "Oh, OK. If you want to get right down to it, it's this. Our chef is asking if you could bring us a living sourdough starter from the kitchens on the Nest. It contains particular bacteria cultures, and you would actually need to feed it twice a day to keep it alive on the NLS. It's a lot to ask of you, but our starter died, and we haven't had any good bread in months. I'm prepared to answer specific questions about how to care for it." His expression changed. It was almost mocking.

"Bread? Did you really make this whole video game to ask for bread?"

"It means more to us that you might realize, but it is a big favor to ask, so please don't feel obligated."

Jacqueline took off her VR headset and placed it on the desk. This didn't make any sense.

It was already late when the invitation had arrived, and Jacqueline just wanted to climb into her bed and forget about it. She'd go to the kitchens on the Nest in the morning.

This seems ridiculous, but I have no reason to deny their request. I don't control the cargo that goes on the NLS when I fly.

****

Jacqueline's sleep was restless. She was having half-lucid dreams of conversations with the Captain. She no longer knew which versions of her conversation were real and which ones were products of her dream state. She tried to clear her mind and focus on her breathing, but each time that she fell asleep the dreams started over again.

After three hours she had had enough. She sat up in bed and tried to think of how to clear her mind. The room was dark, but there was a slight phosphorescent glow coming from her desk.

He said he had recorded 75 answers.

Jacqueline gave up on sleeping. She got out of bed, walked over to her desk and sat down again, then put on the VR headset and waited. There was an evening sky this time.

Within a few seconds, he came walking down the path. "Hello. Thank you for accepting my invitation." He turned and looked around himself at the fields and the circular stone wall. "I miss this place. I was so full of hope, the first time that I came here."

"What did you hope for?"

"I'm sorry, I can't tell what you're asking me."

"What are you hoping will happen?" she asked.

"I'm hoping that you'll ask me a question."

"Do you want me to ask you about the favor?"

"It might be better if we talked about other things first. I don't want to rush into asking this favor of you."

How many different versions of this conversation had her mind invented?

It's a game. Just do it.

"OK, then. Is it lonely on the Outpost?"

Liam smiled. "It does get lonely sometimes. We all have good working relationships. Most of us have friends on the station, and some of us have people who are more than friends."

"Do you have someone special on the Outpost?"

"I hope that you don't mind me confiding in you. I have had a relationship on the Outpost, but there have been problems recently."

"I'm sorry to hear that." She had never even considered it before.

You're so stupid. Did you think he was up there waiting for you?

The Captain was still looking at her as if he expected another question.

It's not real. Just ask him.

"What types of problems are you having?"

"Jealousy." he answered. Was she imagining the look on the avatar's face? Was he looking at her more intently?

This is so personal. "Who is jealous?"

"Chris is jealous... jealous of you."

Jacqueline's forehead was starting to sweat under the band of the VR headset. She chose her words carefully. "Why is Chris jealous of me?"

The Captain took a step closer to her. He was about one meter away from her and she had to look up to see his face. "Because I haven't been able to hide my feelings for you."

Jacqueline's palms were flat on the desk's surface. Her chin was lifted toward him and she realized that she was pulling herself in with her hands, arching her upper body towards him. In the 0.5g, it was almost enough to lift her out of her chair.

"You have feelings for me?"

Nodding, he said, "I think that it started before I even left Earth. Colleen was always so excited when she talked to me about you. Then for the past year, she's been sending me training status on all of you. I've been waiting for the day that I would finally get to meet you. You just left the Outpost yesterday, and the station felt so empty. I started working on this scripted game to send to you."

"Is now a good time to ask you again about the favor?" asked Jacqueline.

The Captain smiled. "Yes, now is fine. When you come to the Outpost again, I want to ask you to meet me in another game like this one. It's called J-loop. I would really like to get to know you properly, but I don't want to cause a stir on the Outpost. If we met inside a game, privately, we could talk for hours and no one would think anything of it. We wouldn't be missed."

"Is that all?" she asked.

"Well, actually, there is one more thing. Our chef is asking if you could bring us a living sourdough starter from the kitchens on the Nest. It contains particular bacteria cultures, and you would actually need to feed it twice a day to keep it alive on the NLS. It's a lot to ask of you, but our starter died, and we haven't had any good bread in months. I'm prepared to answer specific questions about how to care for it." The smile on his face was almost playful.

21 - Contact - Jun 2116 - High-Earth Orbit

Jacqueline

The morning that Jacqueline was scheduled to re-launch from the Nest was one long string of last-minute preparations. The trip to the kitchens took much longer than she had expected. Captain Fourtouna had neglected to mention that the respective head chefs on the Nest and the Outpost were two brothers from Naples Italy. Pietro was the elder of the two, and was so excited to hear that he could send something to his younger brother Luca that he welcomed Jacqueline like an honored guest and insisted on giving her a tour of the kitchens. Along the way, he explained to her that the bread starter that she would deliver to his brother was the same one that they had carried with them from Naples when they joined the Space Agency.

"Signorina, it is easy." he said to her. "It is just like you would do with your bambino. You just have to feed it a little bit every few hours. Here, take these. How many days do you need?" He handed her several small tubes of flour and water paste for the days that she would be traveling, then he went to the back to get a sturdy iron canister with a latching lid to hold the yeast-bacteria starter itself.

"Here you are, signorina. Take good care of her. I don't like to imagine poor Luca with no bread." Pietro gave a short sniff and shook his head quickly, then leaned in to give her two audible air-kisses, one on each side of her face. "You tell him for me that Pietro says hello, and that I am proud of him."

From there, she went to get a technical briefing from Colleen's engineers. After their video call earlier in the week, Colleen had members of her team sit with Jacqueline to get ideas on how to improve the piloting software. In that second call, Jacqueline was the only person on her end, but back on Earth, the room must have held 20 Space Agency engineers. They were all taking notes as she described how she wished that there was a way to tell if a probe that had lost contact with the others was ahead of or behind the pack.

Now, only a few days later, the software on the NLS had been upgraded, and she was invited to a new video chat where they walked her through the new display that would indicate the "Xoffset" as they called it. Jacqueline didn't know why they called it that, but it looked like it would be enough to allow her to restore a probe's alignment the next time that she lost one.

Finally, hours behind schedule, she headed down to medical for a final shower and a flush of her G-tube before suiting up in her COFLEX.

****

Yeah, that's a lot better.

Jacqueline had decreased her dose of sedatives again, and waking up for her zero-g piloting run was getting easier each time. She looked over and saw 132 hours on the mission clock.

As the Outpost traveled farther from the Nest to its final position, it left greater expanses of empty space to be searched by the NLS pilots. Colleen guessed that Andrew would try to take a second reading of the thick dark current that Jacqueline had discovered on her first trip out, so Jacquline's mission plan was to head off in a new direction.

With a voice command and a few clicks, she was out of the cradle and was checking the life support display on the center console. It all looked good, so she took off her helmet. The smell hit her immediately.

Spaghetti?

Jacqueline looked around but didn't see anything unusual. She finally pulled herself around to look behind the cradle. There was no need to look any further. Indeed, something was out of place in the little sphere. Paint-white trails ran along several of the rear sections of the NLS situated behind the cradle, including significant splatter on the lid of her personal, hard-sided bags that were attached to the side-wall of the vessel. In the crushing 75g acceleration, several of Pietro's tubes of flour paste had burst and run like water into every crevice before drying. Jacqueline was starting to wish that she had discussed this plan with Colleen.

After a quick inspection and with a brief sigh of relief, Jacqueline concluded that nothing mechanical or electrical was damaged, and she pushed herself back towards the controls to deploy her probes. There was nothing to be done about the smell.

****

With 128 hours left on the mission clock, things were quiet. There had been no mass detections in her mesh yet, but Jacqueline knew that she had a more pressing concern. It was time to feed the 'bambino'.

I wonder if anyone has ever done this in zero-g before.

The two liter stainless canister holding the starter was attached behind the cradle, wrapped in an electric cooling blanket. It held the beige paste, like pancake batter, that the Captain's avatar had asked Jacqueline to bring with her. She wondered if she was going to arrive at the Outpost to discover that it had all just been a practical joke.

She detached the electric cord and opened the lid carefully. The sticky consistency of the starter paste made it cling firmly to the walls of the container. Below the canister, tight netting held four intact and two ruptured tubes of flour-water paste. Removing the cap from one of the tubes, Jacqueline inserted the tip under the lid of the canister and squeezed it with her gloved hand.

Is it clogged?

The tube was bulging between where she held it and the tip, but nothing was coming out. The lining of the COFLEX made it hard for her to tell if she was applying enough pressure, so she started to squeeze a little bit harder.

Jacqueline regretted that decision almost instantly. She heard a single high note as the tube wall gave way under the iron grip of her exoskeleton. A spray of fast-moving white paste swept in an arc across the netting of the cradle and was sliced into blobs that floated toward the three large instrument panels that would normally have Jacqueline's undivided attention at this point in her mission. Pietro's bambino was turning out to be a handful.

I guess this is why most women take off their body armor before feeding their babies.

Jacqueline wasn't sure if she wanted to take off her gloves to handle the tubes of paste with her bare hands. There was no way to wash her hands before putting the gloves back on, and she wasn't sure that the flour would do to the micromechanical gel that lined her suit. She could already see where her current tube was clogged, but now that the side was split open, Jacqueline just used that opening to squeeze a bit of paste into the stainless canister and close the lid.

I'll mix it later. I need to go clean up my controls before this stuff dries.

****

There were 30 hours remaining on the mission clock when a new gold NLS trail sprung into view. Imagining her own speed was hard enough for Jacqueline without trying to consider how fast two vessels traveling in opposite directions would fly past one another. Regardless, there were five trails now visible in Jacqueline's detection display, and it felt like progress.

She hadn't had another detection as large as the one that almost took her past the Outpost. During their video call on the Nest, Jacqueline had asked Colleen why that large detection had made probes in the ring drift apart in the way that they had.

Colleen gave her a physics lecture to try to explain what happened when her formation of the NLS and its probes flew into or out of a dense clump of dark matter. "It's one of those curved space-time things." she had said. "Space is stretched out and time is slowed down inside one of those clumps of dark matter, so if some of your probes are flying inside a current they have to travel more linear distance and they have less time to do it than the ones that are in emptier space. More distance and less time at the same speed means that they fall behind."

Colleen's answer had only raised more questions for her, but Jacqueline simply nodded and smiled, and they moved on to other topics.

****

OK, bambino. Nap time.

Jacqueline replaced the electric cable that powered the cooling blanket on the stainless canister during periods of 75g when she wouldn't be able to feed it. In spite of her early mishaps, Jacqueline opened the canister often enough to confirm that the beige substance swelled with bubbles after each feeding, then shrank again before the next one, so it must still be alive.

She put on her helmet and began fastening her COFLEX into the cradle. As she did, Jacqueline mentally reviewed the checklist of her steps. She had executed a 180 degree turn and deployed her lightsail. Her Nav displays confirmed that her orientation was correct for deceleration.

****

"Lieutenant, it's nice to see you again. How was your visit to the Nest?" Second Lieutenant Ellis had come into the medical bay at the end of her check-in process, just as he had before.

"It was nice," Jacqueline answered. "I enjoyed talking to Colleen. She has always been very nurturing with me."

Christopher raised one of his eyebrows. "Nurturing? Colleen? It's funny, I frankly never knew that she had that side to her. Could you give me an example of her being nurturing?"

"Well, she said the same types of things that you said, that I was important to the mission, and she asked me to talk to the engineers about how the flight software could be better, and they added new capabilities for me. It's nice that she respects me enough to ask for my input."

"Ah, I see," said Christopher. "Yes, in that case I do see it. If it's about her mission, then she would be encouraging. You know, Lieutenant, if you don't mind my saying so, you should really have a higher standard of what you consider to be kindness. Colleen may be respectful in the context of the mission, but to me, nurturing means someone who wants the best FOR you rather than wanting the best FROM you. Regardless, I'm glad that she has a positive effect on you. How are you finding your flights? Are they very lonely?"

"No..." *Yes*. "I have spent a great deal of time alone in my life. I don't mind the flights, and I enjoy seeing the traces that we're making across the sky. In that sense I'm out there with the other NLS pilots that I knew from training."

"That sounds positive too, if you are feeling connected and with a sense of belonging. I take it that you haven't had the impulse to fly past the Outpost or the Nest since the last time that we spoke?"

Jacqueline looked down, towards the floor. "No. I did what you suggested last time, and I asked the scientists how they would view data that they obtained from a lost NLS ship. Some of them said that they would have moral questions about even using the data. It was very helpful of you to encourage me to talk to them about it. I left the Outpost feeling like I had found family here."

He stood up, and as before she had to crane her neck to look up at him. "Excellent then. Please don't hesitate to seek me out if you'd like to talk about anything. This is especially important if it has anything to do with the crew or officers here on the Outpost. I'd ask that you come to me immediately if you feel that anyone on this station is acting in a way that makes you uncomfortable." Second Lieutenant Ellis extended his hand to her and she shook it.

"Thank you, I will."

You make me a little uncomfortable...

****

Before long, Jacqueline was on the same dirt path, but this time she had come in through one of the Outpost's full-body gaming rigs. She could feel the uneven ground under her feet and the breeze on her face. There was still no smell from the overturned dirt fields, but regardless, the illusion was amazing.

There were small rocks arranged on the ground in the spot where they had met when she was on the Nest. They spelled out, "BE BACK AT 20:00". It made her laugh. She had already eaten a quick dinner, and the setting was pleasant, so she gladly went for a walk inside the game rather than exiting and re-entering.

The model of the Space Agency grounds was extensive. The dirt path from the G-loop to the 5 km jogging track looked just as she remembered it. She could see the tops of the structures of the training grounds, and the sight brought back vivid memories of hours spent dripping with mud and sweat.

As she got closer, she saw that there were other people there. Hadn't the Captain said that they would be alone? She was just about to turn around and head back to the privacy of the G-loop when something caught her eye. One of the airmen on the four story tower had just lain down on their stomach and executed a flip to descend from one floor to another. Intrigued, she decided to try to get a closer look.

Jacqueline made her way slowly toward the training grounds, trying not to be noticed. As she got closer, she saw that the obstacle course was teeming with airmen doing physical training.

How are there are there so many people here? Did everyone skip dinner?

None of them seemed to notice her presence, and as she watched, she began to see the same events repeat all over again. That's when it dawned on her. She had been the airman who had executed the flips on the tower. This was a recording of something that had happened during training four or five months ago. She saw herself again on the monkey bars, and sliding under the barbed wire. There weren't 40 people on the training course, but they were the same five people, over and over again, on all of the obstacles.

"You're really amazing. Do you know that?"

Kappler

Jacqueline almost jumped out of her skin, but when she spun around he was there. "You scared me!"

Liam laughed. "I'm sorry. Well, I'm mostly sorry. It was a little bit funny."

"What is this? How did you know what happened during our training?"

"Oh, Colleen kept me abreast of the NLS training progress. She knew that I thought of myself as one of the trainers, and we also needed to know when the first pilots would start arriving here at the Outpost, so she sent me this scripted game to show me. I'll be honest, I've never been much of a programmer, so when I needed a game-world to send to you, I just took Colleen's and modified it a little bit. For starters, I deleted the warrior elf with the broadsword."

"Yeah. I find Colleen's avatar pretty terrifying," said Jacqueline.

"I was being sincere though," Liam said. "It's amazing what you can do on this course. You are so strong and graceful. I love coming back to this scene."

Jacqueline looked down at the ground. "I have mixed feelings about things like this. There's no doubt that the time that I spent doing gymnastics helped me here, but those years of my life were like a prison sentence. Their training methods were cruel."

He closed the distance between them and put his hand on her shoulder. She could feel it there, as if he were really touching her. "I'm sorry. I didn't know. I guess that it made you strong, but that strength is yours, not theirs."

"Strong... It gave me this boy's body is what it did."

Liam was smiling with his arms crossed. "You think that you have a boy's body? Seriously? You honestly have no idea what other people see when they look at you."

He paused, and she tilted her head and narrowed her eyes at him.

"We see our future, Jacqueline, and it's beautiful."

Hearing him say her given name sent chills up her spine. Liam looked down and shook his head. "I'm sorry, I mean Lieutenant."

"No, I liked it. It just surprised me that's all. I want you to call me Jacqueline."

"OK, then. So will you call me Liam?"

"That sounds harder. I'll try," she said with a smile.

"I regret to say that I can't stay here much longer. I need to be somewhere tonight. Could I ask you to meet me here again tomorrow at the same time?

"Oh, OK, yes, I'll be here. Goodnight," she said.

"Goodnight, Jacqueline," he said and put his hand on her shoulder again.

It's just a game, do it.

She placed her open palm on his chest and said, "Goodnight, Liam."

He leaned forward slightly, increasing the pressure on her palm, then breathed in through his teeth and let out a sigh before turning to go.

****

When Jacqueline got back to her quarters, there was a message waiting for her.

> Lieutenant,
>
> Where I come from, they have a saying, "No matter where you go or turn, you'll always end up at home."
>
> Today my heart is warm and full. You have brought a part of my home to me, and I don't have words to thank you.
>
> We have made our first loaves of bread from the starter that you brought us. There is a fresh boule waiting for you in the kitchen.
>
> - Luca Vitale

It was like an answer to her most secret desire. She had been nervous during dinner and hadn't eaten much. After days of liquid diet, the thought of crunching into the crust of freshly baked bread was suddenly all that Jacqueline could think about.

It wasn't hard to spot Luca. He looked like a younger, thinner version of Pietro and he was in full motion checking stations and talking to his sous-chefs. Dinner had been over for hours, so she assumed that they were doing prep work for breakfast.

He spotted her immediately, and said in a loud voice. "Stop, everyone! She is here!"

Arms lifted, he walked towards her as all noise ceased in the kitchens. "Lieutenant, welcome!"

Jacqueline scanned the faces of the kitchen staff. They were all looking at her, and her face felt warm. "Luca, hello. When I saw Pietro last week, he gave me a message for you. He told me to tell you that he's proud of you."

Luca's face scrunched up. "Did you say last week? I thought that you saw him in April."

"Oh," said Jacqueline with a wave of her hand and a shake of her head, "don't listen to me. I always get the time wrong."

"Non importa. Here, look. We have a little bread for you. Taste it. It's beautiful."

Jacqueline took the small round bread in her hands. It was warm, with a golden color that faded to white at the bottom. She looked at Luca and he nodded at her. She dug her nails into the crust and tore off a corner. The smell that rose up from it was almost sultry. Looking Luca in the eye, she slipped the corner of bread into her mouth, and he clapped his hands together in delight.

It was beyond delicious, and the two of them continued to smile at each other as she chewed it slowly. He reacted to each little noise she made as if he was watching his own baby take its first steps.

****

"So have you always wanted to be a pilot?" Liam asked. They were walking on the dirt roads in the center of the G-loop.

"I used to love drone racing, when I was a young girl. Colleen hasn't told you about this?"

"No. It was a couple of years ago when she first showed me a file on your background. I saw some gymnastics footage, and she mentioned that you had flown drones before that. I think that she said that she was planning on shipping a modern quadcopter to you to see if you'd start up again."

Jacqueline stopped short, and it took a moment for Liam to notice and turn around to come back to her.

"Jacqueline?" Liam asked.

"She sent me that? Colleen sent me that quadcopter? Are you sure?"

Jacquline's mind flashed back to her grandfather's house, to Amah, to the corner of her closet where she had hidden the package with the drone in it. She remembered the look on Raban's face when he found her with it in the field that day. It was the last day that she had seen any of them.

"Well, I think that's what she said. The conversation was more than four years ago."

I remember that the package was from America. Of course she sent it to me. Who else would have done that?

I'm just another piece in this giant game that she's playing.

"Jacqueline, please. What's going on?"

"That quadcopter turned my world upside down. I'm still ashamed to think about it. I knew that I should have just thrown it away, but I couldn't fight the urge to try it. I dishonored my mother's memory, and it cost me my home and what little remained of my family."

Liam took her hand. It felt so real. "I can see that this is a big deal," he said, "but I think that I still don't understand. I don't want to pry, but I would like to understand if you're willing to tell me."

Jacqueline looked up at him. She had never told anyone these things before. She hadn't even really explained it to Colleen or that FBI woman.

Colleen knew. She doesn't need me to explain anything. She has always known more than I have. She's a liar.

His lips were slightly parted, like he wanted to say something more, but he didn't. He just waited, studying the expression on her face. She closed her eyes and took a deep breath before answering. She spoke slowly, and tried to keep her voice level.

"My mother and my grandmother were killed during the meteor strikes in 2109. The only reason that they were in Kuala Lumpur was because of me. I had qualified to compete in a drone racing championship, and I begged my mother to take me."

She opened her eyes to look at him, but then closed them again and took another shaky breath.

"Jacqueline, I'm so sorry. I didn't know."

"My grandfather never forgave me. He had always been very strict. Even before that, I think that he was ashamed of me, but when I came back to his house alone, without them, it got so much worse. He enrolled me in an intensive gymnastics program that kept me close to home, and it was the only topic that I could safely talk to him about. Ever."

Liam took her other hand and faced her. "What do you mean, he never forgave you? How old were you?"

Jacqueline looked away. "Twelve", she said.

"That's awful, Jacqueline. What kind of man would let a twelve year old believe that she was responsible for a natural disaster. When did you finally realize that it wasn't your fault?"

Jacqueline was silent. Tears continued to roll down her cheeks, and she hoped that Liam couldn't see them in the game's rendering of her face.

"Jacqueline, tell me. When did you first realize? How old were you?"

What could she say to him?

"Jacqueline, I can't believe that I have to say this to you, but you do realize now that it wasn't your fault, don't you?"

"I made them go. My grandfather had refused, and my grandmother told me that I should respect his decision. I didn't listen to her. I cried to my mother about it and she felt guilty. If I had just listened, if I hadn't been so spoiled, my mother would still be alive. My grandmother too."

"Jacqueline, this isn't the type of thing that I should be learning about you inside of a video game. I know that you're supposed to fly out tomorrow, and you should probably be preparing for the mission, but I have to see you in person. I can't let you leave like this. Can we meet?"

****

Jacqueline climbed down out of the haptic VR rig and cleared the play history, which was standard procedure on the Outpost. She looked around at the other rigs, wondering if Liam was in the same gaming bay, but she seemed to be the only person leaving a game at that moment. She headed to the elevator and then back to her quarters.

She slipped off her sneakers in the hallway, then entered her quarters. Looking at herself in the mirror, Jacqueline tried to decide if she would keep the same uniform or change.

This is the best that you're going to do for now.

She opened her top drawer and took out the warm socks that she had placed there on her last visit, then slid them onto her feet. They were soft and they made no sound as she walked over to her sink to brush her teeth. Putting toothpaste on the brush, she realized that her hands were still shaking.

The Ghost of Sphinx

I hope that this isn't a mistake.

The elevator opened on the cargo ring, and Jacqueline stepped off onto the 0.2 g level of the space station. There were wide bulkhead passages in the ceiling every 30m leading into the Axle where her NLS was moored in zero-g. Even though the ceiling was 3m high, with such light gravity, Jacqueline could easily jump straight up through one of the openings in the ceiling and land gently on the outer wall of the Axle. From there, she knew that she could jog counter to the station's rotation, canceling the effect of its spin. With one final jump, she was floating across the 150m expanse of the zero-g hangar. Her momentum carried her within reach of the NLS's moorings, so she extended one hand and let the cable gently glide through her fingers, tugging on it slightly with her fingertips to turn her trajectory towards the vessel.

Jacqueline slipped inside the hatch of the NLS and waited. The exertion hadn't been much, but she was feeling flushed and her breathing was audible. She tried to be quiet and to listen for his arrival. The first sound that she heard seemed to come from the side walls of the NLS itself. The sound must be running along the cable and was coming through the hull of the NLS where the moorings attached solidly to the ship.

Jacqueline held her breath to try to hear him, but there was only silence now. Her heart was racing, and the blood was whirring in her ears. When he spoke, it was clear and close, and it startled her. "Permission to come aboard?"

She looked up at the hatch and saw Liam's broad smile. "Granted", she answered, and he slipped inside. His large frame filled the space that was normally hers alone.

They stayed there, talking quietly for most of the night. Jacqueline showed Liam the instruments inside the NLS and pointed out the stubborn white flour stains in the black netting of her cradle. He laughed, and thanked her for bringing such a valued gift to the Outpost.

Weightless as they were, the first touch was inevitable. All it took was one gesture, one laugh, one moment of inattention to how their bodies were floating in space. As innocent and unintentional as it may have been, the weight of that touch was enough to crush what little resolve each of them had left. How long had they waited to breathe the same air like this?

Jacqueline tried to push away the thought that after tonight, Liam would have to wait for ten months for her to come back to him. She probably only had three or four more hours before she would head to medical and don her COFLEX for the trip back to the Nest.

But you're here now...

She had never felt so warm, so safe, and she lifted her chin towards him. She felt a rustle of air on her neck.

Each touch, each caress, even the lightest kiss caused them to drift apart. Jacqueline slid her feet through the netting of the cradle and bent her knees to hold them there.

He slid his hand around the small of her back, and breathed her in, deeply. In a whisper, he asked for a second time, "Permission to come aboard?"

It was almost morning on the Outpost, and the coarse black stubble on his cheek scratched the palm of Jacqueline's hand and edge of her lip as she repeated her answer, "Granted."

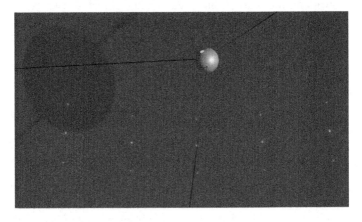

The Ghost of Sphinx

22 - Defense - May 2137 - Houston, Texas

Edward

As he looked out over the faces of his jury, he could feel their judgment. It writhed in the pit of his stomach. Even now, after more than a year, beads of sweat formed on Edward's forehead when he thought about the implications of his own work. So much time had been wasted, so many opportunities lost. He almost wished that he didn't know the truth, and he had weighed the idea of not publishing his results.

"Don't be stupid," Director Pastor had told him. "I'm going to need your help persuading the military to act on your findings, so let's just get you in to defend your thesis so we can get started."

How did we end up here?

The consequences of being wrong were just as bad as the consequences of being right. Assuming that his findings were true, and the GhostMap program really had been ineffective at detecting current threats, then no one was safe, even now. On the other hand, if he had missed something or made some kind of mistake in his research, he would be personally responsible for rendering GhostMap useless for detecting future threats.

He took a deep breath and scanned the room again. They were all looking at him, expressionless. All but Director Pastor. She was nodding at him, so he stood up a little straighter and said, "Is everyone ready?" There was almost no reaction, but Director Pastor was rolling her right hand in a 'keep going' signal, so he continued. "Let's begin with the galaxy."

Edward made a gesture with his own hand and the projection darkened to black, then the double spiral of the Milky Way faded in to fill most of the screen. "The galaxy is rotating clockwise in this view, with the arms of the spiral trailing its movement. Now, if we zoom into the Orion arm, our solar system is shown in yellow."

The flat spiral of the Milky Way began to tilt upward as the scene zoomed in, and the solar system became visible just right of center on the screen, drawn as a thin yellow disk with the top leaning to the right.

"Now, if I add in the area covered by GhostMap, you can see that it projects out in front of the solar system, scanning the dark matter halo along our path through the galaxy." With this, what looked like a long rope, woven of transparent green fibers, faded into view connecting the tilted yellow disk to the left edge of the screen.

"So this is our current state. We have the Outpost far off to the left, and the space scanned by GhostMap along the galactic plane to our solar system in the middle here. The main contribution of the research that I will present today is the following:" Edward advanced the view and a set of small blue clouds appeared on the right of the solar system. The tiny shapes were hard to see, but each one was circled and had a date displayed in bold white digits.

"We'll look first at Enigma. It was the original dark matter structure that interacted with Sphinx-896 in 2109, and its mass is estimated to be comparable to that of Earth's moon."

"The date-stamped blue symbols on the right represent snap-shots of Enigma that we have been able to recover from gravitational probes that flew past the Nest at the end of their mission. Hundreds of probes have continued to fly south in this way, and some of them detected Enigma's gravity. It is from these times and positions that we can trace the path backwards to 2109, and since that path aligns perfectly with the orbital disruption to Sphinx-896, we can have confidence that we are tracking the right object through this recovered data."

Edward risked a glance over at Director Pastor. She looked pleased, but before he could start to speak again, he heard the loud and authoritative voice of the Major General. "Son, I'm a busy man. Do you have a point that you're trying to make?"

Edward froze for a second. "Yes, sir." he said, then advanced the view once more. When he did, the blue clouds smeared to the left forming a single blue path back to the yellow disk. As the blue streak passed through the solar system, its path bent and it continued a different angle off towards the bottom left of the screen.

"As you can see, tracing the blue path of Enigma backwards in time and projecting years before the cataclysm of 2109, its approach is mostly outside of the green volume that is being scanned by GhostMap."

Edward waited, but there was still no reaction from the Major General. "In other words, sir, NLS missions launched from the Outpost's current position, would only have a 12% chance of detecting Enigma before it hit us. The Space Agency's baseline estimate for Enigma's angle of approach was off by a few percent. We now believe that these structures are drifting across our bow, so to speak, carried along by a stellar stream."

"The Outpost's current position?" asked Crespin. His face was twisted into a scowl. "Are you recommending that we change the position of the Outpost station based on a few blue dots?"

"Um, no sir, the evidence is a bit stronger than that."

Edward turned toward the screen and swept his arm in an arc through the air. Hundreds of faint white lines began extending right from the yellow disk of the solar system, and two dozen new blue dots appeared with crisp white dates. As Enigma had done, blue streaks slid to the left connecting the dots and blue paths bent through the solar system extending down and to the left. None of the paths on the left were inside the green area scanned by Ghost-Map.

"Enigma was the largest of the dark masses that we have tracked, but it's not the only one. We have also been able to track the masses known as Scythians, Tiye, and Dischord. These are the galactic halo substructures that caused asteroids Sesostris-4414, Sethos-5009, and Nicomachus-8128 to fall into the sun in the years since Sphinx."

There was a murmur in the audience.

Crespin raised an eyebrow. "Son, we need to bring these people home. The Outpost has already been aloft three years longer than the initial mission plan. Has the Director informed you of any of this, because the idea of asking these people to stay deployed away from their families for another decade sounds like a dereliction of duty to me."

I'm trying to protect all of our families.

"Sir, I hope that it's clear that I am not taking any of this lightly. I would even say that given the negative implications of these analytical findings I have done everything that I can think of to check and verify my calculations. However, I could never forgive myself for missing something. Perhaps if we could find an additional source of data concerning--"

"Absolutely not," interrupted Dr. Pastor. "Major General, if I may interject. Over nine months ago, I thought that Edward was ready to finish his Ph.D. and defend this thesis, but he insisted on driving the uncertainty down to 0.1% before writing the 'conclusions' chapter of his dissertation."

Then, turning to Edward she added, "You have done enough study. More data is not the answer here, and delays come at a cost too."

Edward paused and thought for another moment. He knew that Director Pastor had a point. Turning back to the Major General he said, "If I use your numbers sir, moving the Outpost might cost the current crew five more years, but the only other alternative would be to send up a new crew and a new station for what would amount to at least 15 years by the time we get them into position. Would it be fair to say that there is significant hardship either way?"

Crespin looked at Edward for a long moment, then stood up. "Yes, son, I think that would be fair." He began moving toward the door and added. "Please come see me when the academics are done with you here."

"Uh, yes sir." answered Edward.

As Major General Crespin left the room, he spoke to one of his military staff. "Airman Fisher, would you escort Kaiser here to my office when he's ready?"

"Yes, sir."

When the room was quiet again, one of the Space Agency scientists raised his hand. Edward smiled and pointed to him.

"Your thesis said that you studied signals from the SETI archives in the 8GHz range. Can you explain where those signals are coming from?"

Edward nodded. "Sure, the original laser communications between the gravitational probes and the NLS were designed for 193THz. Now that the probes are moving away from us at .999c we see a redshift factor of 1000, dropping that frequency to 193GHz, but the time dilation of relativity plays a factor too, dividing the cycles per second by another factor of 22 from our perspective."

"I see, thank you."

Another scientist raised her hand. "But without the navigational computers on the NLS vessel, the probes can't locate themselves. How can you be sure that multiple mass detections are tracking the same object if you don't have accurate location data to tie the different observations together? Is there a risk that you're finding different objects of a similar profile?"

Edward nodded. "Yes, good question. As each of these rings of gravitational probes leaves our solar system, it flies towards the Oort cloud situated between 2,000 and 200,000 Astronomical Units from the sun. In all of the signals that I am using, there are dense and sparse bands that we have detected in the Oort cloud, and these offer a kind of signature that we can line up in the 8GHz signals. Looking back 11 light-days from there, we can see if a set of probes detected the dark mass in question."

This Q&A went on for another 30 minutes before Director Pastor and the other members of Edward's dissertation committee adjourned to discuss the results.

****

As he stepped into Major General Crespin's office, Edward thanked Airman Fisher for escorting him.

"Mr. Kaiser, thank you for coming. Close the door, son and take a seat."

Edward did as the Major General had asked.

"So, is it Doctor Kaiser now?"

"Yes, sir. I think so," answered Edward. "They still need to file the paperwork, but my committee told me that my defense was successful."

"Let me get right to it. The situation on the Outpost is dire. I've just been informed that we have lost one of our officers already. The isolation was too much for him, and he took his own life."

"Sir, I had no idea. I have to admit that living inside a space station for so long is very hard for me to imagine. I can certainly see why getting that crew home is a priority."

"Good. It's important that you can appreciate that. Now I actually have a technical question for you. It seemed to me, during your talk today, that you were able to get important data without having a pilot fly along with the probes. Am I understanding that correctly?"

"Yes, sir. Though an NLS pilot got the probes flying, the data that I obtained through SETI came from a point in the mission after the pilot had disengaged."

"Very well. So, given what you know, would you be able to design an unmanned mission to map this threat?" asked Crespin.

"I believe so, sir. I am actually more comfortable, in general, with unmanned missions than I am with manned missions. To answer your question, I would argue that what my research shows is that we can already take advantage of an unmanned phase within all of the sensor runs of the mission that you are currently flying. Moving from that point to wholly unmanned missions seems reasonable."

Crespin nodded slowly. He didn't speak for almost another minute, then finally said, "Excellent. Thank you, Doctor Kaiser. If I may, son, could I ask that you keep this conversation between us? If anyone asks why I called you here, you can just say that I wanted to recruit you to come work for the Space Agency, which would be the truth."

****

Early the next morning, a few hours before dawn, Edward awoke slowly, reluctantly. Disjointed images of wandering the corridors of the Outpost, alone and desperate, were still fresh in his mind. He had heard himself telling his parents to hold on, not to close the door. He tried to tell himself that it was impossible, that none of them would ever step foot on that space station, that he couldn't have recognized their faces. In the dream he had begged them to wait just a little longer, to summon their courage, but as the door closed between them he felt them slip away. He knew that they would succumb to the same hopelessness that had already claimed one of the Outpost crew.

I'm so sorry. I do miss you both.

23 - Sacrifice - Nov 2116 - High-Earth Orbit
Jacqueline

This trip back to the Nest was the longest yet. Jacqueline was going to have almost a week alone at zero-g, and with everything that had happened leading up to her launch from the Outpost, she wasn't sure if a week alone with her thoughts was going to help or hurt.

I need a distraction.

She looked around at her displays inside the NLS, then suddenly remembered some of the new controls that she could try on the gravitational probes. Jacqueline floated over to the detection display and grabbed onto the handhold with her left hand.

They told me I could split the ring.

With her right hand, she carefully applied backward thrust to every other probe: Alpha, Gamma, Eta, Epsilon, Iota and so on through Psi, then she looked over to the center display to see if the updated software would show her where the probes were. *Nice...*

The dense ring of probes split into two sparse rings. One ring stayed in front of the NLS, pulling away slowly while the other began falling backward towards her. The link-status displays began flashing red immediately, showing that half of the probe-to-probe links were broken. It took Jacqueline a moment to remember what the engineers had told her. She would have to redirect the lasers in each group to skip their missing peers. With a few button presses, the blinking red probe names in the link status columns disappeared, and cells compacted and filled in with new green links at the bottom.

With a forward ring and an aft ring, she felt like she was flying a giant barrel.

"As long as stuff passes through both rings," Colleen had said, "the same number of lasers will measure the gravitational delay as in the single mesh, and you'll get an initial approximation of direction and velocity."

Colleen...

Jacqueline had no idea what she was going to say to her during their next post-flight video debrief. There was so much about the flight that she would normally have wanted to discuss during their call, but Liam's revelation about the quadcopter left her feeling as if Colleen had manipulated her.

I'm not sure if I can even look at her.

****

After only about 24 hours flying, a new NLS trace appeared. It was silver and there were several small detections inside of it.

I see you Cemil... That makes three of us now.

Jacqueline turned to intercept Cemil's trace and took follow up measurements on several of the larger dark matter clumps.

Her new cylindrical sensor configuration was fun to watch because the blue mist from the first ring didn't always line up with the bulge in the second green laser mesh. Jacqueline experimented with moving the two rings farther apart and with making the first ring larger and the second one smaller like a funnel. The farther apart she placed the two rings, the larger the mis-alignment of where the detection took place in each.

Worried that she might be corrupting the data by playing around with the sensors so much, she spent the whole of the fourth day piloting the sensors to re-construct a single 24-probe ring.

****

Jacqueline's post-flight medical check-in on the Nest was taking much longer than her previous ones, and they had insisted on doing several additional tests. It was colder than usual in the medical bay, and as she waited, the bright lights, the sterile white walls, and the antiseptic smell in the air were all giving Jacqueline a headache.

"Excuse me." she asked one of the doctors. "Do you mind telling me why this is taking so long? Normally I only need a few simple tests."

"I understand Lieutenant. I think that Dr. Pastor will be here in a moment to explain."

"In that case, I'd like to go back to my quarters and call her. I've been here for almost four hours, and I'd like to get something to eat."

"No, ma'am, I meant that she's coming here. It won't be long now. Please just wait here, OK?"

Jacqueline was just about to protest again that she had several private matters to discuss with Colleen, and that she didn't want to have the video call in the middle of the medical bay, when the door opened.

What is she doing up here?

Colleen strode into the medical bay looking as if it were the most normal thing in the world. "Hi sweetie. How are you feeling? I decided to come see you."

"Colleen, what are you doing here? Why are you on the Nest?"

"Well, I got a message from Liam." answered Colleen. "It arrived about four days before you did, and it seemed like I'd better come up and handle this one personally."

"Colleen, you didn't need to come all this way. I admit that I was very angry with you when I found out, but I've had over a week to think about it and I realize that you were just doing your job. I don't blame you. There was no way that you could have known."

Colleen furrowed her brow and lifted her chin. "Um, give me a second." She touched her AR glasses and Jacqueline could see her eyes scanning something that Jacqueline couldn't see. "Yeah, I'm just re-reading Liam's message, and I don't know what the hell you're talking about. Let's get out of here and you can tell me, OK?"

Jacqueline slid off of the exam table, confused. As she slipped on a pair of socks, Colleen walked over to one of the doctors and said, "Can you send those results to me as soon as they're ready?"

"Yes, Dr. Pastor," he answered. "Some of them are ready now and you'll have the others in 30 minutes."

They took the elevator to the 0.5g ring and headed to Jacqueline's quarters on the Nest. Jacqueline was leading the way and suddenly, she felt Colleen's hand on her back. It was just a quick affectionate rub between her shoulder blades, but it startled her.

"I am so glad to see you. I've missed you." said Colleen.

Why is she acting like this? Jacqueline tried to remember how much time had gone by for Colleen. "How long has it been for you? You know that from my point of view I just graduated a couple of months ago."

"It's been a year and three months for me since you left," answered Colleen. "We had our little video chat about the probe alignment nine months ago, but that was pretty short and it was mostly technical."

They reached Jacqueline's quarters, and she opened the door. "That makes sense. I guess I didn't realize that it had been that long. Come on in while I change, then I need to eat something."

"OK, hold on." Colleen turned away slightly and said, "Hi, Tamara. Could you have someone bring Jacqueline something to eat in her quarters? Yeah, we're going to stay here. OK, great."

Jacqueline just stared at Colleen, open-mouthed. "Was that Captain Kett? Did you just order me room service?"

Colleen seemed distracted. "Yeah, we actually have a crapload of stuff to talk about, and we need some privacy. First things first though, tell me. You were mad at me, and apparently Liam knew about it?"

It seemed odd that she was calling him Liam. She had always referred to him as Captain Fourtouna before. Jacqueline decided just to go along with whatever was happening and to give Colleen an answer. "Colleen, do you remember why I needed to leave my grandfather's house?"

"Yeah, he was going to lock you up in some type of fascist gymnastics camp."

"OK, but do you know why he was going to do that?"

"Did he need a why? I thought he was just a major asshole."

Jacqueline actually allowed herself to laugh slightly. *She doesn't know...*

"OK, in hindsight, I can kind of agree that he was that, but I was already doing gymnastics, and he was satisfied with my progress. The reason that he was going to send me to live there was because he was angry that I had skipped a week of training."

There was still no reaction from Colleen.

"I skipped a week of training because I got a package from America with a drone in it. I hadn't flown a quadcopter in five years out of respect for my mother and my grandmother, but when I opened that package and saw what was inside, my honor abandoned me and I couldn't think about anything but flying again. I live with that dishonor every time I step into the NLS."

"Shit." Colleen was shaking her head. "I didn't realize any of that. So Liam told you that I shipped you that drone, and that's why you were pissed at me?"

"Well, to be fair, that drone cost me my family and my home. I know that it wasn't your intent, but it is no small thing."

Colleen squinted her eyes and tilted her chin to one side. "Meh, I don't really see it exactly the same way. I was there the day that you lost your family, and it had nothing to do with drones. It was all of the shit exploding around us. What you had after that doesn't count as family in my book. I'm not saying that I was trying to fuck it up, that was more of a fringe benefit. Just because you share DNA with somebody doesn't mean that they're your family."

Jaqueline sighed and folded her arms. *I thought that I had forgiven her, but she is so rude.*

Just then there was a knock at the door, and Jacqueline walked over to open it. It was one of the Nest crew holding a tray of food. Colleen made space on the desk as Jacqueline came back into the room with the tray.

"OK, why don't you start eating. All of this is going to seem like ancient history in a minute."

Jacqueline still wasn't really speaking, and it seemed impolite to eat in front of someone, but this was Colleen after all, so resting on etiquette was pointless. She sat down at the desk and took a bite. The food was warm and she started to realize how hungry she was.

"Let's lighten the mood," Colleen continued. "Did anything *else* happen during your last night on the Outpost?"

Jacqueline almost spit out the mouthful that she was chewing, and needed to reach for her drink to avoid choking.

Did he really tell her? Why would he do that?

"Yeah, there we go. Now we're on the same page. So here's the deal, sweetie. The docs messed up your cycles and your pre-flight physical on the Outpost revealed that you were ovulating. It wasn't supposed to be possible. They were supposed to have your whole repro system shut down, but we think that they might have failed to account for the time dilation. Liam found out from the Outpost docs and notified us immediately. The thing is that his message only got to us a few days before you did."

Jacqueline took another sip of her drink and collected her scattered thoughts. "I don't understand."

Colleen scrunched up her face. "You were ovulating, and it would seem that your egg is now fertilized."

Jacqueline could barely believe that she was having this conversation, and it took her a moment to process what she was hearing. "Wait, are you saying that I'm pregnant?"

I sleep with one person one time on the other side of the galaxy and I get pregnant?

"Not exactly, but you will be pregnant in the next few hours if we don't do something. The egg is fertilized, but the embryo hasn't implanted yet. Brass wants you to take a pill and make it go away."

Jacqueline was shaking her head. She could barely believe what she was hearing. "A pill. What kind of pill? Are you telling me to kill it?"

Colleen's answer was just as insensitive as everything else about her.

"Well, it's not quite like that," she said. "Lots of pregnancies never take. Lots of eggs get fertilized but never implant. Until the embryo implants, your body doesn't recognize the baby. You don't start pregnancy if the fertilized embryo stops where it is. It happens to thousands of women every day, and they never even know."

Jacqueline opened her eyes as wide as she could and leaned toward Colleen with balled fists. "Well, I would know, and I'm not taking any pill! I will drop out. They can't force me to kill this baby. If they try to force me to have an abortion, I'll quit."

Somewhere in the back of her mind, Jacqueline thought that maybe she really wasn't afraid to quit after all.

"OK, listen," Colleen said. "I get you. I already have a solution. I'll tell you my idea in a second, but first I need to try to convince you how important this is. You are the best pilot that we've got, and I don't think that it's good for Liam, for you, or even for this embryo if you quit and never step foot in an NLS ever again."

Jacqueline looked back at the tray of food. As hungry as she had been only a few minutes earlier, the thought of taking another bite made her sick.

If I quit, I might never see him again.

Colleen was still looking at her. "Remember, the reason that we need NLS pilots is to try to keep what happened to your mother from happening to anyone else. I can't think of any better way to avenge her death than to fly these missions and to map out this threat so that no other little girl ever needs to lose her family in a meteor strike."

Jacqueline was still quiet. The anger had left her, but she couldn't form clear thoughts.

"Jacqueline, you know that I was there, and that I saw how awful it was, but I have to tell you sweetie, the next time is going to be so much worse. We should all be dead right now. It's a miracle that Sphinx-896 didn't hit us straight on, and what did hit us was just what was left over after most of it had burned up in the sun. We're not going to get so lucky next time. Your best way to protect people, your best chance for bringing Liam home, and this embryo's best chance for having a nice long life is if you keep flying."

Jacqueline lowered her eyes and thought about what Colleen had said, but then stopped. It was happening all over again. Why should this woman always get whatever she wanted from everyone. She should pay a price for manipulating people.

"It doesn't even make sense what you're saying. How can this baby have a long life if I get an abortion?"

"Yeah, that's not what I'm suggesting. Do you know what IVF is?" asked Colleen.

"Is it some kind of abortion?"

"No, it's the opposite. In Vitro Fertilization is when you fertilize an egg outside of the mother then implant it. I want to arrange an embryo adoption. Elenora and I have been working on finding a couple who are open to adopting your embryo."

Jacqueline just shook her head.

"OK, on one level you're right. If you don't keep the baby then it feels like an abortion from your point of view, but nothing bad happens to the embryo. There are people who want to have babies who would adopt the embryo, implant it in the mother, and bring it to term. Elenora will find the right kind of people. It'll be a good loving family with good jobs and a stable life. It will be the type of people that you would have chosen yourselves. We will organize everything."

"How?" asked Jacqueline.

"We could extract the embryo now and cryo-freeze it, just like any IVF family would do. It has some risks, but no more than other risks of early pregnancy. I brought a fertility specialist onboard with me. She's good, maybe the best in the field, and she's ready to do this."

Jacqueline closed her eyes again and bit her lip. She couldn't bear to think of stepping back into the medical bay. All of these people knew. Even Captain Kett knew, and whether she said yes or no, they would all know. If she said no, if she dropped out, how would she support herself? How would they live? Her face got hot as she imagined herself walking through the doors of her grandfather's house, pregnant.

Colleen stood up. Her eyes seemed to be scanning the empty space between them. "OK, I just got the results of your post-flight exam. We can give you about 3 hours to think things over. I'm going to leave you for a little while and check on Elenora's progress, but I do want to say one more thing to you. I'm sorry that sending you a quadcopter caused you pain. I truly am. But Jacqueline, I'm so glad that you're here instead of there. I've been watching you since you were a little girl, and in a weird way I actually think of you as part of *my* family. I'm never going to have kids of my own, which makes me that much happier that I got to meet you. You mean more to me than you know."

****

Jacqueline was sitting up in bed in the medical bay when Colleen entered. "How's your bod?" she asked.

Jacqueline smiled slightly at the odd question. "Compared to 75g this was pretty easy. I've got some cramping and I still feel an odd sort of pressure down in my stomach, but I'm OK."

"Alright sweetie. You've got seven days to get back on your feet. The flight schedule hasn't changed. We have other pilots flying and no way to modify the schedule on such short notice."

"I know." Jacqueline said. "I'll be OK. Is the baby OK?"

Colleen winced. "For now, let's try to use the word embryo, not baby, and yeah the doctors say that it's OK. I'm going to disappear now and take care of this. I promise, I'll do right by you."

Jacqueline looked away and nodded. The white walls didn't offer a single noticeable feature. They were empty and barren, and for some reason they made her want to cry.

Colleen continued. "Here's the thing though. I need you to trust me. Info about you is classified. When you're home, when you're flying, if you're alive, it's all classified. The same thing is true for Liam."

Where is she going with this?

"So, I'll say it again. I've got this and I'm going to make you proud, but I'm never going to tell you where the little lamb is. The only thing that I can tell you is this. If I haven't said otherwise, then things are going great. The kid is great, the family is great, their life is great. I can promise you that I'll see to that, but you can never ask me about it. If you see me and I'm smiling, then everything is great, period."

Jacqueline felt the warmth of the tears on her cheeks as Colleen spoke. "I feel so guilty."

"I know, sweetie." Colleen sat on the edge of her bed and reached across to take Jacqueline's hand. "I feel really rotten, but for what it's worth, I truly believe that you're doing the right thing. The embryo is not the only life depending on you. There are ten billion other lives that need you to fly."

Jacqueline closed her eyes as tears continued to stream down her face. "I'm abandoning this child. The only thing that this baby needed was for me to welcome it in my body. I keep imagining it, frozen and in a box when I should be giving it warmth and a home."

Then, after a moment she added, "This is the worst thing that I've ever done."

They sat that way, quietly for several minutes. Colleen seemed distracted, and Jacqueline squeezed her hand to get her attention. Colleen turned and looked her in the eye.

"Thank you for coming for me," Jacqueline said. "I mean, all of it. Then, now... It would be an honor for me to be part of your family."

Jacqueline thought that she saw a tear roll down Colleen's cheek before closing her eyes and drifting off to sleep. When she woke, Colleen was gone, and she had taken all traces of her visit with her.

24 - Furthermost Limits - 2121-

One Light Year from Earth

Liam/Jacqueline

Liam clinked his glass several times with a spoon as he got to his feet. "If I could have everyone's attention." He gave himself permission to stand there and bask in the moment, looking out on the faces in the room.

"Eight years ago, we swore an oath to each other as we boarded this vessel. We swore to do the hard work to adapt to life on a space station and to leave behind all that was familiar and comfortable. I know each of you personally, and I find both common themes and unique personal motivations in each of your reasons for signing up."

Liam stole a quick glance over at Christopher. He knew that Christopher didn't approve of this part of his speech, and he hoped that he wasn't too angry that he had decided to leave it in.

"Some of you lost loved ones in the meteor strikes. Some of you wanted to do the science that no one on Earth would ever be able to do. Some of you sought the challenge, and maybe even the fame of being one of the few people who would ever travel this far from home. But all of you have told me that your primary pledge and loyalty is to each other."

Liam paused and looked as many individuals in the eye as he could in the few short seconds he had before continuing. More than one of those people gave him a nod and a smile.

"It is my pleasure to give the following command, and it is my honor to share this moment with all of you." he said, as he turned to the Outpost's Navigational chief, Gregory Karabi. "Nav, all stop. Maintain position."

Cheers rang out. Even members of the crew who had never stepped foot on the Command deck knew what this meant. They had arrived at their destination almost 1 light year from Earth.

Liam had wanted to have mementos made for the crew. His idea was to use a 1m long thread with a 1mm bead at each end to represent the size of the solar system relative to their distance, but Christopher talked him out of it.

"I'm telling you, it's a bad idea," he had said. "It's like when two characters in a movie get stuck out on a ledge or something, they say, *'Don't look down.'* You don't want a visual showing every person on this boat just how irretrievably screwed we actually are."

****

Jacqueline shifted her weight repeatedly from one foot to the other as she waited for the shuttle to arrive. Airman Boukali had promised her that he would personally help her prepare the surprise for Liam that she had in mind. When she finally saw the shuttle passengers gliding down the guideline through the Axle, she was relieved.

"Thank you for doing this. I can't tell you how excited I am." she said when she saw him approaching her, smiling and carrying a small black case. "Which ones did you end up getting?"

"Oh, let's see." He opened the case and read the handwritten labels. "I've got a nice mixture of city, wilderness, and seascape. I think that you'll be happy."

Jacqueline laughed looking at the labels. "That is quite a selection. Really, I can't thank you enough."

"It was my pleasure, ma'am. Anything that I can do for those folks, just sign me up," he said, then he handed her the case. They exchanged one more smile, then Airman Boukali turned to take the ladder down to the cargo ring.

Since she was already in the Axle, Jacqueline decided to stow the case in her NLS right away rather than waiting. Her eyes traced the nearest mooring line, and she jogged over to it then jumped. Her momentum carried her towards the center of the Axle, and she took a loose hold of the mooring line to guide her the rest of the way. Once on the hull, she passed head-first inside the NLS and attached the case behind the cradle.

As she pulled herself around again to leave the NLS Jacqueline saw the thick black plastic clock that Colleen had given her for her birthday. It was an antique, with a grey face and oddly shaped black segments that combined to form digits of time and date. Colleen had barred out the first digit of the year with a large black X.

On the day before Jacqueline's 19th birthday, they had set it to December 31st, X018, but now it read September 22, X019. *'As long as you keep it with you, then relativity will affect it the same way that it affects you, and it'll count your seconds just as faith-fully as your own heartbeat.'*

Jacqueline had all but given up on remembering the dates back on Earth. They barely mattered to her anymore. She didn't even mind accepting January 1st as her new birthday on her black clock.

****

The mission timer read 367 hours when Jacqueline came to. She went through her normal process of detaching and deploying probes, then went through a quick review of the new features of the NLS. Each visit to the Nest now brought major software up-grades, and Jacqueline had to spend days of her downtime learning to use the system all over again.

The detection display had been updated to handle the volume of traces that were being logged. Now that there were more than 15 NLS missions in flight at any one time, new controls had been added to sub-select the trace display by pilot, by timeframe, by mass, by velocity, or by location.

Enhanced navigational controls allowed pilots to plot a flightpath through charted or uncharted regions of space between the Nest and the Outpost, and the system would warn the pilot if the path selected would consume more xenon propellant than the lateral thrusters had stored.

The most important upgrade from Jacqueline's perspective was the new NLS to NLS communications ring. It allowed the pilots to send a message to the ship that followed them in sequence, and for that message to be received by the second NLS in just 19 hours. This would be Jacqueline's first trip with daily updates from another human. The information flow in the other direction was less efficient. She could respond directly to a message, but the ship ahead of her wouldn't receive her responses until it began its trip back in the other direction from the propulsion station.

The best part was that Jacqueline's NLS held a position in the rotation right in the middle of her original squad-mates. Andrew had the NLS in front of her, and Cemil was flying the NLS behind her. Kirin had the position behind Cemil, and Jacqueline couldn't help but remember the feeling of passing notes as a schoolgirl.

Do you want to detect dark matter with me? Check a box [] yes [] no

****

When she arrived on the Outpost, Jacqueline reflected on how easy the trip had been. In spite of the annoyance of having to learn a new system every two months, she had to admit that these upgrades were worth the effort. She had easily decided where to fly with a mixture of follow-up readings from her colleagues' detections and new exploration of uncharted areas. The messages and the real-time updates of her peers' progress made her feel like she was really part of a team.

Jacqueline detached the small black case that she had brought with her and handed it, along with her personal bag, to the Outpost crew who had moored her ship. From there she slid down the moorings and headed to medical for her post-flight check in.

****

To Jacqueline's surprise, a psychological evaluation by Second Lieutenant Christopher Ellis wasn't included as part of her medical check in on the Outpost, so as soon as she finished with the other doctors, she got dressed and headed to her quarters to get to work on her post-flight notes. On recent trips, she had learned to bring a uniform with her from the NLS so that she didn't have to walk to her quarters in a medical gown.

There was a message waiting for her in her quarters. It was from Liam.

> Jacqueline,
>
> I'd like you to meet someone. Could the three of us have dinner in my stateroom tonight at 18:00?
>
> Yours,
>
> Liam

'Yours…'

It was the first time that she ever considered that their relationship might be advancing to the next step. Jacqueline tried to be realistic with herself. Could any man really devote himself to a relationship with someone who was so rarely present.

But would he have said it if he didn't mean it?

She needed to think about something else or that little word was going to occupy her mind for the rest of the day.

Once she had finished with her post-flight documentation, Jacqueline went for a run around the outer loop. She put in 6 laps and did a little resistance training, and it kept her busy until it was time to get ready for dinner.

After weeks in zero-g, it felt good to use her muscles. The run had the added advantage of exposing her to more of the Outpost crew. They all knew her, but she was still learning many of their names. As she jogged the outer loop, the floor bent upward in front of her and behind her and she passed people as they walked from one bay to another.

"Hello Lieutenant. Welcome aboard," and "Lieutenant Binti Abdulah, it's nice to see you," were the most common greetings. There were only 50 people on the Outpost, so Jacqueline sometimes went back to her quarters and tried to match faces in the directory to people she had seen on her run.

Chief Sverdlichenko and his astrophysicists were the people that Jacqueline knew best since they worked closely with her on analyzing her gravitational probe data.

Liam had told her that he tried to encourage the crew to use a "three part greeting" consisting of the format "Welcome to the Outpost, my name is XX, I work on YY". To be honest, what Jacqueline heard more often was, "Would you be interested in joining us in game AA? We need pilots who can BB."

Sometimes she even accepted those offers. The immersive games on the Outpost were very engaging.

****

At 18:01, Jacqueline knocked on the Captain's stateroom door. She was holding the small black case in her hand and she was very excited to show Liam the surprise that she had brought for him.

He opened the door and greeted her warmly with a kiss. "I'm so happy to see you. Come in. Can I offer you something to drink?"

"Just water for now, thank you," she answered.

He served her then sat down across from an empty chair. "Can we talk for a minute, while it's just the two of us?"

She got the impression that he wanted her to sit down, so she placed the case near the wall and took a seat at the table.

"I hope that tonight is going to go well, but I have to confess that I am apprehensive."

Jacqueline felt a long flutter in her stomach. She looked up into his eyes, but the expression that she saw there wasn't what she expected.

"There is something that I need to say to you, something important," he said. "I'm nervous, but I've waited long enough already, and I need for you to know."

Jacqueline's mind was racing, but she tried to tell herself to be reasonable and to listen. She took a deep breath and said, "I want to know everything about you."

He slid his fingers into her hand and bent down to kiss it lightly. "You really are an amazing person. OK, there is a chance that you know part of this already, but I told you in a scripted game, and it was a really long time ago, so I don't know whether or not you actually heard it. What do you know about my personal life here on the Outpost?"

Jacqueline thought for a moment. "In the game you told me that you were in a relationship with a woman named Chris, and that she was jealous. But that was months ago and we haven't spoken about it since."

Was it months ago for him? No it was years ago.

Liam was nodding. "Yeah, I understand how you were able to hear it that way, but it's not completely accurate."

Jacqueline opened her eyes wider and nodded for him to continue.

"So one of the things that I need to tell you is that I'm bisexual. When I said Chris, it was a little misleading of me because no one calls him Chris, we call him Christopher."

Jacqueline's mind went blank. How could she have been so stupid? *Did you think that he was going to propose to you?*

He looked at her for a moment then added. "I understand that you might be taken off guard. I'm just going to give you a minute to think about what I've said. We have all night. Remember, I've been bi my whole life and I have had versions of this conversation before, with other people. I have some idea of the thoughts that might be going through your mind."

No, I don't think that you do.

Jacqueline felt like her face was radiating heat. She sat there for a second or two, eyes wide, and then quickly blurted out the first question that came to mind in order to keep him talking and to keep his attention off of her.

"Are you sure?"

Liam smiled. "Yes, I am. That is almost always the first question that I get, even from my gay friends."

"And you've been in a relationship with this person the whole time?" she asked.

"Yes, but there is more that I need to explain. Christopher and I had been monogamous for years. I've told him the truth about you, and he doesn't love the idea, but he has basically accepted that I don't want to stop seeing you. He says that the fact that you're only here for a week every two years and that you're a woman makes it a little bit easier for him to compartmentalize."

Jacqueline still couldn't think of a response.

So what does that make me, his mistress? He had told her that he was in a relationship, and she had never asked him if he had ended it.

"The real question is whether or not it's too much for you," he said. "The last thing that I want to do is to make you feel uncomfortable, but I can't help what I feel. Christopher is a good person and so are you, so I don't want to lie to either of you."

Jacqueline narrowed her eyes, "I hope that you don't expect me to…" She trailed off. She couldn't even think of how to say it.

"No, no, of course not. Nothing like that. I was hoping… I guess, during the week that you're here, I would want to spend it with you. But I want to be honest with you that I am not ending things with Christopher. For the two year spans between your visits, I would want to go back to him."

She let another minute go by. "Is there anyone else?"

"No, definitely not. Listen, I'm not asking anything of you right now, but I wanted to tell you the truth, and am hoping that the two of you might actually become friends."

That would make it easier for you, wouldn't it?

Jacqueline sat and looked at him. She felt so stupid, and his calm tone just made it worse, as if there were no room for her to have a reaction. For months she had tried not to think about why Liam would be satisfied in a relationship with her when she was never there.

I don't have to wonder about that anymore...

Liam put his hand on her shoulder and asked her, "Would I be pushing you too fast if I invited Christopher to join us for dinner?"

She took a quick breath in and looked at the door. "How long has he known about me?"

Liam smiled. "I told him before your last visit two years ago, but he had suspected it long before that. A lot of time goes by for us when you're flying, so he and I have had time to work it out."

She thought for a moment about whether she wanted to face this person right now, but asking them to wait for her next visit seemed like too much. She had to do it now. She looked up at Liam, then said timidly, "I see. I think I can do it."

Liam smiled, nodded, then tapped a button on his wrist. While they waited, he said. "Thank you, Jacqueline. I'm impressed with how well you seem to be holding up. Are you OK?"

She didn't have a chance to answer. There was a knock at the door, and she braced herself for who this mystery man would be. The first thing to enter the room was the cart with a tablecloth and covered dishes of food. The smell seemed to flood the room and it made her mouth water.

The cart had distracted her so thoroughly that she had even forgotten to look at the guest of honor.

Oh no... but...

"Lieutenant, we meet again. I decided that there was no need to chat this morning given that we'd be seeing each other this evening."

Jacqueline closed her eyes and brought one hand to her mouth. "I... I guess you're right." she said. After thinking for another moment, she added. "If I had known what was in store for me, I might have asked you for a double session."

Christopher walked up to her and extended his muscled forearm. "I'm sure that you can imagine that this situation is a little bit difficult for me, but I want you to know that you are not to blame for any of it."

She accepted his hand and shook it.

"Liam has told me a lot about you, and I'm looking forward to knowing the real you. I hope that you will let me start over too. I'm Christopher. May I call you Jacqueline?"

Jacqueline smiled, meekly. "Yes, of course." She was sure that she was blushing. The idea of sitting down for a meal with these two men was almost unbearable.

Just then, Jacqueline saw the little black case that she had brought with her, and the thought of changing the subject was like a lifeline. "Oh, I brought a surprise for you."

Christopher looked back and forth between them. "Maybe I should leave the two of you--"

"No, you can share it. This will be good. Come, both of you. Sit down." She stood and picked up the case from next to the wall, then waited for the two men to sit down.

"OK, now close your eyes and wait for me to tell you to open them." They did, and she opened the case and took out the canister labeled "Cut Grass". It had a small pump on the top of it and a button on the side of the lid. Jacqueline held it in front of the men's faces and pushed the button for half a second. A light spray of air escaped from the canister and made the hair move on both of their foreheads. Both men started to smile as if it had tickled them. "OK, you can open your eyes now."

"What is that? It smells like, like--"

"Cut grass." said Jacqueline. "Here, I have more. This one is Oil Change. This one is City Bus. Oh, and there's Low Tide and Campfire. You just push the button on the side to release a burst of air."

The men were laughing and smiling as they remembered the scents of home. Christopher looked at Jacqueline and smiled. "This was a very thoughtful surprise, Jacqueline. Thank you for sharing it with me. Here, sit down. Let me serve you some dinner. You must be starving."

Jacqueline smiled. "I am, actually. Thank you."

****

On the way back to the Nest, Jacqueline received a message from First Lieutenant Kirin Ballis.

> Jacqueline,
>
> I tracked 5000kg of dark matter on this run and I'm not even done. My detection data shows me that you detected 4000kg. I think that we should set up a leaderboard. I want everyone to know how badly I'm beating you.
>
> Best regards,

The Ghost of Sphinx

-K. Badass

She re-read the note several times, laughing a little harder each time. Kirin had always had a way of drawing her into these little competitions, and it felt good. Jacqueline had turned her back on racing, and much of her involvement in gymnastics had been forced on her, but Kirin was different. She competed for herself, and no one else.

Jacqueline made a mental note to talk to Colleen about the leaderboard idea. It sounded like a fun way to stay connected with her squad.

Thinking about Colleen, Jacqueline wondered if she had known about Liam and Christopher all along. What other secrets was that woman holding onto?

25 - Divergent Distances - 2129 -

High-Earth Orbit

Jacqueline

Jacqueline was whining like a teenager, "Colleen, noooo. Why do you guys keep upgrading the software every two months? It is so annoying."

Colleen smiled over the video link. "Sweetie, it's not two months, it's two years. I have a whole team of engineers. They aren't going to just sit on their hands. Besides, you're gonna love this one. It was crowdsourced from a video game."

Jacqueline paused, and smiled. "The best technology that you've ever given me was that antique clock. The black one. Do you know what my date is today?"

Colleen touched a button and said, "I don't know. April X020?"

"May. May 12th," said Jacqueline.

"OK, listen. I'm going to need to run soon, but I wanted to tell you about this new piloting software for the probes. You can make independent sub-formations of probes now and fly them away from yourself. There are a couple of things to keep in mind though."

"Alright, I'm listening," said Jacqueline.

"First, safety checks in the software will prevent you from directing a probe at the Outpost, at the Nest, or obviously, at Earth. There was no danger before, when the NLS was at the center of the formation, but that danger exists now and it would be really bad if we torpedoed ourselves."

"Ew, yeah."

"Second, you have to be aware that the further the probes are from you, the less responsive they're going to be. It takes time to send commands back and forth, so don't try to fly fancy maneuvers with probes that have a 3 second lag."

"OK, that makes sense. What else?" asked Jacqueline.

"Finally, never break off a formation of less than three probes. It won't be able to detect anything. You always need a triangle, square, or more sides to do detections. The full 24-edge circle-ish thing has the highest resolution."

"I don't get it. I've seen detections that only hit a single laser. Why can't I break off formations of two?"

Colleen massaged her temple with her fingers. "Uhm, so did you ever do geometry proofs in school?"

Jacqueline smiled. "Yeah, I liked those."

"OK, good. So, your gravitational probes are looking for curved space where those proofs break down. The lasers can accurately measure the angles and the distances. If you have a triangle, with all 60 degree angles, but one side is longer, the probes know that it's violating a proof, so they know that gravity is stretching one of the edges. When you have the 24-sided thing that's almost a circle, it's the same concept. If one of the lasers across the middle is longer than the diameter of a circle should be, then we know that the space in the middle is stretched because the circumference is supposed to be bigger than the diameter by a factor of pi."

Jacqueline took a second and tried to visualize what Colleen was saying. "Alright. I'll keep thinking about that, but the rule you want me to follow is triangles, squares, or bigger, no two-probe formations. I can remember that."

Colleen nodded. "Yeah. Listen, sweetie, I'm just about out of time. Is there anything else we should talk about?"

"Yes, quickly, I want your help. I want to get more detections than Kirin on this run. Tell me where to go so that I can win."

Colleen laughed. "Ha, yeah. Let me think. Here, I've got one. Do you remember that big detection that you tried to kill yourself for on the first run? It's been extended, but you could make a special formation just for that one. I'd say, use 12 probes to make a 1000 km circle in the middle, then make four triangles and pilot them around the outside of the stream to find where the edges are. Now that you can pilot all the formations separately, you should be able to scope that one out really well."

Jacqueline's looked away from the screen and placed her hand to her mouth as she thought about what Colleen was saying. "I see, yes!" she said finally. "You're the best Colleen. That's exactly what I wanted."

"Hey, kamikaze, be careful flying inside that dark current," said Colleen. "You seriously almost died last time."

Jacqueline looked down at her hands and thought for a moment. Finally she asked, "Colleen, why didn't I die? I mean, I spent more time out there than the ship's computer said that I had."

"It's super complicated, but trust me. That trick will never work again. Don't ignore your alarms. We changed the way the software works for calculating your angles and time after that stunt. The short answer is that while you were flying inside the gravity of the dark current, you were inside a pocket of stretched space. It meant that you weren't as far off course as the NLS computer thought you were. The angles that your navigation system measured were off because of signals bending as they approached your ship. You're the one who found that bug in the code, and it's fixed, so don't try it again."

****

Christopher gave Jacqueline a professional smile when she came back from giving her samples. "Welcome aboard Lieutenant. How was your trip?"

They had technically been on a first-name basis for her past four visits to the Outpost, but Christopher continued to maintain a professional distance during Jacqueline's post-flight psychological assessments.

"It was amazing! There is new software on the NLS and Colleen gave me an idea on how I could pilot the probes to get a massive detection. I'll warn you now that Kirin is going to be really annoyed when she gets here. I don't think that she's going to be able to catch up from this."

"Heh, OK. I'll add a note to her file. How are you doing with the isolation? You experience about three weeks on a single run, right?"

"It depends on how you count," she said. "It's 24 days total, but I'm usually only awake for 15 of that. Two weeks alone can be hard, but there is a lot to do. Also, It really motivates me to make the most of my time here."

Jacqueline saw Christopher cringe slightly at her words, then he cleared his throat and made a note on his tablet.

"Christopher, I'm sorry. It was really insensitive of me to say that to you."

He pursed his lips and nodded, but then swallowed hard and said, "No, You didn't do anything wrong. I have to ask you for this information for my records. I'm glad that I got a sincere answer."

The expression around his eyes still looked tight, but Jacqueline didn't want to press the issue.

"So, let's see what we can do to make the most of your time onboard," he said. "As it happens, there is going to be a virtual party in one of the immersive gaming venues tomorrow night. I think that you should try to attend, but that only leaves you today and tomorrow to design an avatar."

Jacqueline shrugged, half-heartedly. "Oh, I'm not picky about things like that. I'll just take a selfie or something."

"No, definitely not. People don't want to know who you really are. To pull it off, you'll need an avatar that you can identify with, but that doesn't look like you. Then, during the party, you'll roleplay your character. It should be fun, and it might be a way for you to take some social risks in a safe environment. I'll send you some photos of the time period for the setting."

Christopher gave her another smile, but it didn't quite reach his eyes. Jacqueline did her best to smile back.

How can he even stand to look at me?

****

Jacqueline entered the game to find herself in a small dark room. Light was filtering in around the edges of a closed door, and when she opened it, she had to squint her eyes. Endless blue skies stretched out beyond the decks of a wooden ship. She took a few steps forward then turned to look behind her. Wooden stairways rose up from both the starboard and port railings to meet the raised helm at the back of the ship.

She heard wind blowing, and as her eyes followed the riggings upward she realized that there were no sails. The thick black cords extending up from the decks converged toward massive wooden hoops that hugged the girth of a zeppelin balloon overhead. It was as long as the ship itself with a rudder, like a fish's tail, at the back. The balloon's yellowed fabric was decorated with a large, circular, gold-leaf emblem, positioned perfectly in the sections between the wooden hoops that harnessed its lift.

She walked to the rail and looked downward, 150 meters, to the misty, overgrown streets of the city below. The rooftops of the city reminded her of old photos of 18th century Paris or London.

As Jacqueline looked around at the other avatars in the game world, she was relieved by her choice to dress as a pirate character from classic cinema. Her robe was thick and black with a gold brocade pattern running down the sleeves and growing up from the bottom hem. She wore a tall black leather waistband that ran from her hips to her ribs and which was carved to look like the scales of a dragon or sea monster. On her left hip was a long samurai sword.

She fit right in. As the airship gently approached the skydeck of one of the city's buildings, she saw pirates, ladies and lords strolling on all of the elevated rooftop promenades. She breathed in deeply and pulled her shoulders back. She also made a mental note to thank Christopher for suggesting that she come.

Her airship docked slowly and moored to one of the protruding berths of the skydeck for just long enough for her to disembark with the other passengers. As she walked toward the center atrium, she saw that other airships were lining up to dock on all four sides of the building as guests streamed into the event along multiple walkways.

Once in among the other guests, Jacqueline approached one group of people talking. She had selected a British accent for her avatar, and she loved the way that it pronounced her words. "How do you do," she said, trying not to laugh at the sound of her own voice.

One or two people said hello to her and shook her hand. One man politely asked her about her character, but as she answered, the group seemed to dissipate. Before she even finished answering his questions, it was just the two of them. "You look lovely," he said, but then he turned and walked away from her as well. She was left standing there, where a group of six had stood only moments earlier.

She chose more carefully for her second group, but it happened again. They simply ended their conversations shortly after she joined them. One or two people tried to be polite, but ultimately they went their separate ways.

When the same thing happened with a third group, Jacqueline began to wonder if she had misunderstood somehow. It didn't make sense though. Why would the crew of the Outpost hold a party just to look at each other's costumes?

After 45 minutes Jacqueline had had enough. She couldn't muster the strength to try to break into another group. Taking a look around herself, she saw a path out to one of the skydeck walkways that led back to the airships from the atrium. Though the city skies were still full of impossible and intriguing vessels, none were moored along the edge of the building. She stood at the ledge and looked down at the mists that rolled through the overgrown streets of the city below. Then, slowly, gracefully, she leaned forward and let herself fall. As the wind rushed up towards her, she simply touched her hand to her goggles and exited the game.

****

The next morning, Liam joined Jacqueline for breakfast in the commissary. "I missed you last night. Did you enjoy the party?"

"It was very beautiful," she answered.

"Tell me about some of the characters that you met inside," he said.

"Well, I don't really have much to tell. Each time I went to talk to a group of people, the conversation ended and I would have to spend several minutes trying to find my way into another group. I didn't stay long."

I wish I had spent the night with you.

Liam's face drew down into a scowl. Shaking his head, he said, "This isn't the first time that I've heard of this type of thing happening. The crew takes their fantasy life very seriously, and they feel no responsibility to anyone. Sometimes I wonder if the immersive games don't provide an excuse for some of our worst behaviors."

Jacqueline was shaking her head, eyebrows raised, "No, it's fine. I might try it again some time."

"Listen, let me make it up to you. Let's have a quiet dinner tonight," he said, looking at her through his eyebrows.

"That sounds nice."

He looked down at his empty plate, and took a quick breath. "OK, I'm sorry to run, but I need to get to the Command deck. I'll see you later?"

"Sure," she answered, and Liam stood and cleared his dishes. She watched him walk away, then looked down at her own plate and moved the food around with her fork. She wasn't feeling very hungry.

A touch on her shoulder surprised her. "Jacqueline, may I join you for a second?"

It was Christopher. "Oh, hi, yes, of course. I didn't see you there."

Christopher placed his tray on the table and sat down. He looked straight into Jacqueline's eyes, but he didn't say anything for a few seconds.

"I hope that you don't mind," he said, "but I overheard what you said to Liam about the party. I think that I know what happened."

He took a breath and leaned forward. "I should tell you that I actually saw you at the party. I'm sorry that I didn't do anything to help you. For what it's worth, everyone said that your costume was beautiful and you even received several compliments on your stylish exit."

You told me to go to that party.

It took Jacqueline another moment before a thought occurred to her. Christopher shouldn't have been able to recognize her. "Wait, what do you mean, you saw me? You told me that the crew likes to remain anonymous."

"Right, they do, and that's what I wanted to explain to you. That's actually why some people avoided you last night. They could tell that it was you because you made yourself too young. No one else on this station is younger than 40 years old, but your character was in her early 20s."

Jacqueline tilted her head. "Why should that matter though?"

"Well, it blew your cover," he said. "The others just got too uncomfortable knowing who you were. The anonymity of the game is what lets people lower their inhibitions and have fun. Knowing who someone is inside the game is like knocking over the punch bowl, shutting off the music, and calling the police."

She took a deep breath and let it out again.

"I'm really sorry that this didn't work out. I should have done more to prepare you."

"It's OK," she said. "I guess that I can fix that next time. I'll just have to look forward to another party."

Christopher gave her a lopsided smile, and placed his hands on the sides of his tray to stand up.

"Christopher?" she said quickly, before he could leave. "Why don't people on the Outpost ever dress up as younger characters? If they change other parts of themselves in the games, why don't they change their age?"

"Oh, they do, but people actually have a natural age range where they feel comfortable. I've read studies that show that even people's sexual fantasies fall within relatively conservative age boundaries. I think that it's like half your age plus seven or something. To be honest, it's kind of pseudo-science, but the trends are definitely there."

Am I really 20 years younger than everyone else on this station?
Christopher still had his hands on his tray and looked like he wanted to stand up. Jacqueline had more questions, but it seemed wrong to keep him if he wanted to leave.

"Thank you for telling me," she said with a small nod of her head. He nodded back with a tight smile and got to his feet.

****

As the hours wore on during her flight home, Jacqueline found herself thinking over and over again about her conversation with Christopher. She looked at the calendar and tried to do the math in her head. If Liam was 41 years old, then half his age plus seven would mean that he would want someone at least seven years older than she was now.

Christopher did say that it wasn't scientific, but the thought wouldn't go away that Liam, even in his fantasies, would wish for someone older, more mature, more experienced. He had never shown even the slightest impatience with her and had always followed her lead, but how long could that really last if each visit added almost two years to the difference in their ages.

The next 14 days felt long to Jacqueline, as if each hour that she flew at this extraordinary speed made her fall further and further behind everyone else. How could she ever really share her life with anyone?

26 - The Letter - 2134 -
One Light Year from Earth
Christopher

"Excellent. I think that we're all set then," said Christopher, getting to his feet and rolling the small stool over to one side. "I hope that you have a restful week on the Outpost." Turning to leave, Christopher heard the crinkle of the paper as First Lieutenant Demir slid off of the exam table beside him.

The feel of a firm touch between Christopher's shoulder blades stopped him in his tracks.

"Christopher, I have something for you. Two things, actually."

Turning back to look at the NLS pilot, Christopher kept his face neutral and raised his eyebrows with a smile. "Oh, sure. What is it, Lieutenant?"

Lieutenant Demir straightened his medical gown, then reached behind himself where he had been sitting, and pushed a wrinkled envelope into view.

"First, I would like to ask you to call me by my given name. I am Cemil. I was born a few kilometers from the Mediterranean sea in Antalya, Turkey in 2093. My father was Ahmet and my mother is Zehra."

There had been a slight twitch in the pilot's face as he said that last sentence. "2093," mused Christopher, looking at Lieutenant Demir with fresh eyes. The NLS pilot was easily 20 years his junior. "You're just a few years younger than I am."

Lieutenant Demir bowed his head and closed his eyes for a moment, then looked back at Christopher. "Yes, I have an older brother at home. He's about your age."

Christopher narrowed his eyes in a slight smile and waited for the Lieutenant to continue.

"I actually just saw him," he said. Then, hovering his hand over the envelope again, he added, "I tell you this to explain how I have come to carry this message to you."

Lieutenant Demir swallowed and took a deep breath. "On my last trip home, there was a message waiting for me on the Nest. It was from my mother, and she had written to tell me of my father's passing. In my country, when someone dies, friends and neighbors learn of it the same day, and they come to the family's house. To learn of my father's death this way, months after it had happened was shameful. I know that he wouldn't blame me, but it was difficult for me, knowing that I had not been there to mourn for him."

Christopher bent down and pulled the stool back toward himself, then sat down and reached his left hand for his tablet to take notes.

"No, Christopher," said Lieutenant Demir, waving his hand at the tablet. "I'm talking to you as a friend right now."

"Oh, of course," said Christopher with a nod, and he brought his hand back and placed it in his lap.

"Thank you. What I learned next was a great relief. Knowing that I had missed my father's death and burial, my mother did me a great honor. It must have taken enormous courage. She broke tradition and waited for my return before holding the Mevlit ceremony for my father. I requested leave immediately, and I traveled to my home to offer my recitations in memory of my father."

"Mevlit?" asked Christopher.

"Yes, in my country, on the 52nd day after a loved one's passing, we gather once more to remember them. I was very grateful to my mother. It mustn't have been easy for her. The ceremony was beautiful. My brother was there, as well as my family's oldest friends. We ate and drank, and I was able to say goodbye to my father properly. I returned to Texas three weeks later, but then I had to wait another two months for an open position in the NLS flight schedule before I could resume my work."

"I see," said Christopher. "I had noticed that it was longer than usual since I had seen you. How are you holding up?"

"I am at peace. Thank you," he said. "And now that you know this about me, I feel that I can give you the things that I have carried for you."

Lieutenant Demir took a half step toward Christopher, unfolded his hands, turned his palms up, and gestured for Christopher to rise.

Furrowing his brow, Christopher complied. As he reached his full height, he had an urge to take a step back. They were standing less than an arm's length apart. Fighting the impulse, Christopher tilted his head a little to one side, studying Lieutenant Demir's face. The other man's eyes were dark and deeply peaceful. Even his manner of blinking seemed to play out in slow motion. His eyelashes were very dark and very long.

"So, if I may…" said Lieutenant Demir. He took another half step toward Christopher, and opened his arms. Slowly, he reached up and placed his arms around the taller man's shoulders. Christopher could feel the pilot's wavy hair on his cheek. Closing his embrace tighter, Lieutenant Demir lifted his head and placed a gentle kiss on Christopher's cheek, then released him.

"That is from your father," he said, taking a step back. "I met him in Texas while I was waiting for my return to the Nest. He embraced me, just as I have embraced you, and he asked me if I would carry his message to you."

Christopher's knees shook slightly, and he sat down again without breaking eye contact with Cemil. His next few breaths shuddered in his chest, and he closed his eyes to try to collect himself. When he opened them again, Cemil was reaching back for the envelope on the exam table. He picked it up and turned back toward Christopher.

"He also gave this to me, and he asked me to bring it to you."

Christopher lifted one hand, and Cemil slipped the envelope between his fingers. "He is a wonderful man," said Cemil. "I hope we will find time this week to share a meal. Maybe you can tell me more about him."

With one last touch on the shoulder, Cemil turned and walked out of the medical bay, leaving Christopher with the envelope. The texture of it felt strange in his fingers. He hadn't touched thick paper stock in years. In one corner, the embossed letters spelled out his father's name and the address of his psychiatry practice. In the center was a single line written in sweeping cursive letters, "Please deliver to Chris Ellis"

Slipping his finger under the edge, Christopher worked open the envelope, then slid out a folded page written on the same thick and slightly yellowed paper. There was a rich smell to it that made him think of sitting in his father's office as a young man. He had always imagined that he would work there one day.

Dear Chris,

I had hoped that we'd get to talk face to face one of these days, but it's starting to look like that's not going to happen. It's been a hell of a year, and it's time that I came clean with you.

Last week, I had my last sessions with my remaining patients. I should have done it a long time ago, but I've finally closed the doors on my practice. Everyone is in good hands. I made sure of that.

I know that I should have closed up shop after your mom died, but the work really kept me going. At my age, a lot of men kind of sink into themselves. I've started to realize though that my patients were probably helping me more than I helped them over the past few years. I don't need to tell you how risky it is to engage in that kind of symbiosis, and now that it's over, I'm relieved that I'm getting out before I did any serious harm. They deserve better than I was giving them.

So here's the hard part. Let me start with an apology. I should have told you 18 months ago that I was sick. I've counseled enough families to know that it takes a long time to say goodbye when there's as much unresolved as we've got between us.

I know that I was never crazy about the idea of you flying off when you did. I let your mom do the heavy lifting at keeping us connected all of these years, even though I would have never let one of my patients get away with something like that. Maybe it was a father's pride, or even, on some level, professional rivalry with you, but I see now that expecting you to question your decision was wrong of me. I should have been supporting you, and instead, I let my own ego nourish a rift between us.

Suddenly, I want to know everything. I want to know about the people up there that you're helping and how you keep them going year after year. I want to know about you and Liam and how your relationship has changed over the years. I want to know about the pilots that come and go and how you help them.

It's crazy because one of the things that I was the most upset about after you left was that I wasn't going to get to collaborate with you, and now I realize that I should have been doing it all along.

Here's the kicker, though, little buddy. I probably won't be around long enough to get a reply from you. I hope that you can forgive me one day. I was selfish, and childish, and I wish I could do it all over again.

I always thought that we'd work it all out when you got home, but I guess we're going to have to hope for the promise of something beyond that.

I love you, Chris. I'm proud of you, and your mom was too. I see things differently now. I'm actually relieved that you're up there instead of down here watching me waste away. I feel a little better leaving this earth knowing that I'm not abandoning you.

Please know that you are everything that I ever hoped you would be.

So, here it is, the big goodbye.

All my love,

Dad

****

"Do you want me to carry anything back for you?"

Cemil was already in his COFLEX, ready for departure, when Christopher entered the medical bay.

"No, thank you," replied Christopher. "I've sent him an electronic reply, but at this point, I'm not sure that it'll reach him."

"It's odd isn't it?" asked Cemil.

Christopher was making notes on his tablet, but looked up at Cemil through his eyebrows, then lifted his head before asking, "What is?"

"Knowing that the things that tethered us to a way of being now live only within our minds. The things that tether us to Earth, even."

Christopher felt a churning in his abdomen, and rocked forward slightly. He put his hand on Cemil's COFLEX clad shoulder to steady himself. "Yes, you're right. It is odd to think of it that way."

Cemil took a step toward Christopher and hugged him one more time. The iron embrace of the body armor was tender in spite of its crushing force. When Christopher coughed from the pressure of it, Cemil released him. "I'm sorry, brother. I'm sorry that I brought you pain."

27 - Nukes in Space - 2139 - Houston, Texas

Colleen

"Audacity, bordering on hubris. That's what it takes if you want to hurl steel and bone into space and bring them home again."

She could see that he was squirming in his chair. Why was it so hard for this kid to just step up and own it?

"Colleen, I think that it's just easier for you. That clarity that you have? It's a strength in most situations, but is a feeling of clarity the same as actually being right?"

She asked herself if he was worth it. If he was worth all of these frustrating conversations. All this kid wanted to do was sit in his little cave and crunch numbers. She had handed him the un-manned NLS design on a silver platter, but she had hoped that he would step up and start working on the big missions, the manned missions. The only recent initiative he had shown was to propose another unmanned probe for combing through the asteroid belt, looking for small rocks. He just didn't seem to have the stomach for the big stuff.

"I saw this quote once," she said. "It read, '*Mental toughness is believing, without a doubt, that whatever happens, you've got this.*'"

He had his arms crossed. "Is that bordering on hubris, or is that just hubris?"

"Edward, wake up. Someone is going to do this work. You can't sit there as a conscientious objector and let one of these buffoons plan missions with real people in them. Where is the morality in putting less talented people in charge of protecting human life?"

Edward looked away and sighed.

Heh, the little shit doesn't have an answer for that one.

"Just come with me to this meeting. If you like what you hear, you can sit quietly and say nothing, but you have to promise me that if you hear something that's wrong, or worse, dangerous, you owe it to everyone to speak up and put a stop to it."

"OK. Fine," he answered. His eyes were half closed and Colleen thought she detected a little shake of his head.

Convincing Edward to come with her had made them late, but she didn't care. As they entered the conference room, Colleen saw Tirrell do a double-take at seeing the junior scientist at her side.

He always seemed to look over the top edge of his glasses when he was unhappy. If she could get somebody with Tirrell's ambition and Kaiser's brains, they would make a hell of a Mission Architect.

Colleen nodded at Dr. Tirrell and he began, "Thank you all for coming. As you know, the Presage program is currently evaluating means to deal with the asteroids and comets whose future interactions with GHoSts we can foresee. As is typical in the international community, we use the one-percent threshold for identifying which objects require further study. The higher the probability of an impact with Earth, the more attention we give an asteroid or comet."

As Dr. Tirrell spoke, a list appeared on the display behind him showing the names of solar system objects and their probability of hitting Earth after interactions with GHoSts.

"There are several existing technologies that have been tested over the years for asteroid redirection. Our goal today is to look at each and explain which ones we plan on deploying for these potential threats."

As Dr. Tirrell gestured to the wall opposite Colleen, two separate animations of different types of vessels were highlighted. "Option one is a kinetic impact vessel that guides itself on a collision course with an asteroid. It uses ion thrust powered by a deployable solar array. Option two is the more traditional approach of using nuclear missiles that detonate near the meteoroid or asteroid, thus allowing the blast's radiation pressure to drive the object into a different orbit."

Colleen was fidgeting in her chair and biting her lip. If she didn't do something to stir things up then Tirrell would drone on for another hour about this hundred year old technology.

"Kaiser, what do you think so far?"

Edward jerked upright at being called out, then looked back and forth between Colleen and Tirrell. "I think that I understand the proposal, Director."

Colleen laughed. "No shit, that's not what I'm asking you. What are your specific thoughts on the proposal? Is this the path that you would have taken?"

Edward looked back and forth again between Dr. Tirrell and Colleen.

C'mon kid. Get off your ass.

"Just start anywhere, Kaiser. What would you change, if anything?"

"Well, as you know, I've been looking for ways to study the smaller asteroids. Our surveys of the Main Belt have mainly surveyed objects larger than one kilometer in diameter. I don't see any plan here to catalogue the smaller rocks that could still hurt us if they suddenly fell out of orbit. There are a lot more of the small asteroids, and it doesn't take as much dark mass to divert them, so fixing that oversight seems critical to me."

Colleen raised an eyebrow and stole a glance at Tirrell. He was noting something on his tablet. When she looked back at Edward he seemed lost in his thoughts. He had leaned back in his seat and was looking at a random point on the ceiling.

She was just about to say something when he spoke up again. "On the data analysis side, I notice that the target list is sorted by probability of impact. I think that it fails to factor in things like expected death toll or even *when* it will occur. What if we spend all of our time looking at a 50% object that's 20 years in the future, and we ignore a 0.5% object that is three years away? What if the 0.5% object is timed to fall in a highly populated area?"

"Of course you can sort the target list any way you want," said Tirrell, recapturing the initiative. "What's important is that you act on it."

Edward's far-off look had vanished, and he was nodding to Tirrell, 30 years his senior, like an attentive student would look at his professor.

Colleen was ready to give up. If Edward lacked the basic nerve to push for a better solution, then she was going to have to engage Tirrell herself. She shot Edward a look, then turned her back on him in order to face Tirrell. She was getting ready to ask about the yield of the nuclear warheads when she heard Edward's voice behind her.

"I think that I would also take issue with both mitigation technologies that were mentioned," he said. "Both are self-propelled, requiring terrestrial launch and onboard propellant. As a result, both would have a limited top speed and would require a long time to intercept, which might not be acceptable. Of course, if the list isn't sorted by urgency that wouldn't stand out."

Colleen almost laughed out loud, but she caught herself.

"The thing that really bothers me though is that all of the energy sources seem mis-matched with their task. You've got chemical or ion propulsion for transport, then either a low-velocity impact or a nuclear explosion for asteroid impulse. Why not take advantage of high-value resources like the Nest? I guess I'd be more inclined to use a lightsail craft to transport a boatload of projectiles out to the other side of Mars without consuming any propellant. Then if we had a strong onboard power source, we could fire off tens of high-energy mitigations in a single sortie."

The more that Colleen thought about it, the more sense it made. She turned to the elder scientist and asked, "What about that, Tirrell? Could you find a way to mitigate multiple threats in a single mission?"

Tirrell straightened in his seat and lifted his chin to answer, "Of course, Director. Using option two, as I have stated, the missile could carry up to twelve warheads on a single vehicle. The delivery mechanism would remain the same, and the technology for multi-warhead missiles is well established."

"Yeah, it was designed to kill us all," said Edward.

Finally! We have his full attention. Colleen looked at Edward and prompted him. "Do you think that option two is dangerous, Kaiser?"

Edward turned his palms up and raised his eyebrows, "Nukes in space? I wouldn't know how to start analyzing the risks. We don't know what these asteroids are made of or how solid they are. We don't know how sensitive they are to heat or radiation. If we're talking about existing warheads with a spherical explosion pattern, then I doubt that the subtle collateral effects on other asteroids have been taken into account, and even if they were, we'd only be converting a small percentage of the nuclear energy into actual kinetic energy."

Dr. Tirrell had taken off his glasses and was polishing them with a cloth. He had turned away from Edward to face Colleen. "Director, as entertaining as it may be to allow the freshman staff to participate, shouldn't we try to make some progress on a concrete proposal?"

"Yes, Dr. Tirrell, we should." Colleen didn't usually address the scientific staff by their titles, and it was clear that she had taken Tirrell by surprise. Before he could recover, she turned to Edward and said, "Kaiser, would you care to make a concrete proposal?"

Now Edward was the one who looked surprised. "Um, I suppose that I could prepare some---"

"No, Kaiser, now."

"Director, I'm happy to brainstorm, but you'd be getting my unfiltered thoughts."

"I seriously haven't got all day. Do you or do you not have a different idea?"

"Well... OK... For starters, I guess that I'd prioritize launching probes into the asteroid belts to take a full inventory of anything larger than a Volkswagen that we haven't catalogued yet."

"What else?"

"Then,... I'd probably place a compact fusion reactor on the vessel to power a high-energy kinetic impulse. Let's say a railgun, for example. If you relied on Nest propulsion and a lightsail, that would eliminate literally tonnes of propellant from the ship, and all of that weight can be repurposed to carry more ordinance. The railgun would actually represent a form of propulsion, so you'd need to stagger your targets to control the ship's flightpath."

He paused, looking at the ceiling again. "Now, we don't really want to use solid rails because it could shatter the asteroid, but we could use some kind of simulated soft material to create an inelastic collision. I've read about micromechanical composites that could do it, but they would have to be ferromagnetic to be usable in a coilgun."

Colleen nodded. "Yeah, ferrites. So you've got a railgun and soft rails, then what?"

Edward thought for a minute before answering. "Well, the orbital periods in the main belt are on the order of three to five years, so we might require multiple missions in order to target every part of the asteroid belt. We'll want to drive the targets into the sun so we'd have three basic arcs that we could fire. If you hit an asteroid head-on, it'll fall out of orbit, but if you hit it from behind, that'll drive it into a highly elliptical orbit. That means that we'll have to kick it up at just the right angle so that it'll get pulled into the sun on its way back down. The magnetic coilgun could have enough control over muzzle velocity to launch the projectiles at very different speeds, and for big rocks we could hit them with more than one projectile. The third firing solution would be to shoot out far and high, and then let the projectile hit the rock on its way back down."

Dr. Tirrell had turned his back on both of them and was putting his materials away. He seemed to be making a statement with his deliberate packing. Colleen waited for him to turn back towards them, then said. "I'll come by your office later Leo, OK?"

He looked at her for a long moment over his glasses but he didn't respond. Colleen turned back to Edward and said, "Kaiser, this sounds interesting. Sketch up this coilgun proposal of yours and let's review the design. Try to have at least two of Tirrell's targets worked out on your system so that we can do an apples to apples comparison, alright?"

"Uh, yes, OK. When do you want that?" he asked.

"Shit, I don't know. How soon can you have it?"

"Would one week be too long?" asked Edward.

I wish he knew how long Tirrell had been working on his piece of shit proposal.

"Nah, kid. One week is fine. Hell, take 10 days. I know that you like to double check stuff."

At this point, everyone was packing up. Colleen walked over to Edward and gave him a soft friendly punch in the arm. "Nice job, stud. Are you happy?"

"Well, to be honest I'm terrified, but anything has to be better than nukes in space."

"You know what they say, 'Everything you want is on the other side of fear.' Now get to work."

28 - Life and Limb - 2135 -

One Light Year from Earth

Luca/Christopher

Luca Vitale needed fennel if he was going to get the flavor right for tomorrow's sausage. He could have sent one of the sous chefs down to get it, but he didn't really want them pawing through the case of precious spices that Pietro had sent him.

He took the elevator to the inner ring and tried to remember which direction to walk to locate his storage container. Bouncing along in the light gravity of the cargo ring, he looked at each yellow steel palette with his flashlight until he caught sight of the wooden case that he was looking for.

Ah, there you are...

He walked up to the palette and put his flashlight in his mouth, freeing his hands to open the latches on the suitcase sized wooden box. The bottles inside weren't labelled, so he had to look at each one to find the fennel. He was humming to himself as he lifted the bottles one by one.

Coriander, saffron, bay leaves, sage, marjoram, ah, there you are, fennel.

He wasn't in a rush, and he spent a moment admiring each as it passed through his hands. Their rich colors and their powdery textures brought back memories of family and feasts past, and he could almost smell them without even unscrewing the lids.

Some of the bottles were nearly empty. He knew that he needed to ask Pietro for replacements, but it kept slipping his mind.

There was a sound off to one side of him, but on this flying erector set, there were always sounds. He ignored it until the pain gripped him. It wasn't a collision, just a slow crushing approach between two of the robotic palettes. His vision went white, the pain was so intense.

The palette that held his box hadn't moved, but another of the automated yellow steel palettes had slid up next to him as he stood with one leg on either side of the corner, inspecting his bottles. The two palettes continued to slowly lock together with a high pitched whining sound. His right leg was pinned between them, and any movement that he made sent scorching pain through his whole body.

"Help me!" he yelled, but the Axle was empty at this time of day. Luca didn't wear some of the electronics that the rest of the Outpost's crew wore. He didn't like to have all of that on his arms when he was moving around the kitchens at his characteristic speeds.

"Anybody!" he yelled again, but the sound was hollow. He only managed to holler a few more times before he finally passed out from the pain.

****

Christopher went straight to the medical bay as soon as Luca was out of surgery. "How is he?"

"He's in recovery now. I'm sure that you know, Lieutenant, we would have saved the leg if we could have. The force caused injury to the muscle cells, which in turn released sodium, calcium and organic enzymes. The influx of water and tissue hypoxia only worsened the cellular destruction. By the time he got to us, it was too late to save any of the tissues below the calf."

Christopher was nodding slowly. It wasn't so much that he understood what the doctor was saying, but that the doctor had shown how complex the process was.

As soon as he saw Luca's eyes move, Christopher placed his hand on Luca's arm and squeezed. "Luca, you're safe."

"Christopher?" he asked. "How did I get here?"

He started to slide his arms back and looked like he was about to sit up, so Christopher quickly opened his hand over Luca's chest to keep him from moving. "You're in the medical bay. One of the Axle crew found you on the cargo deck. Are you in any pain?"

"Only a little," he answered, "but my leg feels really strange."

"Luca, the injury was substantial and you were trapped there for a long time. The doctors had to amputate your foot and the lower part of your calf. We've printed a prosthetic for you, but it's going to take time to come back from this. We'll help you."

Christopher lowered his hand, and Luca slowly sat up to look at the bottom of the bed. There was only one foot under the sheet.

"Ah, Madonna santa," said Luca, "why didn't that machine stop? Why can't those things just stay still?"

"The engineers are looking at the rolling palette to see why it didn't detect your presence." answered Christopher. "The palettes move around to balance the weight on the inner ring so that the heavy cargo doesn't --"

Luca had lain back in his bed and closed his eyes, and he waved one hand to put a stop to Christopher's explanation. "Che palle!"

Christopher went still and sat down quietly next to Luca's bed. There was a bottle on the table, half full of green and beige seeds. He picked it up and turned it over in his hands. The sound drew Luca's attention.

"Ah, the fennel. You know, I don't much like the idea of making sausage right now," he said, furrowing his brow again.

"Luca, I'm so sorry that this happened to you," said Christopher, "but this doesn't change who you are or what you're capable of doing."

Luca raised his eyes to look Christopher in the face. "Eh, what I'm capable of doing. I think that you know better than anyone, what I used to do isn't possible here anymore."

"What do you mean?" asked Christopher.

Luca closed his eyes again and laid his head back on the pillow. "Food, it's supposed to bring joy. I feed them, but my wish was always to make them happy. I think that you know how hard that is now. We can try, but joy, in a purgatory like this, it is hard to find."

Christopher tried to keep his face neutral.

"You see it. I know you do," Luca said, with a slow nod, eyes still closed. "Living and surviving, they're not the same."

****

Liam was waiting for him for dinner. The idea of eating sausage made Christopher's stomach turn, but Liam was clearly hungry and was devouring it.

"How is Luca?" he asked. "It's funny, the food doesn't even taste the same when he's not here." He was looking at a piece of sausage on his fork.

"Hmf, the sausage probably needs more fennel."

Liam raised his eyebrows and looked quizzically at the sausage.

Christopher put his fork down. "He's in a bad place though, and I don't know if I can help him."

"Don't be silly," said Liam. "You'll know what to say. You always do."

"Not this time. Luca said something when I was with him, and it's something that I had been afraid to say to myself for a long time."

After a pause, he added, "I can't help him, Liam. I don't think that I've helped anyone in over a year."

"C'mon, Christopher. I know that things have been hard for you since you got the news about your dad, but we still need you here, and we need Luca back on his feet."

Christopher closed his eyes. *Feet...*

"I can't help him," repeated Christopher. His tone was emphatic and he was staring at Liam, almost daring him to answer.

"You underestimate yourself."

"I just don't understand how you go on year after year on this fucking hula hoop!" He threw his napkin in his plate and was shaking his head. "Don't you get it? I can't help him because I agree with him. We're never going home! This station is falling apart around us."

"Christopher, lower your voice!" Liam said in a harsh whisper. "I can tell that you're suffering, but you can't just lose it in public like this. These people are counting on you."

Christopher just pushed his seat back and stood up. "I need to go for a run," he said, and started making his way to the door of the canteen.

As he walked between tables, his only thought was finding the shortest path to the door. His shoulder brushed past someone, but he didn't even see who it was.

"Geez Lieutenant, let me get out of your way there." It was one of Sverdlichenko's arrogant scientists. The tone was sarcastic and there was a shitty expression on the man's face. Before he even realized what he was doing, Christopher drew back and punched the guy, right in the solar plexus. He dropped like a stone.

That's when he heard Liam's voice behind him. It was loud. "Lieutenant Ellis! Please confine yourself to your quarters immediately and remain there until someone from security has come to retrieve you."

He turned on Liam and was about to snipe back a sarcastic answer, but then he saw that everyone in the canteen was watching them. Christopher took a deep breath and drew himself up a little straighter. He stood there a moment and looked at each face in the canteen. Then he turned back to Liam again. The leader, the

Captain. He looked so comfortable in the role. Christopher's eyes felt heavy, but he lifted his gaze to meet Liam's and nodded before lowering his head again and moving toward the door.

He hesitated one last time in the doorway, but he knew that there was no point in turning back.

****

An occupational hazard, thought Christopher as he opened the drawer and saw bottles full of tranquilizers and sleeping pills.

Christopher's quarters were a little cooler than usual, and he had the lights dimmed. There were no windows, no books, no pictures. There was nothing but emptiness. Why was that? Why had he encouraged others to brighten up their personal spaces on the station, but he had never tried to do the same in his own quarters?

Is this what I abandoned my family for?

A tear was rolling down his cheek.

Even if we left today, it would take us eight years to get home.

Christopher opened one of the bottles and slowly poured a line of pills onto the desktop in front of him, then he counted them.

As if any of us really have a home to go back to.

Reaching over the pills, he slid his fingers around his tablet and picked it up. He placed the stylus on the screen and wrote:

> Liam,
>
> My captain, my friend, my love, I'm sorry. I thought that your passion and your conviction were enough to keep me going, but in the end, they were not.
>
> I would have liked to see this through with you, but I realize that I have used my last bit of stamina. It's better for me to stop now before I do any real harm.
>
> I hate the thought of dying here, in this tube, in this blackness. The emptiness will haunt me, and I suppose that I will haunt it too. But blackness surrounds me and I am convinced that there is no way to avoid this death. I take comfort, at least, in choosing when it will come.
>
> I continue to marvel at your vigor and I wish you every happiness,

Christopher

****

Liam hadn't been out of his quarters in almost a week. If it hadn't been for the doctor's ultimatum, he wouldn't have even gotten out of bed that morning.

"Captain, I am truly sorry. We don't have the means to keep a body onboard beyond the initial autopsy period."

Liam just looked at the floor as he answered. "Doctor. I do understand, but ejecting him out into this blackness is against his specific dying wishes. I am only asking you to delay for a few more days. I need to think."

"I can give you a few days, and I can do my best to preserve his body, but I have to reiterate that we don't possess any real embalming capabilities. I can see no other alternative but a burial at sea, so to speak. As you know, sir, regulations prohibit keeping a body onboard. It represents a significant health risk that I can't ignore."

Liam closed his eyes. "I will try to come up with something. Maybe the laser array. I just need a little time."

"I understand, Captain. I am sorry for your loss."

****

There was a knock at Liam's door. It had been more than five days since he had seen the doctor and at least ten days since he had gone up to the Command deck. They must have finally come to look for him.

He had taken some of the same sleeping pills that Christopher had used, but he followed the directions carefully. He just wanted to sleep, nothing more. He stood and slowly made his way to the door, feeling a little lightheaded.

The face behind the door didn't seem possible. It was Jacqueline. *This can't be right. How long have I been in here?*

He was tempted not to answer. *She's just a kid. She shouldn't have to deal with this.* Finally, slowly, he opened the door. There was obvious concern on her face.

"Hi Liam. They told me that I could find you here. Everyone seems to be acting strangely. What's going on?"

Liam didn't answer right away, and he hadn't moved to let her in either. He just stood there trying to wrap his mind around it all. "What's the date? I wasn't expecting you."

Jacqueline looked confused. "Well, for me it's December 18th. I don't know what your date is. I always just look it up when I do my post-flight report. Besides that, I don't ever need it. Liam, what's going on?"

Tears filled his eyes, and his throat tightened. He wasn't sure if he could get the words out.

"It's Christopher," was all that he managed.

"Christopher wasn't there for my medical check-in today. Liam, please, what's happening?"

He couldn't bring himself to say it. As bad as it had been, sitting alone in his room and sleeping whenever he couldn't face the truth, trying to say the words to Jacqueline was so much harder. Every time he tried to speak, the pain flooded in and made him hunch forward.

"He…" Liam stammered. "He…" shaking his head, he gave up on trying to say it. He bit his lip and squeezed his eyes closed as a new wave of sobs shook his body.

Jacqueline raised her hands to her mouth. She began hyperventilating, and each breath out carried a weak shaky moan.

Liam thought that she might fall where she stood. "Come on," he said, putting his hand on her shoulder. "Come in with me."

Liam was holding her arm, and he led her to a chair across from his bed. The only light in the room came from a dim lamp on his desk. The blankets of his bed were twisted and hanging half on the floor.

She sat down, then lifted her eyes to him and asked, "When?"

"Not long ago," he said, shaking his head, "maybe ten days, but I've lost track."

Jacqueline was still looking up at him, and a deep crease formed between her eyebrows, "Was it an accident?"

Liam closed his eyes and shook his head. He heard her gasp again.

He thought for a moment.

Would Christopher have wanted her to read the note?

Finally he said, "Here, this is what I know," and handed her a tablet with the last words that Christopher had written to him.

Tears rolled down her face as she read the letter. "Where is he now?"

"Medical."

Then, after a minute, he added, "They want me to put him out the airlock…"

The word made her recoil. She looked him in the eye, pleading. Her expression was pure anguish. "You can't. He would hate it."

Liam nodded. "The only other idea that I have is to try to use the propulsion lasers as a crematorium."

Jacqueline straightened her posture a little and her head tilted to one side. Her brow was furrowed. Then, after another minute she locked onto Liam's eyes. "I ... I might have a solution."

She was nodding slowly. "He can come with me... when I leave in eight days. I can take him home."

The thought was more than Liam could bear. He leaned forward and put his head on Jacqueline's shoulder. They cried together without saying another word.

****

The mission clock read 367 hours when Jacqueline woke up. She went through her normal process of detaching from the cradle and deploying probes. The sound of the 24 bands retracting had become one of her favorite moments of her flight.

Jacqueline held the left handhold and pushed off with her right hand so that her back floated all the way to one side of the NLS and her body was not blocking any of the displays. She looked back at the large, tightly wrapped black bag behind her cradle and said, "This is my display showing gravitational detections. This mesh shows how the lasers pass between all the probes."

She pushed off and floated over to the cradle. As it approached her, she passed her fingers through the netting of the cradle and pulled her face up close until she could see straight through to the back wall of the NLS.

"I'm glad that you can come home with me, Christopher." She looked over at her antique black clock and confirmed the date. January 1st X021. Looking back towards the black bag she added, "It's my birthday today."

29 - Cascading Failure - Oct 2142 -
One Light Year from Earth
Liam

Liam stared up toward the ceiling wishing that he could tell Jacqueline how sorry he was, but she was asleep. She had been asleep for the past six days.

Now that she was gone, it would be two years before she'd be back on the Outpost again, and Liam would have to struggle to remember how deeply he had hurt her.

The ceiling lights flashed. "Captain, we need you in engineering. Reactor control. Please acknowledge."

"Affirmative. On my way."

Reactor control?

Liam got up quickly and changed into a uniform. By 07:45, he was stepping off the elevator and heading towards the doors of the engineering bay.

Dr. Pyrinas, Liam's Engineering Chief, was waiting for him. "Captain, we are experiencing a Severity 1 fluctuation in the output of our fusion reactors. All eight have been affected. It started about an hour ago, and we have not been able to stabilize things."

Liam knew that Severity 1 implied an immediate threat to the NLS pilot and vehicle.

"Have we lost power to the propulsion laser array?" asked Liam.

"No, sir. Not yet."

"OK, what are your next steps?"

"I need all hands on deck sir. I need people from navigation to help us analyze the propulsion and update the NLS flight plan if we have to modify power output. We need to get Bugs out there to help us diagnose the nature of the problem, and I need every able-bodied physicist and researcher to contribute to forensic analysis of what is causing this."

Liam immediately signaled his Chiefs. "Attention, Phys, Mech, Nav, Sci. We have a Severity 1 situation. I need you to make your way immediately to the Command deck. I will also need each of you to gather a response team for assistance and mitigation. Mech, please have eight Bugs flight-ready in 15."

Turning to his Eng Chief, Liam said "Dr. Pyrinas, please route the relevant visuals up to Command. I'll get out of your way here so that your team can continue to work."

"Yes, sir," responded Pyrinas.

****

When the Chiefs were assembled in the Command deck Liam turned to Chief Fiorrelli. "Mech, where are those Bugs. We need a visual on the reactors as soon as possible."

Chief Fiorrelli, the Outpost's lead machinist, brought up the displays. "They're almost there. I've got video from seven of them here."

The Outpost's fusion reactors were torus shaped, and each was roughly 100m across. From a distance, they were barely noticeable lurking behind each of the eight wedges of the 50km basket woven of black carbon, but without them, the space station had no reason to exist.

"OK, Nav," said Liam, "where are we in the NLS acceleration phase?"

"We need roughly 20 hours more of propulsion to get the NLS up to target speed," responded Gregory Karabi, the Outpost's Navigational Chief. "Current velocity is roughly .963c."

"3%?" asked Chief Fiorrelli. "Do we really need 20 hours to add 3%?"

"Those last few percentage points are crucial," said Chief Karabi. "The difference in time dilation inside the NLS would be a factor of three. At the First Lieutenant's current velocity, the trip would feel like 104 days to her, but the NLS can only sustain life support for 35 days. Any speed below .997c would be fatal for the pilot. She would run out of air before she even got a third of the way home."

"20 hours is a long time, Nav," said Liam. "Is there anything you can do?"

Chief Karabi paged through his information then looked up at Liam, "According to this pilot's records, I think that she can handle up to 100g. If we give her more thrust, we can get her to a survivable velocity in under 16 hours, but it would put more strain on the reactors."

Without taking his eyes off of Chief Karabi, Liam pushed a button on the comm in front of him. "Eng, we're trying to wrap up propulsion ASAP, but it might mean dumping more power into the propulsion array. Can you sustain an increase in NLS thrust from 75g to 100g?"

"It's going to make the whole system less stable, Captain," came the voice back from Chief Pyrinas, "but if it's the best way to protect the pilot, then I'll support it. We'll increase aggregate power to 120 Terawatts immediately."

"Thank you, Eng. Acknowledged," said Liam, then turning to the display from the Bugs, he pushed a different button to open comms to all of them at once. "Bug pilots, report."

"Outpost, this is Bug 1. Visual on reactor alpha is normal. Proceeding in to open the diagnostic panel for further investigation."

"Outpost, this is Bug 2. No obvious trouble with reactor beta. Status is normal."

The roll call continued until Bug 7. "Outpost, this is Bug 7. Request eyes on my video feed."

Liam moved the video feed from Bug 7 to the main screen and looked at it along with his chiefs. "Bug 7, why haven't you closed in on your reactor yet?" asked Liam.

"I'm sorry Captain, but I stopped because something doesn't look right out here. Are y'all able to see the wavy thing going on with the carbon fiber supports?"

Liam did see something strange. Bug 7 had flown at least 5km back from the Outpost with a panoramic view of four of the wedges of the circular station. Viewed from that distance, something wasn't right. The mesh of woven black supports seemed to squeeze and distort at points then to go back to normal. In the blackness, it was hard to see, because the only areas where the Outpost was visible were the points that blocked starlight from the Milky Way, but it was enough. In space, Stars aren't supposed to twinkle, but something was causing the points of light to come and go behind the latticework of the Outpost.

"Affirmative Bug 7," said Liam, "please pull back further to get the other half of the station in your visual as well."

"WILLCO" replied the pilot.

"What the hell is that?" said Karabi.

Liam touched the communication console. "Eng., this is Command. We are seeing a deformation of the propulsion array. Can you confirm?"

The reply took 30 seconds. "Negative Command. Every gridpoint on the propulsion array is reporting stable telemetry," replied Pyrinas.

"Eng, are you looking at Bug 7's feed? This isn't a damn mirage. Something is making the latticework move."

There were several more seconds of quiet, then Pyrinas' voice came back over the comm. "Command, this is Eng. Negative, careful analysis of the visual is not showing a moving lattice. It's the stars, Captain."

Liam turned to Chief Sverdlichenko, the Outpost's ranking Science officer. "Sci, can you explain this? What is Eng saying?"

"Actually, he seems to be making a good point. If the carbon lattice is not moving, then something else must be causing the starlight to refract. Let me go down to Astro. and get them started to analyze this."

Liam breathed out through pressed lips and tried to maintain a collected facade. He waved a hand to dismiss Chief Sverdlichenko, then let himself sink down into a chair in front of a set of displays. His eyes drifted to the feed from Bug 7. It showed the Outpost floating like a shadow, a darkened circle in the speckle of stars. Liam could just make out the Wagon Wheel at the center, spinning around. He let his eyes rest there until they went out of focus.

****

She wasn't even looking at him. She was looking down at the ice spinning in the drink as she stirred it. "It's our 100th night together," she said. "I wanted it to be special."

How could he tell her what he was feeling? Even now, the 100th night thing. Did she realize how long he had been out here? "You've spent more than 100 nights on the Outpost, haven't you?"

"Well, I spend seven or eight nights each time I'm here, and this is my 16th flight. But, we don't spend every night together when I'm here, and we didn't really see each other face to face on my first few visits, so this is number 100."

They had grown so far apart. She still seemed to see this as some kind of honeymoon. "Jacqueline, listen. You have to understand that you and I are living very different versions of this relationship. Doesn't it bother you? I mean, I've changed so much since we first met."

Liam wasn't normally self-conscious about his age, but being around Jacqueline made it hit him a lot harder. At 52, his athlete's physique had softened significantly, and what was left of his hair seemed to sit oddly towards the back of his head.

Jacqueline's eyes fluttered for a second, but then she tipped her head down. He couldn't get a clear view of her face when she spoke, but her voice was unsteady. "No, it doesn't bother me. You're still the same person."

Liam put both hands on the table and leaned toward her. "But that's the thing. I'm not. I have been out here for decades, and I have lost the people who were the closest to me. That changes a person. Jacqueline, we can't even share the little things. I've read about 20 books since the last time you were here, but it's not as if we can talk about them. I'm changing faster than you realize, and to be honest, I don't think that the person you know is still in here."

A tear rolled down her cheek, but her eyes were locked on the ice cubes in the glass of the drink that she was stirring.

"I'm so sorry," he said. "I still love you, but at my age, love is different. It's not that consuming passion that it is at your age. It's protective and nurturing. I love that you are a part of me, but you have to see that I'm turning into an old man in front of your eyes."

"I gave up everything for you," she said.

"I know, and you're not the only person that I've hurt. I've never really forgiven myself for that."

She looked up at him, and he added. "You may not see it right now, but you still have most of your life ahead of you. I want you to live it. I really hope that you have every happiness, and as long as you need me, you will always know where to find me."

She put her spoon down calmly, then stood and left the table. As she walked away, Liam's eyes fell back to the table and the ice that was still turning in her glass.

****

"Captain, can you come over to Astro?"

Liam re-focused his eyes on the Wagon Wheel turning in the dark. He took a second to orient himself.

"Copy that, Sci. On my way."

Liam left Command and headed over to the Astrophysics lab. When he got there, Chief Sverdlichenko was waiting for him. "It could be that we have an explanation for the refraction of this starlight. On Lieutenant Binti Abdullah's last trip out to us, she mapped an elongated Dark Current that lies between us and exactly these stars that seem to be moving."

"You're saying that we are seeing dark matter?"

"No, Captain. I'm saying that dark matter is accumulated between us and certain stars, and it is very probably bending the light. It is actually a mirage, just like you said it."

"So it's just a coincidence? Does this get us any closer to stabilizing the fusion reactors?" asked Liam.

"No. Most probably not."

****

From Engineering, to Astrophysics, to Navigation, Liam made the rounds all day. The investigation teams were eliminating theories as fast as they were being proposed.

All day long, each time one set of reactors stabilized, another set began to falter. There was enough redundancy in the system that functioning reactors took over the load of failing reactors, but that extra load just seemed to hasten the onset of new fluctuations, and the chain reaction repeated. It was a moving target.

Throughout the day, Liam thought about what was at stake.

You should stop this. You should tell them to shut it down and to follow a safe restart protocol. She'll die, but it would guarantee that everyone else could live.

He couldn't bring himself to give the order, and mercifully, no one else suggested it.

At 19:09, the reactors were not recovering fast enough to keep ahead of the cascading failure, and all eight fusion reactors shut down at once. No-one thought to cut power to the propulsion array, and none of the failsafes prevented what happened next. Within seconds, the reserve power that might have been used to restart the reactors was thirstily consumed by the laser array and converted into terawatts of coherent light, projecting outward towards Earth's solar system.

Everything went dark. The floor seemed to move under their feet for a fraction of a second. All of the workstations shut down, and the overhead lights dimmed to black. One by one, crewmembers who carried flashlights turned them on.

Chief Fiorrelli was the first to break the silence. "OK, Let's get all non-critical systems off the grid so that we can activate the auxiliary battery power for life support and inter-ring transport.

We also need to get a radio signal out to the Bugs and tell them to come in."

Liam didn't have any way to know how many of his crew throughout the Outpost understood what was happening. He walked up to the door that led from the Command deck into the corridor and actuated the manual override. From there he walked down to Engineering. Their door was already open.

"Eng, Report." said Liam.

Dr. Pyrinas didn't respond. He looked at the floor then up into Liam's eyes shaking his head. "There is no way out of the energy hole that we're in."

He lowered his eyes again, and gave a twisted up smile. "At this point, Captain, I'm afraid that my best suggestion is that we all go over to the mess hall and finish what's left of the beer."

"You realize, Doctor," said Liam, "there are currently more than eleven NLS ships headed our way, and the Nest is likely to launch another eleven or twelve before they notice that we've gone dark. It's a death sentence. We won't be able to catch any of them."

"I do, Captain," Pyrinas replied. "But, to your point, I'll ask Chief Sverdlichenko to bring his reserves of vodka as well, and we can drink to their courage."

Liam nodded, and extended his hand to Dr. Pyrinas who gladly accepted it in a firm handshake.

"Thank you for everything, Chief. I... I'm sorry," Liam said.

"It has been my honor, Captain. It's a miracle that we lasted as long as we have. Maybe it was time."

****

Jacqueline's whole body was hurting as she started to wake up. She hadn't been this sore on any of her previous flights. It was as if the horrible feeling in her gut from her argument with Liam had spread into her limbs.

She detached from the Cradle, checked life support status and pulled off her helmet. She glanced at the x,y, and z orientation in preparation for deploying her probes, but stopped and double checked the displays. Something wasn't right. Not only was her rotation off by almost 12 degrees, but the mission clock read 921 hours remaining at zero-g.

921 hours? That has to be wrong... She looked back at her life support display.

I only have 729 hours of O2, and that's supposed to be zero-g plus deceleration. What is this?

She did the math in her head. 921 hours of zero-g and another 110 hours at least for deceleration. *That's almost ten days longer than my oxygen supply.*

As the weight of her situation settled in, Jacqueline executed her launch steps by rote. She floated over to the navigational control on her right and fired a few short bursts of yaw to fix her z orientation. Then, absentmindedly pushing over to the center console, she triggered the deployment of her gravitational probes and heard the sound of the bands retracting all around her.

Just focus on what you need to do to get samples.

Jacqueline fired radial then forward thrusters to set the probes in motion, then floated back to the cradle to think. The mesh of lasers established cleanly, and there were already small detections, but Jacqueline's mind was elsewhere. She knew that there would be plenty of time to think once the probes were deployed. She tried to concentrate on the work, but a single thought bubbled to the surface of her consciousness.

You're going to die in here.

****

By the time the mission clock read 820 hours remaining at zero-g Jacqueline had formed her plan. She would spend another hour composing a letter to the people whose faces were rushing through her mind. Then, she would turn the NLS around and fix her navigation for an intercept with the Nest. No excursions on this run. She would deploy her lightsail, 33 days early, and go back to sleep. It was her only chance of making her O2 supply last 35% longer than it was meant to. She hated the idea of sleeping away what might be her last days of life, but it was the only idea she had that would give her even a chance to survive.

But first the letter:

> Dear Friends,
>
> I hope that we can read this letter together some day, but in case that doesn't work out, I should tell you all what you have meant to me.
>
> To Andrew, Cemil, and Kirin. I have loved weaving this web in the sky with you over these past 16 trips

to the Outpost and back, and I have appreciated what you have taught me along the way.

Andrew, I have missed our morning jogs, but I learned from you how to hold onto my dreams even when things looked bad.

Cemil, you gave me courage when I was scared and alone, and you found a way to keep us connected through all of this.

Kirin, you showed me that it is OK to be strong and competitive. You make fierce beautiful, and I am still learning from you.

To Director Pastor and Major General Crespin, who turned the technological dream of this mission into a reality. I was honored to be a part of it.

Colleen, you seem to appear in my life every time that I need a hand. I am counting on you to keep the promises that you have made to me.

To Liam, I wish that we could have met under different circumstances. It broke my heart each time that I had to leave you, but in the end, I was the one who fell behind. I don't blame you for anything. I wish that I could have shared those years with you, by your side for every second.

Finally, if anyone is capable of finding them in Sarawak, perhaps someone can send my regards to Mr. Raban, to my Amah, and to my grandfather.

Thank you, Mr. Raban, for saving me, twice. I have had the chance to drink deeply from life these past four years, and I owe that to you.

Amah, for so many years your warmth and kindness were all that I had. I love you, and I have missed you.

Grandfather, I know that you ache for them, and I want you to know, I miss them too. I would love to close this distance between us. We don't need it anymore.

Sincerely,

Jacqueline

She saved the letter with her navigational notes where she knew it would be found by anyone who obtained the snapshot of the NLS memory that was typically transferred during the braking phase.

Jacqueline took a deep breath and looked around the NLS one more time. Faint traces of flour stains dotted the metal fixtures behind the cradle and parts of the netting itself. Her eyes floated there for a moment then fell closed as she pictured that first night that she had spent with Liam, inside this same ship as it sat moored on the Outpost. It was only two and a half years ago for her, but it had been so much longer for him.

Within a few minutes, the ship was turned and locked on target, and her lightsail was deployed. Jacqueline had to override half a dozen safety protocols to enable the prolonged sleep that awaited her. Securing her helmet, she re-attached herself into the cradle, and issued a voice command to initiate her sleep sequence. Those final moments cost her greatly, staring at her displays and repeatedly fighting the urge to cancel the command. Then, as she began to slip away, Jacqueline struggled to cling to those last few seconds of consciousness. She had no way of knowing where she would be if she ever did wake up again.

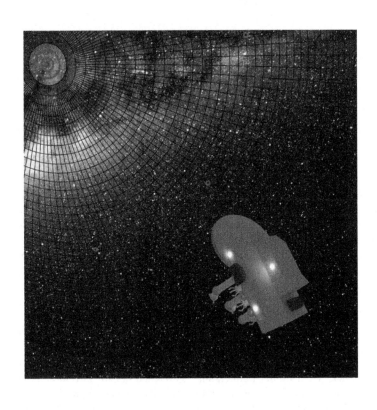

The Ghost of Sphinx

Colleen

As Colleen settled into her chair, Edward signaled his team that they could begin. "Director, thank you for coming. We'd like to bring you up to speed on the detailed designs for the Comber Probes, the coilgun, and Helix projectiles for the Crossbow program. Let's start with the probe."

As he spoke, a member of the research team activated the visual display on the walls and in the air overhead. The title on the wall across from Colleen read "Counter-Orbital Main Belt ExploRer [COMBER] Probe." The animation beneath it showed the dense and light bands of the main belt rotating slowly in a counterclockwise direction. A translucent 3D model of the Comber Probe itself filled the air in the center of the room.

"Since the comber probes will be orbiting the sun in the opposite direction as the millions of asteroids being surveyed, our first step was to quantify collision risk. With asteroids orbiting counterclockwise at roughly 18 km/s, the comber probes will be passing by them clockwise with a combined speed of roughly 36 km/s."

"For this reason, we had considered placing comber probes in orbit in the Kirkwood gaps, but that increased the difficulty of creating accurate scans. Instead, we've decided to place the probes at the median of each dense band of the main belt. From those positions, the probes will rely on their own scan data to make minor navigational adjustments and avoid head-on collisions with the asteroids that they are surveying."

"I understand," said Colleen. "This is fine. To be honest, I never took the probability of collision very seriously. Let's move on."

"Oh, OK…"

Edward looked around for a moment, then said quietly "Jump to section 3." The Comber probe disappeared, and a list of known asteroids replaced the animation of the main belt on the far wall.

"Here is our current list of high-value targets. Each of these is a previously charted main-belt object that is likely to be disrupted in the coming decades by Substructures in the Galactic Halo."

To one side, a panel cycled through a few at-risk asteroids and showed possible intercept trajectories to mitigate the threat they posed. Some trajectories were short and straight, hitting their target head on. Others were long and heavily arced, intercepting their asteroids at nearly right angles.

Edward continued. "We have chosen the codename Helix for the self-guided, self-uncoiling projectiles that will be fired from crossbow, and they offer various firing solutions for initiating an orbital change or triggering abrupt orbital decay into the sun. Now, since none of these asteroids have masses greater than --"

The door opened at the back of the conference room, and Airman Penthos entered. "Director Pastor, I'm sorry to interrupt. I have an urgent message from Nest command."

Edward stopped and looked back and forth between Colleen and Airman Penthos.

"Penthos, we're sort of in the middle of something here. How urgent is urgent?" asked Colleen.

The airman looked around the room. He didn't seem to want to say any more.

"Dammit Penthos, speak," insisted Colleen.

"It's the Outpost ma'am. We've lost contact with the Outpost." he answered.

"Shit!" said Colleen as she got up from her seat. "Kaiser, I think that there are no surprises here. Send me the data and highlight anything that you want me to double check. I'll look it over tonight."

Edward nodded in acknowledgement, and Colleen followed Airmen Penthos out of the room.

The walk from the civilian to the military wing of the Agency felt far too long to Colleen, but within three or four minutes, she was in mission control and was wearing a headset.

"Nest command, this is Director Pastor. Talk to me. What's going on?"

"Director, it seems that at 06:50 on October 7th, the Outpost began experiencing a cascading failure of its fusion reactors. Each time the reactors were restarted, others seemed to fail. During the event, there was an active propulsion, an acceleration, in progress. The last signal that we received from the Outpost is timestamped 19:09 from the same day."

"Dammit, who was the NLS pilot?" asked Colleen.

"Lieutenant Binti Abdullah, ma'am."

"Arrrgh. What is her status?"

"We are still determining that, ma'am, but we do know that the NLS had reached 0.96c before the trouble began."

"She's gonna run out of air, dammit. Did you say October 7th? That means that she's at least a week away. Tell the Captain that I'm coming up. I'll be there in 72 hours."

"Very well, ma'am. Copy that."

"Pastor out."

****

It took Colleen longer than the 72 hours that she had estimated to reach the Nest. By the time that she was on the space station, Jacqueline's NLS should have been 24 hours away from arrival. At that distance, the Nest would have been able to detect light reflected back off the NLS' lightsail. However, no such reflection was visible yet.

Engineers at the Space Agency and on the Nest had been analyzing logs received from the Outpost's final hours on October 7th. The events that they were reconstructing had unfolded almost twelve months earlier, and the log data from the Outpost had traveled nearly a full light year to reach this team. If their calculations were correct, Jacqueline's NLS would have reached 0.994c. It was slower than Colleen had been hoping for, but there was still a chance. They should only have to wait 8 more hours to start to see reflections from her lightsail.

Upon arriving to the Nest, Colleen headed straight to her quarters. She knew that she needed to be ready for whatever was coming next, so she took a sedative and laid down, hoping to catch a precious few hours of sleep.

It had been an exhausting week already. They were now fairly certain that the Outpost had not regained fusion power. If they didn't receive any indication in the next six days that the Outpost had restored power, then First Lieutenant Cemil Demir would miss his window for executing a safe braking phase at the remote propulsion station.

Both propulsion stations, the Nest and the Outpost, worked seven-days-on and eight-days-off with roughly one month dedicated to each NLS ship, for braking, housing, then re-launching each NLS pilot.

With a two year round trip there were currently 23 NLS ships in flight. As disgusting as it was to imagine the deaths of the 11 pilots who were lined up behind Jacqueline in their flight path to the

Outpost, the other 12 pilots who were launched from the Nest after October 7th seemed even more tragic somehow. There was no way that they could have known, but they were being launched towards a destination that might have already been dead.

Colleen had spent several sleepless nights imagining what it might be like for the NLS pilots as they realized somewhere along their journey that there was no longer an Outpost capable of catching them. She even thought that some of them might take evasive action trying to sacrifice themselves in a futile attempt to protect the Outpost from a collision.

When she had first learned about the incident, her immediate concern had been finding a way to save Jacqueline from a failed launch. However, at the present moment, it was beginning to look like Jacqueline was the only person who had even a chance of surviving.

The sedatives took effect slowly over the course of an hour, but even then Colleen's sleep was restless as her mind raced, looking for any way that one of the pilots or part of the Outpost crew might have found to survive. In a state between sleep and wakefulness, she convinced herself that there was a way that no one had thought of yet.

It's worth a try...

Colleen sat up on the edge of her bed, clinging to hope that she might be able to save a few of them, but as the fog of sleep began to fade, the realization hit her that it had just been a dream.

If they're really dead, then they died almost a year ago. You're too late.

Don't let it be for nothing.

Forgetting the reduced gravity in her quarters, Colleen stood up too quickly and immediately lost her footing. She tumbled forward, covering several meters, and struck her head on one of the edges of the desk. It was painful, and she was sure that it would leave a mark. She rubbed it for a moment as she opened the console on the desk and typed out a brief and blunt message to Edward.

Edward,

It looks bad. There has been an accident on the Outpost, and we are probably going to lose all in-flight NLS pilots and vehicles. There are 23 of them. I need you to find a way to recover all of the gravitational probe data that they have collected before it's lost too.

Colleen

Just then, the ceiling lights in Colleen's quarters flashed. "Director, this is Nav. We have visible confirmation of an inbound lightsail. Blueshift indicates that it's moving more slowly than we expected, and we have reduced the power slightly on the laser array in order to compensate."

****

"Bug 6, this is Nest command. Please proceed with manual removal of NLS lightsail. Pilot is not responding."

"WILLCO"

Colleen watched from the Command deck as Jacqueline's NLS floated slowly toward them. The ship seemed to be offline. Colleen knew that the NLS would shut down non-critical systems when the onboard power supply dipped below 15%, but the fact that the ship wasn't sending out any telemetry data was deeply concerning.

They watched, as the Bug, with its articulated arms grabbed hold of the NLS. With four arms it captured the vessel, then used the remaining two to saw through and break off the struts holding the lightsail in place. It was like watching a spider devour a butterfly. When the last of the lightsail supports was severed, Colleen heard, "Nest command, this is Bug 6. Lightsail is detached. Proceeding to Axle with the NLS vessel."

"Roger Bug 6, proceed."

"Nest command, this is Bug 2. Moving into position for lightsail retrieval."

"Roger Bug 2."

That was all that Colleen needed. "Notify medical to meet me in the Axle." Then, turning to Captain Kett she said, "Tamara, I'm going to need help moving around in zero-g. Can you assign someone to me?"

Captain Kett nodded. "Yes, I'll call down. She'll meet you in the cargo ring."

"Thank you," said Colleen, then she left the Command deck and headed for the elevator. She needed to be there when they opened the NLS.

C'mon kid, don't be dead....

Colleen stepped off the elevator in the 0.2g ring and had to remind herself to move slowly. She didn't want a repeat of what had happened in her quarters earlier. A strong looking but petite airman approached her immediately.

"Director Pastor. I'm Airman Elpida. Could I ask you to put this harness on, ma'am?" She was handing Colleen what looked like a backpack with a solid handle on it.

"Thank you, ma'am. Now let's head into the Axle by way of that ladder over there."

The two women passed through the bulkhead in the ceiling, then stepped off the ladder onto the outer wall of the Axle. They watched overhead as the bug and the NLS floated into the center. Nest crew were already attaching the mooring lines to the NLS sphere.

"OK, ma'am. On three, I'm going to need you to jump as hard as you can, OK?" said Airman Elpida.

At the count, Colleen jumped, and she felt herself yanked around a bit by her shoulder straps. Soon they were gliding along the mooring lines toward the NLS. They started to slow to a stop just as the Nest crew opened the hatch.

To Colleen's relief, she saw a couple of flashing lights inside the vessel. *OK, something is still working in there.*

She spoke loudly to be sure that they could hear her. "Remove the pilot's helmet before trying to detach her from the cradle. She's going to need oxygen."

After another 30 seconds, she heard one of the medics say, "I've got a pulse!", and she breathed a sigh of relief. Slowly, two of the medical crew positioned outside of the NLS extended their hands and took hold of Jacqueline's limp body.

One of the medics called out, "Can somebody get these gloves off of her? I need to get an O2 sensor on her finger."

Colleen was right next to them now. "I'll do it." she said and touched a few controls on the left forearm of Jacqueline's COFLEX. At the same moment, another of the medics was strapping an oxygen mask over Jacqueline's face.

"Oxygen saturation is at 60%. Let's get her to medical." The two medics quickly pulled Jacqueline towards the outer wall of the Axle and disappeared through one of the bulkheads.

Colleen turned to Airman Elpida and said, "Help me follow them, please."

"Yes, ma'am. I'm gonna pull on you a bit." The young woman grabbed the mooring line in one hand and Colleen's harness in the other and pulled hard. Colleen realized that she had basically used her as a counterweight to propel their glide back to the outer wall.

Soon they had descended the same ladder that they had used to enter the Axle and Colleen was headed back to the elevator.

****

Every hour for twelve hours, Colleen had either called down to medical or stopped in, but Jacqueline hadn't regained consciousness. Finally though, she was starting to stir, and the doctors had called up to Command.

"How is she?" asked Colleen as she entered.

The doctor gestured for Colleen to follow him and escorted her to Jacqueline's bedside. "She's doing really well, considering. In the past 30 minutes, her eyes have fluttered a few times. She's not fully awake yet but her EEG shows that she is regaining consciousness. At this time, there are no signs of anoxia, which would have been the primary risk given her initial blood oxygen levels."

Behind Jacqueline's bed, Colleen noticed pieces of the empty COFLEX strewn in front of the wall, and the micro-mechanical active gel was stagnant and dirty looking. Half of the electrodes hooked up to the 20 liter glass bottle were dangling, and it occurred to her that the post-flight crew must not have had a chance to do their work given Jacqueline's critical condition.

As Colleen reached her bedside, she was relieved to see that Jacqueline seemed to have some color in her face. Her deep skin tone and dark features showed a healthy contrast with the stark white of everything else in the room.

"Do you think that there will be any complications?" asked Colleen.

"We are hopeful that she can escape any lasting effects on her cognition," answered the doctor, "but it's hard to tell with such a long period of sedation. You could think of it as an induced coma, but normally we would never induce a coma for 40 days straight. It carries too many risks."

"It was a genius move," Colleen said. "There's no way that her air would have lasted if she hadn't put herself under."

As Colleen spoke, Jacqueline awoke suddenly. Her eyes were wide, and she was pushing her head back into the pillow as she stared at Colleen. "Ibu!? Ibu, ia benar-benar anda?"

"Jacqueline, are you OK?"

Tears were coming to Jacqueline's eyes. "Tetapi awak mati."

Colleen picked up Jacqueline's hand. "I don't understand you sweetie." Then, turning to the doctor, she asked, "What the hell's going on?"

The doctor was hurrying around to the other side of the bed. "Patients coming out of prolonged induced comas can experience severe hallucinations. You don't have any idea what she's saying?"

"Ibu, adakah saya mati?"

"She thinks that I'm her mother," Colleen said softly. "She probably thinks that she's dead."

"Jacqueline, I'm Colleen. You're safe and you're on the Nest."

Jacqueline just closed her eyes and sobbed. After another minute, she drifted off to sleep again.

Colleen took a deep breath and clasped her shaking hands together to try to steady them. *This poor kid.*

The only other time that Colleen had heard that word, *Ibu*, was that night in Kuala Lumpur when Jacqueline was screaming it as a child.

It wasn't just that memory though. Colleen was starting to come face to face with the horror of the situation.

They're all dead. She's the only one left.

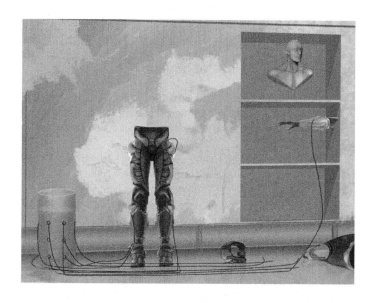

31 - Solo Mission - Nov 2143 - High-Earth Orbit

Jacqueline

"I wasn't sure if you would want this." said Colleen. Jacqueline looked down at what Colleen was handing her. It was the small antique clock with its odd black-on-grey geometric digits. It read September 30th X022.

Jacqueline felt numb, looking at it. It was her eighth day on the Nest, but for the first time in almost three years, she wasn't suiting up for another trip to the Outpost. Instead, she was sitting side-by-side with Colleen on the large aluminum trunk that contained her COFLEX. They were in the inner ring, waiting for the shuttle that would take them to the SPISE summit station.

Jacqueline hadn't been to the Axle yet to see her maimed NLS ship, and she was dreading the thought of passing it on her way to the shuttle. Colleen told her that they had been forced to sever the rigid support structure for the lightsail in order to fit her ship into the airlock. The sawn-off stumps were still sticking out of the sphere.

It had been more than two weeks since the last signals had been received from the Outpost, and there was no longer any hope that someone might be left alive inside. The station's auxiliary power could have only driven the CO_2 scrubbers and the station heat for three or four days without fusion power. Thinking about it made Jacqueline's stomach turn.

The two of them had been sitting there in near silence for almost a half an hour, and Jacqueline was relieved to see the shuttle crew approaching to take her trunk. Both women stood to get out of the way. As the crewmen lifted the case, Jacqueline noticed how much the Space Agency decal and other markings along the aluminum surface had faded.

Colleen and Jacqueline climbed a ladder into the Axle and watched the arriving shuttle passengers slide down a guideline from where they had docked. Jacqueline couldn't help herself, and stole a glance over at her NLS, but then looked away again. The thick twisted and broken struts marred the beauty of the sphere. It made her think of a rotting potato that had been left in the dark for too long to grow eyes.

It was their turn to follow the same guideline up to where they would board the shuttle. As they passed through the hatch, the shuttle commander, an older man with sharp eyes and a thin frame, looked at Jacqueline and smiled.

"I saw them load your trunk," he said. "You know, I flew you to the Nest from the SPISE summit station years ago. It was one of my first trips. Gosh, you haven't changed a day since then. It seems so long ago now."

Jacqueline couldn't think how to respond. After a few seconds Colleen answered in Jacqueline's place. "Thank you, Commander," she said softly. He tipped his head one last time and withdrew, giving the women their privacy.

There were virtual windows on the ceiling over the seats of the shuttle, and more and more of the Nest came into Jacqueline's view as their vessel fell back away from the station. Within a minute or two, the view rotated and Jacqueline saw Earth. It was small, and only about half of it was brightly lit by the sun. The other half was black, but between the lines of city lights along the west coast of North America and the hole that it left in the stars, her mind could fill in the circle.

Jacqueline felt a short backward thrust as the shuttle commander shed speed to let them start falling toward the geostationary orbit that held the space elevators' summit stations. For most of the final hour of the trip, Jacqueline could see their destination through the same windows. The SPISE summit station swept with the rotation of the earth from west to east, and soon another thrust would match its speed and end the shuttle's fall between orbits.

****

Once strapped into the bulky recliner chair in their cabin on the climber, Jacqueline looked out the narrow virtual window that extended from floor to ceiling on the outer wall. She was able to see the Nest retreating slowly behind them in its high orbit, and tears began rolling down her cheeks.

Colleen turned to look at her, but she didn't say anything.

"They should have let me die," whispered Jacqueline, wiping the moisture from her lips. "Why didn't they just let me die? Why did they…" she couldn't finish the sentence.

"I don't think that they realized, sweetie. They thought that they would be able to start the reactors back up again if one failed. It's not your fault."

"I have killed everyone who I have ever loved, and you're probably next. You should stay away from me."

Colleen was shaking her head. Her eyes were low. Quietly, almost to herself, she said, "I'm the last person you should be worried about. I should have called them home years ago."

"What do you mean?" asked Jacqueline.

Colleen just shook her head and looked out the window.

A few minutes later, she said, "Jacqueline, I've been thinking. You're not obligated, but some people say that getting back to work and keeping busy is helpful after a loss. If you want to, you could take over something on campus, like the NLS training program. You're the best pilot that we've ever had."

Jacqueline's stomach twisted in knots. The idea of stepping back into NLS training, where Liam had been just an idea, just a fantasy made her want to curl up into a ball and weep.

"Or whatever, it doesn't have to be that," Colleen said quickly. She must have seen Jacqueline's reaction on her face.

"You could help out in PR."

Jacqueline narrowed her eyes.

"Do you know Katherine Othoni?" asked Colleen. "She's like the head lobbyist-slash-lawyer in the Space Agency. She's been crafting a press release about what you and the other pilots accomplished during the mission. You could help her, and we could even turn it into your official statement."

There was something about the idea that seemed wrong, but she couldn't put her finger on it. The two of them looked at each other for a few seconds.

"The accident has put us in the spotlight, and you've become something of a celebrity down on the surface."

Jacqueline closed her eyes. She could feel the muscles in her jaw clench and she pursed her lips. She tried to tell herself that it wasn't Colleen's fault that Liam had died, that Colleen hadn't forced his hand, but on some level, she couldn't fight it. She did blame Colleen that everyone was gone, but she didn't know why, really.

Part of her even blamed Colleen for changing so much. *She is so old...*

There was her characteristic shock of pink hair, but Colleen was now in her 60s and it showed in how she moved and in the wrinkles around her eyes and mouth.

It was against nature. Young people are supposed to catch up to their older siblings and family. The distance of age was supposed to shrink the longer you knew somebody. NLS travel had taken even that normalcy from them. The whole world had aged and the people around her were dying as Jacqueline stayed frozen at 22 years old.

"I don't want to talk to the press," said Jacqueline finally. "I've seen the news in the US. They always ask the same thing: How does it feel? How does it feel to have missed 24 years on earth? How does it feel to be a time traveler? How does it feel to look 22 years old when you're really … whatever. How does it feel to be responsible for the deaths of everyone you ever knew?!" Jacqueline started to cry again.

She tried to look Colleen in the eye, but she was out of focus and her own voice sounded like she was drowning. "I feel like I'm 22 and like he's 30. I feel like you're supposed to be in your 30s too. I feel like I was recruited four years ago. I don't want to be 40 years old! I feel young and I need for that to matter. All that I want is for people to see me the way that I see myself."

Colleen closed her eyes for a moment, then said, "Shit, sorry honey. You're right. It was a crap idea. I'll tell Katherine to forget it. You don't have to think about anything. Let's just look out the window."

Jacqueline looked at Colleen for a moment. The scientist's eyes were strained at the edges, and her jaw quivered a little bit as she took an uneven breath. Closing her eyes, Jacqueline took a few deep breaths of her own then drifted off to sleep.

When Jacqueline woke up, Colleen wasn't in her chair, but there was a noise behind her and she turned to see Colleen floating in zero-g near the cabin door. Jacqueline had a brief urge to smile at her, to welcome her back, but then she remembered what she had been feeling right before she fell asleep. Turning forward to face the virtual window, she thought about the billions of people down on that blue ball.

Colleen settled quietly into the chair next to her and buckled her restraints. She still hadn't spoken.

"Colleen?" said Jacqueline after a minute.

"Yeah, sweetie? What's up?"

"I just wanted to say… I'm really glad that you're here. I don't think that I would have been able to face coming down to the surface without you."

****

Major General Alesandro Crespin was standing behind his desk, placing items in a cardboard box when Jacqueline knocked on the frame of the open door. His office was in a half empty state with books stacked in piles and opened boxes on every surface.

The sun was shining brightly through the window behind him. Jacqueline had been on solid ground for almost two weeks, but she was still a bit sensitive to bright sunlight. The doctors had given her sunglasses, but wearing them indoors seemed disrespectful to her.

"Captain, please come in." he said to her.

Jacqueline hadn't gotten used to the new title yet, and it still took her a moment to realize that people were speaking to her when they addressed her by her rank.

"Thank you for coming. I wanted a word with you before I left." he said with a gesture to his packing.

Crespin paused for another moment and looked at her. She felt her face getting hot. Was he waiting for her to say something? "Sir, I heard that you were leaving us. I don't think that I can technically vote, but it would be an honor to have you represent me in the US Senate."

"Nonsense, I'm counting on your vote. From what I understand the paperwork for your citizenship went through years ago. The same was true for several members of your squad."

He went back to putting personal items into the box that was on his desk. "On that score, Captain, I know that the loss of one's comrades is very hard to deal with. I'm sure that it's taking its toll on you."

"Yes, sir. It has been difficult."

"The fact that anyone at all survived Dr. Pastor's suicide mission is a miracle. Now this Kaiser is different, and his plan for finishing what you all have started seems sound to me. He's promised me to transition Crossbow to unmanned vessels in the second generation, but he is going to need pilots for the first generation of ships, so I hope that you'll give the Crossbow mission serious consideration."

"Crossbow mission sir?"

Crespin paused what he was doing and looked up at her quizzically. "I had assumed that the Director would have briefed you. Was I mistaken?"

"I'm sorry sir, but I am not briefed on the Crossbow mission."

Crespin was shaking his head. "If any good comes of all of this, it will be that this woman will finally be exposed for what she is, and when it happens, the Agency is going to be significantly better off. Do me a favor, Captain, just go straight to Dr. Kaiser. He's a civilian, a scientist. The Crossbow mission was his idea, and it is the most promising plan that I've heard for mitigating the asteroid threat. If we had had him 30 years ago, this whole thing would be over by now."

"Yes sir. And this new mission needs pilots?" asked Jacqueline.

"Yes, and there is a g-force requirement as well. You might represent the fastest way to get that program unblocked."

"Thank you, sir. I'll look into it. It has been an honor to serve under you, sir."

Crespin finally stopped packing and really looked at Jacqueline. "The honor was mine, Captain." Then he added, shaking his head again. "I'll be darned if you don't look exactly the same as you did on your first day of training. I am no fan of Dr. Pastor, but she did manage to see the potential in recruits like you, I'll give her that."

Jacqueline was speechless. She offered a curt nod and waited to be sure that she was dismissed. Military protocols still felt artificial to her. When Crespin went back to silently packing his box, she decided that was cue enough. She turned and left his office.

****

Jacqueline had started out toward Colleen's office, but the idea of another tiring and frustrating discussion was enough to make her head outside for a quiet walk around campus.

Ultimately, Jacqueline found herself back in her own office and looking up any reference she could find on the Crossbow mission and on who this Dr. Kaiser was. She located a description in the internal technical briefings that matched what Crespin had told her. The mission was to consist of an analysis team, some new spacecraft, and an operations team.

The analysis team took the best galactic halo data that the Ghost-Map Mission had been able to collect, and there were new probe designs to survey the asteroids and comets that were too small to detect from Earth. Together, they would be able to predict the greatest risks for when and where Ghosts would interact with objects in the solar system. From there, the team would maintain a list of targets, that is to say comets and asteroids in the solar system that might have their orbits disturbed, as had happened to Sphinx-896.

The operations team for the first-generation ships would be made up of pilots like Jacqueline who would fly missions to deploy the new probes and to work down the list of targets, eliminating the threat from comets and asteroids that were on collision courses with invisible masses in the galactic halo. The details of the probes, vehicles, and techniques of the operations team were classified and need-to-know, so at the moment, Jacqueline didn't have access.

In spite of that, the information that she did have appealed to Jacqueline more than any idea that she'd heard since she had landed. Finally there was something that would give her a purpose. If she could contribute to a mission that took action on the data that her friends had died to obtain, she could finish what they started. It felt right. She needed to find Dr. Kaiser and see if Crespin was right about her suitability for the program.

The other point that the Major General had made was still nagging at her. Why hadn't Colleen mentioned this? Of all of the stupid things that they had talked about during three and a half days of SPISE descent, why not mention the one mission that would honor those whom she had lost?

Jacqueline paced in her office for a few minutes, deciding what to do next. She looked at the clock. It was already 6pm, but she couldn't imagine waiting until morning to find out more. Maybe she could find Dr. Kaiser immediately to see if he could give her access to the other files. She probably had the right clearance level, it was just a matter of getting read into the program. She went back to his profile page which had his video dial number and a highlighted office location on a campus map. It was in a section of the civilian wing.

Jacqueline grabbed a tablet for taking notes, transferred the high-level mission description onto it, then walked over to the civilian wing to locate Dr. Kaiser's office.

The office itself was what she would have expected for a Space Agency mission architect. The desk was large with several ultra-resolution viewing surfaces and she could see the lights on the training field through the wide windows behind it. The sun had just set over the narrow patch of woods that led to the G-loop. Large book shelves filled the wall furthest from the door, and there was a long couch than ran along the wall opposite the windows.

Dr. Kaiser himself was nothing like what Jacqueline was expecting from a Space Agency mission architect. He was about her age and he had thick black hair and a large frame. It was clear that he was a civilian, but his arms showed lean muscle just under the surface of his olive skin.

Jacqueline was about to knock when she noticed that he had already seen her. The glossy coating from the viewing surface on his desk was highly reflective, and they made eye contact in the reflection as the display dimmed to black. It felt strange, as if she had been caught staring.

"Uh, excuse me, Dr. Kaiser?" she asked.

He turned to face her. "Yes, but, please just call me Edward. What can I do for you… uh Captain is it?" he was squinting to see the insignia on Jacqueline's left breast pocket in order to determine her rank.

"Yes, sir." She lifted the tablet slightly so that he could see it. "I have been reading about the Crossbow mission. Major General Crespin recommended that I do so. I'm a pilot and I would like to learn more about the operational team in case my background is a fit."

Dr. Kaiser's chin dropped down, and he hunched his shoulders forward a bit. "Oh, I see," he said. "I have to confess, recruiting has been a sticking point. This mission isn't for everyone, and there are several complicating factors that we should discuss before we go to the trouble of granting you access to the detailed specs."

Jacqueline nodded. "I see. Could I ask if you're free to discuss it now?"

He hesitated, then said. "I was just about to head over to the commissary for some dinner. If it's not too unconventional, we could discuss it there. I can give you the high level sketch, and if you're still interested, we can take the other steps to check your clearance and read you into the program to gain access to the details."

Jacqueline tilted her head, wrinkling up her brow. "Oh, I don't mean to keep you though. We could meet tomorrow."

Edward smiled. "Keep me? From what? The only people who would ever wonder where I am are walking these halls, and most of them stay up later than I do." He stood up and grabbed a tablet of his own from his desk. "I've got some animations here if we need them."

As he walked around toward her, she took a step back into the hallway. There was something nagging at her that she couldn't place. Maybe it was how different this scientist was from Colleen.

Dr. Kaiser wasted no time in jumping in to describe the Crossbow mission. He began by talking about how the GhostMap mission had collected data using gravitational probes. He even described the NLS flights that left from and returned to the Nest and he went into great detail about how landing on the Nest was complicated given its orbit around the Earth and Earth's orbit around the sun. It almost made Jacqueline laugh to hear the mission described from his terrestrial point of view. When they got to the commissary, they split up to fill their trays.

Jacqueline was still reacclimating herself to the cafeteria on the Space Agency campus. It was a cross between an air force chow hall and a posh Silicon Valley cafe. She picked up an aluminum tray and scooped some rice into one of its separated sections. Leaning over the counter, she inspected the meat to see if she wanted to try it. She picked out one or two small pieces, then walked over to pour herself a glass of water. Just as Jacqueline was placing her tray on the rails in front of the water glasses, someone let a loud blast of steam escape from the gleaming espresso machine. It made her jump and bang her tray against the counter with a clatter, but no one seemed to notice.

She caught Dr. Kaiser's eye on her way toward the seating area, and they rejoined each other, sitting on opposite sides of a long table. "So the idea is simple," he continued. "We have all of this beautiful data from the GhostMap Observatory, but so what? If we don't figure out how it could hurt us, then it's useless. So we take all of the orbits of stuff that we know in the solar system, augment it with the small stuff that we're not tracking yet, and intersect all of that with any Ghosts that might fly by."

As he spoke, his volume grew louder and he was gesturing with his hands. Jacqueline could tell that the subject excited him. She wasn't the only one to notice. There was an older man, another civilian, staring at them over the top rim of his glasses from a few tables over. He looked slightly annoyed.

"Even still, so what, right? So we know that our solar system is going to fly past some Galactic Halo Substructure and it's going to screw up orbits. That's where the operational team would come in. I would have preferred moving straight into the unmanned phase, but as it stands, we need pilots to launch the probes and to carry out multiple mechanical functions on the ship so that we can get started dropping the first wave of at-risk asteroids into the sun. That will buy us the time that we need to do a full unmanned design for the second generation ships."

He was smiling at her, waiting for a reaction.

"What do you mean by 'drop'?" she asked.

Edward gave an excited nod. He had just taken a bite, but that didn't stop him from answering, "Yeah, that's the important part. We throw heavy stuff at the asteroid to knock it out of orbit. After that, it falls into the sun. The Crossbow vessel is a coilgun capable of firing a special cable called a Helix with both distance and accuracy. The coilgun doesn't have perfect aim, but it's really good, and the Helix has just enough self-guidance to correct for errors in targeting. I can give more detail if you sign on to the program. Some of the tech was developed for military use and it's still classified."

She decided to ask the obvious question. "So this sounds very exciting. What are the complicating factors that you mentioned? Why isn't this mission for everyone, as you say?"

Jacqueline felt as if she saw the scientist deflate in front of her eyes. "Two reasons: g-force and solitude. The railgun has a killer recoil. To fire projectiles that far and that fast, it needs to apply a force equivalent to 150,000 tonnes, and in space that makes the whole vessel recoil violently. We've come up with a design to cut that down by a factor of 40 in the pilot's cabin, but it still calls for a pilot that can withstand 98g for several seconds. Also, the missions are long. A single sortie might last for six months."

Jacqueline laughed slightly.

Edward blushed and twisted up his mouth. "I know. The design is irresponsible, and it asks too much of the pilots. I would like to re-design the Crossbow vessel, but our first design needs to be able to launch three delicate probes then be re-fitted during flight to fire heavy projectiles. There are far too many things that could go wrong during that refitting to try to automate it all. The ship also has to operate in a region with a twenty-minute signals delay from Earth, so that just adds to the complexity. I'm sorry if you feel that I've wasted your time."

"Oh, no, it's not that. I was just surprised by how serious you sounded when you said 'several seconds'. I think that I left out an important detail. I was an NLS pilot."

Edward turned ashen. "Oh, my god. I'm ... I'm sorry. I didn't. I mean. Now that I see your name... I realize, but it just didn't occur to me that you were the same... Captain, I really am sorry for what you've been through. I can't imagine what it's like to suffer so many casualties on a mission."

Jacqueline's smile vanished, along with the mild amusement she had been feeling moments earlier. She looked away for a minute, hoping that he couldn't tell that she was fighting back tears.

"No, it's OK." she said finally. "I just meant that the demands of this mission seem on par with what I've done before. I think that I would like to take the next steps to obtain that additional information that you mentioned. I'd like to apply."

Edward knitted his brow and tilted his head down towards her. "But, these are solo missions, and you're a Captain. It's months of isolation for a single sortie. Given who you are, I would assume that you would have your choice of assignments, with a crew of your own."

Jacqueline shook her head slowly. "Edward, you've been honest with me. Let me be honest with you. It's not the right time for me to try to lead a crew. The NLS missions were solo flights, and the people that I did know, the people that I cared for, are gone. The one bright spot, the one ray of hope that I have felt in weeks is this mission, your mission. If there is even a chance that I can make their sacrifice worth something, then I have to take it. I want this. I don't mind the solitude or the g-force. I have withstood worse."

Edward held Jacqueline's gaze intently for a few moments, then he extended his hand, and Jacqueline shook it.

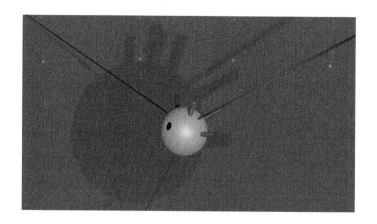

Act-III

Reckoning

The Ghost of Sphinx

32 - Struggle - Jan 2144 - Houston, Texas

Edward

"Hey, slugger. We need you in Katherine's office."

Edward looked up from his work to see Colleen standing in his door. "Katherine's office?" he asked.

"Yeah, the shit just hit the fan in DC," answered Colleen, "and we need to respond. You're going to be out in front on this one."

"Wait, what does that mean, out in front?"

"Just follow me. I'll explain when we get there."

Edward stood and picked up a few items that he wanted for the meeting. Colleen had already started walking, so he had to jog a few steps to catch up to her.

"Colleen, what's going on?" he asked.

Instead of answering, she grabbed his arm and turned it so that the tablet in his hand was face up. Then, with her other hand, she touched her glasses and text appeared on Edward's tablet.

> "The Committee has a responsibility to ensure that the tragic accident, and those events that led up to it, are understood and assimilated into all levels and activities of the Space Agency so that safe manned space flight can be resumed."

"What's this?" he asked.

"We're grounded, pending the outcome of an Investigative Congressional Committee. It looks like you got Crossbow deployed just in time.

****

Edward had never been in Katherine Othoni's office before. It was larger than Colleen's and had traditional dark wood furniture, as if the Space Agency's lead counsel had transplanted a white shoe legal office into the high tech center. Katherine was standing behind her desk, apparently waiting for them.

As they entered, Edward was greeted by a deep voice beside him. "Dr. Kaiser, welcome." It was Major General Crespin. He stood and took a few steps toward Edward to shake his hand. The Major General was smiling broadly in a way that Edward hadn't seen before.

"Hello, General," he said. "I'm surprised to see you here."

"Please take a seat, Dr. Kaiser," said Katherine. "We have a lot of ground to cover today."

From experience, Edward knew that the best spot for him would be between Colleen and Crespin. All four of them sat down and Katherine continued.

"Congress has passed a bill to form an Investigative Commission to be led by a retired member of the transportation safety board, Delphine Temple. Their charter will be to investigate the Outpost disaster. We have agreed to ground all planned launches in order to prepare for the investigation. Congress now has 30 days to appoint committee members. Given his experience with the GhostMap program and his current free-agent status, I have asked the Major General to volunteer for the Committee."

Edward turned to look at Crespin, who bowed his head towards Katherine. "It would be an honor."

"Yeah, and it'll get your name in the papers too," said Colleen. "That's got to be good for your senate run."

Crespin leaned forward to look around Edward at Colleen, but Katherine raised her hand before he could say anything. Crespin looked up at her, then leaned back in his chair again without speaking.

"I have also asked Colleen to recuse herself from leading the internal investigation," continued Katherine. "That means that we need someone to step in as Acting Director for the next few months. Colleen has chosen you, Dr. Kaiser, for this role. Is that acceptable to you?"

Edward felt hot all of the sudden. He had never considered filling any non-technical role in the Agency, and he certainly wasn't interested in dealing with Congress. "Um, if I could ask, why me?"

"Who else can I choose?" answered Colleen. "Face it, kid, you're the only reasonable option unless I pick somebody from outside, and I don't think that anyone wants that."

Katherine started consulting her notes again. "Dr. Kaiser, it's important that you be ready, willing, and able to carry out this role. Let me just recap the full scope of what we're dealing with here."

"We have received warnings from nearly all of our industry and academic partners in the GhostMap program that they could withdraw from the collaboration if this gets out of hand. Some are even threatening to take legal action to recover what they invested in the Observatory if the scientific value of GhostMap were called into question. By the way, I get those calls directly, since I helped recruit those partners years ago. They are by far the least enjoyable part of my day."

"If we lose the support and funding of our Observatory partners, we will have to decommission the Nest and bring everyone down. According to Doctor Pastor, if our partners pull out, we won't even have sufficient mission funding to disassemble the Nest safely."

"Obviously without the Nest, we would be forced to cancel the unmanned NLS mission, and if I am not mistaken, the Crossbow mission would suffer as well. The situation is dire."

Katherine was on a roll. "Now, to wrap it up, families of the deceased NLS pilots and the deceased crew of the Outpost are considering taking part in a class-action lawsuit against the Agency for the wrongful death of their loved ones."

She looked up at him. "So, Doctor, I can't emphasize enough. Do not accept the position if you are not ready to deal with this crisis."

During the time that it took Katherine to outline the situation, Edward's posture shifted from upright and attentive to slouched forward with his hands on his knees. His mouth had fallen open and he was looking at Katherine through glassy eyes. So much so, that when she stopped, he didn't react right away.

Slowly turning to Colleen, he said, "Colleen, I'm really not sure that I can do this. I want to help, but this is completely outside of my experience."

"Listen, I hear you, but I know that this is something that you can handle with a little bit of support," she said. "I'm not going to disappear, I'm just not going to be in charge. I'll help you."

Edward was still shaking his head slightly. "I… uh"

"Listen, don't answer right now," she pressed. "Go take a walk or something and think about it. The missions that stand to lose the most are both yours, and Jacqueline is deployed. We owe it to everyone to put the best people on this."

Edward nodded, slowly, and turned to look at Katherine, who leaned back in her chair and folded her arms.

"Can I take a few hours to think and get back to you in the morning?" Edward asked.

"Yes, Doctor, please do," she replied

Edward stood and the others followed suit. As he turned to leave the office, Crespin put his hand out and grabbed Edward's shoulder. "I hope that you accept, son. I have often thought that you'd make a good Director."

Edwards' eyes followed Crespin's arm from his shoulder up to the Major General's face.

"Thank you, sir," was all that he could manage.

****

Edward felt like the walls were closing in on him. He brought his things back to his office, but all he could think about was getting as far away from campus as possible. He headed for the front door, and the second he stepped outside, he could feel that it was the right decision.

There were cars lined up in front of campus, and Edward got into one and directed it to take him to downtown Houston. When he saw the green of Hermann Park, he signaled that he wanted to get out. It was a pleasant January afternoon, warm but definitely not hot. The car dropped him off near McGovern Lake.

There were ducks swimming in small groups, and a fountain at the center of the lake shot water high into the air. Edward meandered around the water's edge then turned right to walk past the 10 meter obelisk and along the side of the reflecting pool that led towards the planetarium. A family passed by him, headed in the other direction towards the Zoo. His feet slowed, and he just let his eyes follow them.

Throughout the park, families and young couples strolled, enjoying the sun, the blue sky, and the green of the trees. Everything that surrounded him represented things that the crew of the Outpost had given up: sun, air, green, family, children. They would never have any of it.

I wonder how many of them knew that they wouldn't be coming back.

His whole life, Edward had been afraid of making mistakes that could hurt people. It wasn't always rational, but the feeling had colored every decision he had ever made. It drove him to be as certain as he could be in his research. He wrapped himself in control and certainty like a blanket, but they were asking him to give that up. Whatever mistakes that led to the reactor failure on the Outpost had been far more devastating that anything Edward had ever tried to consider. His hands were trembling just thinking about it.

He took one last look back where he had come from, and he noticed the flag. Past the obelisk, past the fountain in the middle of the lake, there was an American flag flying at half-mast. Was it for them, for the NLS pilots and the crew of the Outpost? He squeezed his eyes shut for a moment to clear his vision, then turned away.

So am I just a coward?

Colleen said that she would help, but he would still be answering for all of it. Edward wasn't sure that he could function in the face of so many lives lost. So much potential squandered.

He kept his eyes low and walked towards the Houston monument. Colleen had said that she could find someone external. Would that be so bad? What difference would it even make?

If they put a politician in charge, they would just make excuses for the events leading up to the Outpost going dark and for the losses that they had experienced. Planning a mission was supposed to be about controlling the future and about avoiding surprises. If you could plan for everything that might happen, if you could foresee all possible problems, and put contingencies in place, then you could win.

There was no way to win this. All of the battles were already lost, but at least they should try to learn from the mistakes, mistakes that should have never been made. They were going to spend months looking at avoidable mistakes that had led to real deaths. It made his stomach turn to imagine it.

He turned right and headed past the planetarium. Soon he was in the McGovern Gardens. He had meant to walk up the spiral walkway to the viewing area, but he was lost in thought and took a wrong turn. When his eyes came into focus, he saw that the path in front of him had ended. He would have to double back to walk a different way. As he turned though, Edward saw a bronze statue of Dr. Martin Luther King Jr. At the bottom, it said:

> "...because any time is the right time to do the right thing."

He read it again. There was a nagging thought in his mind.

These were Jacqueline's colleagues. If you don't even try to explain how they died, you dishonor them.

He closed his eyes. If you ignore her pain, you dishonor her too.

Edward pulled out a set of AR glasses and slipped them on. He looked back at the statue, and bubbles with other Martin Luther King quotes filled his view. There was a theme to all of these famous words, and as he read each quote, the question in his mind grew louder. Even now, in his late twenties, he couldn't think of a single time that he had ever been truly courageous. He had always let his fears dominate his actions.

> "Human progress is neither automatic nor inevitable... Every step toward the goal of justice requires sacrifice, suffering, and struggle; the tireless exertions and passionate concern of dedicated individuals."

If the Crossbow mission were cancelled, then they would have died for nothing. These people who had lived in captivity for decades, had done so with the belief that it would make a difference. The only way to honor them was to carry on with their struggle, to keep trying and to succeed at the work that they had made possible.

Even if you fail, the only thing on the line is your career. They gave you their lives, and if we lose Crossbow, millions more could die.

Edward stood a little straighter. He turned and started his walk back, back past the reflecting pool, back towards the zoo. He passed more families, and he thought about living for decades, a light-year from home.

Did they have anyone that they could call family?

It made his eyes sting, thinking about it.

Who are you to talk?

Edward felt a sudden urge to do something that he hadn't done in years. He found a quiet spot between the trees and put his glasses on again. When the video link stabilized he felt tears coming to his eyes. "Hi Mom. How are you?"

"I was hoping that we could make a plan to get together soon."

"Yeah, I know. I think that the last time was almost three years ago."

"Where's Dad?"

****

At a few minutes before 9pm, Edward knocked on the door of Colleen's office. She looked up at him and said, "Ah, you decided to come back. I honestly wasn't sure if I was going to see you again."

"Yeah, to be fair, I wasn't sure either," he answered.

"So what's your plan?"

"I'm still working out some details. If you don't mind, I'd rather give it to you tomorrow, fully formed. What I can tell you is that I'm in. I'll accept responsibility for the investigation."

"Just the investigation?"

"Well, not just the investigation, the current missions too. I accept responsibility for everything. I've got this."

"Hmm, do I detect a note of hubris?"

Edward looked out the window for a minute and ran his fingers through his hair. Looking back again, he said, "I hope you know that I mean it in the best possible way when I say, fuck you, Colleen."

A smile formed slowly on Colleen's face. "There it is..."

33 - Probe - Feb 2144 - Houston, Texas

Edward

No one seemed surprised to see Colleen, Katherine, or even Colonel Kett behind the podium, but Edward and Dr. Ishida were drawing stares. Edward kept a smile on his face and tilted his chin up to greet a few colleagues, but the thump of his own heart pounding in his chest seemed louder to him than the murmur of the 200 people who had gathered to hear their announcement.

The rolling tables of the canteen had been cleared away, and the chairs were rearranged to face front. They had agreed that Edward would speak first to establish himself as the host of the meeting, but he was regretting that choice now.

Holding himself very still, Edward tried to visualize the next 24 hours. He and Colleen were leaving immediately after the meeting to board a 9 hour flight from Houston to Paris. From there, they were going to split up.

Colleen would take a short flight to the south of France to work with the nuclear physicists at ITER who had designed the reactors for the Nest and the Outpost.

Edward would fly another six hours south to Abidjan in the Côte d'Ivoire. A military aircraft would take him the rest of the way to the Gulf of Guinea International Space Elevator located at the equator off the west coast of Africa. He was scheduled to take a GuISE climber up to the Nest in two days time.

When he opened his eyes again, his co-presenters were looking at him. He must have let his thoughts wander for too long. Turning to the room, he could see that most of the seats were full.

"Thank you everyone for coming," he said, but his voice cracked and he had to clear his throat before continuing. "Hehem. We've asked you all here today to announce a few organizational changes that will put us in the best possible position to respond to the investigation by the Temple Commission."

Edward paused there and turned slightly to face Colleen. She smiled at him then addressed the room. "It's good to see this group assembled," she said. "So many of you represent the next generation of scientists and engineers here. You are the new blood of an organization whose tradition stretches back to before we even knew how to leave the surface of the planet. The time has come for me to hand over the reins to all of you. During the next few months, Dr. Kaiser here will take over as Acting Director of the Space Agency to lead us through the congressional investigation."

Just as they had rehearsed, Colleen stepped back to let Edward continue. "We need this investigation," he said. "We owe it to the NLS pilots who will never return to the Nest and to the crew of the Outpost who bore the burden of so many years in space. They sacrificed their chances at family and home so that future generations might hold out hope for both."

As Edward looked around the room, he saw what must have been a hundred heads nodding. "I'd like to take the next few minutes and tell you what we plan to do about it."

Edward gestured with his left hand. "Dr. Ishida here to my left will be taking over direct technical oversight of the Crossbow and unmanned NLS missions. He will oversee their temporary ramp down in order to pivot to an extended safety audit. New launches are likely to be grounded in order to ensure that we can proceed with every confidence when we start back up."

Gesturing the other way, he said, "After decades of distinguished service as commander of the Nest, Colonel Kett has been selected as the military head of Space Agency operations, filling the post that had been occupied previously by Major General Crespin."

"Dr. Pastor and I leave today to jump start technical investigations into the root causes of the Outpost's power failure. Dr. Pastor will be recruiting academic help in understanding what was happening inside our fusion reactors, and I will travel up on the Nest station to carry out failure exercises that will recreate the conditions of the Outpost's final hours. Explaining the chain of events that led up to the fall of the Outpost is both a moral and a technical imperative for this Agency."

Edward hadn't expected the applause, but when it came he stopped talking and waited. This message was overdue. He knew it. These people had suffered a loss, and they wanted answers just as much as anyone in Congress or in the general public.

"Let's turn now to the Temple Commission. I hope that you will all give it your full cooperation. Investigative Commissions like these are common in the wake of an accident, and they are for all of our benefit. Major General Crespin will be joining the Commission in Washington to serve both as mission liaison and a crucial investigator to help us prevent anything like this from happening in the future."

Edward paused again and looked at his co-presenters. They all nodded, but no one offered to add anything. He turned back to face the room and said, "Thank you all for coming today. It is an honor to work beside all of you. Let's open the floor to questions."

No one moved for a few seconds, but then one of the engineers raised his hand. "Why is General Crespin eligible to sit on the investigative committee when he was part of the original mission planning and recruitment?"

Edward turned to Katherine. "Ms. Othoni, do you want to take this one?"

Katherine stood up and faced the engineer. "He's definitely eligible," she said. "This isn't a trial. Congress investigates issues like these in order to better oversee federal programs and to write new legislation helping them do that. There are good reasons for the Major General to contribute his expertise. He will be able to speak openly about his involvement in the program, and regardless of his seat on the committee, he might still be called to testify. Given that he had been a vocal critic of aspects of the program in the early years, the committee will both welcome and value his perspective. With his history and influence in the missions, we think that the public will see him as a crucial participant in finding the truth."

Another hand went up. This time it was one of the enlisted airmen. Edward pointed at him.

"Yes, how long will we be grounding launches of new missions, and what does that mean for missions that are currently flying?"

Edward turned towards Colonel Kett this time. "Colonel?" he said.

"Until we have the full backing of Washington, our top mission is to find and fix problems," explained Colonel Kett. "This will last for several months, if not a year. Missions in flight, such as Crossbow-1 are vital to our defense, and must carry out their most urgent mission objectives, but even Crossbow will curtail lower priority mission objectives in order to hasten everyone's safe return to Earth."

The Q&A continued for another 25 minutes, and with each question, Edward felt more and more confident that the people in that room wanted the same answers that he did.

The overnight flight from Houston to Paris represented Edward's last chance to try to understand what Colleen was looking for in the reactors. They had meant to use the time to get their plan straight for the coming weeks, but the logistics of having a productive work conversation were proving difficult.

They were both wearing AR glasses so that they could share the same view of the technical specs of the Outpost's reactors, but the 3D projection extended through the row of seats ahead of them and gave the illusion of more space around them than actually existed. More than once, one of them tried to point to a part of the system only to end up thumping their hand up against the back of the seat in front of them. In one instance Edward accidentally ran his hand right between two seats and had the unsettling feeling of having his fingers brush up against warm skin. He pulled his hand back as quickly as he could and apologized.

Within an hour, most passengers were trying to sleep, and the flight attendant had asked Edward and Colleen to quiet down.

"Let's just stop, Colleen," said Edward. "I'm AstroAero and a data jockey. I'm no more qualified to debug a fusion reactor than the guy whose face I just palmed."

Colleen closed the models with a swipe of her hand. "OK, we can go through this again with Captain Torres and Chief Yukimoto once you're on the Nest," she said. "I've been in touch with one of the physicists who worked on the original design, and he confirmed that the simulation models of the Outpost reactors can still run on modern computers. My first priority, when I get to ITER, will be to get them to build a more complex simulation with eight reactors combined in the same configuration as on the space stations."

"I thought that each reactor was a closed system. What does simulating them buy you?"

"The way that they were wired together might have made them less independent, but we won't know until we investigate," answered Colleen. "Once you're on the Nest, you'll have access to all of the log data from the Outpost. If we can get a simulation to match that log data, then it'll be like seeing inside the Outpost's reactors in real time."

Edward woke to his alarm at 4am in Abidjan, Côte d'Ivoire. He needed to get from his seaside hotel in the plateau district to the Gendarmerie Camp Agban before dawn. His flight from Paris had touched down at 6pm the day before after almost 36 hours of travel, so Edward had gone straight to bed, hoping to get as much sleep as possible before the next leg of his journey.

The Gendarmerie camp was alive with action when he arrived, in spite of the predawn hour. There were several people running on the exercise track and others going about their business as normally as they would have done in the middle of the day. Edward and 15 or so other GuISE passengers were instructed to wait together at the edge of a grassy field at the center of the camp.

The first light of dawn was becoming visible over the horizon as their aircraft approached fast from the east. It slowed to a stop over the field with its enormous rotors pivoted upward on the wings for a vertical landing. Light shining up from the horizon glinted off of the craft's flat underbelly as it descended. In the relative darkness, the fuselage of the aircraft was nearly invisible, but at the tips of each of the elongated rotors there must have been small lights, because two glowing circles floated in the air over the craft like a dual halo. The effect looked almost alien, and Edward could have imagined believing that he had seen a UFO.

At 500 km/h, they reached the GuISE platform in an hour and a half. By 7am Edward was entering his cabin on the GuISE climber. He set up his terminal and got to work. His first order of business would be to check on the status of the Comber probes.

It had been almost two weeks since Crossbow-1 had launched the probes into their backwards orbits aligned with the three dense rings of the main belt. Crossbow's Helix munitions were designed to launch at a muzzle velocity of 180 km/s, but the goals for the probes were more modest. They needed an orbital velocity of 19 km/s to stay aloft at three AU, but to get it they would have to be shot backwards at roughly twice that speed to overcome the forward velocity of the Crossbow vessel itself.

After so much administrative work in the past few weeks, Edward eagerly dug into the telemetry data from each of the Comber probes. Their respective launches and reconfiguration into reconnaissance mode had gone according to spec, and each was already sending back a catalogue of previously unknown asteroids.

It was a thrill to see things going so well with Crossbow, but regardless it was time to curtail the mission objectives and recall Captain Binti Abdullah. In spite of his technical aspirations, he was almost relieved to have a reason to shorten her deployment. Six months was too long to stay isolated so far from home.

He composed the first message and sent it to Houston to be re-layed.

> "Captain, we need you to update your mission plan. The Space Agency requires your participation with the investigation into the Outpost disaster. We need you to proceed to the immediate deployment of your Helices against the existing high-priority targets only, then return to base. Thank you."

After proofreading it and sending it off, he got to work looking at what the detailed Comber telemetry had revealed. It looked promising. As expected, the outer belt was dominated by C-type asteroids that were very dark and hard to see from Earth. The M-type and S-type asteroids of the middle and inner belt were at least twice as reflective.

None of these newly discovered asteroids were on a collision course with GHoSts, and the only asteroids that would remain within the "urgent" category after an abbreviated Crossbow sortie were still more than 8 years away from any negative interaction with the galactic halo.

It was approaching noontime, but Edward's body clock hadn't quite shifted to his current time zone, and he drifted off to sleep in his big recliner. He woke to a chime and saw that he had received a message from Houston.

> "Negative, base. Please note that Crossbow is not technically the Director's program. The mission plan requires another two weeks to reach my apex, and we risk sub-optimal firing solutions if we deploy Helices before finishing fine-grained triangulation of all targets. There is an additional risk of missed target opportunities unless we wait for sufficient Comber coverage of the reachable portion of the main belt. I respectfully request that someone else assist with the investigation so that Crossbow-1 can remain on task. Over."

Wow, that's not what I expected...

Edward knew that pilots weren't obligated to comply with instructions from scientific staff, but he had assumed that the Captain would have had enough trust in him to go along with his request. Reading between the lines, Edward wondered if she felt like he had abandoned her by handing control of the Crossbow mission over to Dr. Ishida. In retrospect, he should have sent her a message explaining that decision, and also explaining that it was only temporary.

Perhaps a softer tone would do the trick. If this didn't work, he would send Colonel Kett a message, bring her up to speed, and ask her to take over. The Colonel would be in a position to issue a direct order.

This was a side of Jacqueline that Edward hadn't seen before. He wrote a new message to Mission Control in Houston to be relayed.

> "Captain, I sincerely applaud your dedication, but we need you down here. I have grounded the Crossbow mission. The investigation requires your direct observations regarding the mental state of Captain Liam Fourtouna and the conditions on-board the Outpost Station just prior to its destruction. Please transmit your existing target opportunities, await firing solutions, and then return to base under hybrid coil propulsion."

An hour later, Edward received a brief response from Houston. "Crossbow-1 acknowledges. Preparing to deploy Helices and return to base."

He couldn't help but feel disappointed that the conversation with Captain Binti Abdullah had gone poorly. Somewhere deep down, Edward had been holding out hope that the two of them might become closer.

For now though, he had more immediate concerns. In three days, he'd be on the Nest, trying to force its reactors into the same state as the one that had claimed the lives of everyone onboard the Outpost one year earlier.

34 - Recoil - Mar 2144 -

250M km towards Neptune

Jacqueline

The survival instinct of humanity.

Jacqueline didn't really believe in astrology, but when she learned that her flight out to the asteroid belt would include a close flyby of Mars, it felt significant. Earth and Mars only aligned for a few weeks every two years. As soon as her acceleration away from the Nest was complete, Jacqueline spent much of the first month of her voyage reading about the ancient symbolism.

There was a long list of things that Mars was supposed to represent, like action, desire, competition, courage, and passion. They all seemed like words from her old life. The idea that she liked best from her reading was that Mars represented the survival instinct of humanity. That was why she was out here, and she repeated the phrase to herself often as one of her daily meditations.

The fiery orange-red planet had been the visual highlight of the journey, but even now the view was magnificent. The sky was a perfect black with brilliant points of light that Jacqueline had begun to recognize by their shape and color. With a little help from the onboard computer, she could lose herself in faraway galaxies and nebula for days on end. The blackness that surrounded her made these objects that much more brilliant. It was total, complete, and even comforting.

In another two weeks, she would reach the apex of her elliptical orbit around the sun. Like a ball thrown high in the air, her ship was naturally slowing down as it climbed to the far end of its arc. From that vantage point, Jacqueline would be able to refine the firing solutions for her urgent targets in the main asteroid belt, and she had already initiated long range scans to gather data for future missions.

The preceding weeks had been dominated by the launch of the Comber probes. Each explorer module had a mass of over two thousand kilograms, and Jacqueline had to load them manually into the chamber of the coilgun. Before launch, the probes were packed tightly into an eight meter long steel cylinder that encased and shielded the delicate vehicles. Once they were away, they shed their casing and transformed themselves into a more recognizable form factor consisting of solar-panels and a communication dish.

The launch from the Nest had made reliance on thrusters unnecessary, and one result was that her ship had been perfectly silent for weeks, like a hunter lying in wait. The only sound onboard came from an occasional sensor firing, but Jacqueline had been inching the volume lower on those as the days in total silence slipped by. Her heart beating and the air going into and out of her lungs were the loudest sounds around her. Like the blackness, the silence was complete and comforting.

Breathing deeply, Jacqueline closed her eyes and imagined herself dissolving into mist like a spirit haunting her vessel. Her mind and her biology were perfectly compatible with her host, but on some level, she knew that it was more than flight experience and g-forces that made her a good fit for this mission. There was something about the blackness and the quiet that she craved.

What was it like for them in those final days?

Jacqueline had thought about what she would have done if she had been on the Outpost when the lights went out. She would have taken Liam in a Bug and done what she was doing now. She would have shot out into space and joined the stars.

Just one more orbiting body.

Jacqueline's role in preparing for the Crossbow mission had been different than in the NLS mission. She felt a real sense of ownership for the program and its outcomes. Dr. Kaiser, Edward, had been an excellent colleague, and he always referred to her as the mission co-lead in meetings. It was inspiring, and Jacqueline felt invincible sitting atop a magazine of 21 micro-mechanical Helix projectiles, a compact fusion reactor, and a five kilometer coilgun modeled after the Stanford Linear Accelerator.

The asteroids and comets that she was tracking were small, but they were no less deadly. After more than 4 billion years of peaceful orbit, Jacqueline was going to hunt them and drive them down into the sun, but she had no choice. For humanity to survive, these majestic objects needed to die.

Her high priority target list had been finalized before leaving Earth, but in the past month or so, the sensors on Jacqueline's ship had been fine-tuning their data on the orbital paths of her targets. Since some of the Helices were going to be shot out on a multiyear parabolic arc before their eventual impacts, the calculations had to be precise, and the angles had to be perfect, but there was no rush. She could take her time. The earliest encounter between these objects and inbound GHoSts was still several years away. She would aim perfectly, and get this just right.

The living quarters of the Crossbow vessel were small, but complete. There were screens, tablets, and speakers to cater to any need. Full libraries were at Jacqueline's fingertips. For the first month or two, she took advantage of the media and novels, music and movies, but more and more Jacqueline appreciated the quiet.

The ship had four total bays outside of the long hull of the coilgun. Jacqueline's quarters took up most of one such bay. The others housed supplies, munitions, and the reactor. Each of the four bays was roughly the size of a double-decker bus, and they were positioned at the top, bottom, port and starboard around the long cylindrical hull like the feathers on an arrow. A magnetic bearingless ring held them in position without actually touching the cylindrical hull of the coilgun, and Jacqueline could move from one bay to another through arched passageways.

Looking forward over that hull, she let her eyes run along its length. A few months ago, it had seemed unnatural to her to be able to see a five kilometer line of lights extending perfectly out in front of her with no horizon, but it looked completely normal to her now. Like the silence and the blackness, the geometry of her vessel was undeviating.

"Attention Crossbow-1, this is base."

The sound of the comm was like an explosion, shattering the silence. Jacqueline was so startled that her heart thumped several loud beats before she realized where the voice was coming from and turned down the volume.

"Message from Director Space Agency. Captain, you are requested to update mission plan. Space Agency requires your participation with investigation into Outpost disaster. Proceed to immediate deployment of Helices against existing high-priority targets, repeat existing targets only, then return to base. Please acknowledge."

It took a minute for her heart to slow to its normal pace, but at the same time, thoughts were piling up in her head. It didn't make any sense. Colleen wasn't even active in the Crossbow mission. *Why is she interfering?*

Jacqueline wasn't surprised that Colleen would try to take a short-cut around procedure for her own ends, but Edward was the Mission Architect and he deserved to be treated with some respect. She wondered if Edward was even aware that Colleen was meddling in Crossbow.

Why would she even need to involve me? There are over ten billion people on Earth. What kind of problem could they have that only I can solve?

Jacqueline composed her response, "Negative, base. Please note that Crossbow is not technically the Director's program. The mission plan requires another two weeks to reach my apex, and we risk sub-optimal firing solutions if we deploy Helices before finishing fine-grained triangulation of all targets. There is an additional risk of missed target opportunities unless we wait for sufficient Comber coverage of the reachable portion of the main belt. I respectfully request that someone else assist with the investigation so that Crossbow-1 can remain on task. Over."

Her message would take more than 20 minutes to reach Earth. They would need time to compose a response, and that message would take another 20 minutes to come back to her. Jacqueline sat by the comm for the entire hour, waiting to see what the *Director* would have to say to try to make a difference. Her peaceful journey, far from home, suddenly felt turbulent.

Jacqueline folded her arms tight across her stomach and rocked forward and back as she thought about what an investigation into their past would entail. Then she thought about Edward and the thrill in his eyes whenever he talked about the Crossbow mission. She couldn't be a part of taking that from him. He didn't deserve to have it derailed by Colleen.

No. I'm staying out here. It's the best thing for all of us.

Nonetheless, a long response came back an hour later. "Attention Crossbow-1, this is base. Director Space Agency states: Captain, I applaud your dedication, but we need you down here. I have grounded Crossbow mission. Investigation requires your direct observations regarding mental state of Captain Liam Fourtouna and conditions on-board Outpost Station prior to destruction. You are instructed to transmit existing target opportunities, to await firing solutions, and to return immediately to base under hybrid coil propulsion. Please acknowledge."

Jacqueline's breathing stopped. The mention of Liam opened the floodgates and images of Christopher, Liam, Cemil, Kirin, and Andrew made her squeeze her eyes shut. She saw herself jogging along the up-curved corridors of the Outpost and sending messages with her squad in her NLS. She saw Liam sitting across the table from her, leaning in to try to make her understand. His last words to her had been spoken in kindness, but she hadn't even answered him.

In the silence, she could still hear her heart beating, and it was beating faster than it had in a long time. She looked out at the millions of bright stars in their perfect black surroundings, but they didn't look the same. The black wasn't perfect anymore. It was riddled with reflections and distortions.

She's so sarcastic... 'I applaud your dedication'

As Jacqueline started breathing again she could hear that the rhythm was all wrong. Her breath was irregular and there was a smell in the air. Was it a smell or a taste? She could barely remember the difference. It was salty.

How is this even happening? How could this be reaching me out here?

If Colleen was ready to use Liam as a tool to manipulate her, after everything that they had been through together, then it was checkmate. She would have no choice but to comply, but she took a moment to steady her voice before pushing the button on her comm.

She never wanted to make the mistake again of letting Colleen know what she was feeling. Slowly, she slid her finger over the button and pushed it. "Acknowledged. I am transmitting my priority list of targets as it stands. I will spend the next 4 hours running a full systems check, after which point I will commence firing Helices. I am requesting a fully optimized set of firing solutions to minimize reliance on thrusters for course correction."

Jacqueline began the systems check and tested all relevant mechanisms. She actuated the cluster of four bays forward and back along the hull of the five kilometer coilgun. Taking one of the arched passageways toward the starboard bay, she carefully extracted one of the 500kg Helices from its shock-resistant storage sheath and loaded it in the chamber of the coilgun. Finally, coming back into the pilot's bay, she tested the super-cooled magnetic coils and the targeting thrusters.

On cue, four hours later, she could see the flashing on her console as firing solutions began arriving from base. She had finished securing all objects in her quarters, and was ready to snap into the attachments that would connect her body armor to the skeletal structure of the bay. For firing, she would face the rear of the ship, where duplicate displays showed her the scene over the bow of the vessel.

Crossbow-1 pivoted into position for the first deployment. A green light confirmed readiness of the 500kg Helix projectile in the launch chamber. Looking out onto her beautiful black space again, she was calm. There were only eleven targets available at this stage in the mission, and seven of them were large enough to require two Helix impacts for successful mitigation. With roughly one hour per projectile to re-target, she could do four hours on, four hours off for the next two days. The combination of the recoil force from each of the 18 launches would double her acceleration towards Earth during that interval. Then it would be just thrusters for the remainder of the trip.

The pin-straight line of white lights moved slowly past one of her stars. The gentle sweep of the Crossbow's muzzle, like a hunter's rifle leading its prey, kept the coilgun perfectly aimed towards a point in space that an asteroid would pass 600 days in the future.

Jacqueline looked over her displays and narrated her firing checklist.

"EM systems ready. Capacitors fully charged and reactor at nominal power."

"Coil integrity and cooling confirmed."

"End to end resistance below one femto-ohm."

Jacqueline closed her eyes and imagined what was coming. Laws of nature dictated that the whole system remain in balance. The forward momentum of the projectile could only be created by injecting an equal and opposite rearward momentum into the ship. Neither Jacqueline nor the reactor would survive the full force of such a blast, but the four arrow-feather bays were coupled to the ship by a bearingless magnetic mounting designed to slide along the length of the five kilometer hull during firing.

A small light shone green on her controls. Targeting was complete. Jacqueline lifted a safety shield protecting a large red button and pushed it. A series of beeps marked the five-second countdown to firing, giving her time to bring her arm back down into its support. Beep, Beep, Beep, Beep, BEEEEP. Jacqueline's ship and the Helix parted ways.

The railgun was blasted back like a naval cannon recoiling. But unlike a naval cannon, the Crossbow was floating in space and was tethered to nothing. In an instant, the five kilometer hull of the ship was hurtling violently backward at 2200 m/s.

Jacqueline's survival and the stability of her reactor relied on two basic factors, the length of the hull and the magnetic drag applied by the bearingless mounting during the crucial two seconds after firing. The ratios had to be exact. Too little drag and the bays would fly off the end of the hull and into space. Too much and Jacqueline would be crushed.

As the X-shaped configuration of bays came to rest near the muzzle of the coilgun, all components of the vessel were finally traveling at the same speed. Emptied of its precision-targeted projectile, the Crossbow could safely fire up its thrusters and reset all four arrow-feather bays to the aft of the ship without disturbing carefully calculated targeting angles.

Once launched, the Helices would fly in their coiled position for days or even months as they silently arced towards their prey. Each Helix would uncoil to a 1km linear cord hours before contact. This provided a soft impact with 100% of the kinetic energy used to divert the asteroid without causing it to break apart.

The survival instinct of humanity...

Jacqueline wondered if it was time to rethink her own survival instincts, the ones that always seemed to lead her far away from Earth.

She shook her head and looked out onto the blurry and sparkling panorama of black and white. Memories of action and desire, courage and passion were calling her home for a final reckoning.

It'll be OK. I have two and a half months to harden myself. I can be ready.

Kappler

Edward

Edward hadn't slept much. The half gravity in his quarters was sufficient to keep his space sickness at bay, but only if he lay very still.

The trip up on GUISE began with his tense exchange of messages with Jacqueline, then took a turn for the worse when the climber passed fifteen thousand kilometers of altitude. Edward started feeling nauseous, and he spent the following two days vomiting four or five times per hour until he reached the Nest.

As soon as he arrived, they rushed him to medical and kept him there for 24 hours to treat him for dehydration. Edward's first meeting with Captain Luciana Torres was a bedside visit, and he could still picture her standing over him, next to the chrome pole that held his IV, as he lay there receiving fluids.

A chime sounded on the desk in his quarters. It was probably Colleen calling.

Working up his courage, he sat up slowly, then held still to give his head time to stop spinning. With one hand, he pulled off his blankets, then slid his legs to the edge of the bed. Finally, he pushed himself forward, put his feet on the floor, and waited again for a few seconds.

OK, not too bad.

Slowly, Edward got to his feet and took a few steps over to the desk. He sat down and put on his glasses to answer the call.

"Oh, good, you're there," said Colleen, when the video connected. "I was just about to give up."

"Yeah, sorry, it took me a second to find my glasses. I'm glad that you called though, I have a few things that I'd like to discuss with you. Did you get all of the data that you needed from Chief Yukimoto?"

"Mostly," said Colleen. "He sent me the logs from the Outpost's reactors and other power subsystems, but he didn't send me the navigational logs. Could you ask him to forward me any data that's available in Jacqueline's NLS and to include the data from the Outpost propulsion array?"

At the mention of Jacqueline's name, Edward looked down at his own hands and traced one of the lines in his empty palm with his thumb. "OK, I'll ask them to do that today."

"Great, thanks. Hey are you OK?" she asked.

"Yeah. It's just been a long week. Our first test didn't turn up any new information, and I have a sinking feeling that this next test could prove that the only way for Captain Fourtouna to have saved the Outpost would have been to shut down the propulsion array. I'm still not clear why he didn't do it. I'm not even certain on how the propulsion went as smoothly as it did given all of the reactor fluctuations."

Colleen's eyes darted off screen for a few seconds then came back to look at Edward. "Well, there's no point in speculating. You'll run your tests and you'll publish your findings. There's only one way forward from here."

"Yeah, I know. It's just that second guessing how people behaved in a life or death crisis feels cheap. They're not around to defend their actions. Also, I can't begin to imagine what the news will do to Captain Binti Abdullah. You know, knowing that her life came at the cost of everyone else's."

Colleen sighed. "Edward, I get it, but we don't have a choice. You're there to do a job. You're not attacking anyone."

He took his glasses off for a second, rubbed his face with his left hand, then put his glasses back on. "I know. You're right."

There was a pause, then he added, "I actually need to get moving. We're going to execute the combined scenario today. We did a dry run yesterday and everyone is bought into the recovery plan in case we find that sending power to the propulsion array keeps us from restarting the reactors after shutdown."

"Wow, it's finally happening," said Colleen.

"Yeah, it's a big day, but I'll get those extra logs to you after that, and then we can talk again at the end of the week."

"Great, thanks. Good luck with everything today, stud. You've got this."

"Ha, yeah. See you, Colleen," Edward said with a thin smile, then ended the call.

****

Captain Torres gave the order. "Nav, this is command. Engage propulsion at 85% power." It took a moment for the status lights to click on.

"Command, this is Nav. Confirmed, laser propulsion at eight five percent."

"Eng, this is Command," she continued. "Reactor Control, please shut down reactors alpha through eta while confirming no disruption to reactor theta."

Edward looked at the dark scenes displayed on three of the external monitors. Video feeds from three of the "Bug" vehicles were showing different points along the exterior cabling of the Nest's power grid. Ten days earlier, before their first exercise, Engineering Chief Yukimoto had overseen a modification to the exterior cabling of the space station, disconnecting one of the fusion reactors from the power grid of the Nest.

For this exercise, they were activating the propulsion array, so all three Bugs were positioned safely on the convex side of the parabolic station, and out of the path of the powerful lasers.

"Roger, Command, this is Eng, shutting down seven out of eight fusion reactors in 5, 4, 3, 2, 1. Reactors alpha through eta are shut---"

The floor seemed to move under Edward's feet, and he took a step forward with one leg to keep his balance.

"What the hell was that?" demanded Captain Torres.

Before anyone could answer, the overhead lights dimmed. Every system on the Command Deck shut down, and the room was pitched into darkness. Edward put his arms out in front of him and leaned forward until his hands came to rest on the console that he knew was there.

Quietly, and surprisingly close to his ear, Edward heard Chief Yukimoto murmur, "To the depths of terror, too dark to hear, to see."

One by one, crewmembers who carried flashlights turned them on.

Edward saw Captain Torres shine her own light onto herself. "Eng, what happened?"

"Radiation pressure," answered Yukimoto. "The stabilizing thrusters spun down along with the reactors, but the propulsion array seems to have remained active for a few seconds. There was nothing to cancel out the radiation pressure from the lasers, that's why we felt it."

Navigation Chief Sastry got to his feet. "Captain," he said, then waited for Captain Torres to shine her light on him. "That nudge that we felt would have pushed us off course, I'll need thrusters back online ASAP to restore orbit."

"How long do we have before the situation becomes critical?" asked Edward.

"Five minutes, Director. Ten at the most," responded Chief Sastry. "We're lucky that the thrust imbalance didn't last longer than it did."

"Eng, bring us back please," said Captain Torres

Chief Yukimoto clicked a few controls then said, "Reserve power is at zero. We're going to need to reconnect reactor theta."

"Acknowledged," said Torres.

Chief Yukimoto unclipped a hand-held comm from his belt and spoke into it. "Bug 2, we need you to re-connect reactor theta immediately. Bug 1, detach power couplings for the laser array. Bug 3, detach connections to the reserve power storage array."

"Bug 2 to Command, roger."

"Bug 3 to Command, WILLCO."

"Bug 1 to Command, requesting 60 seconds to get back into position. I lost my alignment when the station moved."

"Command to Bug 1, understood."

Edward shot a look to Captain Torres, then at the Engineering and Navigational chiefs in turn. None of them were reacting.

"Bug 2 to Command, reconnecting reactor theta."

Edward turned to his right and snatched the handheld comm away from Chief Yukimoto and pushed the button. "Bug 2, stop, hold position. Do not reconnect. I repeat, do-not reconnect!"

"Director?" asked Chief Yukimoto, blinking his eyes several times as he looked back and forth between Edward and Captain Torres.

It was Chief Sastry who answered. "No, he's right. I should have seen it. We have to wait for Bug 1 to detach the laser array before we restore power or it'll push us further out of orbit. We have to hurry though. It's going to take a minute or two for the navigational systems to restart once power is restored."

Edward handed the comm back to Chief Yukimoto, and the Eng chief accepted it in both hands, then tilted his head in a slight bow. Edward returned the gesture.

****

Edward's space sickness during his trip down wasn't quite as bad as it had been on his ascent. Regardless, he still didn't eat or sleep until the climber had descended to an altitude of thirteen thousand km, offering him 25% gravity to soothe his stomach. The doctors on the Nest had sent him with four liters of oral rehydration solution, and Edward was able to take a spoonful at a time in zero-g then cupfuls once he was able to drink again.

Trying to work only made his nausea worse, but a number of messages had piled up requiring Edward's attention. Among them was a video message from a Dr. Marius Bonaciu at ITER with the title "Results of Eight Reactor Sim."

"Dr. Kaiser, we have completed the latest phase of the Outpost reactor simulations and I think that we have found the clue that your agency was looking for. We now have a simulation that recreates the internal state of the reactors to match the log data that you sent us from the extinct space station."

The display showed a faint shadow of a circle representing the Outpost with its eight wedge-shaped slices. Half-way up each wedge was a disk shaped symbol for a reactor. Edward noticed that the reactor labels, alpha through theta were rotated from where he would have expected them to be.

"In this animation, the color of the reactor indicates its operating temperature. The colors of the control lines indicate heating and cooling commands that the crew is sending to each reactor. For these older fusion reactors to operate correctly, the conditions, particularly the temperature of the reaction and the homogeneity of the magnetic fields, must be maintained within narrow tolerances. Too hot and they can melt down, too cool and fusion ceases."

Edward's mind wandered for a moment. Pausing the message, he looked back at the recipient list and confirmed that the message was actually meant for him. Colleen wasn't even copied.

Do they expect me to explain the reactor failure to congress?

Looking back at the video, Edward unpaused the message, and Bonaciu's voice continued. "If I skip past the periods in simulation when nothing is happening, then the entire crisis can be viewed in just minutes. As each event starts, you will see reactors turning blue as they become too cool to support fusion, then red control lines activate to try to heat them back up. Later, different events cause those same reactors to turn red as they start getting too hot, and blue control lines activate to cool them back down. This fits the data that we found in your logs. At this point, Doctor, we have completed the original study outlined by Dr. Pastor. We will wait to hear from you before doing any further research in this area."

With that, the message ended.

Edward looked out of the virtual window in his cabin of the climber. The Earth below him was in sunshine, which meant that it was daytime in Europe. He checked the time in France and saw that it was just after 1pm, so he tried to establish a direct connection to ITER to see if he could speak with Dr. Bonaciu directly.

As the video link established, Dr. Bonaciu came into view. "Allo, ici Marius Bonaciu," he answered. Dr. Bonaciu didn't look French. His facial features seemed more eastern European, and he had a cleanly shaved head and a two day old beard.

"Yes, Doctor, thank you for taking my call. My name is Edward Kaiser. I am just looking through the simulation results that you've sent to me."

"Ah, yes, Doctor Kaiser. I hope that you found the results as interesting as we did."

"Well, I'm not sure," said Edward. "I reviewed the video, but I'm not confident if I know what it really means."

"Oh," said Bonaciu. "I see. Let me explain. What is interesting, more interesting than the actual events, is the way the conditions spread from one reactor to another. You see that I have turned the station on its side to make the events move across the screen. In my animations, first blue sweeps across from left-to-right, but only on top. Then blue sweeps across the bottom, from left to right again. An hour later, red sweeps across the whole station from left-to-right."

As Bonaciu spoke, Edward restarted the video message. He was able to see it now. The movement from left to right was the constant factor. Everything else was variable, but the movement was always in that direction.

Bonaciu concluded. "To me, Doctor, these look like clouds passing in front of the moon then clearing again. Sometimes the cloud blocks the whole moon, sometimes no. The one thing that the simulation doesn't help explain is, clouds of what? After all, this is not the moon, and we are not looking at it through Earth's atmosphere."

"I see," said Edward. "Thank you, Doctor."

"Of course."

"If I may, Dr. Bonaciu," asked Edward, "why are you sending this information to me, specifically? Did Dr. Pastor ask you to send me a copy of your results?"

"No, Doctor. In fact, we are no longer in contact with Dr. Pastor. She left here rather suddenly, almost one week ago. We did try several times to reach her in Houston, but we were unable to do so. In the end, Dr. Kaiser, we saw no alternative but to send the final simulation data to you."

36 -Televised Hearing - May 2144 -
Washington, DC
Edward

There was still no word from Colleen. Edward had sent her a message on every medium and electronic address that he could think of for her, including sending in-game messages to some of her private online personas, but she didn't respond to any of them. Ultimately, the only idea that he had left was to reach out to Elenora Voskos at the FBI. He asked her if she had any news from Colleen or if she thought that Colleen might actually be missing.

One thing was certain, he was going to be on his own for writing up the scientific progress of their investigation, and from the time that he arrived back in Houston, he only had ten days before he was scheduled to testify to Congress.

Katherine Othoni was helping him adapt his technical findings into a written progress report that could be understood by the members of the Temple Investigative Commission. She explained that he would attend the Commission meeting as a witness, but that it was his written testimony that would carry the most weight in the Commission's final report.

The Committee's charter was to prepare a full and complete account of the circumstances surrounding the Outpost disaster, and they had agreed to hold open hearings so that the press and the public could stay abreast of any findings of their investigation as they emerged.

****

Edward flew to Washington on a Sunday and spent the night in a DC hotel. Katherine had given him stern warnings. "The media are tricky," she had said. He should assume that any person he didn't know was a reporter trying to get information from him. Katherine would be meeting him there. She was attending the hearing too, not as a witness, but as the lead counsel for the Space Agency.

It was 7am on the morning of the hearing when Edward woke to the sound of buzzing coming from the hotel nightstand. Startled awake, he groped for his glasses, put them on, and answered.

"Good morning, Doctor." It was Crespin. "I hope that you've had a chance to read through the message that I sent you with Dr. Tirrell's written statement?"

Even though there was no video link, Edward was shaking his head. "Good morning, sir. I haven't read Tirrell's statement. I have barely had time to prepare my own. I have to confess, sir, that I have a history with Dr. Tirrell. I'm not terribly interested in his point of view."

"I would suggest that you read it, son. If you'd like to meet me for breakfast this morning, I could go through it with you prior to today's hearing."

Edward wasn't fully awake and he hadn't had time to think about his plan for the morning or how he was going to get from his hotel to the hearing. "Umm, no, sir. I don't think that I'm going to be able to do that. Thank you for the offer, but I think that I can just hear it at the same time as everyone else."

"Very well, Doctor. I'll see you there," said Crespin and he hung up.

Even though there was only a one hour time difference between Houston and Washington DC, it still felt early to Edward. He slipped back off to sleep and woke up an hour later. He was glad for the extra sleep, but now he was worried that he'd be late for the hearing. By 8:30am he was showered and dressed. He grabbed a cup of coffee in the lobby, then found a car to take him to the government building where the hearing was to take place.

The car dropped him off, and Edward headed inside. There were throngs of reporters in the hallway, and once inside the conference room, Edward had to show his ID to get down to the witness area. Within seconds, the cameras turned on him, and people were shouting questions. "Director, do you think that the Commission is taking too long to find the cause of the accident?"

Edward reacted as Katherine had coached him to do. He had come prepared with three or four answers, and was planning on sticking to those answers regardless of the question. He started with, "I'm satisfied with what we have uncovered recently."

He made his way to the front and took a seat in the row that was reserved for witnesses and their counsel.

Crespin entered moments later. As they had with Edward, the press swarmed him. "What revelations do you have for us today Major General?"

Crespin looked directly at the reporter who had asked the question and said, "Let's get started, miss. That way we can all get our questions answered." Looking over the heads of the reporters, Crespin kept walking as if there were no one blocking his path. The reporters simply moved out of his way, and he strode down to the front of the room where the committee would be seated.

The conference room had a wedge of theater style seating and an open presentation area. To the left of the presentation area was a table with microphones on it and two chairs. To the right were two rows of panel desks for the Commission members. The second row of desks was raised half a meter higher than the first, and white name tags with large font spelled out the name of each Commission member. Crespin stepped up to the raised row and took the seat behind his name.

Before long, Ms. Temple brought the meeting to order with a clack of her gavel. "Our first witness this morning will be Dr. Leo Tirrell. Would you please come forward?"

Tirrell stood up from the front row and walked over to sit at the table that was opposite the Commission members. Once seated, he positioned his tablet in front of him and bent the microphone stem to the right height.

"Good morning sir," continued Temple. "Would you begin by identifying yourself and giving a little background of the experience you've had with the Space Agency?"

Tirrell complied, "Yes, ma'am. I am Dr. Leo Tirrell, and I have been employed in the civilian branch of the Space Agency for roughly 30 years. In that time I have contributed to the GhostMap program, including the Near Light Speed, Nest, and Outpost spacecraft. During the same period, I have also had close professional contact with Doctors Colleen Pastor and Edward Kaiser as well as with the Major General."

Temple interjected, "Let the record show that the witness is referring to Major General Alessandro Crespin. Major General, at this point, may I ask you to lead the questioning of the witness?"

Crespin replied, "Certainly Madam Chairman," then, directing himself to Tirrell Crespin asked, "Dr. Tirrell, can you tell me your scientific view regarding the cause of the Outpost's reactor failure?"

Tirrell's smile seemed out of place. "General, in my professional opinion, the most commonly held belief is that Dr. Kaiser's proposal to move the Outpost from the position where it had operated safely for years resulted in destabilizing the fusion reactors."

"I see," said Crespin, "and why do you say that this is a widely held belief?"

"I first heard the theory espoused by Dr. Colleen Pastor, sir. I am convinced of it, and I can provide a list of other names as well."

Edward had never heard this theory before from anyone, least of all Colleen. This must have been what Crespin was calling about that morning.

Crespin followed up, "And why do you think that Dr. Pastor allowed this risky move of the Outpost station to continue if it raised concerns for her?"

Tirrell's eyes lit up and a little smile formed on his lips. "Bias, pure and simple. Director Pastor seemed to have an unprofessional affection for Dr. Kaiser from his first days at the Space Agency."

"Unprofessional? Could you clarify?" asked Crespin.

"Yes. The Director indulged in using pet names to refer to this young scientist. Names like *stud* and *babe*. If I'm not mistaken, she had been grooming him from the time that he was in college, and she showed a clear favoritism for him in every interaction that I observed."

"I see," said Crespin, "and can you offer a specific example of Director Pastor's supposed bias?"

"Unfortunately, several come to mind. Most recently, when the Director recused herself in this investigation, she named this same young scientist as Acting Director in spite of his clear lack of experience and in spite of the fact that his own research is to blame for the accident. Before that, she pulled him into meetings of experienced staff, and heaped undue praise on his efforts."

Every press camera in the room turned towards Edward, and he tried to keep his expression neutral.

Crespin consulted his notes. "Thank you, Dr. Tirrell. Besides the unprofessional behavior of Director Pastor, do I understand correctly from your written testimony that you have additional concerns about abuses of power inside the Space Agency?"

"Yes, General. I'm afraid that it relates to another young Captain. I observed Dr. Kaiser trying to persuade her of something over dinner late last year. At one point in the conversation, the Captain became visibly distressed. I suspect that Dr. Pastor's crude habits have set a bad example. The abused has learned to become the abuser."

Katherine had raised her hand to speak, but Edward couldn't stand listening to any more. "This is absurd. This man is throwing out wild accusations based on nothing but his own flawed perspective."

Katherine turned to him and shot him an expression that could only be read as 'Shut up!'

Tirrell turned to face Edward. "My perspective on the culture of abuse in the scientific programs of the Space Agency goes back to well before your time, Doctor. Would you be surprised to learn that in 2116, I personally witnessed Doctor Pastor bring an abortion doctor onboard the Nest? I don't think that you even realize the type of person that we're dealing with here."

"That's enough, Dr. Tirrell," interrupted Crespin. "Madam Chairman, I request that we restrict ourselves to the written testimony. To wit, we have now covered that material, so perhaps we should simply move on to the next witness."

"Quite," said Temple. "At this time, the Commission would like to call Acting Director Dr. Edward Kaiser as a witness."

Tirrell's mouth was twisted up into a sort of pout, but his eyes darted around to soak up the reactions of the room. He stood and collected his things before walking back to his seat in the front row. As he passed Edward, he said quietly, "Well then, I'll be going." Edward didn't react. He kept his eyes low and continued towards the table to take his seat.

Once he was seated and looking at the Committee members, Chairman Temple spoke, "Yes, so good morning to you sir," she said. "As before, would you begin by identifying yourself and giving a little background on your role in the Space Agency?"

"Yes, Madam Chairman. My name is Edward Kaiser. I have been a Mission Architect and I am currently the Acting Director of the Space Agency."

"And how long did you hold the role of Mission Architect, Dr. Kaiser?" asked Temple.

"I was promoted to Mission Architect roughly four years ago, Madame Chairman."

There was an audible murmur in the room, and Edward suddenly wished that he hadn't listed his previous title when introducing himself. "I would also like to go on record with my objection to elements of the previous testimony. Some of it seemed to be outright fabrication."

"Thank you, Dr. Kaiser. You will have the chance presently to testify to your version of events. I believe that you are to give us an update on the status of the Outpost safety investigation."

Edward nodded briefly and continued. "Yes, ma'am. We have spent two months investigating and performing simulations of reactor failure scenarios. I personally travelled to the Nest last month for this work, and we have determined that one of the power control systems was capable of leaving the station vulnerable to an unrecoverable blackout. We immediately put in place a mitigation strategy and have begun the process of designing a replacement solution."

"Contrary to the wild theories of Dr. Tirrell, we are still in search of the root cause of the failure of the fusion reactors, and we have made concrete scientific progress in that investigation. We believe that we will have a definitive answer within the next few weeks. At this time, I have brought some animations with me that explain the current line of investigation if the Committee would like to see them."

"Perhaps, Doctor, we should wait until you have solid conclusions to share with us, rather than airing speculative ideas in this forum," answered Temple.

Edward fought the urge to object. The committee had listened patiently to Tirrell's conspiracy theories but they were declining to hear about actual scientific study. Regardless, Katherine had made it clear to him that he should refrain from appearing argumentative with this chairperson, and he had already risked enough mis-steps for one day.

"Very well," said Ms. Temple. "If there is nothing else, then I'd like to thank the press for their presence today. Hearings like this one, carried out in the open, are an important part of how we are meant to govern. We will reconvene before Congress in one month's time for sworn testimony."

Edward opened his mouth and began to raise a hand to object. Katherine must have seen it because she quickly stepped towards him and said, "Just wait. Don't say anything."

Edward closed his eyes and took several deep breaths. That idiot, Tirrell, had lied to the world in a live broadcast with incriminations that were beyond ridiculous. The damage was done. Now that his accusations had been made, some fraction of the public was bound to believe them.

"Wait here," Katherine said, and turned to approach Crespin. The two of them spoke quietly, then Katherine nodded. She came back to Edward and said, "OK, follow me."

Edward followed, and soon they were in a small office. She closed the door behind them.

"What's going on?" asked Edward.

He didn't have to wait for an answer. A second later, Crespin opened the door and entered.

The Major General closed the door behind him and turned to Edward. He seemed to be waiting for Edward to speak first, and Edward was eager to oblige.

"What's this all about, General? Is this some kind of stunt to help your campaign? How could you let that idiot lie to the world in a direct broadcast?"

"I don't have any evidence that he was lying," answered Crespin, "and you didn't provide any, son. Let me remind you that you chose not to prepare a direct response to Tirrell's statement."

"Listen, General," said Edward, "I defended your appointment for this Commission based on my respect for your integrity, but I can play this game too. You are complicit in everything that has gone wrong with the Outpost. You spent years feuding with Dr. Pastor instead of finding real solutions. You were directly responsible for mission safety, and you failed. You should have launched an investigation months ago like the one that I am leading now, but instead you chose to leave for your own personal gain. If we are out to destroy each other's careers, maybe I'll just call a press conference of my own and end your candidacy for Senate today."

Crespin had fire in his eyes. "So, you think that you're my equal now, do you Doctor?"

Katherine stepped in. "This was a mistake. General, if you would excuse us. I think that you know me well enough to take *me* seriously, at least?"

That seemed to dampen Crespin's appetite for a fight. He broke eye contact with Edward and turned towards the door. As he reached for the knob, he said quietly, "If you'll excuse me, I have somewhere to be." He opened the door and left without saying another word.

As soon as the door had closed again, Katherine turned to Edward and said, "Listen to me. You are the Director of the Space Agency, and as such, my first loyalty will always be to you and to the Agency. Please help me keep this under control. We need to look into Tirrell's claims immediately and either prove or disprove each one of them."

37 - Triple Helix - Jun 2144 - Houston, Texas
Edward

Edward recognized Elenora approaching from behind the security desk in the FBI field office in Houston. He stood up from where he was sitting and stepped forward to greet her. "Hi Elenora. Thank you for meeting with me. I imagine that you must be very busy."

As Special Agent in Charge, Elenora was the top ranking field agent in the Houston office and was responsible for its operation, its recruiting, and its coordination with other law enforcement in the state.

"Edward, of course, come in," she said with a smile. There was an unspoken familiarity between them as a carry-over from their respective close relationships with Colleen.

Elenora led Edward to her office and closed the door once they had entered. Walking around to her desk she said, "So now, what can I do for you? Is this about Colleen's unplanned trip?"

"Uh, no. Why? Do you have news? Is she OK?"

"Yes, I've been in touch with her," said Elenora. "She was pulled away on a family emergency that couldn't be helped, but she's fine."

"Oh, thank you. I'm incredibly glad to hear that. However, that's not why I'm here today. I've come about the Congressional investigation. There has been an accusation made that relates to time that Colleen spent on the Nest, and I'm hoping that the FBI can help us look into it. We need to investigate the claim to see if anyone who took a ride up or down on SPISE in 2116 was an OBGYN who performs abortions. The claim is that the Space Agency forced one of our pilots to abort her pregnancy."

Elenora was taking a sip from her water glass as Edward answered, but she started to cough mid-sip and some water splashed out of the glass and onto her desk. She looked away for a moment to regain her composure. "Oh, that does sound serious. When was this supposed to have happened again?"

"The only information we have is that the year might have been 2116," answered Edward.

Elenora's eyes were still watering after having choked on her drink a moment earlier. It added a strain to her voice as she tried to speak. "OK, I do think that I can help with that. I'll look into it then follow up with Colleen."

"No," Edward was about to correct her when a high-pitched chirp sounded in his pocket. He managed to continue answering her, but he was distracted. "You'll have to follow up with me on this..."

The chirp was a particular sound that didn't correspond to his normal notifications and it took him a moment to recognize it.

It sounded again. "I'm sorry Elenora. Do you mind if we finish this up over messaging? I think that is one of my warning systems and I really need to check it."

"Of course," she said, "Let me walk you out."

****

The ride back to the Space Agency campus took almost 30 minutes, and Edward was looking at trajectories on a flexible display during the whole trip. Comber-3 was orbiting the sun in a reverse direction at a distance of three AU, and it had just detected a previously uncharted asteroid. According to its position and velocity, the asteroid's orbit would intersect the path of a GHoSt in less than one year's time. When it did, there was a very good chance that it would fall in Earth's direction.

Edward quickly ran the simulation to see what time of day the asteroid might theoretically reach Earth. Whichever time zone corresponded to midnight at the moment of impact would be facing directly away from the sun during the collision. Though minute-by-minute calculations were hard to determine, the initial estimate showed that the asteroid would reach Earth when Indonesia, parts of China, and the west coast of Australia were in darkness. In aggregate, it represented over half a billion people.

This was exactly the type of threat that Crossbow had been designed to mitigate, but the timing could not have been worse. Captain Binti Abdullah and Crossbow-1 were only 16 hours from rendezvous with the Nest and less than two hours from beginning her braking phase around Earth. Deploying Helices this close to Earth was well outside of the intended mission parameters.

As soon as the car glided up to the curb, Edward folded his display and jumped out before the vehicle was even fully stopped. He ran towards the Agency's main entrance and sent out messages to coordinate their next steps before he reached the door.

"Colonel Kett, Dr. Ishida, this is Edward. I need you to meet me in the Aero-Astro lab immediately!"

"Nest command, this is Acting Director Kaiser, please open a voice channel for me to Crossbow-1."

The sun was hot, and Edward was already sweating. He slowed down to show his badge to security then broke into a run along the hallways leading to Aero-Astro. Once inside the lab, he transferred each of the trajectories that he had been analyzing to a different high-definition viewing surface.

"Director Kaiser, we have a voice link to Crossbow-1."

He was turning in circles, looking at the mathematical curves that he had transferred to the walls. "Stand-by Crossbow-1." He walked up to each chart and tapped a few controls. "Crossbow-1, do you see the trajectory calculations that I'm sharing with you?"

"Not yet, oh, yes, they're showing up now."

"Excellent, please stand by, Captain," said Edward. "I'm waiting for Colonel Kett and Dr. Ishida, then I can explain our situation to all of you at once. If we all agree, then I'm going to need you to reverse your orientation and prepare to deploy Helices."

"Helices?" echoed Jacqueline. "Did I hear you correctly?"

Edward could see Colonel Kett and Dr. Ishida coming down the hall. They were walking, calmly and it made him want to open the door and scream at them to run. He turned his focus to Captain Binti Abdullah in order to keep from losing his cool. "Yes, Captain. You heard me correctly. I'll explain everything in a second."

Still walking Calmly, Kett and Ishida entered the Aero-Astro lab and smiled at Edward. "Hey, what's up?"

He pointed a finger up and tilted his head toward the ceiling. "Captain, can you hear us?"

"Yes, Doctor, go ahead."

"We have an inbound threat," said Edward. "Comber-3 has detected a 300 meter asteroid that is on a collision course with a GHoSt in just under one year. What's worse, Earth will be coming into phase with the asteroid at that same time. This is a substantial threat to a large population area, and we need to decide if Crossbow-1 is in a position to mitigate it."

"She's supposed to start her final burn in two hours," said Colonel Kett. "Crossbow-1 isn't physically configured for Helix launch at the moment, and the Captain has been exhausting the last of her propellent over the past two weeks in order to match

Earth's orbital speed around the sun. I don't think that she can take the shot, Doctor. Is there any alternative to mitigate this threat?"

"I hear what you're saying, Tamara, but I don't think that there is. Here, look," he said, pointing at a display. "Earth is moving fast to the other side of the sun. With each day that goes by it becomes harder and harder to find a firing solution that can strike this asteroid before it's obscured by the sun. It's on a collision course with a substantial GHoSt, and predicting its exact trajectory after that might be impossible."

Dr. Ishida was nodding his head and pointing at one of the displays. "He's right. Even in one month's time, the sun's gravity-well would make a firing solution impossible. Are you saying that Crossbow-1 can't fire Helices at this point in the mission?"

Edward tilted his chin up to the ceiling again. "Captain, have you been listening?"

"Affirmative, but I have not been able to follow along with the charts that you sent me."

"OK, let me talk you through them. The first one shows the circular path of earth moving counterclockwise towards the 9:00 position. The elliptical arc coming down from the other side of Mars at the top of the chart is your ship. It reaches Earth at the 9:00 point then loops once around to shed speed."

"Yes, I see it. That's my existing flight plan."

"The second chart shows a small dot at roughly 2:00 on the main belt. It's moving slowly upward towards 12:00."

"Yes, I see that too."

"The third display shows a Helix labelled alpha fired from where you are currently positioned. The trajectory starts out diagonally toward the 1:00 position on the main belt, but it will bend due to the sun's gravity. The trajectory straightens out and intercepts the asteroid just above its current 2:00 position out at three AU."

"OK, I see that too. What does the fourth display represent?"

Edward swallowed hard. "The fourth display represents one more Helix that you'd have to fire off to reverse the effects on your ship of the first one. Colonel Kett was correct when she said that you are almost out of propellent. If you fire off Helix alpha, the recoil will throw you off course and you won't have enough thrust to slow down for your rendezvous with Earth. Firing Helix beta in more or less the opposite direction should put you back on course to rendezvous with the Earth and ultimately, the Nest."

There was a long silence. Edward looked away from the displays to see how Ishida and Kett were reacting. Kett looked calm, but Edward thought that he detected a small flinch in one side of her face when she looked back at him. Her eyes seemed narrower than usual. Ishida just sat down and put his head in his hands.

"Can you quantify the risk that Crossbow-1 could miss her final approach?" asked Kett finally.

Edward shook his head as he answered, "I can think of a handful of things that have like a one in a hundred chance of going wrong, so I'd say five percent aggregate risk to Crossbow-1."

"That's unacceptable," said Kett.

"I agree with you, but I don't see any other choices. All launches are grounded. Even if we got authorization to launch another Crossbow vessel, it would be too late. We would need Earth's momentum to catapult a vessel into an elliptical orbit towards this target in the main belt. That's impossible now because we're moving in the wrong direction, away from the target."

"Um, Edward?" It was Dr. Ishida. He was leaning over a workstation, squinting and running his fingers through his hair. "Have you seen the spectral breakdown off that rock?"

"No, why? What's wrong?" asked Edward.

"I know that it's in the outer belt, but it's not a C-type asteroid. It's an M-type, mostly nickel and iron from what I can tell. That means that it's about four times more dense than you accounted for in your firing solutions. The muzzle velocity that you calculated on Helix alpha won't be sufficient to guarantee orbital decay."

"Shit," said Edward, "what do you recommend?"

Ishida did some more calculations. "The highest confidence path will be to fire two Helices at 75% power at the target, then do an about face and fire two Helices at 100% power to course correct."

"I see. OK, I think that you're right," said Edward.

"Base, this is Crossbow-1, please confirm? Did someone say that the plan is to fire four Helices?"

"Affirmative, Crossbow-1," said Kett.

"Base, be advised. Crossbow-1 only has three Helices remaining in the magazine at the present moment."

Kett was opening and closing the fingers on both of her hands. She was looking back and forth at the two scientists. "Can someone please propose a plan that will bring this pilot home safely?"

"OK," said Ishida, "I have one. Here, look at these firing solutions."

He pulled up a chart with Earth near the bottom. Crossbow's path was drawn as a dotted line bending down then spiraling once around Earth. Thin yellow lines showed the paths of the Helices shooting off from the dotted path. One yellow line shot up to the right. A few millimeters below it one shot down to the left. There was one more that shot nearly straight down from the point where Crossbow would start bending around the Earth.

"She can fire off Helix alpha at 110% power, then turn 165 degrees and fire off Helix beta, also at maximum power. That will put her back on the right course, but she'll still be going 10% too fast. She can then pivot one more time and wait to fire Helix gamma to shed the last bit of excess speed before slingshotting around."

Kett was shaking her head. "There has to be another way."

They were all looking at each other when Jacqueline's voice came back over the comm. "Base, this is Crossbow-1. I understand the nature of the problem and I have a recommendation. I suggest firing all remaining munitions at the target and calling it a day."

Colonel Kett walked over to one of the screens and muted the audio in the room. "She's right. This is basically a suicide mission and we don't even seem confident that it will mitigate the threat."

"Look," said Edward. "I understand your position, but I believe that she can pull this off. We're talking about a 50/50 chance of saving millions of people versus a five to ten percent chance of losing one. I hate these odds, but there is only one way to make this call."

Kett still looked skeptical, but she unmuted the audio to re-open the channel with Crossbow. "That's a negative, Crossbow. Your courage is noted, but I respectfully request that you await orders."

She turned back towards Edward and said, "I hate your odds too, but it would seem that she has to take the shot. Can you take at least 15 minutes and get some additional verification on your numbers." Then, talking to the ceiling she added, "Captain, please bring the muzzle of Crossbow-1 around toward Mars, prepare the ship for Helix deployment, and await your firing solutions."

"Roger," answered Jacqueline.

Edward sent out a message to the entire scientific staff, "I need all available Aero engineers to pitch-in on an urgent peer review and independent verification of some trajectories. We have a situation, and Crossbow-1 will need to deploy Helices during her final braking and rendezvous phase. Please refer to--"

Edward turned and looked at Dr. Ishida, who responded with "Firing Solutions Crossbow-Alpha-Gamma-Two."

Edward touched his temple again and repeated, "Please refer to Firing Solutions Crossbow-Alpha-Gamma-Two and contact me with any concerns."

The screen in front of Dr. Ishida started to light up with icons showing that tens of Space Agency personnel were poring through his last set of calculations. Bubbles of annotation were popping up on equations and trajectories. Both Edward and Shinya looked closely at what the team was finding.

After roughly ten minutes Edward stood up straight again and said to Colonel Kett, "We're ready."

"Crossbow-1, is your ship ready to deploy Helices?" Kett asked into the air.

"Affirmative, Base. Crossbow-1 is ready to receive firing solutions."

"OK, Captain," said Edward, "we're going to need you to begin bringing the ship around to the second firing solution as quickly as possible. This will mean resetting the bays to firing position immediately after recoil then coming about. Normally, you'd want to stay secured in your harness during bay reset, but you may have to detach early in order to save time on Helix reload. Are you able to do that?"

There was a slight catch in Jacqueline's voice as she replied, "Affirmative."

"OK, I want a visual," said Colonel Kett. She walked over to one of the displays that was showing a copy of the original asteroid detection and tapped a few controls. The display changed to show the inside of the pilot's bay of Crossbow-1. Jacqueline's COFLEX helmet was on and she was hooked into the ship's firing harness. Behind the harness was a view of the 5km long shaft of the Crossbow's coilgun. Its white lights were pulsating slowly.

"Firing solutions for Helices alpha and beta are programmed in. Targeting will be complete in 20 seconds. Helix alpha is loaded and ready. EM systems ready. Capacitors are fully charged. Reactor is nominal. Coil integrity, cooling, and end to end resistance are nominal."

There was a series of beeps, then the camera juddered for a split second. As the image flickered, the long string of pulsating lights rushed toward Jacqueline in a streak of white, vanishing completely before the scene stabilized again.

"Helix alpha is away. Resetting bays."

There was a high pitched whine as magnetic pulses pulled the bus-sized arrow-feather bays back to the aft end of the Crossbow's coilgun hull. Through the video feed, this simply looked as if groups of white lights were flying away as the long hull of the ship slipped back into firing position.

They watched as Jacqueline detached herself and moved out of sight. It took a full three minutes, traveling at 100km/h, for the bays to retrace the five km length that had shot through the bearingless mountings in a two-second blur during the previous recoil.

Once the hull was extended back out to its full length behind the pilot's harness the scene became static other than the pulsating lights of the coilgun. Jacqueline was nowhere in sight.

A tone sounded, and Colonel Kett said, "Helix loaded, she's coming back."

Jacqueline floated back into view and touched a few controls with one hand as she hooked herself into the firing harness with the other. The stars began to swirl around as the vessel turned towards its new heading. The pivot slowed, and after two more minutes came to a stop. "Preparing to fire Helix beta," said Jacqueline.

"EM, Capacitors, Reactor, and Coil are all nominal. Firing in Five, Four, Three..." The scene repeated itself, with a pixelization of the video resolving, a blur of white lights, then a scene of empty space. For the second time in 5 minutes, the hull of the Crossbow had jolted out of sight.

"HHhhhhhsssss, ahh," came over the comm.

"Crossbow-1, report status," said Kett.

"Crossbow-1 is nominal. Helices alpha and beta are deployed, but I think that I might have fractured my forearm. The last countdown got ahead of me by about a second and my right arm wasn't positioned properly in the support."

"Are you able to use it, Captain or are you incapacitated?" asked Colonel Kett.

"Yes, ma'am. I can move it and wiggle my fingers. I am increasing compression on that side in my COFLEX for additional support."

Turning towards the scientists, Kett ordered, "Dr. Ishida, navigation report."

"Stand by," said Ishida. He was watching the display intently in front of him. After another 30 seconds he said, "Navigation is good! She's on course for orbital braking. Our next Helix won't be fired for another 35 minutes."

"Yes!" shouted Kett, and punched the air.

Edward fell backwards into a chair, covered his eyes with his left hand, and rested his elbow on his knee.

****

The Aero-Astro lab was full to capacity. All of the engineers who had helped verify the previous firing solutions had rushed to the lab and word was spreading that Crossbow-1 was minutes away from a crucial maneuver.

Everyone was watching the telemetry of Crossbow as it rounded its first 15 degrees of Earth orbit for its final braking phase. Dr. Ishida was still sitting in the seat in front of the main navigational display. "She's close," he said.

"Captain, are you in position to fire Helix gamma?" asked Kett.

"Affirmative. EM, Capacitors, Reactor, and Coil are all nominal. Heading is verified," responded Jacqueline.

"Shinya, proceed carefully," said Edward. "She mustn't fire too early or with too much force, If she gets too deep into the atmosphere, it'll cause that coilgun to wrap around the ship like a windsock."

"Right," said Ishida. "Captain, please confirm that target muzzle velocity is set to 59.76 km/s," said Ishida.

"Affirmative, 33% power, five nine point seven six kilometers per second."

Turning to Kett, Ishida said, "Colonel, do you want to count her down?"

Kett took a step forward and double checked the trajectory. "Crossbow-1, this is base, prepare to fire Helix gamma in ten seconds."

"She has reached escape velocity. The thrusters aren't slowing her down enough," said Edward.

"Nine, eight," said Kett, marking the rhythm with a drum beat movement of her right hand.

At the moment that Colonel Kett said the word 'six' Jacqueline reached forward and touched one of the controls in front of her. Beeps accompanied the remainder of Kett's countdown."

"Three, two, one."

The video juddered, then pixelated and went black.

"We've lost video feed," said Ishida.

"It's probably OK," said Edward. "Based on her current position, we were relying on a beam-forming array for the satellite relay. It probably wasn't able to track her through the recoil. It should come back in a minute."

"Captain," said Kett. "Crossbow-1, are you receiving?"

"Shinya, have you got any telemetry?" asked Edward.

"Not yet."

The room was silent with at least 30 people looking at displays that were all frozen, like a computer that was grinding to a halt, about to crash.

"I have an independent telemetry signal from Helix gamma," yelled Ishida. "It's away and its trajectory looks good."

Suddenly, as if someone had pulled a cork out of a bottle, all of the beeps and clicks that should have been sounding for the last 60 seconds rushed out of every electronic device in the room as the systems caught up from where they had gotten stuck.

The video feed went from black to blocky to pixelated and finally clear at high resolution. Jacqueline must have flipped the display from the camera that looked out into space beyond the coilgun to the one that was currently pointing down towards Earth. The blue ball was small in that view, and only half of it was illuminated by the sun as she crossed over towards the sunny side of the planet.

"Base, this is Crossbow-1. Orbital velocity is nominal. I am on track to rendezvous with the Nest in 13 hours."

"Confirmed," said Ishida. "Orbital altitude and velocity are on target!"

The room exploded in cheers. Kett and Edward exchanged a look. "How long till we know if it worked?" she asked him.

"Time to intercept is just under 38 days, but we should have target acquisition data from Helix alpha in ten days' time," he answered.

Kett gave him a hard look, and Edward felt himself lowering his head a little for whatever was coming next. Though he wasn't sure, Edward thought that he detected the hint of a nod when she finally said, "Let's hope that we have time to reload and relaunch before your little probes turn up any more surprises."

38 - Awaited Arrivals - Jun 2144 -

High-Earth Orbit

Jacqueline

"Attention Crossbow-1, this is Bug-3, prepare for docking."

Jacqueline heard a thud somewhere below her and activated the magnetic seal between the bug and her ship.

"Crossbow-1, we have docking seal. Opening hatch," she heard.

"Acknowledged, I'm on my way," said Jacqueline.

She had to tap a series of controls to enter into the vessel management console. From there, she selected the mode named, 'station-keeping standby' and activated it. The lights dimmed all around her and the lighted console went dark.

Taking one last look around, Jacqueline glided over to the arched passageway that led away from the pilot's bay and toward one of the munitions bays. From there, she continued through another passageway to the reactor bay where the docking airlock was located.

She opened the hatch and looked through to the inside of the Bug.

"Can I give you a lift, Captain?" said the Bug pilot.

"Sure, thank you. Is there room for my bag in there?"

"Yes, ma'am."

****

Captain Luciana Torres was waiting for Jacqueline in the Axle.

"Welcome home, Captain," she said.

"Thank you, Captain Torres."

"Let's get you to medical, then if you're free for dinner, I'd love to hear about your mission," said Torres.

"Yes, please! Dinner sounds great. I've been on a liquid diet for months."

The doctors took an x-ray of Jacqueline's arm and told her that she had an impacted radial head. They gave her a sling to wear for a few weeks, but they told her that she could stop wearing it when it didn't hurt her anymore.

As she sat on the edge of the exam table, waiting for the x-ray results, the paper crinkled under her, and the sound brought her

The Ghost of Sphinx

mind back to some of her early post-flight check-ins that she had done with Christopher, before she really knew him.

Jacqueline met Captain Torres on the Command deck at 18:00, and the two of them walked together to the cafeteria. For their first hour, Captain Torres grilled Jacqueline about technical details of the NLS program and the Crossbow mission. Though Jacqueline had never actually had a job interview, she imagined that it would feel something like dinner with Captain Torres.

Once her curiosity had been satisfied, however, Torres lightened the mood and told Jacqueline about her first few months in command of the Nest.

"I had barely learned my way around the station when the Director himself came onboard for almost three weeks to do disaster drills. The poor guy spent his first day vomiting into a bag. His last day too. Fortunately though, the 0.5g of his quarters was enough to keep down his dinner each night."

Jacqueline tilted her head and asked, "I'm sorry, Captain. Did you say, *he*?"

"Yes, Acting Director Kaiser," she answered. "He came up to oversee some disaster recovery exercises with the fusion reactors."

Acting Director? Edward?

"Where's Colleen?"

Captain Torres lifted her chin with a smile and said, "Ah, it looks like no one bothered to tell you. Dr. Pastor had to take some family leave, but even before that, she had stepped down as Director to let someone else handle the Congressional investigation."

"Oh," said Jacqueline, "I got a message from the Director about two months ago. I had assumed that I was talking to Colleen. Are you saying that it would have been the Acting Director?"

Torres raised her eyebrows and nodded. "If it was two months ago, then yes. It would have been Dr. Kaiser."

I'm going to owe him an apology...

****

Jacqueline was able to take a non-stop flight from the new airbase in the Line Islands north of SPISE. Her plane touched down at 6am in the George Bush Intercontinental Airport in Houston. She took a car to the Space Agency campus, but it was still early when she arrived.

"Good morning, Captain," said one of the Airmen behind the security desk. "I don't see any quarters assigned to you, and the station chief isn't in yet. Can we call you with a bunk assignment in two hours?"

"That's fine," she answered. "I'll use the showers in the gym."

Jacqueline dragged her hard-sided suitcase behind her through the Agency hallways. When she reached the gym, she pulled open the glass doors with her good arm and held it open with her foot as she slid the suitcase inside. Under normal circumstances, she might have liked to do a little cardio, but her arm was still throbbing from the long flight and lack of sleep.

Jacqueline was just beginning to cut a path through the resistance machines on her way to the showers when she spotted Edward on one of the treadmills. He had a lean frame and strong legs, and he was running at a good pace. Judging from his sweat soaked T-shirt and the droplets of water on and around his treadmill, he had been on that machine for a while.

There must have been something displayed in his glasses because in spite of her slow approach, he didn't seem to notice her. Finally, reaching out with her good hand, she placed it gently on the console of the machine to get his attention. She regretted the decision almost immediately. Not only was the machine wet to the touch, but Edward was so surprised to see her that he stumbled and almost fell.

"Oh, Captain, you're back!"

Jacqueline winced. "Yes, I'm sorry for surprising you." She discreetly turned and picked up a towel from the rack behind her and held it in her hand until she couldn't feel the moisture any longer.

"No, no, not at all," he said, looking at the console of the treadmill. He pushed some buttons and the whir of the track began to wind down slowly. "It's so good to have you home safely, especially after that marathon we put you through on your way back into orbit. How's your arm?"

He still hadn't looked back at her.

"It's OK, thank you."

Looking down at his own clothes he said, "Ugh, I'm soaked, and I'm going to need about half an hour to cool off and get showered. Could we meet in my office at 9am? I have several things that I need to go through with you."

"Sure, that sounds fine," answered Jacqueline.

He looked up quickly and gave her a short smile, then he nodded, turned his back to her, and walked toward the showers. Jacqueline stood there and watched him walk away. The treadmill next to her was still soaked with sweat, and she wondered if he was going to leave it that way.

She already had a towel in her hand, so she bunched it up thick and wiped off the handrails and the console of the treadmill. Looking again toward the end of the gym where the doors led to the showers, she saw that he was already gone.

It was like he couldn't get away fast enough.

Jacqueline bit her lip and looked at the equipment around her. She threw the dirty towel into a basket and pulled a clean one off of the pile.

Edward's words had been friendly and professional, but it wasn't like him to speak to her without making eye contact. She draped her clean towel over the handle of her suitcase and walked toward the locker rooms herself.

At 8:45, Jacqueline was showered and wearing a fresh uniform. She wasn't hungry yet, so she walked towards the wing where Edward's office was located. She knew that she might end up waiting for him, but there was nowhere else to go.

His office was empty when she arrived, so she lingered in the doorway and let her left hand run up the door frame. The painted metal was textured and cool to the touch. She took another half step into the office, but then stopped herself.

With one foot inside the doorway, she looked around his office as a smile grew slowly on her face. The couch was crumpled, and she wondered if he'd been sleeping on it. She imagined him there with his tousled black hair matted to one side and his long legs extending over the end.

Jacqueline turned her head back towards the hallway to see if he was coming. Edward was different from other men that she had known. The scientist was unkempt and vulnerable, but he had built her a sturdy ship and brought her home safely. She looked at the objects on his desk, nodding her head, and imagined him using each of them during his working day.

When she looked over her shoulder again, she saw him walking towards her. Jacqueline tilted her head to acknowledge him, and he responded with a quick smile.

OK, at least he's smiling...

She started to speak, but then waited another few seconds for him to get closer so that she wouldn't have to yell. Finally, she said, "Edward, I think that I owe you an apology."

He furrowed his brow and his steps slowed a little as he reached her. "For what?"

She didn't want to discuss it in the hall, and she stole a quick glance inside his office.

"Oh, come in, let's sit down," he said.

Jacqueline stepped inside and took a seat on the couch. She sat up as straight as she could and waited for him to sit down behind his desk. "It's just that, I realize now that I was communicating with you in March regarding the update to the Crossbow mission plan and the return to base."

He lowered his head and looked at her through his eyebrows. "I don't understand," he said. "I remember the conversation but what do you mean by, you were communicating with me?"

"Yes, that's just it," she blurted. "The messages just said *Director*, they didn't say your name. No one told me that Colleen had stepped down, and I thought that she was the one sending me those messages. I was angry that she was interfering with your mission."

Jacqueline looked down at the ground and added, "I thought I was defending you."

He didn't answer, so Jacqueline looked up at him. He was laughing to himself. His lips were pursed and his eyes were drawn off to one side.

"Oooh, my…" he said. "That *is* funny. I'm sorry for not being more clear, and I have to confess, I have been worrying about parts of our exchange. You were right to resist though. If I hadn't recalled you when I did, the heroics that were required in the final hours of your mission could have been avoided. Coming home two weeks early put you in a bad position for targeting that asteroid."

She put her hands out in front of her, remembering too late to take it easy with her right arm, and a quick flare of pain shot out to her fingertips.

"No," she said. "I'm so embarrassed. It's only when Captain Torres mentioned that you were on the Nest and she called you Director, that it clicked for me."

"To be honest," she added, "it actually made me realize that my relationship with Colleen is a little bit unprofessional."

Edward's eyes were rolled up toward the ceiling and he was nodding his head. "That's not just you, Captain. I think that might be all of us." After another pause he added. "OK, so let's chalk that one up as a great story."

She didn't know what to say, so she just smiled, scrunching up her eyes a little bit.

Edward looked down and scanned the displays on his desk and nodded again. "Coming back to the mission though, I have to congratulate you, Captain. Your performance on Crossbow-1 went far beyond anyone's expectations. The initial kinetic impacts have kicked off precisely the orbital changes that we were looking for, and our tracking of the high-arc Helices show that their trajectories are ideal. We also have very high confidence that your Helix alpha is on track to trigger a successful orbital decay of the 300 meter asteroid in the outer belt."

"It was my honor, Director," replied Jacqueline. That elicited a short laugh from him.

"Just, Edward, please, and the honor was ours," said Edward with a smile.

His expression changed quickly. "Now…" he said, rocking back and forth in his chair a little.

"I take it then that you haven't been tracking news coverage coming out of Washington regarding the Space Agency."

"No, I'm just arriving back this morning," answered Jacqueline, "and to be honest, I don't really pay much attention to the news, even when I've got my feet on the ground."

"OK, so let me bring you up to speed. We are taking a thrashing. The Space Agency has been in the news and we have been the subject of negative stories for months. We're under investigation by Congress, and that investigation is ongoing. I personally had my head handed to me in a public hearing last month. It was one of the worst days of my life."

Jacqueline nodded, but the idea that an angry meeting could represent the worst day in someone's life made her realize that she had a very different history from this man.

"With your permission," Edward said, "I'd like to ask you a few questions before I go any further. I need to emphasize that if at any point, my words make you uncomfortable, you have every right to tell me, OK?"

Jacqueline drew her chin back, "Uh, OK?"

"Great," he said, shaking out his hands. "First, I want to ask you if I should apologize for the first time that we talked about the Crossbow mission. I suggested that we discuss it over dinner, but maybe I shouldn't have done that."

Jacqueline blinked her eyes a few times and said, "Nooo? I don't think that was a problem. To be honest, I really enjoyed our first meeting. I have even thought back on it over the past few months. You made me feel as if I was part of the program from the first moment."

"OK, well let me just say again, that it was never my intent to treat you as anything other than a colleague."

Jacqueline looked at him for a moment and she felt her nostrils flare. "Fine," she said finally, crossing her arms and leaning back slightly in the couch.

"OK, thank you. Next is the Investigative Commission. At this point, it looks like having you testify will be unavoidable. Basically, you were the last person who interacted with the crew of the Outpost before the disaster. They are going to want to ask questions about what things were like onboard. Specifically, they are likely to have questions about Captain Fourtouna, and if he seemed himself."

How Liam seemed on our 100th night together…

Edward said something else, but she missed it. She sniffed, sharply and said, "I'm sorry, I was thinking about something else. Would you repeat that?"

He squinted a little and leaned towards her. "Captain, if this topic is too stressful, we can discuss it another time, or in a different format. Perhaps written?"

Jacqueline shook her head. "No, this is fine, could you repeat your last question?"

"Yes, do you have any reason to believe that Captain Fourtouna's judgement was compromised with respect to the decisions that he needed to make on that final day?"

Jacqueline started to answer, then stopped. "He…"

Well, was he thinking clearly, or did he let everyone die to save me?

"I can't say for sure. I don't have any evidence that his decision making was impaired, but certainly you can see how I might wish he had decided differently than he did."

Edward took in an audible breath through his teeth, and he was looking a little flushed. "That's probably enough for today. Let me just give you this," he said, handing her a tablet. "It contains the findings of the investigation to date as well as a transcript of last month's hearing."

Jaqueline took the tablet and clicked through page after page of information.

"Katherine Othoni will want to work with you to get you ready. She knows Washington, and she is the best person to help you prepare for your testimony. You should try to get on her calendar as soon as possible."

Jaqueline wasn't really reading the documents on the tablet, just flipping through to get an idea of how much information there was, but one line of the transcript caught her eye.

"Would you be surprised to learn that in 2116, I personally witnessed Doctor Pastor bring an abortion doctor onboard the Nest?"

The room went quiet, and Jacqueline began to hear the sound of her own pulse whirring in her ears. She lifted her eyes to Edward, who was still talking, but she couldn't hear what he was saying.

She remembered her own words from three years earlier, '*This is the worst thing that I've ever done.*'

Was it? Still?

Every NLS pilot and everyone on the Outpost had died while she lived. Giving up her baby wasn't her worst crime. Her worst crime was living, when people she loved were among the dead. It had been her crime when she was 12 years old and it was her crime now.

"Captain?" Edward was looking at her.

"I'm sorry, what?" she said.

Jacqueline didn't wait for him to speak again. She stood slowly and tried to form a sentence. "OK, thank you. I'll contact Ms. Othoni. I appreciate the time that you took for me today."

Edward smiled. His eyes were lifted to look up at her from where he sat. "No Captain, thank you. Thank you for your perfect execution of Crossbow, right down to the very last seconds, and thank you for coming back to help us with this. You're a true hero."

I'm a curse...

****

During the week that followed, Jacqueline had several meetings with Katherine Othoni. As head counsel for the Space Agency, Katherine had a specific idea of how she thought that Jacqueline could project the program in the best light. She wanted her to present a lay-person's view of the extraordinary science, and the up-close view on how well things were going with the Crossbow mission.

Jacqueline had to admit that it sounded very inspiring, even if it was a little bit whitewashed. There really were things to be proud of in these missions.

Here and there, Jacqueline continued to see Edward in the hallways of the Space Agency. They were having lunch one day when she asked him to stop calling her Captain. It took him a few tries, but after that they were officially on a first-name basis.

She was only a little bit surprised when he contacted her the following week, inviting her to have dinner. "I could use a wingman," he had said. "It's just that I haven't seen my mother in a really long time, and I'm not sure if I can make it through a whole dinner without any distractions."

"I'm a distraction?" asked Jacqueline.

"If you only knew…" he answered, and she laughed.

When Jacqueline's car dropped her off in front of the Greek restaurant, Edward was already on the sidewalk waiting for her. The restaurant had a funny name, a play on words, "The Prince of Thebes".

Edward's mother was already seated when they arrived. She stood as they approached the table and smiled brightly at her then at Edward. They all sat down, and Edward's mother rubbed her son's arm vigorously, leaning toward him.

"It's so nice to meet you Jacqueline, please call me Mericiel. Oh my goodness, what happened to your arm?" she asked.

"It's nice to meet you too, Mericiel." It was an unusual name, and Jacqueline had to say it slowly the first couple of times. "I injured it last week, but it's nothing serious."

"She injured it while bravely risking her life for our mission," said Edward.

"Oh my goodness! Edward told me that you're a pilot! That's so exciting."

"Yes, I actually flew in a ship that your son designed. It is an amazing vessel." answered Jacqueline.

Mericiel's smile reached her eyes as she leaned toward Edward and repeated the arm rub maneuver.

"I can't believe that it's been so long since we've seen you, Edward," she said. "You know, your father is still holding out hope that you'll come home and take over his business."

"What kind of business does he have?" asked Jacqueline.

"Oh, he has a small data firm that does analysis for companies who can't afford to have full time analysts on staff." answered Mericiel.

"Ooh," said Jacqueline, then turning to Edward, she asked, "Did you ever work summers at your father's company?"

Edward lifted his hand to his mouth and held it there for a moment before responding, and Mericiel looked away from the table and leaned forward as if searching for their waiter. "Umm, no. I actually haven't been home since I was 16 years old."

He reached over and put his hand on his mother's arm.

He looked at Jacqueline, then at his mother, then back to Jacqueline before continuing. "I used to have these terrible nightmares," he said. "It's hard to explain, but I had them basically every night, and they got worse as I got older. I was tired all the time, and I had this irrational fear that everyone around me was going to die, and that it was going to be my fault."

Jacqueline jerked back slightly at his words, but she caught herself quickly. She didn't want to make Edward feel self-conscious for how close he had come to describing her own history.

"So, when I got a chance to go to college early, I took it." He squeezed his mother's arm again and turned and looked her in the eye, "I'm sorry, Mom. I stayed away too long."

Mericiel's chin quivered, and she was blinking her eyes quickly. She drew herself up and turned her attention to Jacqueline. "You know, Paul and I had two dear friends who left to become pilots at the Space Agency. It's been so long since we've heard from them though. The four of us were so close in college."

Edward pulled out his AR glasses, put them on, and asked. "Oh, what were their names? I can look them up here."

"Well, it was Liam and Christopher. I don't know if I remember their last names. Oh, I think that Christopher's last name was El-lis. Jacqueline, you should have seen these boys. They were so handsome. Poor Paul had an inferiority complex for years."

Edward took off his glasses again and put them away. "I didn't find them."

Jacqueline couldn't help but notice that he hadn't actually touched his temple to enter in the names.

Mericiel's head was tilting to one side as her gaze floated up toward the ceiling. As far as Jacqueline could tell, she hadn't noticed their reaction. "We held out hope of finding them for the longest time," she said. "We wanted to make them Edward's god-parents. Liam actually introduced me to Paul, and I know that Paul still misses him."

Jacqueline tried to change the subject. "So, what was Edward like when he was a boy?"

"Oh, he was so smart, and he loved those video games. It's no surprise that he ended up here. He used to play space games all the time when he was a child. You're too young to remember, but his favorite game was about the terrible meteor strikes in 2109. I could never really stomach it though."

Just keep going...

Jacqueline looked back and forth between Edward and his mother and asked. "So who does Edward look more like, you or your husband? I take it that your husband has blue eyes?"

Mericiel laughed. "Oh no, neither of us have blue eyes."

She looked at Edward, gave a quick nod, and raised her eye-brows. He nodded back at her, and she closed her hands into two fists. "I have a great story to tell you," she said.

Edward interrupted. "Uh, I have actually heard this story already. If the two of you will excuse me, I think that I'm going to use the restroom."

Mericiel watched him walk away, then turned back to Jacquel-ine and raised her eyebrows again. Jacqueline nodded and smiled, encouraging her to continue with her story.

"Paul and I had wanted to start a family for years, but nothing was working. Everyone was telling me to adopt, but for me that missed the point. I just didn't think that I would feel like a real mother, like a real woman if I couldn't feel that baby growing inside me, you know?"

Jacqueline's stomach was starting to hurt, so she folded her arms low in front of her and rocked forward. "Of course. I understand," she said simply.

"Right." said Mericiel. "So I was almost ready to give up, and my OB asks me if I'd consider embryo adoption. I had never heard of it. We looked it up and it seemed like a gift from the heavens."

Jacqueline bit down hard on her lower lip, but she kept nodding. Sooner or later this was bound to happen. She was going to meet someone who had done an embryo adoption.

"It was very mysterious though. The woman who contacted us wouldn't tell us anything about the biological parents or why they were giving it up, but that didn't stop her from asking us hundreds of questions about our careers and our families. I guess that's her job though."

Jacqueline smiled. "That sounds stressful," she managed.

Thankfully she saw Edward coming back from the restroom and she tried to think of what she could say to him to change the subject.

"Is everyone ready to order?" he asked.

"Oh, no, I still need to look at the menu," said Mericiel. "I was just telling Jacqueline about that Elenora woman. God, she was a tough cookie."

Edward's face showed a flash of recognition and a lopsided smile. "Ohhh, I had forgotten that that was her name. I guess I don't know that story as well as I thought I did."

"I'm so sorry," said Jacqueline. "I-- I'm actually not feeling well, and I think that I need to go home."

Edward opened his eyes wide and let his jaw drop slightly. "Are you OK? Do you want me to call a car? I can ride with you if you're not feeling well." He looked back at Mericiel, and she nodded encouragingly.

"No, thank you. It's not as bad as that," answered Jacqueline. "I've been fighting it for about 20 minutes now, but I think that I need to go lie down. It was so nice to meet you though. I'm sorry that I'm doing this."

Mericiel was shaking her head. "Oh, no, it was wonderful to meet you. Thank you for coming all this way. Are you sure that you don't want Edward to ride with you?"

"No, thank you. I'll be fine."

****

Jacqueline heard the keys jingling. She saw a shadow slithering along the walkway between the shrubs. A silhouette, backlit by the lights in the street, followed the shadow. It was late, but the lights on the side of the building lit Jacqueline's face.

The silhouette stopped for a second, and she heard. "Jacqueline, is that you? What are you doing here?"

Jacqueline took a deep breath and spoke slowly. "Hi Elenora. Can I come in for a few minutes? I have something that I want to ask you about."

The Ghost of Sphinx

39 - Congressional Testimony- Jul 2144 - Houston, Texas

Colleen

Colleen tapped on the frame of Edward's office door. "Hey, Director, can I come in?"

"Holy cow, you're here." Edward leaned back in his chair and looked at her for a moment. "What the hell, Colleen? One day we were collaborating, the next day you were MIA."

She walked into Edward's office and let herself fall back into his couch. "Toughen up, kid. Katherine says that you were a natural."

"Seriously though, I'm really happy to see you. Where should we start?" asked Edward.

"I read your report on the disaster recovery drills up on the Nest," she said. "That looked really good. I take it that Marius has brought you up to speed on this cloud thing?"

Edward was already turning a viewing surface towards Colleen "Yeah. I have been poring over this." He pulled up the animation that Dr. Bonaciu had made with the white disks changing to blue and red in a sweep across the screen.

"So, this seven minute video splices together all of the reactor events that occurred during the Outpost's final 13 hours. You see how, regardless of the type of event, it sweeps from left to right over the span of a few seconds?"

"Yeah, I've seen this." she answered.

"OK, so first I tracked the frontmost pixel of each event, and made a vertical line that intersects it." He clicked and the same simulation played but with a vertical white line sweeping from left-to-right with the edge of the event.

"Then, I erased the background and made them all start one second apart." This time, there was just a black screen. Along the bottom edge was a white ruler with 60 tick marks labelled 1km, 2km, 3km up to 60km. One after another, all of the white lines appeared at the left and swept across to the right. They didn't bunch up or separate. They were all traveling at the same speed.

Colleen gritted her teeth. *Shit, that's what I was afraid of.*

"Just to confirm," she asked, "am I right in assuming that you didn't adjust the rate? You only changed the phase?"

"Right. I only set their relative start times. All of the events were traveling at the same speed. If you look at the gradient at the bottom, you can even calculate it."

"Colleen, it's 80,000 kilometers per hour."

"Yeah, that can't be a coincidence," she said. "This proves that the timing of the fusion reactor failure was a function of the Outpost's velocity."

"Right. I don't know if it was cosmic rays or radiation from the stellar stream, or maybe something else entirely, but it looks like whatever caused the instability in the reactors was stationary."

Colleen sighed. "OK. Nice work, kid. Can you send me these visuals?"

"Sure."

Colleen paused for a moment. She tried to sound as natural as possible. "Oh, I almost forgot why I came down here. Where are we storing the 3D models of the Halo Substructures?"

"Here, I'll forward you the directory name. Do you need me to find a particular formation for you?"

"Nah, I got it. Thanks." She turned and left.

As Colleen walked down the hallway towards her office, she touched her temple. "James, things are going super-critical here. I need your numerical results on those weak interactions ASAP."

****

The congressional hearing was two days away. Colleen had been working with Katherine on her strategy. To everyone's surprise, she had been coming in early all week, and was already at her desk when a video call from Switzerland came in for her at 7:55am.

She stood up and closed her door before answering. "It's about time, James."

"Yes, well I do have other work to do Colleen. Dark leptons aren't going to find themselves."

"OK, so where did you get to with the WIMP hypothesis?"

"At this point, I think that I've proven that it is in fact probable. The densities in the structures that you sent me would have been more than sufficient to change the rate of fusion. The control systems on those old reactors would never have been able to adapt quickly enough."

Colleen kept her face impassive as she nodded.

"OK, thank you, James. Can you please send me your writeup so that I can add it to my report?"

"Certainly. I'll do it now. Good luck, Colleen."

****

Colleen was scheduled to testify to Congress in the morning. She was sitting in the hotel bar in Washington DC, trying to take the edge off. She didn't see Elenora until the Special Agent In Charge was sitting next to her.

"Hey, are you avoiding me?" asked Elenora.

"I'm avoiding everybody," said Colleen. "How are you Elenora? Are you ready for tomorrow?"

"Yes, I am. This isn't my first time presenting to Congress. On that score, I wanted to talk to you. You know that this is my career here. I work for the federal government, and I don't have any wiggle room. When they ask me, truth, whole truth, nothing but. I have to say yes and I have to mean it."

Colleen took a sip of her drink and said, "Don't be melodramatic."

"Colleen, I'm serious. Tomorrow, when it's my time, they are going to get the whole truth from me."

Colleen was shaking her head. "You can't do that, Elenora. You'll ruin her life. She's just a kid."

"You underestimate her, Colleen. She came to see me last week. She already knows."

Colleen closed her eyes for a few seconds, until the stinging stopped. She wasn't sure if Elenora could tell or not, but touching her face would be a dead giveaway. "What do you mean, she knows?"

"I mean, she knows. She's figured it all out. Every last detail. She's pieced it together."

"Shit," said Colleen, then she finished her drink and signaled the bartender for another.

****

The light shining off the white columns of the Rayburn House Office Building didn't help Colleen's headache one bit. Reporters were following her the whole way in, barking questions, but they were easy enough to ignore.

The room where she would be giving her testimony was large. Two imposing rows of paneled wood desks lined the wall in front of the room with 20 black leather chairs in each row. Both paneled rows were elevated, but the back row was higher than the front. None of the Congressmen were seated in their chairs when Colleen took her seat. There were still reporters filling the floor all around the table that she would soon occupy.

The reporters stayed standing between the witness table and the paneled desks as one by one the black chairs filled with Congressmen and Congresswomen. It was only as they closed the back doors and called the hearing to order that the swarm of standing reporters found seats on the floor in two clusters. Those with their backs to the paneled desks aimed their cameras at the witness table. Those with their backs to the witness table aimed their cameras at the Congressmen.

The congresswoman seated in the center desk clicked on her microphone. "The Investigative Committee will come to order. Without objection, the chair is authorized to call recesses to the Committee at any time. We welcome everyone to today's hearing on the investigation into the Outpost space station disaster and oversight of the Space Agency's plan to ensure the safety of pilots and crew in current and future missions."

Colleen wasn't really listening. The Congresswoman seemed to be talking to hear her own voice. It went on for a few minutes, until she heard, "I will now introduce today's first witness, Dr. Colleen Pastor, Former Director of the Space Agency. Dr. Pastor was the Mission Architect for the GhostMap Observatory which includes the Nest space station, the Outpost space station and as many as 30 Near Light Speed vessels. We welcome our distinguished witness and we thank you for participating in today's hearing. Now, if you would please rise, I will begin by swearing you in."

Colleen stood and moved forward toward the chair that she would occupy at the witness table. On the table were microphones and a pitcher of ice water.

The congresswoman said, "Would you raise your right hand, please? Do you swear or affirm under penalty of perjury that the testimony you are about to give is true and correct to the best of your knowledge, information, and belief, so help you God?"

"Yes," said Colleen.

"Let the record show the witness answered in the affirmative. Thank you, you may be seated. Please note that your written statement will be entered into the record in its entirety. Accordingly, I ask that you now summarize your testimony in five minutes. Dr. Pastor, you may begin."

"Congresswoman, at this time we believe that we have identified the root-cause of the failure that led to the loss of the crew and vehicles of the Outpost and 23 of the Near Light Speed ships. As of this week, we have conclusive evidence that the Outpost station effectively collided with what we call GHoSts. These are invisible, but in many ways tangible substructures in the galactic halo."

"Our findings have confirmed that the crucial part of this collision, so to speak, was the movement of the fusion reactor cores through dense accumulations of what are referred to as dark matter WIMPS or Weakly Interacting Massive Particles. Since the process of nuclear fusion depends on the nuclear weak force, bathing the reactors in clumps of weakly interacting particles caused fluctuations in their rate of fusion."

Colleen turned and signaled for the animations to be shown. She paused to give people time to absorb the scene that was playing on several large screens around the room."

"Let me explain what these animations are showing. We can see a head-on circular view of the Outpost moving through halo substructures shown as blue translucent clouds."

A virtual 3D tangle of long blue smoky clouds of dark matter moved across the screen. As the Outpost passed through these clouds, the disk shaped reactors changed from white to blue to white to red, but given the context of the swirling veins of dense dark matter, the changes in reactor color seemed to flow naturally from the other moving pieces of the scene.

"You can see that as the Outpost's reactors enter or exit these dense clouds, the weakly interacting particles of dark matter lead to changes in the rate of fusion, and the crew of the Outpost was forced to react to each change over the course of several hours. It would have all been completely invisible to the crew, other than these seemingly random fluctuations in the power output of their reactors. They would not have been able to look out into space and see the clouds of dark matter."

"As Dr. Kaiser and others have previously published, once the reactors had failed, a design flaw in the failsafe circuits for maintaining reserve power prevented the reactors from being restarted. To our knowledge, the Outpost station has not regained power, and we assume the crew to have died in the ensuing weeks."

Colleen's throat was tight. "Tragically, each month since the Outpost lost power, Near Light Speed ships have flown past the propulsion station with no hope of stopping or coming home. We are still receiving signals from some of those vessels. A few of them have not even had a chance to realize what is in store for them, and there is nothing that we can do to stop it."

Colleen paused, closed her eyes, and took several uneven breaths. Tears were streaming down her face.

The chairwoman leaned forward and asked into her microphone. "Doctor, are you saying that some of these pilots are still alive?"

Colleen nodded, and tried to steady her voice to answer. "Yes," she managed.

Colleen focused her mind on the next section of her statement. This is what she had come for, so she needed to do it right.

"There has been some speculation in the press about the genesis of the idea to put the Outpost station in harm's way, so to speak, but please note that before this mission, we had no way of seeing or measuring the degree of risk that this entailed."

"Though I can confirm that Dr. Edward Kaiser provided both the tools and the arguments for aligning the Outpost station directly along the path of the dark matter substructures that we were trying to measure, I would like to state clearly that acting on this research was entirely my decision."

Colleen swallowed. This was the moment of truth.

"Most importantly though, let me state that I and I alone bear responsibility for another factor. We should have brought those people home and used unmanned craft to continue the GhostMap program. I take personal responsibility for failing to move to an unmanned program in a timeframe that could have saved lives."

The congresswoman leaned forward again. "Are you stating, Dr. Pastor, that you accept responsibility for this accident?"

"Yes, ma'am. I knew what I was doing. I gambled with the lives of the people whom I admire most, and I lost. We all lost." The last sentence was spoken in a whisper, but with the microphone so close to her, it echoed in the chamber around them.

There was a commotion of cameras and reporters jostling for position on the floor to try to get a clear shot of Colleen. Yet other reporters in attendance were trying to sneak outside to be the first to file their stories.

The noise was not dying down, and the chairwoman banged her gavel on the desk. "At this time, the chair calls a 30 minute recess. I would like to request that when we come back, the audience should observe the rules of the hearing and remain silent."

"Dr. Pastor, thank you for your testimony. You are dismissed."

****

The chairwoman took the floor to reopen the hearing. "Welcome back, everyone. I will now introduce today's second and last witness, Special Agent in Charge of the FBI's Houston field office, Elenora Voskos. Special Agent Voskos has had a long history of assisting with investigative matters related to the Space Agency, and through her more than 30 year tenure, has seen and assisted with the missions in question. Namely the Outpost station and the Near Light Speed or NLS program. We welcome our distinguished witness and we thank you for participating in today's hearing. Now, if you would please rise, I will begin by swearing you in."

Elenora stood and took a few steps from the front row towards the witness table.

The congresswoman said, "Would you raise your right hand, please? Do you swear or affirm under penalty of perjury that the testimony you are about to give is true and correct to the best of your knowledge, information and belief, so help you God?"

"Yes," said Elenora.

"Let the record show the witness answered in the affirmative. Thank you, and please be seated. As before, please note that your written statement will be entered into the record in its entirety. Accordingly, I ask that you summarize your testimony in five minutes. Special Agent Voskos, you may begin."

Elenora looked down at the tablet that she had placed in front of her and touched a control. She then looked back up and the assembly of Congressmen and started speaking.

"Good morning, Congresswoman. In June of this year I was tasked with investigating claims that one or more female pilots or crew had become pregnant on either the Outpost or Nest space stations as well as the claim that such persons were then forced to abort the fetus."

"This is a serious matter, involving possible infringement on the safety and dignity of female pilots in the NLS program. In the course of my investigation into the question, I found that though certain aspects of the accusation did match the facts, others did not. Through both my investigation, and as it turns out my personal experience, I can definitively state that only one female pilot or crew member has conceived a child onboard either the Nest or the Outpost space stations, and in this case, the embryo was given up for adoption and was carried to term by the adoptive mother. The investigation revealed no other cases."

"With her consent, I am prepared to name the pilot involved in that case. The pilot in question, who is in the hearing room with us today and who will testify before this body in one month's time, was then First Lieutenant Jacqueline Binti Abdullah."

"The pregnancy occurred on the Outpost space station, and the biological father was Captain Liam Fourtouna. Captain Binti Abdullah can attest that the relationship, the embryo extraction and subsequent adoption were all consensual. The embryo was cryogenically preserved, and over the ensuing weeks, I personally arranged that the embryo be adopted by a close friend of the biological father. At that time, I did not inform the adoptive parents as to the identities or circumstances of the biological parents."

"Both Dr. Colleen Pastor and I felt that, though the identities of all involved would remain secret, there was an opportunity to make a choice that perhaps the biological parents might have made themselves, had they been presented with the options. You could call it a secret kindness."

Colleen didn't dare turn around. She knew that the press had cameras on her, and it would be too easy to betray what few secrets remained in this room.

Edward

"You should have told me."

Colleen must not have seen him come in, and she jerked her head around when he spoke. "You're going to have to be more specific, amigo. I've kept a lot of things from a lot of people."

"You should have told me that you suspected that aligning the Outpost along the path of the GHoSts caused it to fail."

Colleen lifted her head to look at Edward under the visual displays in her "chair". It was a cross between a VR rig and engineering workstation with giant displays mounted on the 1.5 meter rings that surrounded her. The chair could rotate forward or backward to any angle, and Colleen was swiveled back, reclined almost flat and looking toward the ceiling. She pushed a button to pivot upright so that she would be able to get to her feet.

The rest of Colleen's office looked like a rainforest, with an oblong green carpet on the floor and live plants covering one of the walls. Long curving benches of natural wood lined an irregular swerve of bookshelves.

"It was just a hypothesis. It wasn't even mine. Tirrell said it a few months ago and it made me think. Naturally, he wasn't considering the particle physics. He was just looking at the simple angle that everything was fine until we moved it. Later, when Marius' Cloud hypothesis started to take shape, I asked a friend at CERN to run the numbers. None of it was confirmed until I put it in my report to Congress."

"And you should have told me that you knew who my biological parents were."

"When? When should I have told you that? Shit, Edward, I wasn't even supposed to meet you. That was Oldfield's idea."

Edward shook his head. "That was eight years ago, Colleen. We've had dinner together 200 times since then."

Colleen had extricated herself from the "chair" and was finally standing. She signaled Edward to one of the wood benches near the plant wall and she took a seat in the chair facing it.

"OK, let's get it all out there. More than nine months before you were born, I carried you from the Nest and delivered you to Elenora. She brought you to Corinth where Paul and Mericiel adopted you. Elenora kept tabs on your family, but I wasn't supposed to have any contact with you. I did send a couple of high-end video games to your parents, and things started to change for me when I found that 'Monocle' mod you uploaded to 'After the Sphinx'. I took your idea and baked it into the NLS software that same year. When you went to college, I asked Oldfield to keep an eye out for you. We funded your graduate research and I stepped in as your advisor when Oldfield was ready to give up."

Edward opened his mouth to speak, but then closed it again.

Colleen leaned in and lowered her voice. "Now realistically, how was I supposed to work any of that into conversation? You would have either run away screaming or you would have tried to have me committed."

Edward stood up and took a few steps away from her. He had always thought of Colleen as his mentor, but this was so much creepier than he could have imagined.

"So I didn't earn any of it?" he asked. "Did you get me accepted to college too?"

"I honestly don't even remember," she said.

He turned away from her again and paced a few steps toward the window then back again.

"Don't get all deflated, you're just as much of a hot shot as always, you just had a few opportunities that most people never get."

"So Tirrell was right. I've gotten unfair advantages and favoritism from the beginning?"

"No, it's not like that. I don't regret any decision that I've made with regard to you. Tirrell is an ass, and he sure as shit deserved every bad thing that he's gotten recently. I had promised Jacqueline that I'd watch out for you, and I made good on that promise, but Edward, that doesn't change anything about what you did with those opportunities."

"I came here to resign," he said. "This just makes it easier."

Colleen was shaking her head. "I get it. 73 people are dead, among them, your biological father. There's no doubt, that's a bad day at the office, but resigning is not the answer. Not for you anyway. You're not a nuclear physicist. There was no way for you to know that the dark matter was going to make the reactors glitch out. Even my guy at CERN was surprised that we had accumulations dense enough to cause that. You can't take responsibility for everything."

"You don't get it, Colleen. I've always known that this was going to happen. I've always felt that it was just a matter of time until I would overlook something and someone close to me would suffer for it."

"Just try to think about this rationally," she said. "If it weren't for your investigation into the Outpost disaster, we wouldn't even have this information. If you want to take responsibility, then take it, but you can't walk away and be responsible at the same time. We need to keep on with some of this stuff. What about your fixes to the power grid on the Nest? What about Crossbow?"

The word Crossbow stopped him cold. For a moment, he pictured the way that Jacqueline had looked at him the last time he saw her in DC and it made his whole body shudder.

How was he going to face her again. Over the past year, he had started to think of her as the co-lead of Crossbow. He had built her up in his mind, hoping that maybe…

"No, I think that this career isn't right for me," he said. "The risks associated with failure are just too high. It only takes one digit misplaced, one chemical interaction overlooked, and people die. I don't think that I can go back to it. You did me a favor by telling me about the unfair advantages that I've gotten. It makes the decision easier. I don't belong here."

Colleen stood up and took a few steps toward him. "Listen, Edward, please. Please think about this for more than a few hours. I know that you've had some bad breaks recently, and I know that your confidence is shaken, but tell me this, who do you trust to do better?"

He didn't have an answer, but he tried anyway. "Anybody. Somebody who actually earned their place here."

"I never said that you didn't earn your place, and turning your back is not the answer. If you feel that you have a debt to pay for the privilege that you've received, then pay it. Pay it forward. Go find someone who deserves a break and give it to them."

"Your resignation is not accepted. Go away and get your shit together. Take time off if you need to, I don't care, but there's too much important work to do, and I doubt that I'm going to be around for very long."

Edward turned his head and looked out the window again. There was no use arguing with her right now. "I don't think that I'm going to change my mind," he said as he started to walk towards the door in her office.

As he reached the door, he heard her yell after him, "You know who could use your help is Jacqueline. She has to testify at the end of the month. Why don't you start there and pay it forward? I promise you, she's deserving."

Edward went back to his office to think. He couldn't shake the sluggish feeling that he'd had since he got back from Washington, so he closed his door and slumped into his couch.

****

"Edward, are you in there?"

Edward's eyes opened and he realized that he had fallen asleep. He sat up and looked at the clock on his desk. It had only been a half an hour, but it felt as if he'd been in a deep sleep. His thoughts were fuzzy.

"Edward?" It was Jacqueline's voice.

"Oh, sorry. Yes, come in."

The door opened, and Jacqueline entered, but she stopped just inside the office, rubbing the knuckle of one hand with the other. She flashed a quick smile, but it didn't reach her eyes. "Colleen told me that maybe it would be a good time to come see you. I've been giving you some space. To be honest, I was hoping that maybe you wouldn't figure it out, but I knew that it was a long shot."

"No, it's fine. Thank you for coming. I mean, thank you for making the first move. Where should we start? "

She sat down on the couch, less than a meter from him. He had an urge to stand up to put some space between them, but he fought it.

"I guess the most important thing that I wanted to do was to tell you how ashamed I am for giving up my baby."

Your baby. That's such a weird way to say it.

"It used to make me cry even to think about it, but for a little over a year now, I've been able to talk about it without getting upset. That doesn't mean that I'm any less ashamed. It just means that I have accepted it, the shame, as something that I can't change."

Wow, obviously she thinks of it in the dilated timeline. It's still fresh for her.

"I'm sorry, Jacqueline, I actually didn't realize. You're still learning to process this trauma. I'm 27 years old, but for you this all just happened a few years ago. Listen, you shouldn't feel ashamed. I have had a good life. They did everything for me that you could have asked for. They cared for me, helped me find my love of science, and they even let me go when I wanted to leave for college early."

He had a bitter taste in his mouth. "Any problem that ever occurred in my family came from me. I was always terrified that something was going to happen to them and that it was going to be my fault."

Jacqueline's stare felt like it went straight through him. There were tears in her eyes, but her face was quiet. She was completely in control. "Is that what you were talking about at dinner with your… with Mericiel? Your nightmares?"

"Yeah. I know that it's irrational, but when you see something enough times, it feels real."

"I can't think of anything more real," she said. "It's happened to me. Twice."

Twice?

"Jacqueline, what happened on the Outpost was *not* your fault. It was actually *my* fault. I'm the one who proposed moving the Outpost to align it with the GHoSts that we were measuring."

"They died trying to save me."

"I know," he said. "I would probably feel the same way that you do. I've imagined the situation a thousand times. Being a survivor can be devastating. Sometimes I wonder if it's not worse."

"That's why I gave up drone racing," she said. "For a long time, I blamed myself for the deaths of my mother and my grandmother. They took me to a drone race in Kuala Lumpur in 2109 and they both died there. For years I refused to think about flying. I felt like I owed it to my mother to deny myself."

"I've never talked to anyone before who understood what I was so afraid of," said Edward. "You're a real survivor, Jacqueline. The more I learn about you, the more I admire your strength."

She leaned towards him and looked him in the eye.

"But I'm flying again. I'm doing it because I believe that it's the best way to honor my mother and even Liam and Christopher. It was actually the Crossbow mission that taught me that. The way to be a survivor is to carry on and fight to preserve what they believed in."

Jacqueline was quiet for a minute, then she looked down towards the floor. "Edward? Can I tell you something? It's not really my place, but I feel strongly and I want to say it."

"Sure, of course. What is it?"

"You should go home," she said. "You should go see your family. From what you tell me, I would have given anything to have a family like yours. You should go home and make things right with them."

Edward looked around his office. He couldn't imagine getting back to work that day, or even in the next few days.

She's right. I should.

He looked back at Jacqueline and said, "On one condition."

She raised her eyebrow and waited.

"You come with me. If you think about it. They're kind of your family too."

****

Jacqueline and Edward landed at the Albany airport at 6 pm. They stepped out of the terminal onto the airport roadway, a car pulled up in front of them, and soon they were headed north. Having left home at 16, Edward didn't actually know the way, but the car said that it would only take 45 minutes to get to his parents' house in Corinth, just north of Saratoga Springs.

Paul had offered to meet them at the airport and ride north with them, but Edward preferred keeping the visit as simple and contained as possible. Stepping foot in his parents' house was intimidating enough without sealing himself in a small car with them for 45 minutes.

It was still light when they arrived in the little hamlet, and Edward was struck by how different everything looked to him in spite of feeling familiar at the same time. It was so much smaller than what he had remembered.

The house's exterior had alternating sections of log cabin and grey stone, with two high gables and large picture windows. A stone chimney cut through one of the high gables. Jacqueline and Edward hadn't even made it up the front path before Paul and Mericiel opened the door together. Mericiel immediately rushed out and hugged them both.

"Come in, both of you! I can't believe that you're really here. Jacqueline, Paul made me a spreadsheet so that I could see how old you were at different points over these past years. It's so fascinating. Gosh, just look at you. I can't believe that you could have been born in 2097. I was born in 2090. We could have been sisters, well, we're almost sisters already."

"Mom, slow down. Please," said Edward.

"Right, of course. Come into the living room. Here, sit down. Can I offer you something to drink? Dinner is ready too, but we don't have to eat if you're not hungry."

Paul put out his hand to Jacqueline, and she shook it. "It's very nice to meet you, Jacqueline."

Edward tried to think of a subject that would take the focus off of Jacqueline for a minute. "Hey, dad, guess what I learned this week. Do you remember that monocle mod that you made for me? Colleen says that a version of it was actually ported into the NLS software."

"That's remarkable. From the video game?" asked Paul.

"I guess so."

Jacqueline opened her eyes wide and looked back and forth between them., "What about the NLS software?"

"Colleen's old company actually published a game based on GhostMap and I used to play it as a kid. Apparently, Colleen used to take ideas from people who played the game and use them to upgrade the NLS software."

Jacqueline pursed her lips. "You know, those software updates used to make me crazy. Which one are you talking about?"

Edward turned towards her. "I used to get frustrated playing that game, so my father added a 'detach' key so that the probes could keep going without following my ship back to the Outpost."

Jacqueline crossed her arms. "So I have the two of you to blame for that one?"

She let her arms fall again and laughed. "Actually, I have to admit. That was a helpful upgrade. I used it on every flight after it was introduced." Turning to Paul, she said, "Mericiel tells me that you knew Liam and Christopher?"

"Yes," he said, "I was roommates with Christopher, and the three of us played lacrosse together in college in Troy, New York. I used to help Liam with his programming assignments."

"A colleague of ours, Colleen took your place," said Jacqueline. "I saw him copy one of her games once, rather than writing his own."

They all laughed a little.

"We are very sorry for your loss, Jacqueline," said Paul. "I had forgotten how much I missed both of them. When I learned from Edward that they both lost their lives in the Outpost disaster, it brought back a lot of old feelings that I had never really dealt with. I don't want to impose, but I would love to hear some of your stories about them if you have any to share."

Jacqueline's face tightened. She looked at Paul through squinted eyes and her lips formed a thin line. Edward wondered what she was thinking about. "Yes, of course, I would like that, but I should tell you something first," she said. "Liam died in the Outpost disaster, but Christopher died before that." She hesitated, then added, "It was an intentional overdose. I'm sorry, I don't remember what year it was, but it would have been several years ago for you."

Edward felt a chill. "I think that it might have been around the time that I defended my thesis. Crespin told me about a suicide that year, before I even joined the Agency."

Mericiel stood up from the chair that she was in and squeezed herself in between Edward and Jacqueline on the couch. She hugged Jacqueline again with one arm and rocked her a little. Edward was worried that Jacqueline might feel overwhelmed, but she seemed completely at home.

"You've had so much loss in your short life, Jacqueline. The pain doesn't really ever go away, you know. It's just that you find a place to put it in your mind so that you can have peace most of the time."

Without taking his eyes off of Mericiel, Edward rocked forward and leaned an elbow on his knee. It was almost as if he was seeing her for the first time. There was so much more to his mother than he had realized as a boy.

Paul cleared his throat. "Jacqueline, Mericiel tells me that you've flown one of the Crossbow vessels. So, tell me. How are you two going to get these missions back up and running?"

Jacqueline leaned forward in her seat and looked around Mericiel at Edward. She was still looking at him, rather than at Paul when she said, "Actually, Paul, that's not a question for me. It all really depends on Edward here."

****

The sun was already bright outside when Edward woke up. He heard the familiar bird calls that he had known as a child, walking in these woods around his house. A smile slowly formed on his face as the memory of the previous night came back to him. All three of them had relentlessly argued against his reasons for wanting to walk away from the Space Agency. They kept at him until he finally admitted that he couldn't name a single person that he trusted to keep the missions safer than he would. Before the night was over, he had decided to go back and pick up where he had left off.

Edward rolled over and looked at the clock. He had slept late, and the house was quiet. He wondered if the others might have gone out already. It was another minute before he realized it. He had actually slept, soundly, all night. He hadn't had even a single dream.

41 - A Final Appeal - Sept 2144 - Washington, DC

Jacqueline

The afternoon before heading back to Washington, Jacqueline was on the Space Agency campus, in her quarters. She was going through her testimony in her mind while she packed a bag. Katherine had been preparing her for weeks, and Mericiel had helped her put together a really powerful slideshow to accompany her testimony.

There had been a news frenzy following their last appearance in Washington. Jacqueline in particular was receiving frequent invitations to appear as a guest on talk shows, but Katherine felt strongly that they should keep a low media profile until the Congressional hearing was complete.

Jacqueline had just closed her small hard-sided suitcase when there was a knock at her door. She opened it to find Colleen. "Hey, sweetie, can I come in? I have some news that I need to share with you."

"Hi, Colleen. Sure," said Jacqueline as she turned her body to let Colleen in. Once she had entered, Jacqueline closed the door again.

Colleen walked over and sat on the bed next to Jacqueline's small suitcase. She ran her hand along the top of it and scratched at some of the white stains that were still stuck in the textured crevices. It made Jacqueline smile a little to think about Bambino.

"So, maybe I'll start with the fascinating man who swept me away on my extended vacation." said Colleen.

"What man? Do you mean when you were on leave?"

"Yes, it was very sudden. He invited me to Borneo," said Colleen.

"Wait, what? Where in Borneo?" asked Jacqueline.

"We went to lots of places. We ate in the open air market in Kuching. We saw the inside of several administrative buildings in Sarawak and even a Shariah Court. I had expected it to be hot, but it's no hotter than Houston, just more humid."

"Colleen, who do you know in Malaysia, and why Sarawak?" asked Jacqueline.

"Well, unfortunately, I have to start with some really bad news. I'm sorry to tell you this, but your grandfather passed away a few months ago. Raban called me as I was wrapping things up in Europe."

Jacqueline just stared at Colleen, then turned, and slowly sat down on the bed with the suitcase between her and Colleen. She remembered thinking when she joined the NLS program, that she could quietly slip away and let the years flow past her. Had she wanted this? On some level, did she know that he was going to die while she was gone?

Why didn't I go to see him?

She sniffed and looked around her quarters for something that she could use to wipe her eyes, but there was nothing, so she rubbed the back of her hand over the corner of each eye.

"Did you say that Mr. Raban called you? How is that possible?"

"Yeah, about that. He has known for a long time that you were here with us, but apparently he didn't tell anyone. That's why he called me. He needed me to prove that you were still alive so that we could list you as your grandfather's next of kin."

"He's really gone? When?" asked Jacqueline.

"It was early April while you were up in Crossbow-1. You can get more information from Raban when he gets here. He has a couple more legal hoops to jump through, but then he's coming to visit you."

Jacqueline nodded slowly. She wasn't making eye contact with Colleen. Her eyes were directed at the floor next to the bed.

"So there is one more thing," said Colleen. "I hate to bring it up, but it's kind of important. We did succeed in establishing you as your grandfather's heir. I believe that it's quite significant. It makes the 25 years of untouched pilot's salary look like small change."

Jacqueline nodded again. The thought of money was so foreign to her. She had never thought about it when she lived in Sarawak, and it had been irrelevant during the time that she had been flying.

Colleen stood and turned so that she was facing where Jacqueline was sitting. "I won't be here when you get back from Washington. I'm sure that Katherine told you that your only focus now is saving the missions. I won't ever be able to make up for all of the mistakes I've made, but you're really important to me, and I hope that you can forgive me."

Jacqueline looked up at her and smiled. She lifted her arm, took Colleen's hand and said, "No family is perfect, Colleen."

****

Katherine had reached the end of her testimony, and Jacqueline sat in awe of her presence. This was someone who felt completely at home in front of a panel of 40 Congressmen and women.

"There is no question that mis-steps have been made," said Katherine, "but that does not diminish the need for these missions. I want to thank Director Pastor, who has ended this saga by her own hand. She tendered her resignation to me yesterday, and it has been accepted. Dr. Edward Kaiser has been named Director of the Space Agency. He has the right experience to safely carry our missions forward for the common good. His audits are complete, and our systems are hardened. I can personally certify that the Space Agency is renewed, and we are once again flight-ready."

After a brief pause the Chairperson of the committee responded. "Thank you, Ms. Othoni. At this time, I'd like to call a 30 minute recess, and when we return, we will hear the testimony of Captain Jacqueline Binti Abdullah."

During the break, Jacqueline stood to stretch her legs. She was too nervous to talk to anyone, so she stayed close to her seat in the front row of the hearing room. Scanning the chamber, she saw the large screens where Mericiel's slideshow would be displayed, and mentally reviewed what she was going to say.

Major General Crespin was present. He offered her a polite nod during the recess as he moved toward one of the exits at the back. Before he made it out of the room, Edward approached him and extended a hand. Crespin stood and looked at him for a moment, but he didn't raise his arm to shake Edward's hand. They were too far away to hear, but Crespin said something, then continued out of the room. Edward shrugged and went back to his seat.

That's when Jacqueline saw Raban. He was sitting between Edward and Mericiel, and he was staring at her with almost no expression on his face. She lifted a hand to wave at him, and he gave her a slow, noble bow of his head. When he lifted it again, there was a smile on his face, but the expression in his eyes was tight and strained.

OK, you need to clear your head.

Jacqueline waved one more time, but then turned and sat back down. She waited there until it was time to start up again. Soon, they were swearing her in.

"... raise your right hand, please? Do you swear or affirm under penalty of perjury that the testimony you are about to give is true and correct to the best of your knowledge, information and belief, so help you God?"

"Yes," said Jacqueline.

"Thank you, and please be seated. Captain Binti Abdullah you may begin."

Jacqueline lowered the microphone to her height and sat up as straight as she could. "I am the sole survivor of the disaster that struck down the crew of the Outpost and 23 of my Near Light Speed squad-mates. Through magic that I can barely understand, let alone explain, I sit before you, 24 years of age, in spite of the fact that I was born in the last three years of the 21st century."

A picture of Jacqueline in her COFLEX, emerging from her NLS projected up on the screen.

"Each time that I entered my ship and flew between the Nest and the Outpost, the journey for me took only a few short weeks. It is perhaps a result of that difference in timescale that I remain in awe of what these missions have accomplished. I was 12 years old when large and powerful meteoroids struck our planet, killing hundreds of thousands. My own mother and grandmother died that night as a result."

The slide changed to a photo of Jacqueline as a child with a first-person-view headset pushed up onto her forehead. She had a drone controller in one hand and the other hand raised into the air. In the background, the colored lighting of the drone track was visible. "November 9th, 2109 Kuala Lumpur" was displayed in a white font in the bottom corner.

"That night, I saw first-hand what this threat looks like on the ground, and how a small piece of rock can knock over buildings if it falls from a great enough height. In the years since, I have travelled to heights as great as anyone can imagine to see what this threat looks like at its source. I need for you to believe me that even though it is invisible, it is massive, and it is tangible. We need a way to know where it will be and when."

The projection screens updated again, showing a photo taken from space of the Nest station. The giant black lattice bowl was visible only in the sections whose silhouette extended in front of Earth's blue and white surface.

"We all agree that the Outpost fell, but let's not forget how it fell and why it was there in the first place. The Outpost fell because it encountered the same veins of dark matter in the galactic halo that made Sphinx-896 fall. It fell because an invisible mass passed through it, unseen and without warning. It fell because it was there, watching, waiting, and protecting us from the very thing that brought its destruction. Liam Fourtouna, Christopher Ellis, and other heroes who lived on the Outpost did so for us. They willingly left Earth and stayed aloft for longer than I have been alive. It was a sacrifice that they made for each of you."

The slide changed to a picture of the NLS pilots on the training course, muddy, but dynamic. Some were in mid leap and some were on the ground, crawling.

"We needed these people and we needed this mission. I and others in this photo flew faster than any person has ever flown, in order to be able to trace the outlines of these vast, invisible objects. The science that makes these things possible is staggering, and I have watched it advance at a pace that bewilders and amazes. I know. I know that it has seemed long and expensive to all of you, but if only you could see it for a moment from my point of view."

The slide changed to one showing Jacqueline floating inside her NLS with the gravitational detection display behind her. The green mesh of the laser array had a clear twisted bulge and smoky dark trace.

"What required human pilots when I started can now be done with unmanned craft. This means that we no longer require the kind of sacrifice that the crew of the Outpost made, and we will no longer need to risk the lives of NLS pilots like myself and my friends who have flown away from us with no way to return. These advances are thanks to the very people whom we are accusing of negligence."

The slide changed again to schematics from the Crossbow mission. The long coilgun with four arrow-feather bays showed at one end, and an animation of a Helix intercepting an asteroid showed at the other. Firing trajectories and flight paths for the Comber probes were drawn over the speckling of the dense bands of the Main Belt.

"I'm telling you. I was just up there. This is working. We have the technology to know where the danger is and to simply step aside and let it pass us by. Please don't mis-understand me. I wish more than I can ever express that I could rewind the clock and tell Captain Fourtouna to just let me die. I wish that they had shut down the reactors and sacrificed me to save the others, and, yes, I wish that technical and scientific knowledge could have prophesied these events so that we might have escaped this fate. But wishing doesn't make it so."

The slide changed to show a room full of Space Agency scientists, cheering and punching the air in the Aero-Astro lab with different Crossbow trajectories drawn on the display surfaces around them. In the background was the image of Jacqueline tethered into the firing harness of Crossbow-1.

"I wish that we could have saved these hundred lives, but that wish is nothing compared to my fierce conviction that 10.5 billion lives are at risk if we stop here. I have the list of asteroids that might fall on us. There are eleven of them that I scratched off of that list myself, but there are 200 more that still need attention. You don't need to take my word for it, the data is public. You can all go and look at our maps and at the speed that our solar system is headed towards these veins of dark matter in our galaxy's halo. If you let me, I will go back to work and scratch off more names until there are none."

"Thank you."

There was silence for almost 10 full seconds. Later, Edward told her that it was Mr. Raban who started clapping first. The applause spread through the chamber, through the audience in the beginning, but then through the rows of Congressmen and Congresswomen too. It lasted for about a minute, and then the hearing came to an end.

42 - A New Mission - Nov 2144 - Allen, Texas

Jacqueline/Colleen

Jacqueline admired the November stars over the open-air stadium in Allen Texas, until a bright white flash of light momentarily blinded her. The deafening sound subsided, leaving a ringing in her ears, and the moment of silence that followed spiked panic in the pit of her stomach. There was still smoke swirling around them, but it was starting to clear. Red lights streaked across the crowd of thousands of people who had gathered for Crespin's election night rally.

Crespin stepped onto the stage and walked out in front of the band. He took hold of the microphone and scanned the front rows of the crowd, looking for her. He was going to call her up there.

"I'd like to introduce you to someone special," he said. "Tonight, we have the privilege to welcome Captain Jacqueline Binti Abdullah. Captain, please come up here and join me."

Crespin's campaign manager had asked Jacqueline to attend and had asked for her permission to call her out as a special guest. She was just one in a list of cameos that night. Like the band, she was part of the show to keep the crowd entertained as they waited for the election results to roll in.

"Now please give the Captain a true Texas welcome, and thank her for her service."

Security stepped aside and pointed to the stairs that Jacqueline would take up to the stage. Her heart was pounding as she reached the top step and turned to walk to the center. A bright spot light fixed on her, but she could still see the red lights sweeping across the faces of 20,000 people. It felt as if every last one of them was watching her.

"Captain Binti Abdullah is famous for her Near Light Speed flights and she is one of the heroes that we have to thank for our safety down here on Earth today."

The crowd roared.

Crespin extended his hand, and Jacqueline shook it. "I want to thank you personally for your support Captain and for your service. Above all, I want to say welcome home." He took two steps back and continued applauding her. Jacqueline turned towards the crowd and looked out at them. She lifted one hand to wave, and the applause grew even louder.

She looked down to where Edward, Mericiel, Paul, and Raban were standing. The three men were clapping, but Mericiel was jumping up and down cheering for her. Jacqueline thought about the odd little family that had formed around her. The lines between sister, mother, brother, father, and son were blurred among them, but she didn't care. She felt connected to each of them. They were all hers, and she would do anything for them.

The band began playing again. Drum crashes and music rose up behind her as flashing lights and smoke machines re-engaged to fill the stage with swirling color. She waved one more time, then made her way back toward the stairs that she had come up a few minutes earlier.

Retracing her steps back to where she had come from, Jacqueline realized that she wasn't afraid anymore.

What would I work for if this were my election night? What would I try to achieve for them? The question intrigued her.

As she reached the stairs, she heard Crespin's voice behind her "Ladies and gentlemen, Captain Binti Abdullah!"

She was 24 years old.

EPILOGUE

It was late when Edward entered the bar in Allen Texas. He paused for a moment to scan for where Colleen was sitting. The rally was showing on TV.

"Hey, sorry it took me so long to get out of there. Did you see when they called Jacqueline on stage?" he asked her.

"Yeah, the kid did great."

Up on the screen, Crespin had the microphone, and they heard him say, "I have just had a call from my opponent. He has conceded the race! We are going to Washington, and my mission starts today. It is finally the time to fix the problems that big science, big tech, big pharma, and a weakened military have caused for this country."

Colleen put her drink down and signaled the bartender. "Could you turn the volume down on that? I can't stand that guy."

Edward chuckled as the bartender came over and turned the volume down on the TV.

"Maybe Crespin's campaign manager had a point, denying you access to the venue tonight. I mean, there's no way that you would have said anything good about him if the press had asked you why you were there."

"Ah, screw him. Let's get really goddamn drunk and pretend that Crespin didn't just get elected to the Senate."

****

Colleen could just make out the numbers on the clock. It was 11:17am. Her head was splitting, and she had only fuzzy recollections of getting back to the hotel from the bar.

The maid was talking to her through the chain on the door. "Miss, are you there? I have to clean the room."

She rolled over and saw that Edward was passed out, fully dressed, on the other bed.

Why is he in my room?

He was still wearing the dark sunglasses that he had bought the night before, joking that he couldn't bear to see the future that lay ahead of them.

"Hey, boy genius. Wake up. It's past checkout time."

Edward just groaned. "Oh, I am in agony-- Wha... Why can't I see anything?"

A Map to the Play

Every part of this chapter contains major spoilers.

Do not read any of it until you have finished the book.

Introduction

Act III of this story is a modern adaptation of Oedipus Rex by Sophocles. As such, Acts I and II represent a sci-fi prequel to that 2500 year old play. Each of the main characters in this story maps directly to a character from Oedipus Rex as shown in the table below:

Original Char	First Name	Last Name
Oedipus	Edward	Kaiser
Laius	Liam	Fourtouna
Jocasta	Jacqueline	Binti Abdullah
Creon	Alesandro	Crespin
Tiresias	Leo	Tirrell
The Shepherd	Colleen	Pastor
Merope	Mericiel	Kaiser
Polybus	Paul	Kaiser
Chrysippus of Elis	Christopher	Ellis
Second Shepherd	Elenora	Voskos
The Chorus	Katherine	Othoni

Below are specific scenes in the story that were meant to re-create the setting of Oedipus Rex in the 22nd century.

Act-I

The Champion & The Architect

The asteroid Sphinx brought great suffering to the people of Earth, and the staff of the Space Agency are held accountable for failing to predict it. They mobilize to try to find a solution. Throughout most of the story, the Space Agency is meant to represent Thebes. In this way, the threat of another asteroid is analogous to the plague of the Sphinx in the original play.

The Captain

Liam falls in love with Christopher and teaches him to fly an airplane. He then persuades Christopher to follow him to the Space Agency and betray promises that he had made to his family.

In Greek mythology, young Laius falls in love with Chrysippus of Elis and carries him off to Thebes while teaching him to drive a chariot. For this action, Thebes and the family of Laius are punished by the Gods.

The Prodigy

Edward grows up in the town of Corinth, NY, raised by Mericiel and Paul. He thinks of them as his true parents. Likewise, Oedipus is adopted by the queen and king of Corinth, Merope and Polybus.

Phocis is the region of Ancient Greece that held the town of Delphi, which in turn was the seat of the Oracle of Apollo. The game that Edward plays is one of many Phocis games that are meant to help the scientists see future possibilities for the mission.

Edward is plagued by fears that his parents will come to harm by his inaction. This is a parallel to the fear that Oedipus felt that he would harm the queen and king of Corinth, Merope and Polybus.

A Commission

Liam becoming captain of the Outpost is akin to ascending to the throne of Thebes.

Christopher tells Liam that his family is distraught at his willingness to go along with Liam, and even believes that Liam is a harmful presence in Christopher's life. This was meant to reference the betrayal felt by Pelops, the King of Pisa, who had entrusted Chrysippus of Elis to Laius for training in the art of war.

Act-II

Signals

Partly based on the fears expressed in Edward's nightmares, he leaves his home town of Corinth at a young age to attend college just as Oedipus leaves Corinth to try to escape the prophesy that he will murder his father and marry his mother.

Once in graduate school, Edward has a technical epiphany while observing a place where three walking paths meet, when he looks at a tree and imagines its roots extending under the earth. Likewise, in the play, Oedipus is challenged by Laius' traveling party at a place where three roads meet.

At this point, Edward begins to uncover the secret of how to solve for the trajectory of "Enigma", the dark mass that allowed Sphinx to cause death and suffering. In the play, after leaving the crossroads, Oedipus encounters the Sphinx and is challenged to solve her riddle.

Her Captain

Christopher warns Liam "If you sleep with her, it'll mean the end for us." In Greek mythology, Laius received a warning from an oracle that told him that he must not have a child with Jocasta, or the child would kill him and marry his wife.

Defense

During his dissertation defense, Edward's findings push Liam and the Outpost off of their original path, which ultimately leads to their destruction. In this way, he is bound to the mythology in which Oedipus unknowingly forces Laius off the path, killing him and his whole traveling party.

Only the Shepard survives this interaction. Though not explicitly stated in the story, the inference here is that Colleen Pastor (The Shepard) must have visited the Outpost during its construction, and thus is the only surviving member of Laius' traveling party.

Sacrifice

Jacqueline discovers that she has conceived a child, but its existence threatens the survival of Earth. She is convinced, against her will, to entrust the embryo to Collen Pastor, who carries it away, frozen and practically lifeless. Colleen delivers the frozen embryo to Elenora Voskos who carries it to Corinth, NY where it can be adopted by Mericiel and Paul.

This closely mirrors the shepherd taking the baby Oedipus to the mountain and giving the wounded baby to a second shepherd. Note that both Pastor and Voskos are simple translations of the word Shepherd in Spanish and Greek respectively. The second shepherd offers the baby to the queen and king of Corinth, Merope and Polybus, and they become its adoptive parents.

Nukes in Space

In this book, Edward is timid, and must learn to become audacious in order to grow into the character of Oedipus. This chapter begins with the following encouragement from Colleen. "Audacity, bordering on hubris. That's what it takes if you want to hurl steel and bone into space and bring them home again."

Naturally, he argues and resists change, but by the end of the chapter, he is taking bold risks and beginning his journey towards fulfilling the character traits of Oedipus.

This is also where we meet Tirrell, who is proposing the Presage program to predict the future of where dark matter will pass in the solar system. Tirrell represents the blind oracle Tiresias from Delphi who knows the truth about Oedipus.

Some of Tirrell's technical blunders leave him open to Edward's disdain, just as Tiresias' blindness opens him up to insults from Oedipus.

Life and Limb

In some versions of the myths, Chrysippus of Elis kills himself with his own sword, just as Christopher uses the tools of his trade, prescription medication, to commit suicide.

In other versions, he is thrown down a well, which could be compared to the blackness and isolation of space.

Cascading Failure

The Outpost falls. Liam and his traveling party perish based on events that were set into motion years earlier by the conception of a child between Liam and Jacqueline. In the same way, the conception of Oedipus, heedless of the warnings given to Laius, ultimately causes the death of Laius and his traveling party.

Act-III

Struggle

The Space Agency is in crisis. Its lifesaving missions are threatened, and the General Council, Katherine Othoni, is asking Edward to lean into the investigation. By the end of the chapter, he vows to do so. In the original play, it is the Chorus that entreats Oedipus to do something about the suffering of Thebes.

Probe

Edward and Katherine defend Crespin's role in the Investigative Commission, just as Oedipus sends Creon to seek guidance from the Oracle of Apollo. Edward takes on a serious investigation into the disaster, looking for the root cause, and not realizing that, like Oedipus, his investigation will lead him back to himself and his role in the destruction of the Outpost.

The large meeting that opens this chapter is reminiscent of the opening scene of Oedipus Rex, where Oedipus pledges to get to the bottom of the current blight on Thebes.

Some inspiration was taken from the play for Edward's and Colleen's words:

- "new blood of ancient Thebes, why are you here?"
- "Here are boys, still too weak to fly from the nest, and here the old, bowed down with the years,"
- "and here the picked, unmarried men, the young hope of Thebes"
- "I'll bring it all to light myself"

- vs. -

- "You are the new blood of an organization whose tradition stretches back to before we even knew how to leave the surface of the planet."
- "We owe it to the NLS pilots who will never return to the Nest and to the crew of the Outpost who bore the burden of so many years in space."
- "They sacrificed their chances at family and home so that all of us might hold out hope for both."
- "I'd like to ... tell you what we plan to do about it."

Storms Clouds

During the technical investigation, Chief Yukimoto mumbles a direct quotes from the Sophocles play:

"To the depths of terror, too dark to hear, to see."

In a previous version of this chapter, he also used the following quote when asked to deliver detailed log data, "grudge us no message plucked from the embers." However, streamlining chapter 34 took precedence over retaining this bit of connectivity to the original work.

Televised Hearing

Major General Crespin calls Edward in the morning and asks him if he wants to hear Tirrell's testimony in private. Edward discounts the value of Tirrell's statement and refuses Crespin's offer. This is similar to the opening of Oedipus Rex in which Creon returns from Delphi and offers Oedipus to "go inside" to hear his report, rather than hearing it "in the presence of these people."

The head of the Investigative Committee is named Delphine Temple, in reference to the Temple at Delphi from which the truth of Oedipus' curse is revealed.

Tirrell states that he believes that moving the Outpost off of its path led to its destruction, including the death of Liam. Tirrell and Edward exchange barbs during the congressional hearing, just as do Tiresias and Oedipus in the play.

Throughout, Katherine Othoni counsels Edward to be calm and collected, in the same way as the chorus counsels Oedipus in the play.

This chapter ends with a conflict between Edward and Crespin, mirroring the conflict between Oedipus and Creon where Oedipus accuses Creon of being a traitor. Katherine, like the chorus, declares her loyalty to Edward in the conflict.

Note that in the play, this is where the relationship between Jocasta and Creon is explained as brother and sister, just as Crespin and Jacqueline share the bond of military brotherhood.

Awaited Arrivals

Just as a budding romance develops between Edward and Jacqueline, she learns the truth by recognizing aspects of Mericiel's story. She speaks to Elenora and confirms her deductions. She hopes that Edward never learns the truth, that she is his biological mother.

In the play, Jocasta is the first to realize the truth that she is Oedipus' mother, and she tries to keep Oedipus from learning.

Just for fun, the restaurant is named "The Prince of Thebes."

Congressional Testimony

Colleen Pastor confirms that it was Edward's doctoral research that led to Liam's death and the destruction of the Outpost. This follows the original Sophocles play wherein the messenger/shepherd recognizes that the man at the crossroads and the baby that was carried to Corinth are one and the same. Like the shepherd, Colleen resists making this public declaration.

Aftershocks

Having learned his adoptive origins, his role in the death of his biological father, not to mention the current crisis of the Space Agency, Edward wants to be exiled from the Space Agency, which continues to serve as the metaphor for Thebes. Once again, he mirrors the desires of Oedipus during the corresponding point in the play.

Colleen recounts the story of how the two "shepherds" took charge of the child along his path to Corinth. She also re-states the link from Edward's research to the death of his biological father.

Edward says, "You don't get it, Colleen. I've always known that this was going to happen." This is again meant to reflect the fact that Oedipus tried to run away from Corinth and away from the prophecy that he would kill his father, only to do so on his journey to Thebes.

A Final Appeal

Katherine Othoni quotes the original play with the words "who has ended this saga by her own hand." She does so referring to Colleen not to Jacqueline, and the death is professional not literal, but the parallel to the original story is upheld referencing Jocasta's suicide.

A New Mission

Crespin wins his bid for Senate, just as Creon ascends to the throne of Thebes. This ends the strict equivalence between the Space Agency and Thebes.

Epilogue

Edward's hangover and the dark glasses that he purchased for himself are intended as a humorous nod to the self-inflicted blindness suffered by Oedipus at the end of the play.

Endnotes

To reduce the cost of the paper version of this book, the end-notes have been removed. Most end notes are internet URLs that are both available and clickable in the kindle version of the book.

Acknowledgements

I owe many people thanks for the help that they gave me in writing:

To my sometimes co-author and full-time collaborator Sabrina Kappler. Your Midas touch has added vibrant color and texture to every scene that you chose to revise. I look forward to our future collaborations.

To Katya Kappler, who got me to understand evocation and who guided me on how to translate expository text into a narrative told from the character's point of view. The story was transformed through your lessons.

To Annika, Cleo, and Iggy who listened to chapters with me as we got things cleaned up for the final draft.

To Dr. James Gill, you were the ideal reviewer and consultant for a story like this one. Between your doctorate in theoretical physics and your deep insight into the structure of character, story, and fruitful conflict, I found each of your suggestions to be profound and essential. I can't thank you enough.

To Ellie Ellerman whose insightful suggestions around Edward's relationship with his university, Jacqueline's relationship with the US, and the Agency's relationship with the public have made the story much stronger.

To John Roll and Alvin Wen. In 2016 I survived my own high adrenaline adventure together with both of you. Thank you for helping me with this story. John, your question regarding "why now?" has become central to chapter 2, and Alvin, your insights into technical and emotional clarity of scenes has made crucial parts of the story stronger.

To Tamara Kett, the insights that you and Keith added on the economics of farming added crisp detail to a vague chapter, and your keen eye for precision on the evolution of military technology and on life in the military made the corresponding chapters come alive.

To Kimberly Stoker, you are the fastest reader that I have ever met. Your comments were surgical and insightful, and the new scene that you recommended in the middle of the book made that chapter so much better.

To three women who gave me early feedback that helped the story take shape in 2019. Kimberly Fine, thank you for your careful commentary and encouragement, and your coaching on how to make parts of the story more accessible. Robin Kappler, thank you for your careful review and your suggestion to put illustrations in the story. Sandy Frachetti, thank you for helping me find the balance between not enough description vs. too much.

To Edmund Jorgensen, thank you for your advice on how to live like a writer, how to publish, and how to find artists interested in collaborating on projects like these.

To Srikanth Sastry and to Rohith Unnikrishnan, thank you for encouraging the addition of chapter 26 to make Christopher's troubles clearer for the reader. Srikanth, I look forward to our next collaboration.

Finally, Dr. Joel Christensen, a lecture that you gave to visitors to Brandeis University in November 2018 inspired me to try something that I've never tried before. To my amazement, one year later, you took me in as an adopted student, reading the full book and giving me crucial feedback on the story and guidance on the next phases of the revision process.

Made in the USA
Middletown, DE
04 June 2021

41088551R00205